THE
GHOST TOWN
PRESERVATION
SOCIETY

— A Novel —

JULIE CLARK SIMON

RIVERBEND
PUBLISHING

The Ghost Town Preservation Society

Copyright © 2019 Julie Clark Simon

Published by Riverbend Publishing, Helena, Montana

ISBN 978-1-60639-097-9

Printed in the USA

1 2 3 4 5 6 7 8 9 FN 22 21 20 19

Cover and text design by Sarah Cauble, www.sarahcauble.com
Cover artwork by David Swanson, www.davidswansonart.com

Riverbend Publishing
P.O. Box 5833
Helena, MT 59604
1-866-787-2363
www.riverbendpublishing.com

Each age writes the history of the past . . . with reference to the conditions uppermost in its own time.

—Frederick Jackson Turner, *The Significance of History*

A True Accounting

THIS IS A STORY ABOUT THE CIRCUMSTANCES OF MY BIRTH. OR MAYBE IT'S a collection of stories about the ghosts I raised when I went looking for a mother who didn't want to be found.

Now isn't that a peculiar locution for a 21st-century woman: "circumstances of my birth"? But you have to understand that I am a historian, someone who wants to know what's knowable, to solve mysteries systematically, to find patterns in the past. So I set out to do what historians do best, to conjure rags and bones into a plausible narrative, one that casts a backwards spell that somehow makes it possible to go on. Like Lot's wife, I ignored everyone's orders to keep my eyes front and forward. Whether I was right to insist on looking back, I'll leave it to you to figure out. I'm still trying.

Oddly enough, in this real life "ghost town" that knew so much well-publicized violence, almost all of it by men upon other men, the only ghosts I've been able to dig up have been those of women, children, and animals.

—Debra D. Munn, *Big Sky Ghosts*

1966: The Past Is Prologue

MY MOTHER STOPS DEAD CENTER IN THE MUD OF WHAT USED TO BE THE ghost town's main street, the hanger in her hand quivering.

She's not exactly afraid.

The wailing skims the surface of the April wind, then sinks beneath the throaty mutter of the hens.

"Shut up," she thinks, forgetting to say it. "Shut up!" she whispers to the hens as she tries to listen. And they go quiet—at least for the time it takes Evie to draw an unsteady breath.

They have followed Evie like white shadows, at least a dozen of the scarlet-combed Wyandottes, their heads bobbing toward her clenched fist, waiting for the usual cascade of scratch. Their greed is so strong that Evie almost can smell the grainy dust of their oats and cracked corn. Sheila, the leader of the flock, pecks at Evie's tennis shoe. My mother loves all the hens, but Sheila is the only one who allows Evie to take her warm eggs without a fight. The rest have to be riled into pecking the ax handle while Evie does her thieving.

Except for the hens, Evie is alone in the ghost town—she is sure of that. She would have heard the rattle of any vehicle jouncing in from the two-lane state highway five miles away. She is alone with the lingering smell of fresh bread from her father's early baking and the sharp fragrance of sagebrush rising with the false spring. With the nearby chortle of the amber water frothing through Grasshopper Creek with the start of the April run-off. With the broken-windowed stare of the school, gold stamp mill, church, jail, and once-grand brick hotel. With the tumbled cabins and houses, empty shops and saloons, all silvering under the shadow of Bannack Peak. Only her parents' house still resists decay, shutters freshly painted green, the attached bakery glinting white.

Alone with her secret. Well, almost alone.

Her parents left for Misfire at six this morning, the way they do every Monday and Thursday, except, of course, when the Montana winter locks down the state highway. This morning, after checking the sky, her mother pulled on a Levi jacket over the corduroy tent dress she had made herself; Evie knows that her mother will take off her coat for the deliveries. Her father supplemented his baker's best—starched shirt and pressed trousers, both spotless white—with his wool peacoat. As always, the homemade shelves in the back end of the panel truck were carefully stacked with white cardboard cartons, each holding newly laid eggs, or fresh loaves, or angel food cakes, or fruit pies.

It's Easter Monday, a school holiday; otherwise Evie would be sitting beside them, carving herself a small space from their intimate silence, fiddling with the radio all through Badger Pass. Distant Butte is as hard to reach as a rattlesnake coiled in the cleft of a limestone cliff on a blistering day. Usually, though, the Misfire signal can be coaxed to emerge for at least part of the ride. When Evie is lucky, she hooks the hit parade. "Wo! I feel nice, like sugar and spice/I feel nice, like sugar and spice/So nice, so nice, I got you." She loves howling along with James Brown. As long as she keeps her face reasonably steady and her hands relatively quiet, her parents don't even try to read her lips.

There are advantages to having deaf parents. They never care what you play on the radio. But there are more advantages to boarding Monday through Thursday in town with her older sister, even though Elizabeth rarely remembers to talk to Evie, not even to ask if she needs help doing her homework or ironing her homemade blouses. Busy as a bumblebee, Elizabeth leaves Evie free to do what she wants.

Evie watches a lot of television at her sister's house, even though Elizabeth and her husband make do with an old-fashioned set, a blank gray eye that opens in a massive mahogany cabinet. Still, to Evie the television is magic, from the six o'clock news during supper to Johnny Carson past her bedtime. You can't get even a single channel in Bannack. Or so her parents have assured her.

"Go on back, get away you stupid things!" Evie whips the hanger at the hens. They explode squawking into the sagebrush, two of them flapping up the stairs of the Methodist church, in better repair than most of the structures in the ghost town. But they begin bobbing their heads almost immediately, pausing to scratch at the few clumps of dried grass left by the wintering mule deer. The hens won't flush so much as a grasshopper from the drooping heads of last year's growth. It's too early.

Even though she is not exactly afraid, even though the sun is warm for April in Montana, even though she is wearing an old shirt of absorbent flannel over her sweater and dungarees, a shirt she plans to bury afterwards, Evie shivers.

Truth is, she doesn't know quite what to do with the hanger, even though she's a smart girl, a reader, a tenth-grade honor student who can make a clever metaphor by comparing the screen of her sister's television to the eye of the Cyclops, either before or after Odysseus blinded him, depending on the deep inner meaning intended. To distract herself from thinking about what comes next, she stops in front of Mrs. Parsley's scabby picket fence to untwist the strands of wire that form the hook. Lace curtains pattern the wavy glass of Mrs. Parsley's front parlor.

Looking at their delicate tracing, Evie thinks of the way her father signs to her mother to watch him perform his favorite trick: pinching the paper doilies from the top of his nearly black chocolate cakes to reveal the web of powdered sugar below. Evie's mother never fails to smile, the curve of her mouth pushing up her Gaelic cheekbones.

Evie sometimes wonders if her parents had made more of an effort to include Elizabeth in their finger-flying conversations than they did her. Maybe so. Elizabeth was, after all, their first daughter, born early in their marriage. But maybe not. Having escaped Bannack to board in town her first year in high school—the year Evie was born, Elizabeth never moved home again. Even summers, Elizabeth found reasons to stay in Misfire— swimming lessons, a waitress job at the Golden Hour, classes at the college open to a select group of high school students. Maybe Elizabeth just couldn't stand the silence? It isn't a question Evie can ask.

Evie's parents don't mean to shut her out. She sees them making an effort to include her in their gestured conversation, to sweep her into their world. Truth is, though, they don't need her—haven't needed anyone since her mother flung her first greeting to her father down the gleam of the hard-polished floor of the wide hallway of the state school for the deaf and blind. "Hello," her hands fluttered. "Are you new?" At the time, her father hadn't known sign language. He had learned fast.

It used to be easier to forgive them their happiness. But that was before Mrs. Parsley had been persuaded to move to a Butte nursing home by her Salt Lake City second cousin, her only acknowledged family member. He had avowed concern for an old woman living alone in a ghost town with only the deaf bakers and their gangly daughter for neighbors. The rest of the buildings were empty—most of them labeled with signs that proclaimed "Montana Highway Department Property" in a black-on-white design that looked a lot like the state's license plate. Personally, Evie thought the second cousin simply had grown tired of waiting for the check that the state kept waving under Mrs. Parsley's nose as the bureaucrats and local history buffs tried to puzzle out how to turn the ghost town into a tourist attraction.

It would be easy for Evie to stop here at Mrs. Parsley's house, to scramble through the weeds to the outhouse. The extra key is waiting, taped under the lid of the outhouse seat, the thawing stink rising gently from below. Evie doesn't have to banish herself to the far edge of town, to the dirt-floored dugout she made her own when she stumbled across it the summer before she started first grade. She could do what she plans to do—must do—in the comfort of Mrs. Parsley's house. Maybe she could lie down on Mrs. Parsley's bed and rest when it's over.

Normally, Evie isn't a procrastinator. Normally, she runs up to her tiny bedroom in the turret of her sister's stately Queen Anne to do the algebra she hates first thing. She used to hurry because of the television. Now she races to finish before her brother-in-law's gentle knock, the only sound in the house except for the clock tapping out the time in the downstairs entryway. As the wife of Misfire's high school principal and a former teacher herself, Elizabeth feels she has certain obligations, especially since she and Nick have no children. She volunteers as an after-school reading tutor, giving the principal and Evie plenty of time to share ideas about the meaning of life. There's nothing more beautiful to Evie than the way the afternoon sun magnifies the craters on the principal's skin into a landscape as pock-marked as the surface of the moon. No one but Evie knows how lonely he is, how he suffers from Elizabeth's impersonal cheerfulness and unrelenting efficiency. He has taught Evie to recognize her sister for who she is.

My mother leans her forehead on the cool glass of Mrs. Parsley's bay window. There's no comfort in the shadowed view. The parlor is stripped down to its rose-bordered linoleum rug. The second cousin has trucked away Mrs. Parsley's nearly new Montgomery Ward living room set. It makes Evie sad to think how proud Mrs. Parsley had been of it. Hating the emptiness, Evie walks around the corner of the house and peers through the sag between the slats of the blinds.

In Mrs. Parsley's bedroom, the second cousin has left everything in place. Maybe he hopes scavengers will loot the old stuff and save him the trouble: The carefully pieced quilt on the bed. The hand-tinted photo of Old Faithful erupting on the wall. The hope chest full of important family documents and keepsakes. The fancy dresser with the faceted glass pulls, a piece of furniture that even Evie recognizes as a bona fide antique. It all looks as sad as some stray dog abandoned to snuffle roadkill and tip over garbage cans.

Looking in from the outside, Evie can almost see her younger self perched on the rocker, Mrs. Parsley at the dresser brushing her handsome grey hair, set once a week in Misfire's best beauty shop. On the dresser among the empty perfume bottles is a framed studio portrait of Mrs. Parsley's daughter, Lisette. Evie knows now the story Mrs. Parsley used to tell about her daughter—that she had died in a tragic accident—was a prevarication. Prevarication is Evie's favorite new word, taught to her by the principal, who has assured her the truth is too complicated for the average person. Mrs. Parsley probably did see the loss her daughter to the life of a Las Vegas call-girl as a tragic accident, the principal said in the low, compassionate voice that Evie found so thrilling. Elizabeth had gone to high school with Lisette. Had Elizabeth ever been tempted by feathers and sequins? Evie tried and failed to imagine that she had.

"Tell me a ghost story," Evie used to beg Mrs. Parsley, her own voice echoing a hint of the aging woman's lightly lilting accent, itself an indirect inheritance from her Confederate grandfather. He had been among those to pan for gold in Grasshopper Creek when Bannack was bursting with greed and hope while the rest of the country was still bleeding from the Civil War.

Advised by their family doctor to make sure Evie grew up hearing the sound of human voices every day, her parents had regularly deposited their infant with Mrs. Parsley.

Evie imagines herself babbling in the bottom drawer of the dresser, which still holds a supply of her baby blankets. By the time she was five, she was conversing with a lilt of her own.

Mrs. Parsley spoke ever so carefully to Evie, enunciating as clearly as she could, recapitulating the elocution lessons of her own childhood. To speak was her job, after all, one she was paid for in eggs and bread and cake. As the years passed, she would have done it for nothing—in fact did, since she fed most of the bread and cake to a child who would have preferred the crispness of apples. Mrs. Parsley was content with a bowl of oatmeal at five thirty, a grilled cheese made with Velveeta at noon, just a cup of tea before her nine o'clock bedtime. Her body was so slight that it barely disturbed her long, straight skirts, her snowy blouses with their Peter Pan collars. Her voice, feathery with a slight tremble, was perfect for the telling of tales.

"Shall I tell you about how Bertie Mathews saw the drowned girl?" Mrs. Parsley asked, sipping her tea at her dressing table.

"No," Evie groaned in pretended terror, even though she had spent many Saturday afternoons sitting cross-legged in one plaster-shattered room or another of the ghost town's Meade Hotel, listening for the mice to scuttle in the walls, waiting for the drowned girl to appear in her drenched blue dress, her long hair streaming onto the uneven wooden floor. Evie found the story deliciously frightening because it featured someone she knew from church in town: Miss Mathews, the matron of the county seat's Normal School, a handsome woman who wore immaculately tailored suits and no makeup at all. For Evie, it was much easier to imagine the drowned girl than the severe Miss Mathews as a frightened adolescent, working as a chamber maid in a dying hotel, gasping in terror when her former playmate appeared.

"Well, shall I tell you about the lost babies then?"

Evie would nod: the story was her favorite, although it was nearly as sad as the one about the dying cries of the Lemhi Indians: drunken prospectors had massacred them in their own camp that bordered a Bannack subsiding from boom to bust.

"It was the flu epidemic of 1918, you know."

Evie did know.

"Or maybe it was one of the earlier epidemics—typhoid or measles. It's hard to remember. So many children died in those days. It might have been earlier, but I don't think so. I think it was just after the cyanide mill opened and the town was full again."

Evie made an encouraging sound. She had heard it all before. She always wanted Mrs. Parsley to get to the good part. "The Grim Reaper took more than his fair share that year. There were so many sick—and not only the babies. Anyway, they had to go somewhere, and the hospital in Misfire was overflowing. So someone got the idea of turning the abandoned cabins into nursing stations."

As Mrs. Parsley's story flowed around her, Evie imagined exhausted women stooping helplessly toward the babies. Pictured the hurried burials, not in the old Boot Hill graveyard where the outlaws were interred, but in the respectable cemetery a few miles outside of town. Heard the wailing of the infants seeping into the thick log walls of the house, the crying so persistent that it still echoed. Anyway, that's what Mrs. Parsley said. And Evie believed her.

Then.

Now she is a tenth grader too sophisticated to believe in ghosts. Evie pulls her forehead back from the glass. Her breath has fogged a halo around the oval where her face has rested. Sheila and the rest of the hens are nowhere in sight. The wind makes a convincing argument that April is not spring in Montana. Evie decides she should hurry; the threat of a storm could bring her parents home from town early.

She skirts the back of the house, following the deer path that parallels the creek. The dugout jammed halfway into a hill at the far edge of town looks lonely. The state hasn't yet bothered to brand it with its black-on-white plate. The yellow grass and greening paddles of prickly pear stick up from its sod roof like spikes of uncombed hair. Evie finds her pry bar still hidden where she had left it, under the wild rose someone had transplanted when the town was still a town. The swollen door resists and resists and suddenly gives way

Inside the dugout, the cold earth exhales. Evie gropes her way to the table she had left set for imaginary friends before she started school in September. By the time she reaches the table's rim, her eyes have adjusted enough that she can see the gleam of the Aladdin's lamp, the white shadows of the mismatched china she has collected from the town dump for almost as long as she can remember. A careful girl, she has left it filled with oil, expecting she would return her first weekend home. She didn't know then how quickly she'd lose interest in her childhood fantasies.

Just as she fishes a match out of the coffee tin, a sudden change in atmospheric pressure shoves the door into a creaking moan. The sound doesn't stop when the wind takes a breath.

My mother runs as fast as she can, leaving the hanger behind.

Me, she takes with her.

If nothing tangible could be discerned by a visual survey of otherwise promising country, the prospector was still by no means at a loss. Feeling in his bones that something worthwhile ought to be about, he would hunt up a suitable camp site, make himself and burro comfortable, then lay out his tools in preparation for a search for a float. This term embraced mineral particles and scales eroded from a load and carried away by water action. By finding float and tracing it back to its point of origin, the prospector might well discover some kind of lode.

—Otis E. Young, Jr., *The Prospectors: Some Considerations on Their Craft*

2010: A Wide Spot in the Road

NOTHING MUCH SEPARATED ME FROM RHETA—OR AT LEAST THE WOMAN I assumed was Rheta. She was in the right place at the right time, behind the counter of the *Sun-Tribune*, ripping pages from a newspaper, heavy rings glinting above swollen knuckles. Her lipstick was three shades too orange for a small-town Thursday morning and for the mental picture I'd formed of her. But the illegal lift of smoke from an oversized ashtray matched the rasp of the voice I'd heard on the phone.

I wondered afterwards what might have happened if she hadn't looked up, eyes clear as creek water.

As my unrestored '53 Bel Air ticked at the curb on the street, its sturdy six-cylinder engine cooling in the morning chill, I told myself that I could still leave. In fact, I knew I should leave. I should climb back in behind the sedan's toothy chrome grin and lose no time dodging the potholes in the deserted street. I should hustle myself past the line of 19th century false fronts rusting above the bars and tackle shops and T-shirt outlets that constituted the business district in Misfire, Montana. In five minutes, I could be back on the highway again, following the sleek avian arrow of the Bel Air's hood ornament, congratulating myself for having the insight, for once, to recognize that I was about to do something irrevocably stupid. Already euphoric with the prospect of making the right choice, I decided to leave immediately before anyone, especially me, got hurt.

The worst kind of lie is the lie you tell yourself. Rheta was too close, and she probably already had guessed who I was, even though I had rolled into town hours ahead of schedule.

Closed, the *Sun-Tribune*'s heavy glass door would have provided me a buffer. But despite the surprising cold of the mid-April morning, it was propped open with a newspaper dispenser. Rheta was so near that I could smell her cigarette burning, hear the rasp of newspaper against the straight edge she was holding tight against the counter with one hand as she made a clean tear with the other. She didn't bother to look down as she picked up another broadsheet. She didn't smile. Her stare, windowed by the spotless lens of her bifocals, gave nothing away.

I hated to imagine what she saw, a woman whose short red hair still bristled from a half hour spent some two hundred and fifty miles back between heavily chlorinated motel sheets with an out-of-work logger whose abilities in bed hadn't reflected the name of his town—Superior. But my rule has always been "no regrets."

Still, something was making me shudder now besides the wind. I knew of only one thing that would cure what ailed me: returning to Powerglide through the snow-shadowed mountain passes I had descended without encountering more than a half dozen other vehicles, the Bel Air's faded body paint absorbing the colors of sky and reflecting them back again—Horizon Blue, with both the horizon and the blue always changing. From where I stood chilled and unhappy, the mountains—not only the ones I had traveled through, but all the others cradling and caging the town—seemed seductively close, flattened by the quartzite light, sharpened into cartoons, featureless and benevolent.

Stranger though I was, I had troubled myself to learn the names of those mountains and the others that were beyond, but not very far beyond, the reach of my vision. The Recreational Map of Western Montana, spread pretty as a paper quilt over of the front seat, the fabric of its gentle ridging asserting itself untorn under the map's pastel patterns. Greens marked BLM and Forest Service lands. Deeper tints of yellow, gold, and orange laddered up the slopes. To the south, the Blacktail Range escaped the stretch of I-15 that leashes Southwest Montana to Salt Lake City. To the northwest, the Pioneer Mountains struggled to penetrate the cool reserve of the sky. To the northeast, the Rubies and the Tobacco Roots thrust up edges blunted by snow that I knew wouldn't melt until July.

What does it say about me that I took obnoxious pride in knowing more about the genesis of the map than most of the locals probably did: that the Ruby Mountains were the source of a river that Meriwether Lewis had tried to name the Philanthropy. But that name, far too philosophical for the terrain, hadn't stuck. Not surprisingly, Ruby had. Never mind that the rubies in the riverbed were really garnets. Never mind that, scooped up by the handful, those garnets dried dull. Under the moving water, they flickered with a real and lovely light.

I do go on, don't I? One of the advantages of digression, besides the pure pleasure of the ramble, is that it buys you a little time. That morning I needed a beat or two to give myself the chance to breathe as I paused in front of the *Sun-Tribune*. I couldn't even plead ignorance as a defense.

I knew what a dangerous thing it was that I was doing.

So I stood there, gawking around, afraid for once to make a move, in case it was the wrong move. I strained my eyes trying to see the mountains that the map told me sprawled farther south than the Blacktails. The Tendoys, I knew, had been named in honor of the Lemhi leader who used his influence to keep his people out of fights and in the reservation that they had come to regard as home—a rough country that they loved as desperately as a child can love her adoptive parents, however harsh they may be. Tendoy must have been a smart man, presenting an agreeable face to the Anglo invaders who had stayed when the gold gave out. He rode paint ponies in their parades, appeared to give into federal pressure that demanded his band's removal to another reservation, and stayed planted with his people for twenty-five more years.

This is just another example of the type of thing I love knowing, God help me. Which explains, at least partly, the bundle of documents in the large manila envelope hidden under the map on the passenger side of the Chevy's front seat. Not coincidentally, it also accounts for the fact that I was standing mired in the remembrance of things past, unable to take the necessary step into my planned future.

If I'm remembering right, and I'm probably not, it was a stock truck that shook me forward as it rumbled past, its load of sheep bleating hopelessly, patches of dirty wool pressing through ventilation slits. Or maybe there was no truck that morning, but there could have been. For that matter, there could have been (although April would have been early for it) a mob of cattle occupying the street, kids on mopeds helping to push them along to their high country warm season grazing on public land. But no: I would remember (I'm almost sure) the pleasurable shock of a downtown cattle drive, the Angus (the red Hereford cross, not the black of clichéd restaurant fame) bawling, dropping steaming manure onto the streets and the edges of the bluegrass lawns that take so much tending in high, cold desert places.

I'm also certain that the only vehicle parked along Montana Street was my ivory-roofed Bel Air, my surrogate sister. The Chevy is older than I, but not by as much as people tend to assume, given my jeans and T-shirts and my unlined face, untended to a degree unusual in a woman who had already crossed that dangerous border between her thirties and her forties.

Standing exposed by my car, I felt about as safe as the last shot of scotch in the bottle. I don't know why I didn't leave right then. Maybe I was just too tired. The surge of adrenaline that had propelled me out of Seattle and tumbled me through Washington and Idaho had evaporated even before the Montana border. My restless stop in Superior had not helped. Still, at Missoula I abandoned the speed of the interstate anyway. On old U.S. 93, the fresh snowdrifts would have obscured the asphalt if not for the piercing reach of roadside reflectors meant to warn against steep drop-offs and sudden curves. Springtime in the Rockies, I remembered from a childhood punctuated with sudden moves, is a season with an identity crisis.

Still, I didn't consider turning back: I wanted a long, hard trip. One that would toughen me up for what was to come while nudging my arrival just a little further into the future.

As I picked up Route 43, the snow slid into slush, but the Bel Air, broad-beamed and ponderous, held steady. In a few miles, the lift of dawn would offer up the valley that in 1877 had absorbed the blood of the ninety or so

Nez Perce men, women, and children killed in a surprise attack by the U.S. Army. No one knows exactly how many died that day. Despite their first shock, survivors organized a desperate fighting retreat. When they at last surrendered short of the Canadian border, newspapers praised their Chief Joseph for his tragic courage, while conveniently ignoring the condemnation of his people to a deadly captivity.

The road to the Battlefield looked pretty clear, but I pulled over short of the turnoff, steadying my map against the steering wheel. The dome light showed that the confluence of Route 43's solid slash with the broken line of Montana 278 was only a few miles away. From there, the turnoff to the ghost town of Bannack would demand no more than forty minutes—as long as the road hadn't spiked a shroud of black ice.

It hadn't. After I left 43, the Chevy skimmed 278 so quickly that the sun was barely settling from dawn into day when a sign announced the Bannack turnoff. My foot hesitated. Just twenty-four miles to Misfire—a stretch so short that it seemed suddenly irresistible. No matter that I would arrive hours early for the appointment that I was considering breaking.

Taking the first (and last) exit into Misfire, I felt the town close around me. The road devolved into a street so narrow that it enforced its own speed limit. The gothic heap of the local teachers' college walled off my lane. On the other side, a Taco Time, a Dairy Queen, and a couple of gas stations broke a straggling line of Victorian homes whose original grandeur had decayed into peeling paint and sagging porches.

My hopes of decompressing over a New York Times and a decent breakfast plummeted as I braked for a pack of dogs sniffing the carcass of something unidentifiable in the middle of the street. At the edge of the pack, a hound—long, low, dangerously skinny—lifted his nose in my direction. I honked, but gently. I knew my own face was a desirous human version of his: crumpled with impossible yearning and unjustified hope

I had arrived. The trouble was, I couldn't quite remember why.

In lieu of a purpose, I scraped the curb to park in front of the *Sun-Tribune* and disembarked. How long had I been standing here, my shoulder blades twitching? To postpone the necessity of deciding which way to jump, back into the Bel Air or forward to the newspaper's open front door, I fumbled in the pocket of my jeans for a quarter. The parking meter tipped streetward, echoing the slight tilt of the *Sun-Tribune's* facade. I fought the desire to lean in synch to get the world in balance again. Rheta watched me without comment, stopping the rhythm of her work to take a delicate sip from her heavy white china mug. Coffee, I could smell it. Bad coffee, brewed up from the cheap stuff, bought on sale. Measured out in an unsuccessful attempt to make up in quantity what was lacking in quality. Left to stew.

"Metermaid doesn't come around until after lunch." Rheta's voice was gravel at the bottom of a streambed.

I continued to hold my face into a semblance of a gawk. In truth, I didn't have to fake my interest in the *Sun-Tribune's* facade, its crenellated cornice crowned by the arrow of its gable. I recognized the false front as the type that had been stamped out of metal and shipped West to dignify the squat rawness of frontier business districts. Always a sucker for 19th century pretensions, I stood studying the facade's fussy details: the date of 1888 picked out in gilt that someone had kept bright, the border of acanthus that embroidered every available edge, the line of medallions running above the upper story's bank of windows, the miniature Corinthian pilasters whose fake columns emerged from the facade's surface like the tip of an iceberg in a spot where there was no iceberg and never had been. The pilasters separated rectangles of glass that once had loomed nearly as tall as the upper story they delineated. I winced to see that some latter-day fool had cobbled in the original window openings with plywood and stuck in squinty substitutes framed with cheap aluminum. It was a relief to look away.

"I won't be parked here very long," I told Rheta brightly and then tried to think of a graceful exit line. "I just wanted to take a look at the building." I watched her face, smooth as silk-cut tobacco, no nicotine-induced wrinkles visible. She didn't challenge my explanation. For a breath or two, I imagined I might still escape. "That's an iron facade they shipped in from St. Louis, isn't it, a Mesker?" I added, made nervous by her continued silence. A half-second too late, I realized I had just demonstrated that I could read the history coded in the curves of the fleurs-de-lis.

"You must be AJ," Rheta said, snubbing out her cigarette. "I thought you might show up early, and I worried what you would think if you found the door locked. We always open late Thursday to give ourselves a little break after the paper comes out on Wednesday."

"Thanks," I said, expressing insincere gratitude for the second time in a couple of minutes.

"No problem. Always plenty of work to do around here. Besides, we're doing a press run this morning for a special edition. Our annual egg edition. It comes out tomorrow."

I paused, not sure what would be safe to say. None of my research had revealed a propensity for raising chickens in Elephant Rock County. The aforementioned sheep and beef cattle, yes, and even a luckless population of hogs whose hooves never touched the ground in what agribusiness euphemistically called a "containment unit." I identified the hogs as the likely source of the stench rising with the wind to mix it up with tang of mountain pines. The resulting combination was not improved by a sigh of stale beer from the *Sun-Tribune's* next-door neighbor, the Antler Bar, its name announced in unlighted neon.

Rheta noted my expression. "The city's having trouble with the lagoon," she said. "The sewage lagoon. They keep promising to get it fixed before summer." She sounded far from confident about that probability. Clearly, Rheta was a woman who had learned to take promises, official and otherwise, with a grain of salt. At least that much we shared.

I was still searching for the right words when a siren's shock rattled the glass of the *Sun-Tribune's* main floor showcase window—not the whine of an ambulance or fire truck, but an end-of-the-world ululation like the ones you hear in old sci-fi flicks. I don't exaggerate at all when I say that I leapt into the shelter of the newspaper office. My body, possessed by 9-11 paranoia, tensed toward a crouch, just in case I needed to roll under Rheta's counter. Bodies have their own inexorable logic, just as stories do. There was no use telling my muscles that it was unlikely that terrorists had chosen a quiet weekday morning in Misfire, Montana, population roughly five thousand souls, counting horses and dogs, as the perfect time and place to wreak havoc.

All the dogs in town were moaning doom, including a golden retriever that was struggling out from under the bench in front of the *Sun-Tribune's* front window. The dog lifted a muzzle aged to the color of over-ripe wheat and gave voice in the canine equivalent of the Mormon Tabernacle Choir: not much complexity but, my God, plenty of feeling. Which I shared. The worst had finally happened. What a relief and why had it taken so long.

Apparently the dogs and I had wasted a surge of adrenalin. Rheta lifted her cup to her bright lips again. The only pedestrian that I'd seen since I'd entered town shuffled into view, burdened by the trash bag stretched over his shoulder, its plastic skin tight against the lumpy push of whatever was inside. Ignoring the siren's fading screams, the bagman kept his eyes down, fixed on his paint-spattered boots, cracked on top, thick of sole below. The retriever's tail quaked as he struggled to his feet and pressed his head into the rusty droop of the bagman's jacket. I wondered if the bagman might be blind when he groped for the retriever, his long-fingered hand white as it emerged from its grease-dark sleeve,

"Nine," Rheta said.

"Nine," I repeated to prompt an explanation, which was not forthcoming. Clearly, Rheta was a woman of few words, and, because I had decided to extricate myself from Misfire and to recognize my pilgrimage here as a fool's errand, that suited me fine. She hadn't even asked me the usual question—what the initials in my name stood for—not that I would have been able to provide an answer.

The last time I'd tried out a name crafted to match my initials was when my short-lived marriage gave up the ghost. For a few months, I'd been Ara (goddess of revenge) Jobina (one persecuted). Before that I'd been the witty doctoral student Aphra (dusty) Jaela (wild mountain goat). Before that, the lonely high school teacher, Amalia (work) Jane (plain by association with J. Eyre). And before that, the shy history undergraduate Aria (singing) Jelena (deer) and—well, you get the picture. Now, however, I was just plain AJ.

"Want to see the apartment?" Rheta's words were absorbed by the hollow chimes of a clock striking the hour from what could only be a Misfire version of Big Ben.

I agreed, even though, after one glance into the inky cave beyond Rheta's counter, I knew that any apartment lodged in the upper regions of the *Sun-Tribune* building wouldn't suit, even if I were planning to stay in Misfire. Which I definitely wasn't. I already hated the newsroom's lowered ceiling blotched with yellow stains, acoustic tiles sagging to meet walls the green-gray color of the mold that grows on imploding oranges. One of the smudges on the wall resolved itself into the shape of an inky hand. Probably the blotch belonged to the same person who'd left footprints smeared into humped carpet. The soles of my own feet tingled. I shook one and then the other before I realized they were vibrating in sympathy with the floor. Since the last of the siren's tremblers had faded, a press must be thumping away not far below. None of this prompted Rheta to break her step to explain or apologize. Reluctantly, I followed her through a makeshift passage formed by a waist-high partition that probably was meant to give the reporters some protection from the public.

Only one of the three desks seemed enrolled in active service. And it was the one that looked much worse for the wear under clouds of clutter. Snarls of developed film. Photos, mostly of scruffy white people grimacing as they gripped hands in front of shabby businesses and basketball players showing their armpits, hairy (male) and smooth (female). Reams of cheap brownish paper, some sheets already filled with blotchy type, some blank, and many crumpled. A scattering of beer cans. A gadget that I recognized as a telegrapher's key. A nearly empty bottle of scotch (The Famous Grouse, not my choice, but of a quality surprising given the newsroom's general squalor), a dusty model of Union Pacific 119 staring down Central Pacific Jupiter to commemorate the 1869 completion of the first transcontinental railroad. Where the desktop broke through the mess, it showed scabrous wood, pocked and ringed. I imagined an angry reader wielding a hammer or some other blunt instrument. Following the passageway past the desk, I realized Rheta couldn't be the *Sun-Tribune's* editor. The crisp drape of her smock signaled she would never allow such a mess if she were in charge.

"Actually," I called to Rheta's retreating shoulders, very square in their protective smock. "Actually, I'd just be wasting your time." I hate it when I lapse into default politeness. Thankfully, it happens less and less as the years go by.

"Rheta!" I had to raise my voice to try to make myself heard over the hard mechanical thump that was getting louder the deeper we penetrated the murk of the office. A chemical smell thickened the already dank atmosphere, and my throat began to close. I had left my purse—a heavy saddle-bag model—and thus my inhaler in the Bel Air, not intending to stay long enough in the newspaper office to need luggage. I had never before noticed any hypersensitivity to bad coffee, bad plumbing, and cheap ink, but when had I ever encountered them in such a combination and concentration?

I was certain that I would not and could not live in such a stew of bad smells and shabbiness, but there seemed no reasonably dignified way to get Rheta's attention. So I clumped up a steep flight of stairs, finally catching up with Rheta on a surprisingly spacious landing.

"You'll get your exercise if you rent from us," Rheta said, not out of breath herself. "No, don't go that way. That's the entrance to the morgue." She paused, dangling the bait. I kept my face expressionless, but I couldn't help asking. "Do you have any of the early papers? What kind of shape are they in?"

"Want to see?"

I nodded.

Rheta pulled a skeleton key from the pocket of her smock and inserted it into a lock so large that it looked as though it belonged on a stage set. It yielded with a click, sharp and clean.

"Light string's just above you," she said. Across the room, dirt-dimmed light seeped in the wink of one of the re-sized windows; no one had bothered to try to disguise the plywood with the balm of paint. I blinked, letting my eyes adjust. The room smelled like dusty paper, a smell I like, even though it makes me reach for my inhaler.

"Damn Conrad," Rheta said. "He probably stole the bulb for downstairs instead of hauling his ass to the Food Farm to buy a new one. Anyway, here's the key. You can look later." The key was heavy in my hand and warm from the press of Rheta's palm. I pushed it into my pocket.

"I think there's enough light from the window to navigate," I said, blinking. My contact lenses felt like corn flakes. Despite the murk, I could make out the caves of empty shelves lining the room. The volumes they had been built to hold were jumbled on the uneven planks of the bare floor, some splayed open, others closed but spilling their contents. I squatted beside one of the most confused of the heaps, supporting the spine of a spread-eagled volume as I folded the marbleized boards of its cover back into place. The date on the cover had been rubbed away.

"Even if these have all been microfilmed, it's a shame to abuse them," I said, trying hard not to sound as angry as I suddenly felt. Silver duct tape had been promiscuously slapped down to half-heal the worst of the damage. Although I knew enough about journalists never to trust a newspaper, I hated to see any of the surviving scraps of the past get carelessly obliterated by the carelessness of the present.

Rheta didn't respond to my comment. Instead she knelt beside me. "These are some of the oldest," she said. "You can recognize them by the fancy covers. A couple of them date back to the 1880s."

I felt a flutter like a leaf falling. The 1880s were too recent to advance the research project I had concocted to give me a reasonable excuse for poking around Elephant Rock County. Given the fact that I had no intention of actually conducting any sort of real investigation, I felt oddly letdown.

Sensing my disappointment, Rheta rose easily, more easily by far than I did. "Of course," she said, obviously rummaging through her mental tackle box for the fly that might tempt the finicky prey, "I could help you try to locate the earlier papers from the mining camps, if you stick around."

"They exist?" I asked, snapping up the hook, forgetting to remember that my project was more or less a fake.

"I have an idea about where a stash of them might be tucked away," she said. I followed Rheta out of the morgue and up the next flight of steps. "The editor of the Tribune, before it combined with the Sun, was one of my best customers. Lord, that man was a saver. He kept everything, labeled it, and filed it. After he died, I heard they took more than twenty pairs of his worn-out boots to the dump, unwearable, but still shined up nice, each in its own original box. I don't know if I believe the story, though. I never saw him with a new pair—and he never took his old ones off, not for anything."

Rheta flashed me a significant look, the golden glints in her sepia eyes sparking with an intensity that seemed unrelated to her words. I couldn't tell why she was telling me all this, nor did I much care. But despite my indifference, force of habit took over, and dipped my chin, ever the encouraging listener. Teaching can do that to you.

"Anyway, he was a talker; most men are, even when they haven't paid for a woman's time. He used to talk a lot about the early newspaper editors— tramp editors, he called them—and about the papers they published. At the time I didn't give him much more than professional attention, but later I remembered he mentioned finding a cache of those papers out at the ghost town before the state started fixing it up for a tourist attraction."

I nodded again, this time less vigorously, finally catching what she was implying about her past profession and reacting with a slight sense of shock, despite my own propensity for jumping into the sack with anyone who caught my interest and many who didn't.

"Well, here it is." But instead of ushering me into the apartment, Rheta paused.

"Some in town hold my past against me. That's why I try to tell people my version first. So what do you think?"

With relief, I realized that Rheta wasn't asking me to pass judgment on her personal history, but on the apartment. Although I sauntered around the murky space, the place was everything I had expected and more. The carpet was a red of such intensity that the overlay of dust, punctuated by heaps of dead flies in the corner and under the windowsills, didn't do much to dim it. A bar covered with rusty vinyl dominated one wall, and a scabby steam radiator ran under the adjacent stretch of windows, as dirty and diminished as the one in the morgue. A kitchenette of sorts had been cobbled into the interior wall. A filthy counter separated a set of upper and lower cupboards that didn't match. The stove offered only two burners. The humped refrigerator was considerably older than I was. Above the scabrous enamel sink, the ceiling was splattered with perforations.

"Those are just bullet holes," Rheta said, offering no further explanation.

I couldn't tell if Rheta's taciturnity constituted a strategy designed to engage my curiosity or a manifestation of her usual communication style. In any case, I refused to ask the obvious question. Rheta's earlier hook hadn't set that deeply: I could still escape if I retreated into a useful indifference. No one could force me to be taken in by the promise of a phantom stack of papers waiting for discovery, despite my longstanding yen for even a scrap of the *East Bannack News Letter*. That little rag was supposedly published late in 1863 or early in 1864 by a man so flexible in his friendships that he contrived to hobnob both with the local Vigilance Committee and with the sheriff whom its members hanged for good cause—or so they claimed.

"Sorry," I started to say, waving my hand to both indicate and reject the apartment. A faint shudder rattled the glass of the windows against the grip of their plywood cages.

"Damn that press!" Rheta said. With a neat pivot of her spotless Keds, she was gone.

Dump: A place for the deposition of waste rock from a mine; or the waste rock piles themselves (which may still be seen over much of the West).

—T.H. Watkins, in *Gold and Silver in the West: The Illustrated History of an American Dream*

Misfire: The complete or partial failure of a blasting charge to explode as planned.

—*Glossary of Mining Terminology*, rocksandminerals.com

Making Camp: "Son of a bitch. Son of a bitch. Son of a bitch."

SOMEONE WAS SWEARING RHYTHMICALLY IN THE REGIONS BELOW, BUT THE cadence was failing to compel the press to action. The chant grew more and more distinct as I steadied my descent to the newsroom with a railing that shifted uneasily on flimsy aluminum brackets. I hadn't noticed its wobble going up. Obviously a recent innovation, the handgrip didn't do much to mitigate the steepness of the risers. I was grateful, though, for at least the semblance of something to hang on to.

How many frontier editors had suffered drunken tumbles before common sense (or OSHA) finally had compelled the railing? It would be interesting to find out whether the agility developed in skipping lightly from town to town with a fifteen-hundred-pound Washington press in tow saved them from the worst injuries. Or maybe they had been protected by their own brand of unshakable Western optimism. Maybe they rarely stumbled because they were so convinced feet could be trusted to find their own way, leaving hands free to grasp the next advertising dollar. Or the next bottle. Whichever was in reach.

Rheta's smock was draped neatly over the end of the paper's front counter. But the *Sun*'s heavy glass door was still propped open, so I figured she must be around somewhere. The phone on the only occupied desk in the newsroom began ringing insistently with a dull brrrr and then stopped. When the ringing resumed two beats later, I gave in and picked up the receiver, black and heavy and cold. If the outside temperature had risen since morning, it wasn't by much.

Without preamble, the male voice on the other end of the line delivered a threat in a tone that seemed all the more menacing for being perfectly pleasant, "Please tell Mr. MacFarlane if he's not able to get to the museum in five minutes to take the photos of the GoldPro representative as per our appointment, he may cancel the bank's full-page ad for the agriculture edition. In fact, he may cancel the bank's ads for the foreseeable future."

Mr. Courteous-Aggressive hung up abruptly without giving me the chance to explain the newspaper was closed for official business, that the aforementioned ag (apparently not egg) edition was already (more or less) in press, that I wouldn't know Mr. MacFarlane (presumably Conrad-the-editor) if I tripped over him, that I couldn't care less about the *Sun-Tribune*'s ad revenues.

Nevertheless, you don't get a PhD without ending up with an exaggerated sense of your own role in making the world run properly. I can leave colleagues and lovers behind with hardly a pang, but I can't easily shrug off duty defined as work. Besides, it wouldn't hurt me to deliver what was evidently an urgent message before I hit the road again. I could make it to Butte in an hour, in plenty of time to dig out the bottle of scotch for my carefully measured daily allowance. Just as soon as I delivered my message, I'd run not walk to the Bel Air. After I arrived in the town that once was called "The Richest Hill on Earth," I could settle down with my maps and my documents to try to think about what I should do, if not with the rest of my life, at least with the next week or two.

I threaded myself through the newsroom, looking for a route to the basement, where, despite the sullen silence that rose with the fug from the regions below, I hoped someone with authority, perhaps Conrad-the-editor, was still administering aid to the press. Beyond the plastic curtain serving as a greasy barrier between the newsroom and the dim space beyond, someone slammed the *Sun*'s back door. The plastic clung to me like a cheap shower curtain as I jogged through a dim room and then a dark one to catch up. A cold wind was stirring in the surprisingly neat alley, but nothing else.

"Rheta!" At least it was warmer inside.

"Conrad!" I amended, though I was reluctant to shout the name of someone I'd never met. By this time, I had back-tracked from the dark space to the dim one. Along one side of the narrow room, a bank of lighted easels glowed eerily above drifts of paper scraps that must have taken months to accumulate. Strips of leftover news stories rustled on the adjacent wall; they were pinned to corkboard like moths in an entomologist's display. The headlines pasted above the as yet unused stories advised "Battle Against Leafy Surge Continues," "Dog Obedience Classes Set," "Western Beef Called More Nutritious," "Jaycee Honey Sale Slated."

Oh the excitements of the Wild West.

I stood considering my options. It took me a couple of minutes to find the basement door because it was half-hidden behind a contraption that looked like a cross between a hospital gurney and a giant camera. When I threw my voice down a shadowy stairwell, it bounced against unbroken silence. Any sensible human being would have considered her duty discharged. But I couldn't help but think of my pre-digital Nikon perfectly accessible in the Bel Air's glove compartment. I always kept it handy as a backup for my Rebel, which tended to run out of charge at awkward moments. The Nikon was loaded with black and white film, the kind I favor for certain kinds of close-up work. Given the snarl of film on the newsroom desk, I knew the *Sun* must have an old-fashioned darkroom somewhere. If so, it would gratify my inner Luddite to play an old-fashioned journalist for a half hour.

It took me only a few seconds to look up the address of the museum in the Misfire section of the Butte area phonebook that I'd found on Rheta's counter. Glancing from the page to the building directly across the street, I realized that I could satisfy my conscience without much trouble. What I'd taken for Misfire's long and low and logged version of a strip mall was, I now realized, the Elephant Rock County Museum. There was still no traffic as I dodged the potholes in Main Street, although a few parked cars had materialized. They nudged up tight against the railroad ties that provided a suitably folksy curb for the museum.

My feet jounced the boardwalk, which, like the log curb, offered another neo-rustic touch with its planks bright and unworn, still resisting the push of quack grass from underneath.

"I-I-I-I'm glad you're here," the docent whispered, after I brandished the Nikon and announced my mission. His jowls were oddly flaccid for a skinny man. He presided over a card table set up directly under the carcass of a polar bear; it had been positioned by a taxidermist, not a very imaginative one, in an upright posture of eternal menace, its claws—long, sharp, and obviously fake—spread wide. Beyond its back, I saw a scene that would have done justice to a swap meet. Arranged on the concrete floor in wavering rows, unmatched display tables offered up what apparently passed for history in these parts: a congeries of Minié balls, beaded deerskin shirts, wire-rim spectacles, gold pans, bustles, china teacups, hunting knives, and hymnals, all forced into promiscuous couplings, arranged without regard for era or place of origin. In fact, I could spot no organizing principle. Probably each time some Friend of the Museum cleaned out an attic, another table was added.

Even as I felt the weight of the Nikon stretching its shoulder strap, I promised myself that before I left Misfire, I'd give myself a tour. I try to hate these sorts of junky local museums. Professionally, I do hate their jumble, their lack of discrimination (a polar bear in Montana, for God's sake), and, most of all, their smug assumption that the past can be both completely known and accurately reconstituted: that inert fragments can invoke the pulsing, networked, and almost entirely disappeared whole.

As the docent gestured weakly toward a hallway that led away from the museum's main showroom, I was still looking back over my shoulder. In a cabinet shaped like Cinderella's glass coffin, a bustled black dress glittered with jet beads—a weighty dress for a weighty event, a 19th century wedding or a funeral. At least the dress had been laid out with the respect due its fragile seams—someone in the museum must have realized its fragility and its rarity. Thrifty seamstresses transformed most such costumes into more practical garments when the long European obsession with voluptuous hind ends diminished.

I knew I would rather wear the dress than climb into the dentist's chair that sat high and mighty, its treadle-powered drill standing under a trio of dangling hangman's nooses—fakes, the weave of the nylon ropes tight and clean and synthetic. Nearby, a coven of seats circled a pump organ. Looking only marginally more comfortable than the dentist's chair, their backframes had been tortured into existence by taking a considerable number of bulls by their horns. Each chair carried a handwritten sign cautioning the visitor not to sit. Who would want to?

To nudge my attention back to the business at hand, the docent stood up, the bear's wide embrace almost catching his misshapen hat, its brim folded back in stereotypical prospector's fashion. The battered headgear didn't match the computer-generated name tag that labeled him as a Bruce. Neither was his hat the best choice to go with the snazzy black parka that the Bruce was wearing zipped up as far as he could force it over the bulk of his overalls, too blue and crisp to look authentic.

Apparently the museum was trying to save on heating costs. If there was a warm spot anywhere in Misfire, this wasn't it. Bruce looked uncomfortable despite his expensive coat, his face clenched under the jaunty hat. The docents I'd known—and as a historian I'd had to cope with a tedious number of them—had tended to be elderly folks cheerfully trying to stave off mortality by doing genealogy in their spare time—which is to say, all their time. Or worse still, they were members of that annoying species, the history buff. The buff's distinguishing characteristic was an obsession with either a particular kind of "collectable" (steam engines or treadle sewing machines or cavalry uniforms) or with a particular famous event that had been burnished in the popular imagination by some PBS or History Channel program.

The Bruce, however, seemed too young for the former and too unenthusiastic for the latter. I couldn't imagine what else would induce a man of his age to don bibbies and shiver away a Wednesday afternoon in the shadow of a polar bear.

"Bruce!" At the sound of his name, the docent startled. The voice was low and cold. I recognized it immediately even before its owner materialized. Mr. Courteous-Aggressive had a sharp-edged, handsome face, a smoker's dull teeth, and a phiz reminiscent of the most famous of the Marlboro men. He glanced at me, pointedly avoiding my eyes but obviously taking in the slim reporter's notebook I'd snagged from a pile on Rheta's counter.

He directed his command not to me, clearly a no-account hired hand, but to Bruce: "If that's the *Sun*'s photographer, please ask her to step into the hospitality room."

"Nice man," I said as he subsided into a narrow hallway.

Bruce gave the door a fretful glance to make sure Mr. Courteous-Aggressive hadn't heard. "W-we'd better go in—they've been w-waiting for at least a half hour." The slight stutter that slowed his words asserted itself more strongly when he added, "He's, he's, he's my father." It was clear from his diffident tone that Bruce was offering the information not to rebuke me, but to prevent me from embarrassing myself further. I don't know what gave him the idea that I was susceptible to embarrassment.

I bit back my impulse to offer Bruce my condolences. Gratuitous rudeness is not my style—or at least it's not my intended style. Besides, I felt rather pleased, as usual, at the spectacle of parental boorishness. Such demonstrations always serve to remind me that perhaps I shouldn't regret my status as an adopted child.

"I've listed everyone in order and double-checked the spelling of the names," said Mr. Courteous-Aggressive handing me a printout of a caption that he'd written in advance and then built the photo op to suit: the GoldProspectives officials pretending to study a hodgepodge of early gold mining equipment—a bouquet of pickaxes, a splintered sluice box, a row of dented gold pans, a half dozen assayer's scales. Unrelievedly male, they looked as much alike as Baptist preachers, except their suits were pinstriped and their expressions far from sincere.

"I'm sure Conrad will appreciate your very kind efforts to aid the paper," I said. The GoldPro officials looked blank. Mr. Courteous-Aggressive allowed himself the pleasure of a scowl.

"I don't think I caught your name," he said, allowing the threat in his voice out for a little fresh air. "Are you new at the paper?"

"AJ Armstrong." He took a leather notebook from the pocket of his western-style jacket, his shoulders made assertively broader, I suspected, with a little discreet padding. I repeated my name. And then I spelled it, twice, stressing each time the fact that my initials aren't punctuated.

Mr. Courteous-Aggressive laughed angrily. I laughed, too—just as angrily. He smelled of smoke and aftershave and alfalfa hay. We shot each other appraising looks, but I glanced away, deciding that I didn't need to complicate my life with an unpleasant new lover.

There was still nobody at home when I arrived back at the *Sun*. I could have left the film on the counter with the caption and a note. But I didn't. Instead, I went out to the curb and started unpacking the Bel Air. Toiling upwards through air that seemed to lose its oxygen to the climb, I lugged my Mighty Mite vacuum cleaner in one hand and a bucket packed with cleaning supplies and washrags in the other, my coffeemaker tucked under my arm.

If I'd learned nothing else from the peripatetic parents' chase after something they could count as success, I learned to pack the important things where I can find them. Maybe that skill was the only good thing that came from a childhood spend being conveyed over highways that were always under construction, the hours barely lightened by counting the posts of barbed wire fences. The roads of memory were always lonely, the telephone poles sometimes crowned by hawks, little white crosses marking the places in some states where someone had died at the scene of the accident. Like many children of that place and time, I'd grown up believing the crosses loomed above actual graves.

As I paused, huffing slightly on the landing outside the morgue, I felt tempted to set down my impedimenta and launch myself into straightening the abused volumes of disintegrating newspapers beyond the splintered door. But I had inherited my adoptive mother's philosophy if not her genes: work before pleasure. And there was plenty of work in the apartment that apparently I had decided to take. It was too bad Bet and I weren't speaking. She was the one person I knew who'd actually want to hear in detail just how dirty my new "home" was and what I would have to do to make it habitable.

Because the hallway outside the apartment door was cleaner than any surface inside, I let my load settle to the floor. Retrieving the coffeemaker, I flattened its carton to create an island of clean cardboard on the kitchenette's gritty counter. Rusty water dribbled into the carafe from the sink's cold tap, matching the rusty stain sagging from the base of the rusty faucet to the orbit of the rusty drain. When the water wouldn't clear, I tried the other tap. Its stream was just as discolored—and just as cold.

In the bathroom, the situation was even more dismal. Something scuttled at the far border of my peripheral vision as I tried to reset faucet handles that had been dropped into the basin the way broken cart wheels had been abandoned along the Oregon Trail. I comforted myself with the knowledge that cockroaches are rare in Montana, maybe because of the depth of the winters. Despite the threat of hantavirus, I prefer mice. At least they're warm-blooded and comprehensible, if not actually companionable. In any case, there was nothing here to help me battle any type or variety of little live thing. The toilet was dirty, which I had expected, but dry, which I had not. The sight made me glad that I had hunted up the museum's restroom, but sorry that I'd gulped down a cup of complimentary coffee afterwards.

Back downstairs in the *Sun*, I didn't have much better luck. When I located the office's toilet at the bottom of the stairs, I found the facilities so blackened with grime that they'd developed a slick patina. A brownish cud was bobbing in the inch of stagnant water in the toilet. My piss dribbled out reluctantly as I crouched, trying not to let the toilet's seat touch mine. Given my experience in the apartment, I hadn't expected hot water and I wasn't disappointed. Fighting queasiness, I felt my throat thicken.

The apartment looked even worse when I returned, the repository not only of dirt, but of despair. What's more, none of the lights or outlets worked; the *Sun* must have had the electricity disconnected in the ersatz domicile to save a few bucks. The squeaks in the stairs were beginning to sing an all too familiar tune, but I needed the extension cord that I always included in my moving kit. I figured it would reach to the outlet in the morgue.

On my way back to the Bel Air, I sold a classified ad to a skinny man in a toupee and a white coverall after I looked the rates up in the most recent edition of the newspaper. The customer shifted his weight, a pendulum of a man, nervous and stringy. "You should have those rates memorized," he suddenly cuckooed. Half-pleased that someone in town hadn't spotted me immediately as a newcomer, I didn't bother explaining I'd been selling classifieds for the *Sun* for about one minute and thirty seconds.

To prevent a repeat of the experience—and to halt the incoming flight of Arctic air, I considered shoving the newspaper dispenser out of the way so I could close the front door. However, the pile of quarters on the front counter made it clear that the honor system worked in Misfire, at least in matters of small change. Besides, the prop was making it a lot easier for me to haul things in from the Bel Air.

Upstairs, the vacuum cleaner revealed stains of an impressive variety of color and size, but its thrum made me feel less lonely. Encouraged, I stripped down to my T-shirt and turned myself into a one-woman bucket brigade, sloshing water through the coffeemaker to heat it for the scrub bucket, after, of course, I'd made a pot of coffee, a rich East African blend and drank three cups straight up, no cream. Where was the closest Starbucks? Butte probably, or maybe Bozeman. In my saddlebag, a printout waited to map my way to the house of someone in Bozeman who had made it clear she didn't want to see me at her door. The medicinal tang of the iron in the water wasn't that bad, I decided.

Pulling on my rubber gloves with surgical snap, I descended to the car, this time for my boombox. Old-fashioned in my way, I hadn't made the leap to iPod and its ilk. Even my cell phone, out of commission since it had slipped from my pocket into a gas station toilet, had not been the smartest phone in the digital neighborhood. Oh well, Katie Webster would whittle my problems down to size with the blast of her blues—and, with luck, even drown out the throb of the jukebox from the neighboring bar. Apparently the afternoon drinkers liked being slapped around by some latter-day rapper. My other old-fashioned accouterment, a hard-shelled leather briefcase with a lock, I left in the trunk. Containing the most fragile of the tools I used to examine documents, it was part of the professional kit that I didn't really expect to need despite my pretense I was here to do research.

Six hours later, the apartment no longer looked like a house of prostitution that had been abandoned to flies, spiders, and mice. Instead it looked like a house of prostitution that had seen better days but was about to reopen. Released from its blanket of dust, the carpet's red was as lurid as— what else?—blood.

Tired, I boosted myself up on the bar to test its potential as a bed. It was long enough to stretch out on, but I didn't dare risk such a narrow bier. Instead I inflated my air mattress and unrolled my sleeping bag onto the floor. The hot cone of light flowing from the gooseneck lamp was all that was left of light. The extension cord snaked away under the door. The dark weighted me down, kept me from doing more than flexing my right foot to stop the clench of a muscle cramp in the calf of my leg.

Despite my discomfort, I couldn't seem to make myself go through the requisite motions to stand up. I lay there in the sleeping bag, my exposed face and arms cold, my body hot, my briefs as clingy and damp as an unwanted embrace. Every time I shifted slightly, I imagined that I heard something scuffle.

The view was barren, consisting mostly of the kitchen counter, which I'd scrubbed down to a surface that might have once been aqua, but was now the color of aquarium water that needed changing. If the counter had been a teeter-totter, the mass of the stack of documents that had brought me here wouldn't have been enough to keep in balance the weight of personal effects on the other end—the coffeemaker, my battered saddlebag purse, my sweater and my jacket. In the center, my suitcase, an expensive souvenir from my mistaken marriage, acted as a fulcrum. It was still closed, its contents waiting to be put away somewhere. There was a closet door cut into the wall behind the bar, but unaccountably it was locked, so I'd been denied the pleasure of stowing my possessions in an orderly way. Oh well. At least this way it wouldn't take me very long to pack up and leave.

A sudden blinking flash punched itself through the window above the radiator, dying my hands and T-shirt a dirty red. Hefting myself up, I lumbered to the window, stiff-muscled, too tired to sleep. The pair of monstrous neon antlers above the entrance of the bar next door had begun tapping a staccato beat. I would have a nightlight whether I wanted one or not.

"Hey bitch!" someone shouted very loudly from the sidewalk below. "Get your ass in here!" The voice had nothing of a joke in it. Logically, I knew the order couldn't be directed at me. Even so, I stood shock still, a deer mouse transfixed by the pulse of neon light. I pictured a predatory owl perched within swooping range.

Motel, I decided wearily. Motel, even though I hadn't an unbudgeted dollar in my checking account and my credit limit loomed on the horizon.

In the still-deserted office, the draft rushing through the open door could have turned water into ice. My wary glance shot up and down the sidewalk. The neon-striped shadows were empty except for the bagman collapsed on the *Sun's* bench, his dog tucked neatly under the seat. The bagman's now-empty sack was folded into a precise rectangle beside him; the bill of his cap was pulled down over his eyes. Seeing me, he straightened.

"Do you need some help, miss?" Each word was presented precisely. My hands were full, a suitcase in one and my coffeemaker in the other with my sleeping bag wedged under my arm, all ready to be returned to their appointed places in the Bel Air's trunk. If I wasn't going to spend the night upstairs, neither would they. I glanced at my saddlebag purse on the counter and decided that it was unlikely the bagman would make a grab for it.

"I can manage," I said, setting everything on the sidewalk, opening the car's trunk and then quickly re-packing the lot. On my next trip down the stairs, I would wear my sweater.

"I'm certain that you can," he said, moving out of my way to stand under the pulsing antlers. His wire-rimmed glasses were secured at the temple with a string that looped under the back of his cap. Inside the bar, whoever was riding the jukebox had switched to one of the old, slow songs turned up to maximum strength. If I needed to scream, no one would be able to hear me over Hank Williams, Sr. "I'm so lonesome," I sang along under my breath, "I could cry." Hank Williams died, I recall, in the backseat of a car crossing into oblivion so easily that the friend who was driving didn't notice until he stopped for gas.

A further show of strength would be wise, I decided. My car keys made a satisfying arc and landed on Rheta's counter beside my purse with an assertive clank.

"You'll want to close that door this time of night, won't you, miss?"

Not deigning to point out that I'd just emptied my hands to do exactly that, I tried to shove the newspaper rack out the door's path with the additional help of a firm nudge from my hip. The rack didn't budge. I shoved again. The dispenser abruptly surrendered.

"You might be careful . . . ," the bagman began. His words were interrupted by a thud: The door had propelled itself shut. I grabbed its lever. It yielded only a fraction before bumping against a solid stop. On the counter inside, my car keys glittered next to my saddlebag.

For a microsecond, I considered finding a rock to ram through the plate glass that both allowed me to see into the office and kept me out of it. Suddenly, the disheveled newsroom looked more desirable than dirty under its fluorescent lights. Now so cold that my stiff back was threatening a spasm, I tried the door again. Then, despite knowing full well that I had left the car locked as always, I walked back to the Bel Air to rediscover what I already knew.

Angry, I skirted the bagman and the retriever without a word. I never locked myself out of anywhere. Never. The dog pulled himself from under the bench and stood, head bowed and tail down swishing like a ragged mop. I peered over the bar's swinging doors just like the ones in a long line of venerable television westerns. A line of middle-aged men in baseball caps and scuffed work boots slumped on stools, drinking from beer mugs and shot glasses at a long, dark-wooded bar. They looked down, not at the wavering reflections in the mirrors that glinted behind the bottles.

There wasn't a woman in the place. The bitch must have decided not to get her ass in the bar after all, good for her. The only female presence was an old-fashioned nude with heavy breasts; she reclined above the three tables occupying the bar's back wall. The whites of her eyes gleamed. She floated in the smoky air, untouched by the slap of sound from the TV mounted on the opposite walls. Utah was behind Denver by one point. But the drinkers were ignoring the painting and the game with perfect impartiality. Hank, whose voice was still washing over the basketball blare, had landed in the right purgatory for converting pain to music.

The drinkers couldn't have heard me creaking one side of the double doors indecisively, but in a single motion they turned alert eyes toward me.

I stepped on the bagman's foot as I took one step backwards. His boots were so thickly glazed with paint that they cracked.

"Sorry, miss," he apologized, as I gyrated. Before I could think what to do, he retreated.

"I might mention that the alley door is open," he said.

I considered my other options. I could sit on the bench and stand the chill until Rheta or Conrad-the-editor showed up. I could hike for a motel room I couldn't pay for, since my purse was inside on the counter. I could brave the bar, beg to use its phone, and call one of the two people in town besides Rheta whose full names I knew—one I wanted to have as little to do with as possible and the other I planned to stalk. Or I could step into the alley with the bagman. Eying his sloping shoulders, I decided he must be at least seventy-five. I could knock him down if necessary.

"I'll just walk around and see if the door's open," the bagman said. "If so, I'll come on through." He adjusted his cap, let the empty sack flow in a ripple of black plastic over his shoulder, and disappeared around the vacant JCPenney store next door, abandoned except for a trio of mannequins, the streetlight catching them naked. Next to the bagman, the retriever bobbed and huffed along.

After a minute, I saw the bagman emerging into the newsroom, the re-triever still following. Both stopped at the editor's desk, the dog half-disappearing under the desk, the bagman picking up a beer can and shaking it. Finding it empty, he set down his bag and made a deposit, and then repeated the process efficiently until the beer cans were gone. Resuming his progress, he stopped only when he reached the front door. He had to shove the newspaper rack out of the way before he could re-open the door. It took a lot more grunting for him to get the door open again than it had for me to close it.

"Thank you," I managed.

"Don't mention it." Whistling for the dog, he touched the bill of his cap in a gesture that I had thought extinct. "The back's locked up now, so you won't want to close this door again until you're in for the night, will you?"

"No," I said, deciding that it would be churlish, given the circumstances, to tell the bagman to go to hell.

The retriever and the bagman looked on with interest as I unlocked the Bel Air's trunk and carefully placed the keys into the front pocket of my jeans. I'd lost my enthusiasm for driving around the dark town in search of a motel cheap and quiet and clean enough. Come to think of it, the room upstairs now approximated all three requirements, even the last, if I lowered my standards until I could meet them. Once again, I unloaded my suitcase, coffeemaker, and sleeping bag and bundled them up into my grasp, grateful that the air mattress was still in the apartment. When I waved curtly to the bagman to dismiss him, he touched his cap one final time. At least he was discerning enough to refrain from offering me help as I lugged my baggage inside and again shoved the dispenser out of the way. The door clicked shut with a definiteness that I liked, now that I was on the inside looking out.

Upstairs, I put the coffeemaker into brew mode once again. The water had finally cleared—or perhaps the rust just didn't show in the light from the gooseneck lamp. One of my contacts blinked out as I bent over the inoperable bathroom sink, probably out of some misguided sense of doing the proper thing in the proper place. As I splashed by hands in the battered dishpan of water I had imported from the kitchen, my damp face floated in the dim bathroom mirror. It was pale as the pit of a sour cherry in the light of the emergency lantern that I had brought up from the car. I couldn't make out the red in my hair or the crisscrossed scratches in the lenses of my glasses. Maybe my contact would reveal itself in the morning light.

I busied myself for a while making a meal of sorts from my emergency kit, tuna on crackers, slices of an apple whose skin slipped over the softening flesh beneath. Finally, I measured out a precise shot of scotch, mine, not the editor's—Glenlivet 18, the best I could afford. I checked the time on my travel clock. It was just a little after ten o'clock, and I never went to sleep before midnight. But what else was there to do? My drink didn't last another five minutes.

After I unrolled by sleeping bag again, I forced myself into its cling and willed myself to sleep. The neon antlers ticked relentlessly. The muscles in my calves cramped as I tried to mimic a relaxed stretch, my hair spiked under my head. My ears strained to sieve out the throb of the bar's jukebox from any creakings that might indicate the return of the prodigals.

Pulling myself up, I snapped in a CD, Billie Holiday. But Billie isn't one to send you to sleep. Giving up the light so that I could switch cords, I made a fresh pot of coffee; my heart was pounding already from the day's overdose of caffeine. Restlessly, I paced and then went back downstairs, not bothering to change out of the sweat pants and clean T-shirt I'd worn to bed.

Back in the newsroom, I poured another scotch, this time from the editor's private stock. I told myself the second one wouldn't count it if didn't come from my own bottle. No one could see me from the street as long as I stayed seated at the desk enclosed by the office's maze of partitions. This was sort of fun, I decided, straightening up the editor's desk in revenge for his disappearance, filling a wastebasket with takeout cartons and converting the avalanche of newspapers on the desk into a neat stack ordered chronologically. Shoving the heavy Underwood Champion typewriter out of my way, I sorted the photos as to type, put all the copy pencils in a mug, and used one old-fashioned paper spike to impale receipts for the Chinese restaurant the editor must favor and another to puncture a series of overdraft notices for both Conrad's and the *Sun-Tribune*'s account. The desk drawers were locked. Resisting the temptation to jimmy at least one open, I thought about going upstairs but decided that I still wasn't sleepy enough.

The easel lights still burned in the composing room. The basement's stairwell opened below into a room bright and surprisingly clean considering the state of the rest of the building. Rolls of newsprint were stacked neatly on one end of the room, opposite the press that stood silent at the other. Although a pool of dirty water leaked from one end of the press, the

moisture magnified the gleam of a stretch of highly waxed linoleum. Curious, I picked up one of the damp newspapers that had been tossed down to
wick up the moisture. The headlines on the front page were blurred. Deciding I didn't care enough about Misfire to try to decipher them, I tossed the
paper down and paced the perimeter of the room to yet another stretch of
curtain, this one dusty and black rather than greasy and plastic. Apparently
whoever was in charge of the *Sun*'s interior design, having found a formula,
was content to repeat it with variations on a theme.

Behind the fall of the heavy drapes, I found what seemed to be the old-
fashioned darkroom that was to digital photography what the Underwood
on Conrad's desk upstairs was to my laptop. (I'm not a complete Luddite.)
Noticing a sink that looked considerably cleaner than the other two I'd seen
in the building, I stepped into the red haze of the safety light and turned on
the tap. In a few seconds, clean, hot water splashed onto stainless steel. Too
bad the sink wasn't big enough to climb into.

There were enough corners, closets, and storerooms secreted in the *Sun*
building to hide a convention of criminals, but I felt entirely safe. Maybe it
was the scotch. Maybe it was the hot water. Maybe it was lack of commonsense. Whatever the inspiration, when I reached the top of the basement
stairs, instead of making my way back up to the apartment, I pushed my
way into the dark space that separated the composing room from the alley.
Blinking, I strained my eyes for a light switch. Should I risk my fingers in
the maze of pipes and cords to my right? Was there a cord dangling from
the oversized bulb I could make out overhead? The muddy illumination
seeping from the composing room didn't allow me to see so much as to
sense the bulges of what were probably canvas sacks. Tripping over something, I landed on my hands and knees in one of the piles just as someone
rapped at the back door.

I expelled one long startled breath and then squared my shoulders.

"Yes. Who is it?" I said in the firm voice I had developed for classroom
deployment.

"No one, Miss." The thin voice easily slipped through the door. "Nicholas Stanislavsky— from the bench. Are you all right?"

"Yes," I said steadily. "Just checking the door."

"I was just double-checking it myself. I'm sorry to have startled you."

"You didn't," I said, not displeased that the bagman and his retriever were patrolling the night. Knowing that I had guards on duty, I decided to attempt my makeshift bed again.

But I couldn't sleep. Lying there, hot and cold in patches, I realized anyone could have slipped into the *Sun* during the long hours the newspaper's front door had been left unattended. More out of a respect for proper procedure than from fear, I dragged a particularly solid desk chair up from the newsroom, tipped its back against the door and balanced my biggest suitcase in the angle of its repose. It wasn't yet midnight.

When the suitcase banged me out of a sticky and restless sleep a few minutes later, I sat bolt upright, too startled to be actually frightened. Hoping I was in the throes of a nightmare with sound effects, I grabbed for my glasses.

"Dammit to hell!" a shadow yelled as it tumbled over the now upended chair. I opened my mouth. When I howled, somebody else howled, too. Now that I had hooked one of the earpieces of my glasses, I could see my assailant was lifting his blunt nose toward the ceiling, his mouth gaping below.

"Get out of here or I'll scream," I shouted, ignoring the fact that both the intruder and I had tried that tactic already, and in unison.

"Who the hell are you!" the assailant shouted, using the chair to struggle to his feet. In the murk, I could see a small man with a large mustache.

"Who the hell are you?" My voice was calmer than his had been. Somehow I found it difficult to fear someone with 19th century facial hair. By this time, I was on my feet myself, my fists clenched at my side.

"I'm Conrad J. MacFarlane, editor of this newspaper, and unless you're prepared to answer to the law, you'd better explain what you and that sleeping bag are doing on my floor."

"I'm renting this floor and all the rest of this rat trap, so you'd better leave right now."

"You're renting this apartment?"

"Yes, I paid a week in advance to Rheta Fox today," I lied.

"You're not with GoldPro, are you?"

"Get out."

The editor opened his mouth. But instead of saying anything more, he dodged the suitcase and the chair and slammed out.

Slightly shaking, I checked my travel clock. Twenty minutes after twelve.

I had thought it must be later. Sighing, I hesitated between the bottle of scotch and the coffeepot. Rejecting both, I found my coat and firmed a fist around my car keys.

No two spring storms are identical.

—Meteorologist Warren G. Harding, in *Montana Weather: From 70° Below to 117° Above*

Three hours later: Outside the Haunted House

THE SKY LUMINESCES WHITE. THE ONE LIGHTED WINDOW IN THE HOUSE across the street blinks through the blowing snow. On AJ's side of the street, the park's tender stretch of April grass gives up the struggle to keep tips atop powdery whitecaps. Powdered snow-white herself, she stands shaking in the wind like the tree hiding her in its shadows. The clack of bare branches reminds her that patience is a virtue, especially when sticking your leaves (or your neck) out at the wrong time in the wrong place can get you into a lot of trouble. Maybe this is the wrong place and the wrong time.

At least her trembling isn't violent enough to separate her shadow from the tangled chiaroscuro of dark branches and white drifts.

If the light in the window means Everonica is awake, she almost certainly can't see AJ. Even if Everonica is staring out the window, her view must be limited to wind-driven waves of snow so insubstantial that they rise and flatten, now covering the dark street and now revealing it again. But, if AJ moves, Everonica might notice. AJ slips a little deeper into the shadow of the not-so-green ash, a member of a species that sleeps late in the spring.

As if to reproach—or reward—AJ's decision, the second-story light blinks out. The tidy shutters, which AJ has been imagining as deep colonial green, melt into rectangles dark against the light paint. Her breath whistles in her ears as the wind sighs to a sudden stop. She rocks slightly on feet that would be happier in felt-lined Sorels. When she left her dismal *Sun* apartment for Bozeman, AJ figured that she could make her mother's house in an hour and a half—a trip so short and easy that she didn't even consider trying to hunt up an internet café (was there such a thing in Misfire?) to check the weather. Still, this snow is nothing, the ghost of winter past, not a real storm.

A wing of drapery flutters at the downstairs window. A knife-edge of light cuts the dark but fails to come close to probing the spot where AJ is playing a sorry-assed snow angel, not yet fallen, but on the precipice. Does the feathery weight on her shoulders represent the landing of Everonica's glance? If the sparrow can feel the glance of the hidden cat, can the cat sense the returning ripple of prehension? Can AJ's mother feel her daughter nerving herself to ford the street? Compelled by atavistic connection, is Everonica fighting the compulsion to throw back the deadbolt and step out on her porch?

More likely, Everonica is drinking a cup of herbal tea in her kitchen—or calling the police to report a shadowy burglar casing the joint. AJ tries to picture Everonica with a heavy white china cup comforting the palm of her hand, but she can't. AJ has no idea what Everonica looks like. When she tries to see her mother, all AJ can see is the specter of herself.

A plow rumbles, troubling the snowlight with the yellow pulse of its beacon. When the plow looms in front of the tree, walling her away from her mother's house, AJ turns and runs.

The small song birds had arrived, and . . . following the storm many small birds were found dead in the snow around the city.

—Meteorologist Warren G. Harding, in *Montana Weather: From 70° Below to 117° Above*

Three hours later: Inside the Haunted House

EVERONICA LOOKS INTO THE BLIND WHITE EYE OF THE STORM WONDERING if she has set out her sweet pea seedlings too early. Across the street, tree shadows dance with the swirling snow; when the wind pauses to catch its breath, the shadows settle into a watcher. Everonica stares hard at the shape and then decides not to worry about it. Commonsense assures her no one would be crazy enough to stand still in the middle of a storm just to spy on her. Just in case, though, she keeps out of view, draping herself in the dimness of the living room like a nude behind a towel. Besides the gurgle of the coffeemaker in the adjacent kitchen, the television provides the room's only pulse of movement and chatter. A genial looking couple is bantering with scripted affection as they cooperate to hawk a fancy juicer practically guaranteed to bestow its user eternal life. Infomercials have become Everonica's companions these last few months when night limps toward dawn. Watching them palliates her very bad case of acid reflux of the soul. It's the memory of that voice that shivers her stomach, a female voice nasal with deep need and too much education. An arrogant voice asserting hopeless hopes based on unreasonable reasons.

At the hiss of Everonica's breath, the half-dozen cats who have arranged themselves in a tableau of feline content twitch off the sofa, hustling to displace a particularly uxorious tom who has been keeping her stocking feet warm with his weight. As he stands up and yawns to display his teeth, Everonica pads toward the kitchen, puffs of fur drifting in her wake. Her floors—all bare wood—are not as clean as they will be when the school year finally drags to a conclusion and she begins a summer of serious scrubbing alternating with serious gardening.

The sweet peas never do well if she lets them develop more than four true leaves before she moves them from their laundry room nursery into the black slice of earth along the front yard fence. Despite the winter storm warning, last evening she patted them into what she hoped would be their cradle, not their grave. Not one to allow herself the futile indulgence of self-doubt, she pushed her worries aside then and does so again now. Sweet peas are surprisingly tough, better able to lift their heads up again after a heavy snow than to survive the light warm waterfall of artificial light inside. She thinks they will make it.

Probably the coffee isn't a good idea, but she will chew an antacid tablet first. She needs the coffee to calm her anxiety, not that she is at all afraid to be alone in this house. She loves the house. Besides, she has always been alone in the house, even when her son was growing up, and even when her husband was home to entertain her with his smooth patter. His stories, irrespective of their connection with reality, are the thing she still likes best about her ex.

Everonica loved her husband more-or-less, first more and later less, but she never trusted him with her secrets. But tonight she would welcome his company. He drops by to clean the leaves from the rain gutters and to ask advice on where he might be going wrong with his relationship with his new wife and her sixth-grade daughter. It is the friendliest of divorces. When he failed to make it home one Friday night after his week on the road repairing computers, she didn't actually notice until lunch the next day. He, knowing that she never checked her e-mail on the weekend and guessing (correctly) that she wouldn't pay attention to his absence, showed up Sunday afternoon. He thought they needed a break from each other. After the first muffled shock, she thought so, too.

When the coffeemaker beeps, the cats try to lead her to the refrigerator, their tails snaky with lust for a bonus bite of the tuna she uses to tempt them inside every cold evening. She glances down with pleasure and shame. With pleasure at the chorus of discordant purring, at the lopsided twitching of ears, tips clipped flat on one side to demonstrate that someone has cared enough to limit their biological imperative to yowl, to spray, and (these preliminaries completed) finally to fuck and (about nine weeks later) to multiply at an astounding rate. In Salem, they would have burned her for a witch, a punishment Everonica is sure some of her latter-day neighbors would endorse. Because these six aren't all. There are another dozen outside, too wild to venture into the warm spot by her flickering television. One is a female that Everonica has been trying to catch since last summer. While she planted her sweet peas, the cat, still half a kitten herself, crouched moaning at the far end of the driveway, her behind arched high, her white feet stamping in rhythmic desperation. Everonica could relate.

She provides shelter for the shy and suspicious outside on her patio in the form of old kitchen cupboards furnished with heating pads, litter boxes positioned a genteel distance away to discourage her charges from digging up her—and more to the point—her neighbors' flowers and vegetables. These measures, combined with the fact that Everonica feeds the multitudes out of sight and isn't afraid of trading on her status as a respectable (if only they knew) teacher of high school history, have worked—so far—to keep the neighbors pacified.

Although the sky outside glows with snowlight, Everonica expects the drifts will vanish with the rising sun. She expects most of her sweet peas will survive. If not, she will cut her losses and seed a new crop directly into the detritus of the storm. Let the dead bury their dead—a good policy, one that limits liability. Everonica leaves her still hot cup of coffee on the counter and pads up to bed. The television is still burbling away downstairs when her alarm rings at seven.

This animal stood symbolically for the whole business of gold seeking. When a San Franciscan told a friend that he'd about decided to "see the elephant," he did not mean that he was going on a toot, but that he intended to take a flier at the mines.

—Stewart Edward White, in *After Old California, In Picture and Story*

The Blind Woman and the Elephant

DESPITE THE COMFORT OF HOT COFFEE, I SAT ON THE FLOOR, STILL SHUD-dering from the aftereffects of the snowy trip to Bozeman, my back against the bar, my paper trail winding white and tan on the lurid carpet. I told myself that last night had been nothing more than a false start. Today was the day that I would follow my train of crumbs back to their starting point. I would reorient, reboot, and reinvent my goal to one that was rational, well defined and possibly attainable. So why was I hunched into immobility, fighting depression, but not fighting it very hard?

If not pride, I should have been feeling at least relief. I had worked hard to get this far. Every fragment of information, except the first, had given itself up to me one painful piece at a time. A year ago in Seattle, I finally talked myself into petitioning Montana's Fifth Judicial Court in Helena to release my birth and adoption records. Six weeks later, I sank to sit on the eroding top step of the front porch of my run-down rental, the rest of the day's mail stuffed in my jacket pocket, the oversized envelope trembling in my hand. It had been almost too easy, too quick.

Opening the clasp of the flap—it hadn't even been sealed—I first saw the hand-written note positioned on top to prepare me for a letdown: the requested birth certificate was enclosed, but the file with my adoption documents had not yet been located. Those records would be sent to me if and when they were found.

For once in my life, however, I saw my glass as half full, not half-empty. When my birth certificate offered up my mother's name typed (the vowels smudged, the serifs of the consonants missing) and then repeated (I presumed) in her own uneven hand. I said her name aloud in the raw Seattle morning. I said it three times.

I had no one with whom to share that dangerous chant. I certainly couldn't tell my mother—that is to say, my adoptive mother. As usual, I was quarreling with Bet, intensely, continuously, and bitterly. Even if we ever reached another truce, she wouldn't want to hear this particular news. She had made that much and more clear.

It was the spring I was sixteen, and a backhoe had been clawing away for days in the cemetery across the street. After the deep subsoil freeze of winter in Grand Forks, North Dakota, the intermittent arrival of hearses made it clear that it was time to plant more than the local gardens.

"The landlord should have warned us about this." As usual, she was crocheting, but I could see she was pulling the cotton thread too tight, distorting the stitches into tight little nooses. Not that it mattered. She made doilies by the dozens and then abandoned them on the kitchen counter of our latest rental whenever we moved.

"I wonder where they keep the coffins all winter," I asked, not at all innocently. I was beginning to develop my mean streak.

I should have shut up then. I had already changed into the nylon uniform for my after-school waitress job, which was for me a symbol both of imminent adulthood and the potential for future stability. Bet and Chas had stayed the whole school year in Grand Forks, an unusual circumstance that had allowed me to settle into the strangeness of an actual routine. Now they were getting ready to move again, but I wanted to stay put to finish my senior year, and I said so again for about the twentieth time in the last hour.

"No," Bet said, her repetitious rejoinder. "Sixteen isn't old enough for you to live on your own."

"Well, what is sixteen old enough for then? Is sixteen old enough for you to finally tell me about my mother, my real mother! How long am I supposed to wait?"

Bet threw the misbegotten doily against the wall next to my head, the spool of cotton thread bouncing down the wall with it.

"After all I've done for you." She hissed like a June bug as she ran the lines I'd heard hundreds of times before. How she had pinched me as an infant, a baby who had been so neglected that I had already learned there was no use wailing. Prodded me to cry to get air into my weak little lungs. Kept pinching and prodding every minute of my life afterwards— always for my own good.

"Nobody could have loved you more," she whispered. A shout wouldn't have been nearly as insulting—or as terrifying. "If you want to hurt me, just keep asking your questions. But just remember—you might be sorry once you know the answers."

It had taken me years to dismiss Bet's words as hyperbole. Her declarations of maternal love kept me from searching, despite decades of having to lie when officials of various sorts shoved forms at me that asked for "mother's maiden name," the incantation guaranteed to abracadabra up an identity as hidden and common as the muscle that contracted in every living chest.

But Bet was the one, the only one, I wanted to tell after I tore open that envelope. Not my adoptive father, who'd always been more of an absence than a presence in my life. Not my ex-husband, who would find a way to use this gelatinous lump of information against me. Not my old friends, not that I had any, really. Not my colleagues, who were interested only in the kind of conversations that could skate without a skip across a coffee shop table.

So I crouched over the envelope on my rented porch, my mother's name tasting like iron in my mouth. I sat alone and tried to like the solitary bite of it, the way it resisted the tongue: Everonica Louise Ohm, a name that zinged. As for my father's name, that line had been left blank.

Still, I was no longer completely bereft of information. Thankful for the rarity of my mother's first name, I began searching for it on the internet when I should have been working on my book, grading my students' exams, writing committee reports. There was a ritual to my hunt. First, I would post a note on my office door, its window papered over with Xeroxed images of Calamity Jane, who, according to unsubstantiated tradition, had given up a daughter herself. The note proclaimed the truth, if not the whole truth: "No office hours today—Dr. Armstrong is conducting research." Locked in, I settled behind the stacks of books that I'd arranged as a barrier between my desk and my computer table to give my enterprise the image of respectability in case someone with a key (the department chair or the custodian) happened to walk in. My bottle of scotch, I kept under a stack of exams in the deepest of my desk drawer. I would measure out the first in a series of single shots into a clean coffee cup, crack the window, and get to work.

Divorced by that time, I was addicted to the distraction of the hunt. I itched sexually, but I wouldn't stoop to seducing a student. Nor would I risk my reputation on our gossip-ridden small campus by slutting around with my professorial peers.

I searched systematically, first by the city of my birth, then by state, and finally by region, staring into the screen for hours, spending more money than I could afford on sites that offered to scan census records. Locate death or birth records. Conduct background checks. Provide names, addresses, and phone numbers of all the hits generated by all possible variations of my natural mother's name. I would stagger away from my computer panting after what felt like a desperate race, one that I had lost.

My initial trouble was famine; my subsequent trouble, feast. There were no Ohms currently listed in Misfire, where I'd been born, and too many Ohms elsewhere, fifty-four in Wisconsin alone. Since I could find no trace of any American Everonica in all the virtual world, I resorted to calling Ohms, two or three a day, asking them if they had heard of my mother. In the meantime, I kept trawling the web for family trees and census records that weren't embargoed, hoping to catch at least a glimpse of Ohms who might have lived in Montana.

Locked up in my tiny office, I strained my eyes staring into my computer screen, neglecting the work I was getting paid to do, ignoring the department chair's messages about the need to come to see her to discuss my teaching evaluations and my progress toward publication. A modestly promising scholar as a doctoral student, I had wrung the requisite number of articles out of my dissertation. But my university expected a book as a condition of getting tenure and keeping my job. And I no longer could pretend, even to myself, that a book was going to appear, unless a scholarly race of elves cobbled one together for me in the night.

Not knowing my past, I was unable to get on with my future.

Since I couldn't discover any Everonica or Eve or Evie in Montana the year that I was born, I started rummaging through internet obituaries and genealogy websites for potential relatives. Discovering nothing. I guessed Everonica's parents were obscure folks who didn't make the news when they were alive and whose obituaries had been published in little local newspapers that were still scrambling to create online archives. For a while I was stuck. It seemed my only choice was to leave the safety of the internet and engage with hazardous reality. But I couldn't afford a trip to Montana, I told myself. What I really couldn't afford was failure at the end of the road.

Finally overcoming my disinclination to ask anyone for help for any reason, I phoned the history department at Montana State University. Wrapping up my need for the information in a plausible professional context, I talked my MSU counterpart into setting his graduate research assistant to work on my behalf. The graduate student located a disconcerting accident report from the Butte newspaper: my grandparents Mr. and Mrs. William Ohm of Bannack, Montana, had died in an accident in April of 1966, about six months before I was born. There were more details in the article about the rollover on snowy Badger Pass than there were about the victims themselves. The obituaries were limited to a brief joint death notice published a day later. There was another survivor listed besides Everonica: a married sister living in Misfire. However, the graduate student found that Mrs. T.N. (Elizabeth) Smith and her husband had disappeared from the Misfire phone book the very next year.

The graduate student, bless him and his dogged determination, decided to try another approach. He sifted through lists of graduates from Montana colleges in the ten years after my birth. Failing to find a match for the Normal School in Misfire, he tried MSU next and encountered Everonica Hunsaker as a secondary education history graduate in December of 1975. Feeling satisfied that he had located a probable match, the RA passed on the information, along with a number he had found for Evie Hunsaker in the Bozeman phonebook.

The only thing Everonica offered me when I called, my voice shaking, was a Biblical quote, "Let the dead bury their dead." Her voice was old glass, bubbled with an emotion I couldn't identify. It shattered when she broke the connection. My letters to her were thrown back at me, refused at the post office. And when I persisted, a letter, formal and cold, warned me to keep my distance or face legal consequences. It was an unenforceable threat, I believed, but one that chilled me to my DNA.

Had she known me, Everonica would have realized that nothing would make me want information more than being denied information. I thought about hiring a private detective. But why should I, a trained researcher, pay someone to do work I could do myself? There might be grizzlies in the undigitized wilderness, but there also could be streams where the fishing might be good.

In truth, there was less and less to hold me in Seattle. Normally at my institution, two weak pre-tenure evaluations get an assistant professor a third year of grace to repair her record—or to find another job. I wasn't about to wait around for the bad news. Possessed by the need to grasp the nettle firmly, I broke university policy by giving my final tests a couple of weeks early. Within hours of filing my grades, I started packing. The day before I left town, the chair of the department told me that she had requested an emergency leave for me to attend to a "family crisis"—the euphemism she used to telegraph a plausible reason for my dismal job performance to the string of committees and administrators that would need to excuse my sudden disappearance. Most of them knew the real story anyway, since my ex-husband (already tenured and a full professor, damn him) made it a point to hobnob with the big fish in our small pond.

"But I'm not coming back," I told Katharine, carefully keeping the anger out of my voice in deference to the fact that my boss had taken a risk by shaping the rules to accommodate what I knew she saw as a form of temporary insanity. It was kind of her, even though that kindness would benefit the department as much as it would me—by saving my position from the budget chopping block until the economy started repairing itself.

"You might change your mind in a few months," Katharine said, a small woman with a big job that she did well down to every last detail, including trying to save the career (and for her, that meant the life) of a junior faculty member. "Besides, the leave will force the university to keep paying for your insurance."

Oh. Okay. Always the pessimist, I did want to keep my insurance. And, always the pragmatist, I knew I would need references when I was ready to look for my next job, even if the job wasn't an academic one. I didn't want

Katharine's pity, but I knew that I would need her continuing professional goodwill. And there was one more thing: there was some small comfort in the fact that someone—even if that someone was an employer with an impersonal sense of responsibility—thought that I was worth taking trouble over.

Now that I was in Misfire, stuck in the mud of an unfriendly spring morning, that thought helped steady me into action. Rising to my knees from my apartment's appalling red carpet, I resolved to send Katharine an appropriately appreciative postcard—and, more to the point, deliver a package she had sent along with me for one of the local history professors. But right now I had to get going. My brother was waiting.

The genuine prospector is always looking about him, is everlastingly cracking stones, has always his eyes wide open for "something kind 'o curious."

—Arthur Lakes, in *Prospecting for Gold and Silver in North America*

The Scenic Route

"Good morning, AJ—or did you get enough sleep to make it a good morning?" Perched on her stool, Rheta was neatly folding yellow sheets of paper—I took them for invoices—and slipping them into envelopes.

"I apologize," called Conrad-the-editor from behind the Underwood, his fingers continuing to pump forcefully at keys that stood up like eye stalks on an alien insect. Abruptly he threw the carriage into position for a new line and, with a surprisingly fluid movement, pushed back his chair and rose to his feet. The Famous Grouse bottle was no longer visible, I noticed.

"Again, I really must apologize." A small white button popped from his shirt and spun across the room. He didn't deign to notice its trajectory—or the bulge of thin white T-shirt that had erupted into the gap right above his belt buckle. Instead, he reached out and snatched my hand.

"Still, I'm certain you won't harbor any ill feelings when you understand the unfortunate comedy of errors that resulted in our little upset."

When I tried pulling my fingers out of his grip, Conrad clasped them more securely and took another half-step in my direction. His breath smelled minty. I tugged more firmly and won my release. "Certain problems with the press yesterday caused an uncharacteristic mental lapse, and I did not understand that the apartment had been rented by yourself."

In the morning light, he looked even less prepossessing than he had the night before: sad, stout, and polyester-clad.

Rheta lit a fresh cigarette with an air of practiced patience. "I did tell you twice, Conrad, while we were loading up the press plates. I would have told you a third time but you were frantic to get me on the road to Bannack."

"Alas, I could not be two places at once, covering that meeting and driving through the blackness of the night to Hamilton."

Never having heard the word "alas" uttered by anyone with serious intent, I couldn't help but imagine Conrad's words in flowing copperplate. Apparently attributing my bemused silence to confusion, he looked at me. "We have an arrangement with our sister publication in Hamilton to help us cope with such problems, rare though they be."

"Rare," Rheta said, her tone calling Conrad a liar.

"In any case, when I finally arrived back in town I suddenly realized I had left without securing the building. Imagine my horror when I drove up to see what looked like the glow of an intruder's light from the upstairs window." I waited for his words to stop the way someone might wait out a cold rain under an awning.

Rheta began stamping envelopes by hand, dabbing each one on a sponge sitting on a cracked plate before placing it precisely in each corner. "I should have checked myself after I got back from Bannack. But I was already late picking mother up from day care at the rest home." She turned her gaze to me. "I tried phoning a few times, but I couldn't raise you. Finally, I just told myself anyone with a doctor's degree would have the brains to close a door. And apparently you were fine—at least until Conrad decided to leap without looking."

Conrad made another lunge for my hand, which I succeeded in dragging away.

"Anyway, my dear, I hope you will forgive my intrusion." Against the burbling of his voice, I forced myself to resist the undertow, to raise my head and take a breath.

"I will, if you get the electricity connected and the hot water going," I said, striking for shore with a pretense at vigor. There. I had tried and succeeded in taking the first step out of the muck of depression by halfway wanting something. Yes. I did want to get cleaned up for my first morning in Misfire.

"I myself am too busy to attend to that errand this morning, but I'm sure Rheta can make the arrangements." Conrad settled back into his chair, picking up a green eyeshade from beside the Underwood. To me the visor looked like the kind of thing that healthy and wealthy grey-haired tennis players (if there were any still left in this recession) wore to protect their eyes from the January sun in Arizona. Under the fluorescent lights, the visor transformed Conrad's skin from pale to bilious.

"Will do," said Rheta reaching for the phone book. "With any luck, AJ, you'll be in business by this afternoon. I can't imagine why the gas and electricity aren't on since we'd decided that it would be best to keep the apartment connected." She gave Conrad a disapproving glance. "We'll have to pay extra to get the gas company to relight the pilot light on the water heater."

"I can accomplish that task—after all, I'm the one who switched it off. A penny saved is a penny earned, is it not?"

"Conrad," Rheta said. Her voice had an edge to it that I guessed had been precisely honed by a long dispute. "Remember the last time? Besides, if you need something to do, you might work on the cleaning. I'm tired of going across the street to use the museum's ladies' room. Why don't you let me hire the Tuott boy to get it done? Wouldn't cost us that much."

"As you know, we cannot afford any extra expense," Conrad said. But he had stopped in midstride. "Why don't you join me this morning in my efforts to return our office environment to a pristine condition?"

"Your turn," Rheta said. "Has been for two months."

"By the way," I said, trying to fix on a desire less complicated than my thwarted attempt to obtain a hot shower. "Is there any place to eat nearby that's not too expensive?"

As Conrad swept off his visor, I noticed his eyes were a deep Liz Taylor violet. He blinked rapidly, either from earnestness or the misplaced middle-aged vanity of contact lenses, a vanity I shouldn't criticize since I shared it. "Perhaps you'll allow me to take you out to show you how sincerely I regret my error of last night."

I heard my internal alarm go off, the one that jangled when I sensed unwelcome amorous intentions. "I wouldn't think of interrupting your work," I said, and immediately regretted my lack of directness. Subtlety, I'd found, was wasted on most men.

"Perhaps I could make up my lack of courtesy to you in some other way." Conrad bounced up from his chair. I stirred myself to take evasive action. He followed. "Rheta tells me you're a historian. Perhaps I could give you a tour of the museum—I'm on its board and have certain privileges there."

Been there, done that. Saying as much, I produced the film I had shot at the bequest of Mr. Courteous Aggressive and graciously (for me) accepted Conrad's thanks.

"Allow me some way of expressing appreciation," Conrad insisted. "I must buy you breakfast to repay you for your work. And then I could take you on a drive to one of our most historic places, the ghost town of Bannack. I'm on good terms with the park manager, and she, on my request, would show you the sights and open archives not often available to the public."

I paused, considering his offer. "You must have a paper to get out."

"The life of the editor of a weekly does have its small compensations," he said. "Although we have an extra edition this week, my successful journey last night allowed the mail crew to get it signed, sealed, and delivered to the post office this morning while you were still snug abed upstairs."

I retreated a couple of steps at the gratuitous insertion of the word "bed" into the conversation. He blinked anxiously, but didn't try to close the gap. "Our next edition won't be published until next week." He made next week sound as far away as New York City.

I paused again. I was hungry, or should be, and on a tight budget, so OK to the breakfast. As for the ghost town, maybe it would disarm my prey if I arrived in Conrad's company. Besides, riding with Conrad would save me a few dollars in gas. The Bel Air was ever a thirsty girl, having been born in a time when gas was cheap and optimism was a sky with an unlimited ceiling.

"Well, I do need to talk to the park manager about Bannack's archives," I said, not mentioning that I'd already suffered through a couple of phone conversations with Delores Tendoy, a woman remarkably taciturn given her membership in that usually helpful species, the park ranger. She had brushed off my inquiries, which was actually all right with me. Research was merely my excuse, not my reason, for my interest in Bannack.

"Sure, AJ, go eat hearty and let Conrad show you the sights," Rheta said. I noticed that she refrained from reminding the editor that he'd just claimed to be too busy to tackle the bathroom. "By the time you get back, you'll have hot water to wash the dirt of the road off."

I preferred cleaning up before breakfast—and said so. Rheta handed me the key to her house and gave me directions.

Embarrassed by her generosity, I nevertheless accepted the key and went back upstairs to get a change of clothes. Her brick bungalow with its cheery blue door surprised me. The old-fashioned linoleum rug in the kitchen was so highly waxed that its pink roses glowed. The refrigerator was a massive contemporary model that seemed at odds with the rest of the room. Its smooth stainless steel surface was unmarked by family photos or crayoned drawings by children. In one corner, a walker suggested that the house did have another occupant, however. I resisted the temptation to peek in the bedrooms to confirm my guess. In the living room, a half dozen oil land-scapes, moody and complex, dominated one wall. When I looked more closely I saw a modest signature in the corner of each: Rheta Fox.

When I returned to the newspaper an hour later, Conrad was waiting by the receptionist's desk. He gave the impression of holding the door for me, even though it was once again wedged open by the paper dispenser. The newly minted headline showing through its window looked crisp and businesslike: "GoldProspectives May Impact Local Agriculture."

"What's the story on GoldPro?" as we walked toward the restaurant. Usually, I avoid small talk, but I needed something to keep me focused.

"Now that's no topic for an empty stomach," Conrad said, lifting his nose toward the scent of frying bacon.

"Whatever," I thought.

The air in the Golden Hour was so stiff with grease that I could feel it scuffing my bronchi on its way to abrade my lungs. Too bad there wasn't a Clean Air Act regulating bacon fat. Trying not to breathe too deeply, I stopped my slide into a booth seat the instant I felt a sudden invasion of moisture into the back of my jeans. My sit-down shifted into an awkward stand-up.

"Allow me." Conrad pulled a large railroad bandanna from his back pocket and began blotting at the sheen of moisture that overlay the vinyl.

"Damn kid spilled her orange juice," said the woman who materialized beside the table with a sponge that reeked of chlorine. Gathering up plates smeared with ketchup and decorated with steak bones with one hand, she swabbed the oilcloth with the other and slapped down two paper placemats printed with the image of a silhouetted outlaw dangling from a gallows. The outlaw seemed to twist slightly as the paper blotted up the leavings of the sponge. My nonexistent appetite decided to light out for the Territories, as I kept clear of the damp.

"Waiting tables today, Lena? I thought that's what the staff was for."
Conrad sounded nervous.

"Have to. New girl can't keep up."

Lena pointed her chin in the direction of a skinny post-adolescent who
was standing empty-handed in the middle of the floor. The girl was tossing
her head like an acned horse, clearly wanting to run, but unable to decide
where.

"Crystal, get yourself over to the other side of the room and start taking
orders." The girl startled in the direction of the nearest customer. I would
have done the same even though Lena was a tiny woman with a face as
round and delicately pink as the shine of a third grader's lip gloss.

"Order?" she demanded without volunteering menus.

"Well, Lena, you know I'm confined to a special diet." Without comment, Lena cut away and returned with two full coffee cups, each with a
spoon quivering against its rim.

"Forget it, Conrad," Lena said, the string of authentic-looking pearls
around her neck bumping impatiently against the halter of an apron that
was still holding onto its starch. "I'm too damn busy today to separate the
bloody yolks from the bloody whites for you."

"You force me into a death defying act, my dear. I'll have sausage and
eggs—but if I pass to the Great Beyond before your very eyes, don't blame
me."

I'd been sitting with my hands in my lap waiting for the oilcloth to dry.
"What do you recommend?" I asked when Lena turned to me.

Conrad watched Lena slice her way to the kitchen. We drank our coffee.
It wasn't at all bad. Our silence was more companionable than our conversation could have been, so I regretted it when he tipped his head forward
and pretended to rub the side of his nose. "She's a harridan now but she
was an Aphrodite in her day." He made this pronouncement with more
satisfaction than I liked. "She was smart enough to retire young from the
Red Rooms. Cooked for a wealthy rancher—he left her all his money. But
she lost it all in the bars playing the poker machines. She'll probably cook
until she dies because . . ."

Lena thumped down two heavy china platters. On mine, a tower of pe-
can pancakes exhaled steam. Conrad's bore a bowl of oatmeal and a side of
unbuttered toast. Having delivered our food, Lena wrested the coffeepot

from the new girl and began scissoring a path between the tables. Hand-printed and computer-generated posters fluttered from the walls at her passing, advertising horse trailers, rummage sales, team roping contests, babysitting, horse shoeing, metal detectors, snowmobiles, seed potatoes, internet hookups, water filters, saddles, vitamin pills, housecleaning, and the stud services of a stallion named seductively My Handsome Flyer. Lena managed a return pass before we were more than a quarter of the way through our meal.

"Well?"

"Delicious," I said, reaching to switch on the small lamp that centered the table. The hotcakes deserved the glow of the yellow shade.

"Not very good sausage and eggs," Conrad complained, stirring his oatmeal sadly.

But he waited until Lena was out of earshot and gave his all to his breakfast. Relieved at his return to silence, I concentrated on the pancakes.

Finishing first, I retrieved a dime for the tabletop jukebox that decorated the wall-side of the table offering a posy of standards from the Fifties. If the cost of the music was any indication, Misfire might end up to be a pretty good place to camp for a while, after all.

"One is not allowed to play the jukebox until after lunch," said Conrad.

"Why not?"

"Lena will not stand for it."

I shrugged in irritation, wondering if Misfire possessed any people I defined as normal—nice middle-class liberals with degrees from state universities, people who believed in wearing cotton, supporting alternative energy, eating organic vegetables, and questioning war as an effective means of achieving peace.

That irritation was inflated by the pressure on my credit card when Conrad fumbled for his wallet and then held up helpless hands, empty even of change for the tip.

At least he didn't ask me to buy the gas for his vehicle, an ancient International Scout suffering from the metallic equivalent of eczema. In a minute we were out of town and off the pavement, gravel popping against the Scout's undercarriage. Conrad didn't cast a single word into the racket. As the Scout slipped from one back road to another, the dust in the cab piled up with the minutes and the miles.

Conrad shouted something about taking "the scenic route." I wouldn't have used that term myself. Although mounds of sagebrush humped like bison toward the horizon, the sides of the road were strewn with garbage, and not just beer cans and grocery store sacks, but a strange and discordant jumble: a life-sized plastic St. Bernard, a section of picket fence, a twisted aqua rag that from its shimmer might have once been a prom dress, a tractor tire, a lawn chair missing most of its plastic webbing, a couch cushion, a tangle of wires.

"As you may observe, this is the route to the sanitary landfill." Conrad bent toward me to force his voice into my ear but then sat up abruptly to keep the Scout from being bucked into the borrow pit by a section of washboard.

"I must write an editorial!" he hooted when he had regained control. I wondered why he hadn't already. The drive, I decided, would indeed have been scenic in its high, cold desert way had it not been for the trash. Spiny hummocks of prickly pear punctuated the sagebrush and the persistent sweeps of dust-glazed snow. The spikes of the bunchgrass were brightening toward spring. The valley floor drew itself up into rolling hills that hurtled toward the defining cut of the mountains. Snow gleamed on jagged rims, the white disappearing here and there into the clouds building themselves into geysers in the endless sky. Montana calls itself "Big Sky Country" with justification.

Despite yesterday's damp chill, the Scout dragged a trail of dust like tattered yellow silk. Not only was grit muddying my still-damp hair and coating my glasses, it was sifting into my airways.

"Could we close the windows?" My voice cracked as I coughed and coughed again. Instead of replying though, Conrad veered to the right, braked abruptly enough to force the Scout into a sliding stop, and fumbled for something between the seats. I decided it was time to unearth the inhaler from my saddlebag purse. The medicinal blast knocked the spasms into the kind of twitching submission that suggested the fight wasn't over yet. Conrad brandished a screwdriver to pry the Scout's glove compartment open. Out sprung a smudged first aid kit, six or seven dusty Kleenex, a coil of exposed film, a handful of plastic pens, and a box of dust masks sealed in a box. At least I was spared a spill of condoms.

"My daughter also suffers from this malady," Conrad trumpeted, not yet having adjusted to the stillness of the countryside. The meadowlark perched on a fence post just ahead of us trilled its joy. Conrad extracted a mask from its plastic housing, saving it from cascading to the floor with the rest of his cache.

Chameleon-like, the white paper of the mask turned brown nearly as soon as I pinched it to my nose and slipped its elastic over my forehead to circle the back of my head. Huffing through my new muzzle, I decided that I might have to start taking the expensive medication that in six weeks or so would give me some relief.

"Observe!" he said pointing like Sacajawea, who, I remembered, had encountered her brother after a long separation not many miles from here. Cameahwait hadn't recognized her at first, but he had been kind anyway— to her and to Lewis and Clark's Corps of Discovery.

I already had spotted the sign off to the right. It didn't strike me as particularly interesting: a humped figure fashioned from wood to resemble what I took to be a sheep.

"Behold the Elephant Garden!" Conrad said, waving toward a vista lumpy with gopher holes. I sighed, wondering if the editor had fallen at an impressionable age into the clutches of an elocution teacher, elderly but re-sisting extinction. I knew the story of the Elephant Garden already, having run across the place name on my map and investigated its origins, which had something to do with the fateful alignment of the pachydermous shape of the county's famous (well, in Montana anyway) rock formation with the coincidental derailment of a circus train.

It was good story that ended with all performers, human and animals, safely deposited in the broad low basin next to the track. Local people had been tickled by the pasturage of real elephants not far from the andesitic formation that early miners had thought looked like the animal that em-bodied all of their hopes and all of their terrors. Maybe they even thought Divine Providence had sent the elephants to them as a sign to stay put after the mines ran out.

Conrad shouted out the story over the road noise, as I clenched my fists with anxiety. Thanks to the Elephant Garden and my good memory for maps, I now knew where I was—on a road that would join the state high-way and, if luck was with me, to the encounter that I had come here for.

I perched stiffly on the Scout's hard seat, letting the wind wash away

Conrad's words, watching slit-eyed for the sign I had strained so hard to see: "Bannack—Vehicles Prohibited."

The buildings were false in material pretense (wood feigning masonry), structural pretense (log party walls supporting a balloon-frame front wall for greater light and display area), and formal pretense (a rectilinear facade hiding a gable or shed roof) . . . . To be sure, the residents were not really deluded; all one had to do was to venture behind the buildings. But the effort to make the "town" look more mature than it was was a forced one, and the visitor to camp . . . often sensed the hoax.

—Kingston Wm. Heath, in "False-Front Architecture on Montana's Urban Frontier"

False Fronts

TAKING ADVANTAGE OF A SUDDEN SMOOTHING OF THE ROAD, CONRAD stepped on the accelerator. Just ahead, the gulch that held the ghost town in a tight embrace waited under the thickening storm clouds jousting with a surprisingly warm sun. Conrad forced the Scout past the visitor parking lot. Jerked into a U-turn. Skidded to a stop in front of a building taller with a soaring veranda. My face was flushing with what was either an early-onset hot flash or the heat generated by doubt and hope duking it out. Hope won—hope that my first flesh-and-blood encounter with someone with whom I shared that flesh and that blood would end happily ever after.

Grey-green clumps of sage spread like bonfires between the town's surviving structures. Managing to restrain myself, barely, from pounding on the Scout's window, I realized that Conrad had parked in front of the Meade Hotel: red-bricked, architect-designed, intended to be as glorious as possible when it was erected as the county's first courthouse. It was not the oldest building along the hardpan road, but it was the one that caught the eye.

"Here we are," Conrad announced with a journalist's gift for stating the obvious. Because I had pulled the snout of the dust mask from my face, my bronchioles were swelling like a cluster of raisins trying to reconstitute themselves into grapes. Still, I didn't like to use my inhaler again before I truly needed it. Letting the mask dangle around my neck on its elastic band, I gave into the compulsion to rattle the Scout's passenger door. Conrad hustled around to my side and forced it open.

"Thanks," I said, feeling no more gratitude to Conrad than a trout does to the catch-and-release angler who pulls the hook from its mouth and lets it swim bleeding away.

"It's always hotter than hell in Bannack—unless it's colder than hell," Conrad said, and waited for me to laugh at his wickedness. I didn't. Instead, I looked up and down the road to see if I could spot the park's Visitor Center, where my putative half-brother might be answering some tourist's questions or selling a Bannack Days poster or revving up the inevitable informative video. Because I hadn't yet fully decided if I wanted revenge on my mother for refusing to see me or a relationship with my brother or both, I set aside my desire to get the whole thing over with and headed for the hotel, my saddlebag strapped over my shoulder, a notebook displayed in my hand to lend me an aura of professionalism.

A wide swoop of wood steps led to the Meade's front porch, deeply shadowed by a second-story balcony. I tried to ignore a new round of tightening in my chest by distracting myself by taking note of inconsequential details—the purple stroller parked next to the hitching rail at the base of the stairway, the solidity of the steps under my tread, the muddy color of the porch rails not yet silvered to match the rest of the building. Clearly, the veranda had been rebuilt by some hyperactive local history group in the not-too-distant past— or perhaps by my very own half-brother whose job description (my internet sleuthing had revealed) included carpentry duties. I could hear a wailing that could be generated only by an infant or a banshee. Huffing even harder than I was, Conrad caught up. He put a restraining hand on my arm.

"Before we go in, wouldn't you like to walk these history-filled streets and meditate on the glory of the past?" His face projected an annoying sincerity.

"You're the expert. Where do you think we should start?" Frankly, I didn't much care.

"Well, I suppose that we should let Delores Tendoy know we're here.

Otherwise, she's likely to work herself into a conniption fit and write us a ticket for illegal parking."

He tuned up the volume of his voice as he looked over my shoulder. "What good luck, Ms. Tendoy—we were just discussing you."

"I hope you were saying you'd better move that vehicle before it gets towed away," said the woman as she emerged from the hotel's front door. She was wearing a variation on the universal uniform of a public lands employee—a wrinkled short-sleeved shirt that more or less matched the sagebrush and faded jeans with dust marks at the knees. Unexpected was the baby, fat-rumped in its disposable diaper. It sprawled over her shoulder, asleep as far as I could tell from the rise and fall of its back. If the infant had been the source of the ghostly howling that had haunted the hotel just moments before, it had downshifted with amazing speed.

Despite the infant, Delores, ebony hair pulled back in a business-like coil, didn't look like the motherly type. She was packing a pistol on her hip. Besides, she was refraining from flashing a Ranger Rick smile.

I stepped forward. "We've spoken on the phone; I'm AJ Armstrong, the historian from the College of the Washington Cascades. I offered her my hand, and Delores gripped it with decisive pressure. Conrad gave me a wounded look for spurning his introduction, but held his peace. "I see," Delores said, "that you've already met our local purveyor of history in a hurry." Her glance at Conrad could not be construed as friendly.

"Dr. Armstrong is doing the newspaper the honor of leasing our upstairs apartment."

"Lucky you," Delores said to me. "No doubt you'll want to see the town and then begin taking a look at our archives, such as they are. I assume you brought your credentials?" Without waiting for my answer, she asked, "Which do you want to do first?"

I wanted to see my brother, but couldn't think of a reason to inquire after the park's carpenter/seasonal worker from his boss. For all I knew, he could be taking an early lunch or hunting a new hammer in Misfire or engaging in an unimaginable number of other activities, any one of which could have taken him far away from Bannack.

"Conrad has offered to show me the sights before it gets any hotter."

"He's the one who can do it—he makes it his business to know Bannack better than most of us." Delores's voice twisted the compliment into irony. "But I guess he'll want to move his Scout first."

"It's a warm day here in Bannack, much warmer than in Misfire." Conrad said ignoring the fact that the rising wind held a bite. "I didn't want the good doctor to walk, especially as she suffers from asthma."

"That must be inconvenient for a historian, dust being your stock in trade." Delores shifted the baby to her other shoulder. It continued to sleep. We all refrained from commenting on its somehow embarrassing presence. Without saying goodbye, she turned and strode away down the boardwalk, snagging the purple stroller with her free hand and pulling it behind her. "I'll probably be in the Visitor Center when you're ready to scope out our documents," she called, not bothering to look back at us.

"Don't mind Delores," Conrad whispered as the park manager sauntered away. "She's a diamond in the rough, but a gem nevertheless."

He hastened back down to the road, climbed into the Scout, which bucked once, and then stampeded in the direction of the parking lot, stirring up the dust that had finally settled. I was left alone in the middle of the town where not only the vigilantes, but, as far as I'd been able to discover, my mother had struggled with conscience and desire. But my mother had been only fifteen and pregnant in a town whose surface gold had played out long ago and whose population had dwindled to members of her own family—mine, too, I guess. They were all gone now as far as I could tell, dead or departed. Except for my brother.

The dank coolness of the Meade wrapped itself around my shoulders. Breathing more easily, I stopped just inside the hotel's double doors to give my eyes the chance to adjust. The half-moon transom above my head strained the rust from the cloudy light of the incoming storm. Something was scraping away the silence: mice scrabbling behind plaster or fingers of sage tapping the first-floor windows. I shivered. A table gleamed in the dimness, its chrome legs and fake marbling obviously decades newer than the telegraph key and sounder it supported. But then again, so were the dry cell batteries tucked to one side of the key and a cable that drooped to the baseboard.

For warmth, I folded my arms against my chest and bent to examine the graffiti lightly scratched into the sloped wall lifting the hotel's iconic grand staircase to its second floor. Surprisingly, no obscenities disturbed the tracings, as delicate as the venation of fallen leaves. I searched the wall for traces of my mother's name.

"Someday I'll catch one of those Vandals!" Conrad boomed right behind me, his voice inflecting the common noun into a proper epithet. Taking no note of my startled gasp, he brushed past me to seat himself behind the telegraph. His fingers began drumming a staccato of what I guessed sounded like dots and dashes to an ear more finely tuned than mine. No, not drumming. Stroking. A side-to-side quivering caress. I looked away.

Conrad didn't notice. At the end of the series, he paused with such a clear look of expectancy, his left ear cocked toward the open face of the sounder's wooden box, I wasn't surprised when the metal rod within began striking a tiny brass anvil. A Prince Albert tobacco can—the real deal, its red paint scoured, its flat sides dented—responded by vibrating in mechanical ecstasy.

"Damn Adon sends too fast," grunted Conrad, as he began scribbling out the message on a strip of paper. As the striking rod stilled itself, he waved the scrap like a flag and bolted for the door. Reluctant to leave the refuge of the hotel, I let him go. Instead, I followed the staircase up to the deeply recessed window above the fifth step. Conrad was nowhere in sight. The sun, too, had completely disappeared, and the wind was shoveling a muddy load of clouds across the sky. My asthma—and my nerves—had cooled in the shadows of the building. I felt the way I often do when I'm strapped in a plane making its post-takeoff climb to a safer altitude: not happy, but irrevocably airborne.

Across the road, Conrad popped out of the flat-faced school house just as a rush of sleet smacked the rippled glass of the window. He glowered at the sky and then hustled back toward the hotel, hunching his shoulders. Thunder startled the storm into a stroke of lightning that linked earth and sky.

"I thought you wanted a tour!" Conrad called up to me, water dripping down his forehead. The storm had turned both his shirt and T-shirt translucent. Even in this dim light, I could clearly make out the shadows of his nipples and navel. The sight was not arousing.

"Where's Adon?"

Conrad gave me a sharp glance, either because of the quaver in my voice or, more likely, because of the oddity of the question from someone who presumably didn't know Adon from Adam's off ox.

"He's right across the street, where I thought we were both going," said Conrad, his tone conveying the fact that he considered himself a patient man for offering a sensible answer to a nonsensical question.

"Well, let's run for it, then." I sprinted until my shoes threatened to hydroplane on the slippery boardwalk. The sleet was already stopping. Cleansed of its burden of dust, the air carried a medicinal tang, a spring tonic. Ok-a-lee! ok-a-lee! A red-winged blackbird rode the freshening breeze up from the willows below. From here, you couldn't see the gravel heaps, still grey and sterile in sun and snow a hundred years after the last gold dredge excreted them.

"Nice, isn't it," said Conrad, not asking a question, but stating a fact. He slapped a mosquito, an early riser not only in terms of the season, but the time of day. A tiny smear of blood smeared his forearm at the spot where the jagged halves of a tattoo, a broken heart, separated.

The school house door was standing open, but Conrad ignored it in favor of the exposed steps clinging to the building's exterior. Lots of tourists probably had a good time imagining children parsing sentences on the ground floor, while over head, vigilantes plotted in the second-floor Masonic Hall. Lucky for tourists, truth rarely gets in the way of a good story: the school building wasn't constructed until years after Bannack's notorious sheriff/outlaw and his alleged gang were lynched. Still, the vigilantes' conspiracy to uphold the law by breaking it haunted the hall's construction. I knew that between the levels, a double floor had been packed with dirt to stop secrets from leaking through.

Happy to note that someone, maybe my brother, had stabilized the steep run, I climbed to where Conrad had already slipped through the gates designed to bar tourists from the hall's treasures. If stairs kept presenting themselves to me, I wouldn't have to worry that Misfire was too small to support a gym.

By the time I reached the top, asthma had re-colonized my breath. I patted my saddlebag, feeling the lump of my inhaler in its outer pocket to reassure myself that it was still there. Behind a barrier of what looked like bullet-proof glass, the unfinished pine floor stretched between a Masonic throne at one end of the room and a massive globe at the other. A carpet, luxurious in deep red, displayed its square and compass pattern under protective plastic sheathing.

In the middle of the room: my brother.

Not knowing what to say, I said nothing. I'd learned at least this one thing from writing history: silence sooner or later invites the story—insists that the narrative begin. Besides, I wasn't sure I had breath to speak.

Adon was stationed at a telegraph set the twin of the one at the Meade, his shoulders, like mine, tending to roll forward; his face, unlike mine, reflecting the topography of a rough country. Someone, knowing we were related, might read a connection in the heavy line of his eyebrows, the sharp bow of our upper lips. I couldn't make out the color of his eyes. He looked, and I use this word not at all contemptuously, nice.

Wheezing, I took in his uniform (the twin of the one Delores wore, sans wrinkles and ornamental baby), the holster on his hip, the way he waited, fingertips resting on the worn brass of the telegrapher's key. The first thing I said to my brother was not a lie. "Happy to meet you," I gasped, taking his hand, stubby, calloused, with precisely manicured fingernails, in my own. It was the first time that I'd ever touched a blood relative. I am not a fainter, but the square and compass carpet pulled me downward. My landing was hard.

"AJ, where's your inhaler?" Conrad's voice was hard to hear through the rasp of my breath. I couldn't answer, but my fingers closed around hard plastic when Conrad thrust the dispenser into my hand. In a minute, I felt recovered enough to feel mortified.

"Where did Adon go?"

"To get his emergency kit—he's an EMT." Conrad was kneeling beside me, his finger pressed on my wrist, calmer than I would have been in his shoes.

At least I'd probably be spared the indignity—and the expense—of an ambulance ride. With the Misfire hospital nearly twenty-five miles away, dialing 911 probably wasn't the first thing people out here probably did when a medical emergency loomed. Which this wasn't anyway.

Delores stampeded into the hall looking irritated. Adon followed, lugging a small plastic case the size and shape of the type used for jet transport of vital organs on their way to transplant candidates. Unlike Delores, he looked worried.

"I'm OK, really—my asthma's usually so mild I don't take anything for it. I've used my inhaler more the last couple of days than I usually do in a month. The local flora must have it in for me." I was babbling, proof enough that I wasn't in any danger. I rose to my feet, using the telegraph desk, fortunately, a sturdy one. My own legs felt wooden. Ignoring Delores's stare of disapproval, I settled in the Masonic throne, trying to find a comfortable spot in its heavily carved embrace.

"You'd better find yourself a local doctor," Delores said. And stop bothering busy people, her tone implied. "Anyway, it turns out that I can't help you with the archives this afternoon because a couple of mining company reps have decided they want to cruise around the park. I guess they want to get ready to swoop down on the carrion if the state decides to sell us out. If you feel up to waiting for a while, Adon will be free after he gets the SOBs started on their soap-making project downstairs." Delores was already disappearing through the door. I wondered what had happened to the baby.

"SOBs?" I asked

"Adon," Conrad said with a soft sincerity that made my brother step back warily. "Adon, do you think you could do me a service? If you could entice the GoldPro spokespersons to visit the schoolroom while the SOBs are there, what a photo opportunity!"

"Members of 'Save Our Bannack,'" Adon said, answering my question, not Conrad's. "They're meeting to plan a rally against GoldPro and for their own proposal." He'd tucked his medical kit discreetly out of view behind the throne—whether out of concern for my sensibilities or that of any tourist who might drop in, I couldn't tell.

"To make a long story short," Conrad began and took a big breath. Adon wedged a whispered excuse into the pause. He had, I noticed, evaded Conrad's request that he help engineer the photo. I was proud of my brother. Nice people aren't necessarily stupid, I sometimes have to work to remember. I hated to see him go, but I couldn't think of an excuse to follow. Conrad clacked on despite my frequent, but futile, attempts to assure him that I already knew the story, especially the bloody parts.

"But where does GoldPro come in?" I finally managed to insist.

Conrad sighed, a teacher who had run through his supply of tolerance for the new kid. "Of course, I forget, not everyone follows Montana politics. (The arc of his eyebrows indicated this was a dereliction of any U.S citizen's duty.) However, you'll have to ask someone else. I can't be objective about GoldPro—and besides, talking about it raises my blood pressure."

As I followed him down the stairs, my invisible tracks overlaid his and my brother's. Conrad's shoulders were erect under the burden of a suppressed rejoinder. He halted suddenly and spun to face me. My grab for the rail stopped me from stumbling into him.

"GoldPro isn't the solution." His voice buzzed with anger. "We want not only to save Bannack, but to improve it!" Mystified, I searched Conrad's face for clues about what the hell he was talking about.

"My editorial in this week's paper lays out the entire proposal," he explained and then explained his vision in Technicolor detail. Barges bearing paying passengers would float down the creek past theme park employees panning gold or running water through sluice boxes or having gun battles with claim jumpers on either bank. After paying to have themselves videoed at a realistically staged hanging, tourists would ride a gondola style lift up to Boot Hill where a roller coaster would be set up—at a discreet distance from the graves, of course—to resemble a gold dredge.

"We're also thinking about making the old stamp mill into a haunted house, but I personally think that would be too much." Conrad waited, clearly expecting a compliment on his good taste.

"Conrad, we need you!" Inside the schoolroom a half dozen middle-aged people were squeezed into grated desks like chickens fattening in a poultry factory. My brother was carefully peeling away the strips of cellophane tape from the corner of a poster affixed to the blackboard. It read "The Vigilantes Will Ride Again!"

"You're free to write messages on the board with chalk," he called back over his shoulder to a woman. "But please don't use tape or tacks." His tone was mild, his expression concerned: Mr. Rogers packing a pistol he hoped he would never have to use. His eyes, I noticed, were almost as green as my own, his eyebrows dark and sloping: mine. His internet photo hadn't suggested these subtle resemblances.

"Remember, Adon, you're here to serve us, not the other way around," said the woman who had called to Conrad. She wore a blue gingham bonnet of the sort that costs about fifty cents to produce in China, but thirty-five dollars to buy from a souvenir boutique. A matched set of plastic Colt 45s, almost big enough for a small child to point at passing strangers, stretched her earlobes. "Conrad," she called again, "we need your help to figure out our plan of attack. Your friend can help—she's your new employee, isn't she?"

Apparently Misfire's information exchange hotline was about as quick and inaccurate as it is in most small towns. Before Conrad could finish introduction, Binah was flapping the poster, still bordered with strips of the offending tape, in the direction of Conrad's nose.

"I'll be in the Visitor Center," I called, deciding with equal parts relief and irritation that I would have to wait until later to engage Adon in conversation.

There was a "Closed until May 1" notice on the door, but it yielded to my push. Inside, polyurethane sealed oak floors. The Victrola in one corner displayed a prominent "Do not touch" sign, and glass cases caged predictable collections of ore samples, assay scales, picks, shovels, photos—the usual.

"Vultures here yet?" I dared to ask.

"Not yet," Delores said, refusing the joke.

I felt a flash of rejection until I remembered all I needed from Delores was her belief that I had a legitimate reason to hang out in Bannack.

"Since we talked on the phone, I've come across something that might interest you," she said. Her office probably had been intended as a storage closet; it wasn't much larger than her desk. I wondered where Delores had stowed the baby and all of its paraphernalia. Somehow I couldn't picture Delores with a husband or significant other. What did she do for a babysitter out here?

There was nothing decorative in the room except a plainly framed group photograph taken to commemorate some 19th century treaty. "My three times great-grandfather, Chief Tendoy, third from the left in the front row," she said, noticing the direction of my glance.

Unlike the others in the photo, the chief was dressed in a vested suit and well-shined anglo-style boots. A hat, wide-brimmed and high-crowned, bridged the gap between his knees, anchored with the index finger of his right hand on one side and the curve of his knuckles on the other. He looked considerably more elegant than the only white man in the photo, mustached and rumpled, standing almost directly behind him. I wondered if the chief had carried the look of Sacajawea, his great aunt, forward a generation.

The chief refused the camera his full gaze; his mouth etched the crescent of an eclipsing sun. A trailing feather followed one of his braids to the lapel of his suit.

Delores explained the original had been taken in 1880 when the chief traveled to Washington to assent to the removal of his band to the sagebrush of the Fort Hall reservation from the salmon runs of the Lemhi Valley.

Seeing that none of this was news to me, she—unlike Conrad—skipped the details.

"Ten-doi-op was a wily one." Delores's tone darkened the compliment. "Some say that he knew all along the band wouldn't vote to ratify the agreement—and surely he would have known the band's feelings. By that time he'd been leading the band for nearly twenty years—ever since the day after his Uncle Naw-ro-yawn—Snag to the whites—had been murdered."

"Near Bannack as he was bathing in Grasshopper Creek, according to the most believed accounts," I said to demonstrate I knew that part of the story. Delores said something else, but I missed it because I was thinking about another Shoshoni who came to grief in Bannack. When that woman had fled an abusive Anglo miner, he and two friends shot up the Shoshoni camp on the edge of town twice in one night.

If I were really serious about my research project documenting births and deaths in Bannack, I'd want to compare existing sources to figure out how many Shoshoni had been murdered during that shoot-up. Histories of the town merely noted that one white living in the Indian camp had been killed and another Anglo wounded. The jury convicted the murderers of manslaughter, but didn't call for a hanging. Instead, the three were sentenced to banishment—after the weather warmed up. For half a heartbeat, I considered the various ways I might reconstitute the native presence in local demographics. If my erstwhile study were real. If I planned to stick around.

"Well," Delores said, raising her wrist and tapping her watch. The park manager retrieved a chain from around her neck. From it dangled a plain gold cross and a small key. Without taking off the necklace, she bent over to unlock the desk's top drawer and pulled a shallow box from under a pile of papers. Looking more closely, I saw that it wasn't a closed container, but a leather slipcase pushed about two thirds of the way down over an inner sheath. It was obvious that the outer case had once suffered an encounter with a couple of inches of standing water. The high tide mark was clear on the wine-colored leather.

"What's this?"

Delores grimaced at the lack of enthusiasm in my question. Her lips were slightly chapped. If she was nursing her baby, she should drink more water. Working carefully, she slowly rocked the outer case off, revealing a daybook or ledger covered with a 19th century version of cardboard.

Delores tipped the ledger toward me so that I could see how tightly it was wedged into the sheath. A mass of what looked like newspaper clippings bulged between its last page and back cover. She pushed the ledger in my direction, forcing me to accept it. "It's stuck. But if you pry at the front cover a little, you can see that there's something there that might be worth looking at." She pointed her chin to indicate she meant for me to take her observation as a directive.

By carefully nudging the exposed section of the ledger open a few fractions of an inch, I created a kind of temporary skylight that revealed two lines of faded copperplate cursive faded to the brown characteristic of iron gall ink:

A True Record
Of Bannack Births and Deaths

A HINT OF A THIRD LINE FOLLOWED, BUT I COULDN'T SEE FOR CERTAIN whether it offered a set of dates. There are times that I wish that I had the patience to cultivate longer fingernails, and this was one of them. Smoothing the top corner of the page with thumb and forefinger, I tried to separate it from the next page. As far as I could tell without tearing or forcing fully open the fragile leaves, the top third of that sheet and the next held a set of inked entries dated by month and day, but not year. My sense was that the handwriting changed between the first and subsequent pages. I couldn't make out much of the later entries, but they didn't seem to connect to births or deaths.

"What do you think?"

"Where did you find it?"

"Actually, I wasn't the one. When I was in town last week picking up some groceries, one of the locals just shoved the box into my cart."

I waited for her to explain.

"Nick Stanislavsky, but I don't know how to describe him."

"I've met him." I tried to keep my voice neutral, but Delores looked impressed at the level of local knowledge my tone implied. "Have you given it to anyone else to evaluate?"

"Nobody yet—every time we acquire some artifact, there's a squabble between the state and the SOBs about who should retain ownership. There's a possibility that I may have to depart from my job suddenly. If so, I don't want to leave any bones for Conrad and his merry little band to pick apart."

Delores's cell clamored with a plain ringtone that revealed nothing about her or her caller. "I'll meet them here—but outside," she said into the phone.

"I'm off," she told me, leaving me alone with the ledger in my hands.

Working the ore dumps of some of yesterday's forgotten old mines has become a profitable pastime indeed! In many instances the company originally operating the mine was seeking only certain minerals or metals. Furthermore, because the human eye could not look inside the chunks of ore, many valuable samples were discarded on the dump.

—Roy Lagal, in *The New Gold Panning Is Easy*

Visitations

"She gave you something, didn't she," Conrad said as we jounced out of the Bannack parking lot. Ignoring what sounded a lot more like an accusation than a question, I scanned the rearview mirror hoping for a last glimpse of my brother. Nuisance though it promised to be, the ledger secreted in the saddlebag between my feet might be a rich source of excuses to visit Bannack and to "accidentally" encounter Adon.

"What makes you think that?" I assumed an expression of innocent confusion, re-settling the mask on my face and cranking down the window, hoping the wind would discourage further interrogation.

"We'll take the highway back, so you shouldn't need the mask."

I shrugged and cupped a hand around my left ear.

"You can tell me what she gave you," he shouted. "I know how to protect my sources."

I closed my eyes, feeling as empty as the now cloudless sky pressing against the horizon.

Conrad subsided for a few minutes and then tried another approach: "Anything she's found at Bannack is public property, you know!"

Swiveling my head to the window, I pretended sudden fascination with the view. "What's that cemetery?"

It wasn't the most subtle of evasions. But Conrad swerved, apparently sharing the common misapprehension that there's nothing a historian likes better than to visit the dead. A meadowlark chimed as the engine clunked into silence.

"This graveyard is interesting, even though Boot Hill in Bannack is older." His voice boomed, still set to counter the wind. I wondered how long Conrad's marriage had endured before his officiousness, his doughy midriff, and his fondness for the bottle in his desk drawer made his wife discount his decency. He scraped the gate open while I dodged gopher holes.

The marble obelisks and slabs were struggling to stand up straight, but the more modest pine markers slumped, their inscriptions long-since scrubbed away by Montana's storms and sun. I stepped carefully around the plots marked only by a certain settling of the earth and by the flames of the prickly pears, the yellow of their blossoms so waxy that I half expected to see wicks rising from their incarnadine hearts. You take certain risks when you walk through old graveyards: the crack of disintegrating coffin wood under your feet, the sudden downward slide of earth.

Did the prickly pears always blossom so early? Conrad said he didn't know, but—unable to resist the chance to pontificate—pointed out that the old gravestones probably captured and held the spring sun better than the stretch of sagebrush flats.

Enclosed again in the Scout, I shut my eyes as Conrad expounded on the difference between unpaved roads that, as he explained in ponderous detail, could be accurately described as washboard (because of their crosscut ruts) and those that should be described as corduroy (which served up their jounces in a lengthwise version). Before it was paved, he claimed, the road to Bannack fit both categories, sometimes alternatively, sometime simultaneously. One spot had been so bad that a Bannack couple had died when the road bounced them into a roll during a spring snowstorm.

"When was that?" I asked. I hadn't noticed an accident story in the new edition of the *Sun*. "Oh, maybe thirty or forty years ago." Maybe my grandparents, I thought. Before I left Misfire, I would have to see if the *Sun* archives offered any more information about their deaths than the Butte paper had.

Now the road was silk by comparison, Conrad said, and completely safe. I corroborated his claim by slipping from pretended to real sleep. When I woke up, Conrad was pulling into a parking space in front of the *Sun-*

Tribune, the one behind my Chevy. There was something stuck under its wiper.

"Sorry about the parking ticket," Rheta said as we walked in. She appeared to be in the middle of writing out a set of old-fashioned paper checks to the *Sun*'s creditors. "I fed the meter until all hell broke loose around here, but then I got too busy to fuss with it. The paper will pay the fine for you, because I should have shown you the free parking spot in the alley." There was a tightness in Rheta's voice that made me think she wasn't using the word "hell" lightly in describing the *Sun*'s post-publication quota of trouble.

"I don't know that we can afford such a frivolous expenditure," Conrad said.

"Then I'll pay the five dollars myself." Rheta waved away my polite protest with what seemed to me uncharacteristic sharpness. But her next words were normal enough. "Anyway, AJ, you have hot water and electricity, so why don't you run up and make yourself at home." Not really curious about the *Sun*'s tribulations, I accepted Rheta's dismissal, but her words echoed in the stairwell: "We have real problems. And I don't know what we're going to do about them."

Upstairs, I undressed for the second time that day, intent on washing away the afternoon's events. Let's see: in the space of one afternoon, I had managed to make a wonderful first impression on my brother by falling faint and to commit myself to evaluating a probably worthless document that came all wrapped up in political entanglements.

The shower's rust-encrusted handles were hard to crank, but the water that sputtered out was, as Rheta had promised, blissfully hot. As the spray blasted away the dust graying my hair, I sang "Papa's Got Your Bath Water On." I sounded good, although not as good as Hattie Hart belting out the blues with the Memphis Jug Band. Later would be soon enough to worry about my new compulsion to scrub everything scrubbable, including myself.

People had moved West, hoping that a few more of their misfortunes and unhappiness would be carried away with every river they crossed. Today, we instead end marriages, start businesses, visit chatrooms, send out resumes, apply to graduate schools, and take lots of showers, hot ones. By the time I'd toweled myself dry, I had convinced myself that falling faint wasn't the worst way I could have initiated my relationship with my brother. At least temporary unconsciousness had made fewer lies necessary.

Clean and dressed in a semi-professional, if wrinkled, cotton dress and matching jacket, I paced between the apartment's the vinyl bar and the kitchen counter. Despite my conviction that the ledger would cost me more time than it would be worth, I felt a compulsion to yank it out of the saddlebag. Fortunately, my scholarly conscience intervened. It would take at least an hour or two to set up a working space. Without patience and the right tools, I could damage the pages. Besides, I had just about enough time before five o'clock to fulfill my promise to Katharine to make a delivery to the chair of the local college's history department.

"I don't want to entrust this to the postal service," she had told me, handing me a padded envelope without further specifying its contents. "Besides, Luke might have an adjunct job for you to help you get through the year." And take you off my conscience, she might just as well have added.

Picking up the saddlebag, I considered showing Katharine's colleague the Bannack ledger, but then rejected the idea. Delores would have told Ingraham about the ledger already had she wanted him to know about it. Sighing, I stashed the saddlebag on the shelf under the bar. Then I fished it out again. I couldn't trust Conrad to refrain from rummaging through my things while I was gone. Feeling burdened, I retrieved my personal papers and added them to the weight I was carrying.

Like my adoptive father, the salesman, I believe in the efficacy of the surprise appearance. With luck, Ingraham wouldn't be in. Katharine, in urging (ordering, really) that I seek him out immediately, had mentioned that the college's spring session was just ending. This late in the afternoon, I probably would be able to get away with a brief contact with a secretary. Even if Ingraham was the type who kept long hours, by dropping in without warning, I would rob him of the time to think up a way he could do Katharine a favor.

The only trick would be to escape the *Sun* without becoming entangled in conversation. As it turned out, the newspaper office was again deserted. The front door was closed and locked, an envelope taped to the inside of its smudged glass with my name on it. Inside was a key. Glad that I hadn't ended up on the outside looking in for the second time in twenty-four hours, I glanced at the newsroom clock. It was already a quarter to five, but the college was only a few blocks south.

The downtown stoplight turned out to be the only one I encountered, and even it was set on flashing yellow. The college was quiet, the parking lot empty. The map I had printed out in Seattle indicated that Old Main occupied pride of place in the center of campus. A winding sidewalk quick-marched me to a splendid 19th century tower that soared about as well as anything made of old red brick could be expected to. Despite my hurry, the distant bong of the courthouse clock warned me that I was probably too late. I paused and then kept going. At least I could figure out where Ingraham's office was. I pushed through a side door into a dark hall. Desks tumbled helter-skelter in the passageway, and the smell of new wax haunted the gloom. I would have turned around, but I could hear voices reverberating in the stairwell.

"I got a nearly new hedge clipper for five dollars, but I lost a nice handyman jack when I set it down for just a second to look at a chain saw." The voice was loud and male—a janitor's I guessed.

The responding female voice was unsympathetic. "Well, you should have known better. Those rummage sales are worse than the Oklahoma land rush. Besides, shouldn't you be getting rid of all that stuff of your mother's instead of dragging home more junk?"

A door stood open in the second-floor hallway. A dark-haired woman in khakis and a crisp white shirt turned toward me with a sheaf of papers firmly in hand, the big silver hoops in her earlobes vibrating in response to the force of her personal energy field. The smile on her face broadcasted the satisfaction of a professor who had just finished the last of her term grading. A man in a khaki coverall lumbered up from a receptionist's desk.

"Excuse me, but could you tell me where Luke Ingraham's office is?" I counted myself lucky not to have to search the dim hallways for a building directory.

"This is Luke Ingraham's office, and here is the man himself. I'm Pilar Bravo, the assistant chair of the history department." She offered a hand, which I took awkwardly, transferring my saddlebag onto my other shoulder.

"Dr. Bravo is too gracious," said Ingraham, sticking out his own hand. "She does almost all of the chair's work now and gets the title, God help her, on July 1." His hand was calloused. He glanced at Dr. Bravo rather than at me, and she nodded. "What can the history department do for you?" she asked.

Annoyed at Ingraham's attempt to shuffle me off and irritated by the friendly atmosphere, I nevertheless willed myself to assume a veneer of graciousness. "Thanks, but I'm just running an errand. I believe Dr. Ingraham is expecting a package from Katharine Kelly." Opening the saddlebag, I reluctantly added, "I'm AJ Armstrong."

"Well, AJ, I'm glad to meet you," he said. "Kate e-mailed me all about you."

So Katharine had been meddling, just as I feared.

"I've been expecting you," he added. "Have you found yourself a place to stay?"

"Sort of," I said, explaining my arrangements with the *Sun.*

"Poor girl—I just wish I could offer you a room myself, but we're in the middle of moving."

Pilar laughed, I couldn't tell why, and waved as she dodged out the door, clearly willing to cede responsibility for me to Luke.

"That's not necessary at all." I refrained from saying something snappish about being called a girl. Instead, I pulled Katharine's package from my saddlebag, trying to tuck back the ledger that slid out with it.

"Now that looks interesting," he said, looking at the ledger, not at Katharine's box.

"This is what you want," I said, pushing the box at him. "The other is just something I might use in my current research project."

"Mind if I take a look."

"Sure—maybe we could make an appointment for next week." My plan to evade anything more than cursory contract with Ingraham—and to foil any plan Katharine had launched to "help" me—seemed to be in danger of failing. "I've got to get back to the *Sun.*" Unable to add more detail, I left the nature of my urgent errand unspecified. My ability to lie convincingly had apparently been exhausted by the frequent exercise it had been subjected to. The diminishing echo of Dr. Bravo's footsteps had died away entirely. I made a move to leave as Luke stashed Katharine's unopened package in a filing cabinet. Because he didn't lock the drawer, I decided the materials she had sent weren't so valuable that they warranted hand-delivery. I could distinctly feel Katharine tugging the long-distance end of a loop positioned directly over my head.

"Well, I have an errand to run, too," he said, "but I wish we could talk for a few more minutes because I have a proposal that I think would help you with your research and get me out of a tight spot." Here it comes, I thought. Might as well get it over with. My face molded itself into a professorial expression of polite neutrality.

"But I really have to go now myself," he added. "I wonder if you could delay your obligation at the newspaper. If so, you could ride out to the cemetery with me and then come home to supper. I'm grilling some trout that Stela—that's my wife—caught this morning. Nothing fancy, but good if you're partial to fresh fish."

Noticing Ingraham had read my excuse as exactly that, a slight sense of panic fluttered under my collar bone. I had planned to dislike him. He was known in history circles for his hide-bound resistance to challenges to the heroic view of frontier history. Moreover, every minute I stayed increased the chances Katharine's long-distance snare would irrevocably tighten. On the other hand, I really didn't want to make another trip to Luke's office. Besides, I was hungry again.

Luke's faded green Chevy pickup was even older than my Bel Air, with more rust than paint and a floorboard awash with gravel. The cottonwoods arching over the street created a twiggy shade, their emerging leaves a nascent gold. We were already leaving behind the white-painted turrets of neighborhoods raised by Misfire's first prosperous settlers, the ones who had made quick fortunes in gold or freight or cattle after the railroad had reached the townsite in 1880. Of course, then Misfire was known, like so many others, as Terminus—the temporary end of the line. The people who had been disappointed in promoting Bannack as the next Chicago turned their attention to making Misfire grow into a metropolis. They christened the city Pleasant Orchard. As far as I could tell, no one ever used that name.

Within a few blocks, elegant Victorian houses gave way to treeless streets clotted with single-wide trailers corralled by chain link fencing. It was restful riding with Luke. He seemed to have forgotten the reason he had invited me along. Or maybe, he had changed his mind about taking me on as a charity project. As the paved street bumped onto a gravel road, he looked out across the sudden stretch of fields as if he hadn't seen them for a long time. The air carried the odors of a country spring—manure and dust and fresh green growth. The road seemed too narrow for more than one vehicle at a time, but I didn't worry about it. The only other traveler I could spot was a sturdy white woman who was hiking down the hill we were climbing, her legs thumping steadily inside of baggy jeans, an empty leash hanging loose in one hand. She lifted it in greeting as Luke slowed to speak to her.

"Nice day, Jane," he called.

"Would be if I could find that damn Fancy. He bolted after a cottontail while I was up working on the family plot."

"Well, I'll toss him into the back of the truck if I see him," Luke said, nudging the pickup forward.

"Jane's a nice woman," Luke said. "She was in fifth grade when I started kindergarten. I fell in love with her the first day of school and never got over it until I met my first wife."

"Do you like teaching in the town where you grew up?" I asked in an artificial voice, failing to remember the last name of even one person I'd gone to grade school with.

"Yes and no. The old folks all remember the time I got drunk and knocked over a half dozen gravestones up here, and before that, the time I started the fire in the junkyard, and before that, the time I got expelled from English class for rolling marbles down the aisle at the teacher and—well you get the picture. As for the ones my age or younger, they think I must have failed out there in the wide world to end up here again."

Luke shifted down so the pickup could make it to the top of the hill. The lawns of the cemetery draped the summit like a scarf, already preternaturally green despite the earliness of the season.

"This is the second cemetery I've visited today," I said. In summarizing my trip to Bannack, I didn't mention my brother or the ledger.

"A lot fancier than Bannack's boneyard, isn't it?" Luke was driving through an iron gate that looked as if it were designed to contain the elephants of the Elephant Garden. The answer was obvious. How many thousands of gallons did it take in this high dry place to keep the thick cushion of bluegrass springy underfoot and the lanes of blue spruce fresh and lofty? Luke didn't slow on the outer edges of the cemetery where the graves were marked not by headstones, but by slabs as flat as paving stones.

"For a while, back in the seventies, the cemetery board banned headstones because they were too hard to mow around," Luke said. "Luckily, my dad didn't die until '76, just after we voted in a new mayor, one who campaigned on the slogan "Head Forward with Headstones.""

Incredulous, I gave him a hostile glance. Despite my mounting list of personal prevarications, I hated it when people told me lies, especially jocular ones.

"No, I'm perfectly serious," he said. "I would have voted for him myself if we'd been here."

"Katharine said that you moved back here a few years ago to be near your mother."

"Yes, but she died the year after we came back." He steered the truck into tire tracks that stopped under the boughs of one of the spruces. Climbing out, he walked around to the back of the truck and hoisted out a planter box overflowing with greenhouse geraniums in full bloom. "It was odd the way she started failing almost the minute we walked in the kitchen door. Maybe it was bad for her to have us around to take care of things for her. When she stopped struggling to sweep the walk and wash the dishes and take the senior citizen bus downtown to the drugstore, she seemed to stop struggling to live."

"I'll take the other planter." I wanted to help despite the crisp, markable cotton of my dress.

"Better not—I just watered them this morning so they're muddy. Besides, the graves are just over here." Luke settled the planter in front of a double headstone and then went back for the other one. The grass over Luke's father was spring velvet. Above his mother, the scars still faintly showed between the squares of sod. The death date hadn't been filled in.

"The stonecutter is behind in his work," Luke explained, dropping the second planter into place. "And since these markers are all bought and paid for, he prefers to concentrate on unpaid work."

Having finished with the planters, he was bending to touch the head of a lamb worn so featureless that it reminded me of the Ivory soap animals I tried to carve as a child. Next to the lamb was a headstone in the form of a chair. The stonemason had centered a book on the seat, carved to look as if it had been left face-down. The inscription on its cover proclaimed: "Our Darling Amy Oct. 10, 1908—Oct. 10, 1918." The flu pandemic had probably swept the child out of life on her birthday.

"My plot is there," Luke said, pointing to the space between the lamb and his parents' headstone. I just hope I'll have earned the right to it by the time I need it."

I didn't understand what he meant. I didn't care what he meant. How could I get out of the dinner invitation that I'd tacitly accepted?

"You must love Misfire very much," I said, taking refuge in banality.

"Sometimes I hate it."

He pulled a kerchief from his pocket, spat on it without apology, and began rubbing away the marks that the rain had left from the polished surface of the rose granite. He glanced at his watch, its silver and turquoise band glinting in the sun. "Forgot to wind it," he said, glancing at the sun. I had never seen anyone do that before, outside of a Western movie. "Guess we'd better get home—I have some cooking to do. It's lucky I made the potato salad before I left for the office this morning."

I could smell the fragrance of trout frying even before Luke negotiated a cattle guard and herded the pickup along a gravel driveway that circled to a clapboard house with a glassed-in front porch reaching across its face like a wide smile. Instead of stopping, he bumped the pick-up onto the lawn. A dozen or more apple trees, some with their limbs propped up with rusting iron stakes, were tempting another spring snow with the sympathetic magic of their snowy blossoms.

"We're living here until we get my mother's house sorted out," he explained, braking in front of a double-wide trailer no one had taken the trouble to disguise. Balanced on piles of concrete block, it shuddered in the wind. There were no steps to the front door, just a blue plastic crate. Luke took a running step, hopped onto it and hoisted himself up by grabbing one side of the door. He then offered me his hand. I was offended that he thought I needed it.

"I was supposed to do the cooking!" Luke's voice ricocheted against the trailer's walls.

"I wanted to make sure these trout get the treatment they deserved!" The throaty voice was sweetened by a Southern flavor, Georgian, I guessed. The short woman who followed it into the short hall was wiping strong brown hands on the oversized towel snugged around a sturdy waist, her thick coffee-colored legs emerging from the fringe of her cutoffs.

"Stela, this is AJ Armstrong, the visiting professor I told you might be kind enough to take my classes next year, so I can actually take my last sabbatical before retirement." He shifted his gaze from her to me. "The adjunct we had hired got a better offer from Missoula last week and left us high and dry." Here it was. Luke was too canny to have let me see sooner. When I didn't bite, he looked back at Stela. "I hope you brought home your limit because I've invited her to supper. And AJ, this is the best mezzo soprano, the best angler, and the second best cook in Elephant Rock County."

I hate that kind of folksy introduction, but cheered up anyway, thanks to the rich scent of the cooking fish, Stela's long look took me in, probably squaring what she had heard about me with what she saw.

Without waiting for her to comment, Luke caught her waist and cinched her close. The floor of the trailer vibrated slightly. I glanced away, cringing. There was something false about the scene: I suspected it hadn't been enacted so much for my benefit, but in some way, for their own. Stela embraced Luke with what seemed more like practiced tolerance than enthusiasm.

"I've got to get back to the trout before they burn!" Stela shook Luke off and touched me lightly on the shoulder in welcome.

"Is there anything I can do?" I asked her.

"Just stay out of the way." Her tone robbed the words of any insult. "There's not enough room to change your mind in here, so settle down on a stool while I finish up."

Stela was right. The kitchen consisted of a single counter crowded with a collection of appliances so small they could have furnished a child's playhouse. I watched her flip the fish in an electric frying pan that straddled the stove's two burners. Luke had disappeared.

"Smells good." I breathed in a fragrance that made it clear even the Golden Hour's substantial hotcakes couldn't last forever.

"I tell my customers at the Dairy Queen there's nothing like a Southern upbringing to teach a cook everything there is to know about handling hot grease. Of course, I use olive oil these days—and we don't eat like this at home very often. Even at the DQ, we offer grilled chicken sandwiches and non-fat frozen yogurt."

"You work at the Dairy Queen?" I asked appalled.

"Sure do—I bought the local franchise when we moved here. There weren't too many choices here for me; I was a music professor at the University of Utah. Luke and I met there when we were both in Faculty Senate.

"She was the president, and I was the gadfly," Luke called from the back of the trailer.

"I was the president, and you were the pain in the ass," she corrected.

She took one step to the waist-high refrigerator and set a bowl of potato salad and a tray of fresh vegetables onto the bar that served as a substitute for a table. Its surface was covered with a fresh layer of striped shelf paper. "Anyway, I still sing—with the Montana Lyric Company in Missoula— when snow and ice doesn't scare me off the interstate."

"Couldn't you teach at the college?"

"The music department did offer me one of their spouse jobs." She looked at me to see if I understood. I did, all too well and all too personally.

"Well, I thought it would be better for me to go into business for myself. Course, that was before GoldPro started talking so much about making us into a boomtown that a McDonald's opened up in the next block."

"Stel, let's not spoil our supper by bringing up that name." Luke reappeared in a clean shirt and jeans.

"Which one—McDonald's or GoldProspectives?" I asked.

"Take your choice." Luke moved to the cupboard above the refrigerator and began setting out a collection of mismatched china.

"Almost all of our stuff is packed since we don't want to start emptying boxes until we sort through my mother's things," he explained.

"That reminds me. Sugar, did you find anyone to help you get ready for the sale tomorrow?" Stela's tone made it clear she had just pitched a fast ball to a batter who was about to strike out. When Luke didn't answer immediately, she turned to open an oven packed with a half-dozen foil-wrapped cylinders that could only be corn on the cob. I was relieved to see she was the type of cook who, even when she wasn't expecting company, made extra.

"Well, I think I'm ready enough." At least Luke was attempting a swing before his miss. "I thought we could just try to sell the leftovers from last week." He looked at me to avoid Stela's stern stare. "We seem to be in the garage sale business—Friday through Saturday every week until everything's gone," he explained.

"People aren't going to keep coming if you don't make the trip worth their while. You've got to get serious about clearing out that stuff, Luke." Stela's voice was quiet, but it held an edge stropped by sharp repetition. I was listening to the kind of argument that runs underground until the company leaves.

To avoid answering, Luke again directed his comments to me. "Stel thinks we need to clean out the place before we move in." His voice was flat as he dropped individually wrapped packages of plastic Dairy Queen utensils next to the plates. Moving to the window above the sink, he stood beside Stela, who was arranging the fish on a plate edged with lemon wedges. He seemed to be trying to gaze through the windowless wall.

"It has to be done," Stela said. The steam from the fish joined and divided them. I had the feeling that I had vanished.

"Maybe I could help with the sale." I paused, wishing I could suck my words back. But it was too late: I had rematerialized within easy reach of their shared vision.

In the Dance House you can see Judges, the Legislative corps, and every one but the Minister. He never ventures further than to engage in conversation with a friend at the door . . . .

—Thomas J. Dimsdale, in *The Vigilantes of Montana*

Boogieman

CONRAD CAN NEVER SEEM TO GET AROUND TO SCROUNGING UP SOME OLD piano for the spot he's saving for it in the *Sun*'s backroom next to the freight elevator. A drinking man has his dreams, but it takes a sober man to carry them out. The trouble is, when Conrad is sober, his dreams don't survive in the afterburner of his ambition.

Considering the way his daddy had gone, scotch shouldn't be his drug of choice. But what else is there for a more-or-less respectable small-town newspaper editor? Sure, he smoked his share of grass in Vietnam—hell, who didn't. But he doesn't seek it out now for the same reason he didn't fuck with anything you had to inject or snort then. His daddy didn't teach him much back home on the family's Indiana farm. But his daddy did teach him, by word when he was sober and by deed when he was drunk, not to gamble more than you're willing to lose.

Conrad would prefer playing to an audience, one whose ability to appreciate music has been enhanced by alcoholic intake. But none of the local bars has a piano anymore. The Baptist Church is closer to the newspaper office, but the Baptists won't have him. The Lutheran church isn't bad, really. He smuggles in his own bottle, which he secrets in the gap between the polished Steinway and the wall. At first, he hid his glass too, but then the pastor began leaving him a clean tumbler cushioned by a thick coaster of the previous week's bulletins.

Conrad doesn't mind the ghost. Pounding away, he glanced up one

Tuesday evening, and there she was, Mrs. Wakasa, her camera cradled in her arms, its old-fashioned flash opened like a sunflower. She looked much the way she always had, the lenses of her glasses suspended from the severe dark bridge, a Shetland wool sweater neatly draped over her shoulders.

"Sorry," he said. "I can stop if you want to be alone."

Mrs. Wakasa had hanged herself from a hook in her darkroom two winters before. Up until that point, she had given no indication. Always completely pleasant and unflappable, she arranged the school children for their annual pictures or posed bridal couples to feed each other bits of wedding cake, year after year after year. People invited her to Sunday pot roast once in a while or for strawberry pie at the Golden Hour. Her daughter, the lawyer, came to visit every year or two. Mrs. Wakasa displayed photos of her grandchildren, their faces showing their yearly development like the time-lapse photography of the division of cells.

"Do you remember Mrs. Wakasa?" Conrad asks. The Lutheran pastor's lower lids sag. His breath smells of the infection that has invaded his sinuses. Certain church members have been leaving brochures on his desk showing the joys of retirement center living.

"I'm hardly senile enough to forget a woman whose business was less than a block away from here."

Conrad ignores his tone. A newspaper editor is used to dealing with testy people. "Was she a member of your church?"

"Of course not. She was a Buddhist."

Conrad soothes the pastor with a sweaty version of "Cow Cow Boogie." Although the pastor retreats to the door of the sanctuary for dignity's sake, he listens to that tune and three more before retreating to his study.

Conrad doesn't raise the subject of Mrs. Wakasa again. She begins dropping by to hear him play almost every week. He never notices her enter. He looks up, and there she is.

She never responds to his playing. She simply sits in one of the pews, holding her camera, waiting, but not for him to leave. She is always gone before the aching in his fingers forces him to stop.

"Can I play something special for you?" he asks sometimes after the level in his hidden bottle has dropped sufficiently.

She never answers, so Conrad tries to leave her alone. He wants her to keep coming back. Boogie-woogie never sounds good in an empty room.

[The park representative] scouts the countryside to turn up bits of Bannack stored away in attics or displayed in area living rooms. In one instance, he retrieved the original bell from the Bannack Masonic Hall by trading a more modern one to the rancher using it for a dinner bell.

—*The Butte Montana Standard*

Small Change

"YOUR SALE IS IN HERE?" I TRIED TO SHIFT MY VOICE INTO NEUTRAL, BUT the sour set of Luke's mouth made me realize I should have tried for reverse. Inside the garage—long, low, probably built in the 1930s—the air twitched with the stink of mice and old gasoline. Reflexively, I pinched the dust mask more tightly onto the bridge of my nose and fastened the top button of my ad hoc protective gear. Stela had outfitted me with a worn pair of overalls and a dun colored shirt with the boxy cut and twin patch pockets of the 1950s. The shirt's label proclaimed in fancy cursive "Silver Star—Sanforized."

"This or the rag bag," she had said pointedly, when Luke raised a palm in protest as I reached out to take the bundle from her. Now that Stela had departed to check on the DQ, I thought he might ask me to give him the clothes right off my back.

Instead, he answered my question: " No, in my father's old woodworking shop—it's not as full, and a lot cleaner—long as you don't count sawdust as dirt."

I was relieved to hear it. In the garage, the only open space was a path that lost itself among towers of cobwebby boxes. Squeezing through them, I remembered that Butte, just 60 miles north on I-15, once had quite the reputation for attracting arsonists who viewed a book of matches and a can of gasoline as an effective tool for tapping insurance money. Perhaps Luke should take a lesson.

Not that he could get rid of the mess that way—too much metal: Motors of various sizes clustered in groupings like destitute families. Rusty loops of towing chain. Open-mouthed Butter-Nut coffee cans brimming with nuts, bolts, nails, hooks, screws, and a bewildering variety of other small parts. And heaps and heaps of tools, pressing down the workbench that hugged the perimeter, humping it up from below: sledge hammers that looked as if they belonged in the hands of John Henry; saw blades with teeth still sharp enough to bite; archaic power tools with tweedy, fraying cords; vises with greasy jaws; drill bits; wrenches; screwdrivers with split or broken wooden grips.

There were burnables as well, I noticed, forgetting my role as a historian and reacting instead as the daughter of adoptive parents who made travelling light into a religious tenet. Faced with this mess, they would have a nice big bonfire going in apple pie order. Where were my putative parents now when I needed them? What highway were they burning up with their gas-guzzling RV? Or had they broken their trip to take on a lucrative estate sale from desperate heirs who just wanted someone else to deal with the mess. Chas and Bet followed a simple, effective policy: buy low, sell high, and get rid of the extraneous trash as conveniently as possible. Chas, who never had considered shredding and recycling a serious option, would reach for his cigarette lighter without a qualm to convert mountains of trash into molehills of ash.

For Chas and Bet, a sale would be even better than a fire, because lots of people would actually pay for the privilege of hauling the junk away. They might smell potential profit even here. In the mousy stacks of *Popular Mechanics*. In the fishing creel dangling from a hook. In the dirt-streaked Barbie stretching her arms toward an anvil. In the jumble of radio casings and vacuum tubes. In the collection of toasters that, had they been lined up in chronological order, would have shown the short evolution of their species.

"Awful, ain't it," Luke drawled. "Every damn summer vacation, I intended to get started on it. But whenever I suggested that I do a little sorting, my mother would get this solemn look. Always reminded me of Lincoln staring out across South Dakota. 'Leave it alone, son,' she said. And I did. Maybe she was right not to trust me to tell the difference between the baby and the bathwater." His face warned me not to take his little joke on himself seriously.

"But you trust me?" I wondered what Luke classified as junk. Probably not much.

Without waiting for his reply, I squeezed past the front of a shrouded Model T, navigating the maze of boxes until I spotted a box that sprouted the handles of a couple of saucepans. Hefting it down, I heard the promise of an interesting clank.

"You can tell the difference, I'm sure. You are a historian," Luke said, the doubt in his voice undercutting his words.

"We'll have to have a big bucket of hot, soapy water and a whole bunch of old towels or cotton T-shirts," I ordered, by way of distraction. And something to price with. I don't suppose you have a gun, do you?"

Luke shot a puzzled glance in the direction of a rifle hanging from hooks on the pegboard above the workbench.

"A pricing gun," I clarified.

"I thought we'd just do what we usually do—let people make us offers."

I grimaced with disbelief.

"Well, the object isn't to make money—it's just to get rid of whatever is useable," he defended himself.

"What would your parents say to that?" I said, thinking of the actual horror with which Chas and Bet would greet such a sentiment.

"I can see that you're the right woman for this job." I pretended to mistake the comment for a compliment.

It was almost midnight before the shelves in the workshop, still damp from the satisfying scrubbing I had given them, were heaped full enough, in my judgment, to tempt. My asthma had slept through the proceedings, even though the elastic of my mask had snapped early on.

"Looks nice," said Stela, who had come out at ten o'clock to announce apple pie, but who had stayed to help in what seemed to be an exception to some sort of marital policy governing division of labor. She had been smart enough, I noticed, to change into jeans and a long-sleeved sweatshirt. Now that I had stopped working, my arms were cold in my Sanforized shirt. The fluorescent lights washed everything ice-blue.

I had talked Luke into holding back a scattering of things I thought might be valuable— furniture, cookie jars, teacups, and the like—until he could get a chance to research their market value on the internet. It was harder convincing him that he shouldn't do the same with two faintly perfumey boxes of empty Avon bottles.

"Believe me, you'll never miss these," I argued. "There's always a heap of them at any estate sale I've ever attended. "

"My mother loved them." He picked up a bath oil container shaped like someone's idea of a Greek statuette.

Stela walked toward Luke and took his arm. "I think that's enough for one night," she said just as we heard some sort of vehicle jounce over the cattle guard.

"The early-vultures must be getting a head-start," Luke joked, but Stela glanced toward the paint-spattered clock on the wall just inside the shop's entrance as if she were thinking about pulling out her cell phone in case she needed to dial the cops.

With a surge of irritation, I recognized the squeal of the Scout's brakes even before Conrad shoved the shop's double doors open.

"Thought I'd find you here." Materializing out of the dark, he gave Stela and Luke a half-embarrassed greeting before offering me a ride. Boggled by exhaustion and even more by the idea that someone that I'd known for less than forty-eight hours would presume to worry about me, I knew I should try harder to resist the solicitude Conrad was shedding like dandruff. Instead, against my better judgment, I hauled myself into the Scout.

At six the next morning, I was showered, dressed in my last pair of clean jeans, and waiting groggy and brainless on the sidewalk in front of the newspaper when Luke's pickup slowed for the stoplight, still blinking yellow.

Climbing in, I muttered a hello to Luke's overly cheery greeting. I unscrewed the top from the Thermos he handed me. To my relief, a promising incense infused the truck's cab with the olfactory equivalent of pure hope. With gratitude, I lifted the cup in Luke's direction in a completely sincere toast. He grinned at me so brightly that I finally noticed that the pouches under his eyes bulged like a night deposit for tears.

"You're not looking forward to this." The sharp air of the obsidian dawn was acting on me like a variation of nitrous oxide—not laughing gas but talking gas. I was sick of the kind of grief that hid itself away in a soundproof cellar. Instead of replying, Luke shrugged.

Acid bubbled at the back of my throat. I felt my right hand tighten its grip on the cup and my left close itself into a fist. My body was insisting on its right to anger, no matter how inexplicable. I didn't know who I wanted to hit more, Luke or my absent and agonizingly silent mother.

Luke bumped over the cattle guard without saying a word. And then he surprised me. "Let me tell you a story about the theory of relativity in history," he said, his voice falling into the cadences of a practiced lecturer. "Over in Bozeman, archeologists have excavated the privies at the Army fort there, and they've found a lot of extremely interesting stuff." Luke stopped the pickup in front of the shop. Neither of us made a move from our seats.

"I'll bet." Despite myself, I was intrigued. Or maybe, sometime hypocrite that I am, I was all too grateful to reach for the diversion of the story, to excuse myself from acknowledging Luke's pain—and my own.

"Yup—they've gathered quite an impressive collection of whisky bottles that had been deposited in the holes along with the usual. Apparently the fort's prohibition against drinking just pushed it underground."

I didn't make him wait for the forced stretch of my smile. "It makes you wonder how pickled the Second Cavalry's judgment was when it came to trying to parlay with the Crows." One more honest encounter had just been averted, and it was just as well since I didn't see a long-term relationship with Luke in my future.

The shop's overhead door was standing open, demanding that we get to work. I wondered if the undefended entrance indicated Luke and Stela trusted that no thieves lurked in Misfire. Or maybe they hoped someone would make the rummage disappear in their absence.

No one had. Scoured by the uncompromising morning light, my careful arrangements on the tables (their sheet coverings revealed as dirty where their edges swept the floor) looked as forlorn as leftovers abandoned on the kitchen counter after Thanksgiving. I picked up the hem of the sheet and tried to brush it clean. "Leave it," Stela said, walking into the shop with a foil-wrapped plate in her hand. "No one will notice." As she dodged a single-speed Schwinn leaning heavily on a rusty kickstand, she handed the plate to me, ignoring Luke.

"Better eat your omelet now—the vultures will be arriving any minute," Luke advised me, picking up a roll of quarters and cracking it into a tray that probably had organized a cutlery drawer in his mother's kitchen.

"He's right about that much, AJ. Go ahead and don't worry about us. We've eaten. At least I've eaten, and Luke has thrown his over the fence to the neighbor's dog." She touched Luke lightly on the shoulder, apparently asking for a truce. "We could handle this without you."

"No. That would be like going home after the funeral to watch TV while everyone else followed the hearse out to the cemetery. Want some more coffee, AJ?"

Before I could accept, a snazzy Prius, shiny as a silver dollar, swept over the cattle guard and made a neat U-turn in the driveway so that its backend was facing the open shop, ready for loading.

"Are you open?" a woman called as she opened her window, but only part-way. She sat tight in her vehicle as though she expected to be attacked by a pack of police dogs. Despite the early morning chill, she wore a sundress, bright yellow against the car's grey interior. Even from several yards away, I could see that she must have spent most of her youth in a bikini, varnishing herself with a tan so thick that it probably crazed the moment she had turned thirty-five.

"Nope! Not until eight," Luke said.

"Well, good. I hate fighting the crowds." She threw open the hybrid's door and, without wasting time by closing it behind her, hustled into the shop.

Within minutes, the woman had cherry-picked the shelves, handed Stela a few dollars, and fired up her hybrid, and sped away, spraying gravel and forcing a couple of vehicles about to cross the cattle guard to stop. I felt terrible. What if the teddy bear, despite its buttonless ear, was a Steiff worth hundreds? What if the vases were lead crystal signed with a famous maker's name so finely etched that its cursive flow hid itself in the vine design that trailed to its base?

"Don't worry about it," Stela said while she unfolded a metal chair and patting its scratched seat as if she were calling an obedient dog to come sit beside her. "For one thing Crystal Starr doesn't really have an eye for quality." Stela repeated Sundress Woman's name to indicate that yes, I had heard correctly. "For another, remember that you saved us from selling that set of wooden golf clubs at a give-away price and from putting that Goldilocks cookie jar out on the fifty cent table."

"Luke, I do need to talk to you about your prices. Don't you think five dollars is a little high for a set of old table linen?"

I recognized Binah's voice immediately, even though today she was wearing a wide straw cowboy hat pinned to brightly artificial curls. The fringes of her scarlet shirt bounced against jeans so tight that they highlighted the snaking path of the varicose vein on her left thigh.

Stela put a restraining hand on Luke's arm. At what point in their marriage had she taken on the role of the reasonable one, I wondered. "I don't think we want to bargain, today, Binah. Whatever we can't sell, we're simply going to donate to the church."

In response, Binah moved to the shelf where a roaster big enough for a 25-pound turkey presided sphinx-like over a collection that included a square angel-food cake pan, a set of Revere Ware, and a half dozen cookie sheets. Thanks to the quick rinse I had given everything, the kitchenware flashed in the strengthening light.

For a half a minute, I considered stashing the pots and pans away for myself. My former husband had claimed ownership of the set of our fancy wedding Calphalon as I was isolating his belongings from mine, and I'd been without even a halfway decent set of cookware since. Not that I'd cooked even in the passing-for-happy early days of our marriage. I'd immersed myself in the life of a tenure-track assistant professor—the damp and dangerous academic equivalent of a long-term seduction that climaxes in the sort of unprotected sex that turns not to be as much of a relief as you had hoped.

Three preschoolers—could they all belong to the harassed-looking young couple looking at the table of Melmac—were swinging the remaining teddy bears by their arms and screaming while a middle-aged man in a cap with "Prospectors Bar and Grill" printed above its bill sighted down a chainsaw as if he intended to shoot with it. The stretch of still patchy grass along the driveway had already filled up with vehicles, and I could see more cars tussling for space outside the white picket fence.

"Luke!" Binah hollered over the din. "You've made a mistake in pricing three—no, four—of my books. They've ended up in the ten cent box."

Again Stela laid a restraining hand on Luke's shoulder. "Oh dear, Binah. We're lucky that you noticed—why don't you bring them over here," Stela said.

"Maybe they should go with the collectibles. The people in my chemo support group are always asking me for autographed copies."

"How are you feeling?" Stela's voice was gentle.

"Better every day. Like I say, where there's a will, there's a way." Binah spoke in the same determined tone that she had used rallying the troops in the Bannack schoolroom, but her voice dropped as Luke and a man with the cap appeared dragging a wooden box full of chisels of various sizes. "Looks like you're making out like a burglar, Brownie," she told the man in the cap. "I just hope you don't use all your energy up bargain hunting. You know we're going to need you at the rally tonight."

"I'll be there, Binah," he said, but he refused to look up. If Binah was offended by his terseness, she didn't show it. "And Luke, we're expecting your support as well. Are we going to get it?"

"I'll wander over to see what you have to say, but I expect that you and I are going to end up on opposite sides of the fence on the theme park issue."

Binah flushed an angry red that went well with her outfit. "If you're not with us, you might as well side with those GoldPro thieves." The shop was now filled with bargain hunters. Drawn by the vibration in Binah's voice, their heads swung with the precision of a compass arrow in her direction. Unembarrassed, Binah turned up the volume even more. "We need every person in this town to get behind us tonight and fight to save historic Bannack!" She waited for applause. When none was forthcoming, she announced, "We'll serve ice cream afterwards, so come one, come all." She bobbed her head to punctuate her sentence; her wig, I noticed, showed no sign of slipping.

"And does that include me?" It was Mr. Courteous-Aggressive from the museum. He looked good, very good to me, with his weathered skin and mean mouth.

"It's a free country," Binah said, counting out five dollars for a set of embroidered napkins without, I noticed, attempting to bargain for them again.

"Thank you for your gracious invitation, Binah. And did I hear correctly, Luke, that you intend to oppose the ill-considered efforts of our beloved Sons of Bitches?"

"I think, John, I'll reserve my judgment—at least for now."

Mr. Courteous-Aggressive saved face by taking a deposit slip out of the back of an old-fashioned check book and shoving it into an embosser meant to raise the name of the Bluebird Mining Company from a sheet of stationary. He pressed the handle down with what I thought was unnecessary force. "I'll give you two dollars for this," he called, after examining the result. The night before, I had asked Luke if he really wanted to sell the embosser. "I guess I don't mind," he had said. "If I don't get rid of it, I'll end up spending six months trying to trace its origins, and I'm getting too old to try to follow every stray lead that I come across. You can have it if you want it."

"No thanks."

"No—didn't think you were a collector."

Luke's observation was perfectly true. It shouldn't have hurt. Mr. Courteous-Aggressive dropped the embosser next to the change tray and hooked his thumbs in his belt, assuming the wide-legged stance affected by men who want the bulge in their crotch observed.

"I'll give you four dollars, but that's my best offer," Mr. Courteous-Aggressive said in a husky voice. The fingers of his right hand twitched. They hovered over his belt above the spot where a holster might have ridden.

"The embosser's not for sale," Luke said. "In fact, nothing's for sale."

Brownie interrupted: "How much are you asking for that mirror?"

"It's not for sale."

"I'll give you twenty-five for it."

"Sorry—we're closed."

Brownie turned his back on the shop and began limping toward the cattle guard. Giving up without a fight, Mr. Courteous-Aggressive also left without another word, his departing strut dragging my glance with it. He stepped up on the plank that bridged the cattle guard, even though Nick the bagman was already half way across. Mr. Courteous-Aggressive advanced without slowing his pace. Nick shuffled backwards to let him pass, but didn't touch his cap in the gesture of courtesy I'd seen him offer Brownie the second before.

Inside the shop, Luke re-settled himself into the metal chair behind the cash drawer. "I guess we'd better give Nick his chance after he's walked all the way out here."

"Right," said Stela. From the way she rapped another roll of quarters into the change tray, I could see that she'd set her anger aside for an afternoon simmer. She was businesswoman enough to convert the heat into fueling warm and apparently sincere smiles. Luke seemed to have forgotten his insistence on shutting down the sale. The customers kept coming empty-handed and leaving clutching plaster cowboys or Pyrex refrigerator dishes or one-of-a-kind items like the jewel box with a ballerina who jerked through a rendition of "Love Is a Many Splendoured Thing." If they felt uncomfortable in the rare presence of a black woman in their woefully homogenous town, they were too busy sacking up their bargains to show it. Still, I wondered how Stela felt living in Misfire, exotic and exiled, serving up pint after pint of soft white ice milk.

"Find anything you want, Nick?" The warmth in Stela's voice sounded unforced.

Nick held up a gold pan. The shallow basin had sustained rim to rim dents, but Luke had printed a fifty dollar price on its sticker the night before. "This was my father's," he had told me. Reaching for the gold pan so that she could see the price, Stela cast a disgusted look in Luke's direction. "I guess you'd better talk to Luke about this one," she told Nick. "I need to go find a couple of aspirin."

"Perhaps this pan still carries some of your father's luck," Nick said as she left. "I remember how fortunate he always was, how he would win on the punchboard at the Stockman's Bar nearly every week. I have often thought that you must have inherited Lady Luck's favor yourself, given your career and your marriage to a woman like Stela."

Although Luke gave no sign that he had noticed Nick's lofty diction, the bagman seemed to realize that he had slipped into high register. With his next breath, he resumed his usual folksy twang: "I saw by the paper just a couple of weeks ago that you won a hundred dollars in the lottery. So I reckon you can afford to drop your price a little on this here gold pan."

"OK, Nick—one dollar. But just don't tell GoldPro if you . . ."

"Thanks Luke—you may rely on me. I'm accustomed to keeping my own counsel."

That last comment worried me. I couldn't help but wonder if Nick would also feel compelled to keep his own counsel about where he had found the ledger. Oh well. I didn't really care about the ledger, did I?

As Nick left, the gold pan weighting the sack on his back into a pendulum that swung with his stride, Luke carried the embosser back to its shelf.

"That guy John isn't part of GoldPro, is he?" I called to him. "I thought he was a local banker."

"John Storey has his fingers in lots of pies, more so now than ever." Luke was rearranging the shelf so that the gap left by the gold pan wasn't so obvious. "I've heard his bank is going to be quietly taken over by the feds one of these weekends. That's why he's so intent on this GoldPro deal: he needs it to keep himself going. Let's close up, shall we, if that Subaru coming down the lane doesn't turn in."

But the Suburu clattered across the cattle guard, forcing the re-emergent gophers to dive for safety. I was surprised at how glad I was to see Rheta emerging from the car. Her lips curved up in her vivid orange-red smile as she spotted me.

"Is all the good stuff gone?"

"Lots more where that came from" Stela was carrying a tray with three drinks that looked as though they had a lot more kick than lemonade. "Just tell us what you need and we probably have it. Of course, prying it away from Luke won't be easy."

"For Rheta, I'll make an exception."

"Do me a favor and take as much as you can carry," Stela said.

"I do want to look around," Rheta said scanning the shop. "But then I want to talk to AJ about a business proposition." When Rheta reappeared she was carrying a doll. "For my neighbor's little girl," she explained. I wondered if Rheta had children of her own; she had shifted the doll to her shoulder with what looked like a practiced gesture.

"OK, AJ. Conrad wants to talk you into playing reporter tonight at the Theme Parks International rally. He's going to be one of the speakers. Normally, I'd cover it for him, but I'm going to be playing the piano like I always do for the Saturday night rest home sing-along."

"I hardly think that I'm the person to ask," I protested.

"Why not? It wouldn't take all that long, and no one could accuse you of lack of objectivity. Can't you write?"

"Of course, I can write."

"Well, why not, then? Conrad's willing to give you a week's free rent for doing it, but I think you can get more if you play hard to get. He never plans ahead, and now he's caught in a bind. Of course, he could write the meeting up himself, and I don't think he'd slant it. But no one would take anything he'd report about this particular issue as anything but propaganda."

"No," I said. A shadow blocked the light from doorway. My brother, neat as a pin, strolled in, gave me a noncommittal look of recognition, and then offered Luke, Stela, and Rheta an encompassing smile.

"Just the person I want to see." I impaled him with my brightest shit-eating grin.

As I advanced, he stepped backward until a set of empty shelves cut him off. Stuck, he decided to make the best of it. "Oh?" he said and waited.

I swallowed hard. Yes, my brother was just the person I wanted to see, but not for any reason I could announce at a rummage sale. He ran one hand along the shelf standards. "Oak," he said. I must have looked confused. He explained, "It's odd to find utility shelves made of oak."

Luke looked pleased. "My father built the whole place out of salvage—I can remember him bringing home a whole load of oak flooring when one of the grand old railroad mansions was pulled down."

"I'd be interested in seeing his finish work sometime," my brother said.

"No time like the present." Luke turned toward the door.

Desperate not to lose my brother before the hook was set, I blurted, "Shelves! I really need to talk to you about building a set of bookshelves for me. As soon as possible."

My brother gave me a look of mild astonishment, but waited politely for me to go on.

My hands shook as I sketched a vision of what I supposedly wanted into the air. A nice set, I asserted too emphatically. With a set of tightly fitting glass doors to keep the dust out.

Adon threw a longing glance over my shoulder to where another late customer was loading up on saws and screwdrivers. I could see my brother trying to figure out whether (A) I was mentally unbalanced; or (B). I had developed a sudden infatuation for him during our encounter in the Bannack Masonic Hall; or (C) Both of the above.

I did feel a strange attraction for him, blinking nervously, packaged in his ironed Mr. Ranger shirt, as nervous as I was, if the dampness under his arms was a clue. I licked my lips, tasting salt and feeling an odd ping of desire. Clearly I was mentally unbalanced.

"Well, I might not have time to get to a very involved project right away," he said, shifting his weight and his head back, tortoise-like, into his starched collar. "Although I do take on a few private carpentry jobs from time to time, I usually schedule them during the winter."

I stared intently into his face. He looked back warily without a hint of recognition.

"I don't need anything fancy, just nicely made and functional." Good: my voice sounded calmer now, almost normal. "I can't work without a way to organize and protect my documents. And, unfortunately, ready-made shelves just don't come in the configuration I need. How soon will you get busy at the park?"

My brother suffered from honesty, I could see that. He struggled silently to formulate a lie and then gave up, admitting that he would be working only part-time until the tourist season officially started with Memorial Day, more than a month away.

"What keeps you here," I asked with a change of subject so abrupt and inappropriate that it made him start edging toward the exit. "Do you have any family around here?" Now I knew what the hackneyed expression "to wait with bated breath" meant. I waited with bated breath to hear my mother's name.

"My wife is from Misfire." He stressed the word "wife" a little too emphatically.

"Does the rest of your family live around here?" I could have been a trap waiting to spring.

"My mother," he said.

"Your mother?" Yes, I thought. Your mother. Our mother. My mother.

"She lives in Bozeman."

"Really?" I said, hoping to encourage him to say more.

But he edged past me without further elaboration. "Well, I'd better take a look at those saws before they're all gone."

"Okie dokie." (I never said okie dokie.)

"Let's meet next week, then. Would Wednesday afternoon be OK? About four?" I was about to add "In my apartment?" but managed to alter that dangerous-sounding suggestion to "In the newspaper office?"

He agreed without enthusiasm.

"It's a date, then!" By the time Adon approached Stela at the cash drawer with a miter box, I had an old-fashioned paper check ready for him, an advance meant to set the hook, with our appointment written out on its memo line. Lucky I hadn't yet given myself totally over to swiping ephemeral plastic. As he folded into a rectangle and inserted it carefully into his shirt pocket, I knew he was the type who would keep his appointment come hell or high water.

"See you later, then!" I called, my voice quavering, as he hastened away.

"He's married," Stela said. "From what I hear, very married."

I shrugged silently. There was nothing in the world I could say.

Only the journalist who has experienced it knows what the man who wrote the news and the editorials had to do in the way of hurdling the difficulties that stand in the way of achieving an accurate picture of the event. He realizes vividly the hazard of projecting a complexity in a simple, limited vocabulary, the danger in compressed messages, the difficulty in bringing the remote near.

—Robert Houseman, in "The Journalist as Historian"

The purpose of agitation is to move the solution inside the developing tanks so a steady supply of fresh chemicals reaches the emulsion at regular intervals. Agitation is vital while the film is in the developer and is also important during later processing stages. Too little or too much agitation can cause problems . . . .

—Barbara London and John Upton, in *Photography*

In the Dark

THE RALLY STORY WAS BEGUN, BUT NOT WELL BEGUN—AND CERTAINLY NOT finished. As Rheta rattled the lock of the *Sun*'s front door, I stayed in my stubborn forward slump. With my forehead pressed against the Underwood Champion's slightly pebbled brow, I awaited release from constipation of the mind, disconsolation of the heart, and, most of all, regret for the series of decisions that had led me to this time and place. "Concentrate!" I told myself.

I was still too shaken to organize the chaotic swirl of facts into a coherent story. Besides, I hadn't actually witnessed the fight that had sent Conrad tumbling to the lawn from the concrete stage the evening before. Bored by the rally's slow start, I had deserted the icy seat of my folding chair in the hope of cadging a cuppa from the museum's tourist coffee bar. I needed something to keep me awake, and I got it—but in a different form than I intended.

"Help! Call the ambulance!" Binah had clomped toward me as fast as her red boots could carry her. "Conrad's hurt! That damn John Storey! My phone's dead!" She galloped back down the boardwalk and disappeared around the corner. On one of the rare occasions when I needed a cell, I was without one. I stampeded into the museum office, scattering the tourists. "But the phone is for authorized personnel only," Bruce the docent protested as I dialed 911.

"Just stay calm," the dispatcher commanded. "Help is on the way—we've already had several calls."

Despite her assurances, I felt compelled to deliver my own version of the message: "There's been an accident at the museum. I mean, at the gazebo stage. Just get here fast!"

"We've had several calls already, Ma'am," the dispatcher repeated. "The ambulance is on the way. Please hang up to free the line."

Pounding back to the stage, I saw Binah kneeling on the lawn by Conrad, who was lying completely still, his chin tipped toward the sky, his eyes squeezed shut. Mr. Courteous-Aggressive was crouched loosely beside Binah, the bouquet of GoldPro protest signs he had been holding tumbled into a forgotten clump. "Mine the Future, Not the Past," they exhorted.

"Did you tell them he's dying!" Binah yelled in my direction. Nick was speaking urgently into what seemed to be his own iPhone, a possession that slightly shocked me despite the circumstances.

"No!" My stomach contracted.

Conrad opened his eyes and groaned. "Those damn volunteers! Unless you tell them someone's dying, they won't come until they finish their coffee."

"Keep still, Conrad," Binah said.

"He's OK." Mr. Courteous-Aggressive's voice was more than half-contemptuous.

"What about the rally?" The Theme Parks International businesswoman, who was supposed to be the event's main attraction, was shouting her question from the stage. She looked more like a sumo wrestler than any

Caucasian female I had ever seen or could imagine. Refusing to trust her skirt to the wind, she was still firmly ensconced in her chair, gripping its edge like a backseat driver.

"I'm OK!" Conrad called up to her. He was struggling to sit up—a wounded John Wayne playing cavalry captain surrounded by his command. Binah's cowgirl bandana was tied around his forehead but wasn't doing much to staunch the seep of blood from his scalp. The makeshift bandage was probably synthetic, I thought, feeling an impulse to tear off my sweater and offer its absorbent cotton. But I was even more concerned about the tinge to Conrad's lips than about the flow from his cut.

"Do you want another nitro pill?" Binah asked.

Not knowing what else to do, I raised the Nikon and focused. In the viewfinder, Conrad looked like someone I had never met. Mr. Courteous-Aggressive, kneeling now, loomed large, his shoulders set in a threatening angle. Binah was still grasping the tiny brown pill bottle.

Conrad closed his eyes, either because the pill dissolving under his tongue was making him feel better, or because it wasn't. He opened them as a lethargic wail announced the arrival of an ambulance.

Remembering that wail, I pulled myself away from the typewriter's surface, the cool color of river stones. The story remained stuck at half mast.

"Help," I whispered. St. François of Sales, the multi-tasking patron saint of both reporters and the deaf, answered in Rheta's voice.

"How's the story coming?" Rheta's determined advance reminded me of a line from a song they made us sing one summer when Bet had sent me to Vacation Bible School in Great Falls, Montana: "Onward, Christian soldiers, marching as to war . . ."

Rheta came to a sharp halt at my elbow. "You're not using your laptop?"

I chinned a "No," although the answer to Rheta's second question was obvious. I had opted for the typewriter because I wasn't sure where or when I'd be able to get access to a printer. As for the matter of the story, it had been at least two hours since I had tossed my most recent draft, number five, into the wastepaper basket beside Conrad's desk and started again, hoping momentum would carry me to some kind of clarity:

Conrad J. MacFarlane, 62, editor of the Misfire *Sun-Tribune* was in serious but stable condition Sunday in Missoula's St. Patrick Hospital after collapsing at about 8:15 Saturday evening during a highly heated argument between the two opposing factions clashing over the undecided future of Bannack State Park. The bitter altercation took place when

"Not bad," Rheta said, leaning over the back of my chair to retrieve the draft I had thrown away. Flecks of wood pulp splintered the surface of the cheap copy paper. During the last ten hours, she had arranged temporary residential care for her mother in the rest home, called Conrad's daughter in Portland to report her father had been Life-Flighted to Missoula, hit the highway for the 200-mile trip to St. Pat's cardiac ICU, and returned to Misfire with no more sleep than one can manage in a hospital waiting room.

"Really, not bad at all." Rheta's voice was too calm and too kind. "It's just too bad the Butte newspaper got inspired to send a reporter to cover the rally. Did you see the story in this morning's paper."

"Yes." It had been a solid account, quoting Binah, the sumo business woman, and Mr. Courteous-Aggressive. The Butte's photographer had caught a shot of Storey looking like a particularly sincere Marlboro man.

"As Number Two, I guess we'll just have to try harder."

My story must be shit. My next breath wheezed. It occurred to me that I didn't know where I had left my saddlebag or the inhaler it contained. Upstairs? In the trunk of the Bel Air? On the folding chair I had abandoned when Conrad took his tumble from the stage?

I started to get up, but I felt Rheta's hands on my shoulders. With the index finger of her free hand she tapped one of the long paragraphs near the bottom of the first page. "But you need to cut out all the adjectives and adverbs. And save the details about the conflict between GoldPro and Theme Parks International for a sidebar. The issue of whether John Storey caused Conrad to fall from the stage by jabbing him with his protest sign might go as another sidebar, don't you think? You did get a shot of Storey kneeling by Conrad, right?

Words quivered on the tip of my tongue, but when I opened my mouth, they transformed into themselves into a gasp. Rheta re-mastered her voice into a soothing tone. "It might be better to finish the story up later. You have to do follow-up interviews tomorrow anyway with the cops and with everyone you talked to at the scene anyway, right? Wouldn't it be better use of our time right now to soup the film? Seeing the photos might help you finish the story."

Like a paper cut, Rheta's implied criticism continued to sting all out of proportion to the original injury as we descended to the basement dark-room. Even though my breathing was relaxing a little more with every step I put between me and the Underwood, I retreated into a vengeful sullenness. I watched with what I hoped would communicate itself as a pointed silence as Rheta sought to share the mysteries of processing black and white film the old-fashioned way with foul-smelling chemicals and splashing water. Distracted by my anger, I had to force myself to pay attention to the first step of what was, after all, a simple procedure: use the bottle opener to pop the cap off the film magazine, insert the end of the film into the heart of the stainless steel reel, and then slip its soft coils through its patterned grooves so that no surface touched another.

"OK, let's try it in the dark," she said after I had loaded a roll of waste film onto one of the reels three times in a row with no problems. When she reached for my hands, I tugged free, refusing further help.

"All done?"

"Yes—it was easy." I had to force myself to resist falling into a dark-induced whisper. Then I couldn't help adding, "Although a digital camera would be even easier." A vinegary stink gave the darkroom's air a bite. I hoped my asthma wouldn't rouse itself to bite back. Of course, I could have asked Rheta to wait a few minutes while I searched out my saddlebag, but I wasn't in the mood to ask for even a minor favor.

Rheta switched on the red safelight. "I'm surprised to hear that you're a digital fan. Isn't your own camera pretty much a twin to Conrad's?" It seemed too much trouble to explain that I also owned a fully charged Canon. I had opted to use my old Nikon at the rally only because Conrad had told me the *Sun* had only one option for dealing with digital photos in the newsroom: none.

Rheta shrugged at my silence. "Well, OK. If you think you can manage alone, I'll go check on my mother —she's being a really good sport about having to stay at the rest home this week. And then I'll pick us up some-thing for dinner. I don't think I've had anything to eat since a God-awful hospital cafeteria muffin this morning in Missoula. You?"

"Nothing but coffee." I wondered whether I should brew a new batch before I started on the film. It should take only a few minutes to load the reels. Once the lights were back on, I could sip with one hand while I agitated the tank with the other.

"Well, we're both overdue. With any luck, you'll have all seven rolls hanging up to dry by the time I get back, and we can call it quits for the evening."

Ignoring all considerations of my current and future health, I told her that I wanted a deep-fried fish sandwich, a double order of fries, and a large chocolate malt—the comfort food treat that Bet used to treat me to after my first day at yet another new school. Deciding the coffee would taste better after I ate something, I forced the darkroom's door along its runners and closed the greasy black curtain that completed the *Sun*'s defense against outside light.

For the first time, I noticed the slow drip of the darkroom's faucet and an unidentifiable rasping. To counter the lonesome creaks of the old building talking to itself, I twisted the lid of a radio made to mimic a catsup bottle. Rheta had warned me that it brought in only the local station, so I didn't bother trying to figure out where the tuner was hidden. A DJ with a bad cold started mumbling public service announcements.

The first four coils of film ran into their reels with speed and docility. Feeling self-satisfied, I dropped the finished reels into their tank, closed the lid tightly, turned on the safelight, and activated the timer. Did I really have to finish the first batch before I loaded the reels for the next one? There seemed little reason to stretch out the process. Since the numerals on the timer were visible even in the dark, it should be as easy as playing spin the bottle to alternate between slipping the remaining rolls into their reels and giving the developing tank a shake at the prescribed thirty second intervals.

But pride ever goeth before a fall. Just as the congested disc jockey was promising me an hour of Elvis (never my favorite), the first roll crackled and balked. Closing my eyes so that I couldn't see that I couldn't see, I started over. And over. And over. When the timer pinged, Elvis was crooning "Blue Moon of Kentucky" and I resigned myself to the fact that I would have to set the naked film aside. Oh well. I should be able to manage the stop bath and the fix for the first batch of film well enough in the dark.

I continued to give the tank falsely enthusiastic shakes in time with "Heartbreak Hotel," "Love Me Tender," and "Are You Lonesome Tonight?" For the not-so-grand finale, plain H2O would have to do. Without a visual clue, I couldn't remember where Rheta had pointed when she was giving me directions about something called the Hypofix.

The dark bubbled up around me as I groped back to the recalcitrant roll. I dipped the reel. The film curtsied and accepted the offer of a dance. Static claimed Elvis, as film and reel developed a close, if temporary, relationship. When the last two rolls also consented to embrace, I decided not to mention my spot of bother to Rheta.

"Almost done," I told myself. On the counter, my hand found the second tank, but where was its light-tight lid? My fingers scuttled across the counter's smooth surface. Wishing for rubber gloves, I knelt to probe the cobwebby spaces on the floor under the counters. Stray wisps of film caught at my fingers. "Fuck a duck," I said with something close to despair.

The hollow clank of the front door and the fast beat of Rheta's determinedly snappy gait announced that the cavalry was coming. The stairs creaked; in a moment her voice knocked.

"I'm back. How's everything going?"

"I couldn't get one of the rolls loaded for a long time, and now I've dropped the lid of the second tank." I meant to simply report the facts, but my voice trembled.

"Poor kid. I suppose you've already checked under the counter."

I nodded, and Rheta responded as if I'd seen the gesture.

"Well, did you check between the curtain and the door?"

"No," I said. Uncertain about which direction the door might be, but unwilling to ask Rheta to keep talking so I could orient myself, I groped until a sweep of clammy fabric suddenly adhered to the palms of my hands. I patted it down like a dangerous suspect.

"I can feel it behind the curtain, but won't I let in the light if I grab it?"

"There shouldn't be enough leakage clear down there to hurt anything as long as you move fast."

It only took me the space of a couple of breaths to set everything right. Rheta stepped inside, her white hair shining like a flame. Sick of the dark, I switched on not only the safelight, but the naked bulb overhead. The old-fashioned type, it hung like an oversized tear bulging toward its final fall. Nobody made that type of light anymore, especially in these days of energy efficiency. My thoughts bobbed upwards, imagining an unused room crammed with boxes of fragile incandescent bulbs waiting for the surge of electricity to break dormancy.

Rheta set the timer. To cover my embarrassment over forgetting that vital step, I rapped the tank on the counter to shake loose any air bubbles and began agitating.

"Rheta," I said having the sense to stop myself from asking what would sound like a crazy question about light bulbs.

"Yup?"

"Nothing." What was wrong with me—first, my panic over the saddle-bag, which certainly had to be in the trunk of the Bel Air. And now this impulse to explore the *Sun* for lofty hidden chambers.

"Is Luke really an attorney?" I asked to cover my confusion.

"Well, yes—he earned a law degree before he went on to get his PhD—always says he figured the best judge is history. But what makes you ask?"

"After the ambulance left and Binah took over the emcee duties, John Storey heckled her from the audience. Said something insulting about how the editor of a small town weekly and a writer of paperback romances had no business attempting to work out a business deal to take over Bannack and run it as a theme park. Asked if anyone in the organization had a law degree."

"And Luke stepped up to the bat? I thought he was against the theme park. Maybe you should call him tomorrow and ask him for an explanation."

"Good idea," I said, feeling a little offended. Rheta must think I might not figure out that obvious course of action for myself. Despite the unintended insult, it was oddly pleasant standing in the rosy glow of the safelight, companionable ghosts. Rheta's perfume, a light lily of the valley, cancelled out the combined chemical reek of developer and fixer, the way orange blossoms are supposed to neutralize gardenias.

"You probably had trouble with the film because the leader got crimped. When that happens, just reach for the scissors." Apparently a believer in tactile memory, Rheta caught my hand and showed it where the scissors hung on a hook on the wall in back of the sink. "Slice off a little bit, and you can start over. I've often thought it's too bad you can't do that in life. "

"But what if you lose a shot?"

"You usually won't, not unless your leader is awfully short. Anyway, if you do lose something you can always brag about the one that got away."

"Dinner?" Rheta asked once the film in the second tank was washing, this time with the benefit of the hypo. "I got us two of the nice chef salads at the Safeway deli."

I returned to my chair in front of the Underwood at five the next morning, but not much before Rheta and the typesetter showed up nearly at the same time. Jana was a rancher who worked two and a half days a week to help the cash flow of one of the last family spreads in the valley. When she saw how short-handed we were, she phoned her daughter-in-law—a woman as raw-boned and competent as Jana was herself—to staff the front desk. Freed from receptionist duties, Rheta flashed in and out, weaving the newspaper office to a downtown that was waking up more wide-eyed than I had yet seen it.

Today fickle April had decided to offer a menu heavy on sweetness and light as it reached toward May. The sparkling day had transformed the sidewalk outside the *Sun*'s entrance into a sparkling stream buoying up a flotilla of shoppers. Waving her notebook in triumph, Rheta appeared and reappeared. "Another one!" she called, giving the ad copy to Jana, who was slapping away at the keyboard of a mastodon of a typesetting machine, lumbering, grey, and caged in its own protective glass booth . What went in letter by letter and line by line came out in long strips that had to be proofread by someone, and that someone was me. I didn't mind, though. Proofreading was something I was good at. And I liked the rhythm of moving between the Underwood to the typesetting booth, where Jana would periodically stop to run out my corrections. With surprising pleasure, I doctored the errors with strips like tiny Band-Aids. That pleasure carried me past the pain of writing and not even Rheta's unrelenting questions returned me to the deep freezer. Where will the burial be? What's the bride's mother's first name? What time is the 4-H meeting? How much will dog licenses go up in the fall? For a woman who claimed she had no ambitions to edit the *Sun*, I thought Rheta was doing a pretty good imitation of tough guy editor Cary Grant in *His Girl Friday*, minus the high drama and heavy on the stuff of everyday life: a newsroom version of *Our Town* played out for real in the foothills of the Rockies.

Through that day and the next, I kept on typing, revising and proofing, happy to be part of the web of work that was transforming the newspaper office into something more than a dank cave. Although I had finally taken the time after Rheta left Sunday evening to satisfy myself that my saddlebag and its documents were indeed safely stowed in the trunk of the Bel Air, I had let them lie untouched since then. Too tired to worry about poking through the *Sun* morgue, I put off that adventure as well, telling myself I would have plenty of time for exploration later, if I was still interested.

I didn't even complain about more immediate concerns—chiefly, Rheta's assumption that I would continue to play Rosalind Russell to her Cary Grant. In reality, I was engrossed in trimming the typeset copy into columns, running them through the waxing machine, and precisely affixing them to paste-up sheets to get them ready for the process of burning them into the aluminum press plates.

With the paper due to go to press in just a few hours, I had to force myself to pause to greet Luke and Stela when they appeared while I was gulping down a lunchtime sandwich while trying to finish the last of the proofing. Because I could hear the old-fashioned wall clock ticking off the minutes until our deadline, I offered only superficial resistance to the gifts they bore. I did notice them parading by with things that I had told them they ought to set aside because of their possible value: a sewing rocker with a delicately spindled back, a brass floor lamp with a creamy silk shade, and a gate-legged table that proved its storability with demurely folded leaves.

"No more!" I begged on their third trip past my desk. "This is too much. Rheta already had a futon frame and mattress delivered for me this afternoon, and, really, I don't actually need . . ."

Ignoring me, Stela began hustling the rocker up the stairs. "If we shove that monstrosity of a bar against the wall next to the closet door, everything will fit," she assured me without slowing.

Luke followed the spiral of Stela's voice, dragging a rag rug wrapped with plastic tarp. I stood up and called after him, "But those pieces could be worth a lot of money. I wouldn't even want to guess about what you might get for the rocker, not to even mention a hand-braided rug like that one."

"We couldn't get anything, because we're not selling them," Luke said, continuing to trot toward the apartment without missing a step. The rug looked heavy, but I noticed with relief that he wasn't even breathing hard. Conrad's heart attack had made me expect that all the middle-aged men I encountered might suddenly keel over. "I suppose that when you're ready to move on . . ." He stopped mid-sentence as Stela dodged him on her way back out to the pickup.

"Don't worry," she said on her return trip. "We have an ulterior motive—-actually several. We really need to get rid of all this stuff. We also need to pay you back for saving our asses by helping us. Besides, we hope you'll lend us a hand again next week." With the flourish of a seller presenting a contract to a recalcitrant buyer, she rattled the cardboard box she was carrying. The clank silenced me: I knew without asking that the box contained the cookware I'd coveted, which had apparently not sold.

They waved and I let them go, almost forgetting their visit as we raced to finish. A quick, intuitive designer, Rheta didn't bother to plan her pages or even to write out and size her headlines out in advance, but everything clicked together. She was more careful with the ads, working from the sketches she had created with her clients and spending time flipping through the huge, heavy clipart booklets that looked as if they predated by a generation the thousands of images accessible through my laptop.

"If this keeps up, we'll be able to pay the electric bill before they cut us off." Rheta grinned as she checked a double-truck ad from the town's lone surviving local department store. I followed her into the room that controlled the camera that would transform the paper page into a metal plate. "Either the advertisers realize they're going to have to nudge people into spending or the economy is getting better," she added. "Whatever it is, I'm glad I'll have some good news for Conrad when I drive up to Missoula after the press run."

"Do you think you'll get to see him?"

Rheta, who had been keeping tabs on Conrad by phoning his daughter several times a day, had been reporting uneven improvement.

"As of an hour ago they were still keeping him drugged up to his gills because of the respirator, but they think that they'll be able to remove it later today," Rheta said, wiping developer onto a flexible aluminum sheet the size and shape of a newspaper page. "His daughter has listed me as his sister, so I'll be able to get into the ICU. Whether he'll be with it enough to track what I'm saying, I don't know. But I want to try."

Under her hands, the photo of Conrad collapsed on the museum lawn began blooming. Although John Storey was kneeling beside him in what should have looked like a posture of concern, there was something menacing in the way the banker's Stetson darkened his face. If bad guys wear black hats, what do not-very-good guys wear? Storey's headgear was printing up in dirty gray. Ignoring him, Conrad was gazing upward, heroically calm, his eyes fixed, or so it seemed, on the emerging headline: "SOB rally continues despite emcee's fall."

"Looks good, don't you think?"

"Better than I hoped."

"Anyway, it might be nice if you could ride up to Missoula with me after we finish the press run at about seven. We could book a hotel room and drive back in the early morning. I'd like the company, and it might do you good to get out of town. They might even let you in to see Conrad for a few minutes."

"I'd better not," I said, suppressing a zing of low-level horror at the idea. One advantage of having adoptive parents who claimed no relatives and who never stayed long enough anywhere to make friends was that I had rarely been obligated to visit hospital rooms.

"Well, if you change your mind . . ."

"Really—can't," I said, half-truthfully. "I have my bookshelf appointment with Adon today—pretty soon, in fact—and one with Luke at the college tomorrow morning to talk about my research. In fact, unless you need help with the press run . . ."

"Nope—we're covered. We're just lucky that Conrad is on good terms right now with Elephant Rock Printers. There have been times that Tom Engles and Conrad have been so mad at each other that neither one would lend the other a Number 2 pencil. And he's bringing his daughter along to fly the press, so we should be just fine." Rheta released me with a friendly wave, but called me back as I started up the stairs. "You're not forgetting about your parents, are you?"

"What?" Stumbling, I grabbed the rail for support

Seeing my incomprehension—or was it fear, Rheta slapped her forehead with the palm of her right hand in mock dismay. "Oh, AJ—I'm sorry. They called while you were at the cop shop yesterday. I must be catching my mother's Alzheimer's."

"My parents called?" I was still hoping I had misunderstood.

"Yes, yesterday afternoon, from Spearfish, South Dakota. Apparently your boss at the university told them where you are. They sounded real nice—said not to worry about finding them a place to camp. They want to look around and find someplace to park their RV for free. They won't be here until sometime tomorrow evening because they want to stop at Mount Rushmore."

I stared, wishing I could stop time or skip the part that involved my adoptive parents bursting into the *Sun*'s door.

But time, as the cliché assures us, marches on no matter how we might wish otherwise. Adon showed up at the newspaper's front counter just as the courthouse began bonging out four o'clock, his wife, displayed a little too ostentatiously at his side. Relaxed in her presence, he gave me a sincerely friendly smile while Nancia offered me her hand. A woman like the sword-sharp leaf of an iris, Nancia was elegant in a silk tunic, storm colored with an expensive drape. Reluctantly I wrenched my attention away from my half-brother and extended a half-hearted reach toward her. Elegant women occasionally force me into the uncomfortable admission that grownups can give up jeans as their daily uniform without betraying themselves. I expected her grasp to be cold and smooth; her fingers were warm and her palms calloused.

"When Adon told me were stopping to see you, I stuck something in my bag for you," she said. "I hope you don't mind." Her carry-all was solidly packed, but she brought up the book on her first try.

Bemused, I read the title: *The Pass*. No one had given me a book for a long time. The sketch on its tattered cover was dominated by a mountain range nonchalantly condescending to rolling hills and a curving river. In the high middle ground, a modest barn and a barely visible house sketched a human presence effaced by a higher power—not God, but the land.

"You'll understand Misfire better once you meet Tom Savage," she said.

"Does he still live here?"

"He did come home once before he died," she said. "You'll start to figure out why when you read him. I'll lend you one of his others when you're finished with this one, if you want."

Despite myself, I was touched. To lend a book is to invite a relationship and to extend trust. To lend a beloved book to a stranger is the equivalent of starting a garden in new place, one with an unpredictable climate and soil of dubious fertility.

Adon was opening his sketchbook, but I no longer felt desperate to force an immediate response from him. As Nancia handed me her phone to let me see a photo of her daughters, I projected a Technicolor future brightened by quick-witted kitchen table conversations with my sister-in-law and laughing games of croquet with my newly discovered nieces.

Nieces. Somehow I had never considered the possibility.

It took just a few minutes for me to approve my half-brother's precisely drawn plans and to sign his simple contract. Looking slightly insulted when I offered him an advance payment, he nevertheless offered a cheery goodbye as he hustled Nancia away for an early dinner.

"We'll have lunch as soon as you're settled," she called over her shoulder as they left.

Left alone, I could no longer avoid thinking about the fact that my next close encounter with relatives was likely to be less pleasant and more complicated. What could I possibly say to Bet and Chas after all these months of silence? I rehearsed possible scripts as I climbed the stairs, none of them likely to end in a warm embrace. I was three steps into the apartment when I stopped confused. In the rush of the afternoon's work, I had forgotten Stela and Luke and their gifts. The braided rug I had last glimpsed swaddled in a tarp now gently bore up the gate-legged table and two ladder-back chairs. The sewing rocker was angled to converse with the newly delivered futon. A silk-shaded lamp tossed light like a gold coin into the braided ripples. Like that famous "round upon the ground" jar conjured up by the poet Wallace Stevens, the circle gathered the slovenly wilderness of my life into a new pattern.

Never had I been so taken in.

The prospector should know how to open his vein or ledge, when he finds it, with pick, shovel and blasting apparatus.

—Arthur Lakes, in *Prospecting for Gold and Silver in North America*

Lucky Strike

PRESENTED WITH THE PURE GEOMETRY OF THAT LOVELY LIGHT, I FLED. Outside, the springtime-in-the-Rockies chill was reasserting itself, even though sunset was hours away. The Bel Air offered me a temporary sense of shelter, but the driver's seat was cold. The engine cranked eagerly. But I had nowhere to go—except, of course, on foot, back up to the apartment. Sighing, I switched off the ignition.

At least I could follow the rule that Bet had drummed into me from early childhood: wherever you're going, make sure you make the trip count, even if the flight you're taking is only a flight of stairs. The Chevy's trunk lid was uncharacteristically sulky about lifting. There it was, right where I had left it: my saddlebag, gleaming in almost solitary splendor, except for my roadside emergency gear and the old-fashioned briefcase where I kept my document evaluation toolkit. I draped the strap of the saddlebag over my shoulder, bounced the lid closed with a clank, and then stopped to reconsider: the cure for my free-floating anxiety was literally within my reach.

Back in the apartment, I stashed the saddlebag and briefcase on top of the bar and began battling the clutch of my new furniture. I shoved the rocker out of its cozy conversation with the futon. Dragged the gate-legged table to the middle of the room. Unplugged the lamp and slid it into the corner at a careless angle. I wouldn't need it as long as the daylight lasted—north light, I knew without having to think about it. Apparently my internal compass had calibrated itself to the lay of the local land.

Having done as much as I could to discomfit the apartment, I hid the

121

luster of the cherry tabletop with one of the sheets that Rheta had left folded on top of the futon. Rheta, I noticed with relief, did not iron her sheets. Not allowing myself to feel anything but a prosaic sense of purpose, I extracted Delores's ledger from the saddlebag and disinterred my tools from the briefcase: a handheld lighted magnifier, three document spatulas in graduated sizes, a folder of acid-free paper, a ledger of my own for taking notes, two sets of white cotton gloves—one for handling the outside of bound materials and the other for working with interior pages—and my digital camera to document each page as I encountered it. I arranged everything precisely, ending by adding the last two ballpoint pens and lining them up as equidistant as railroad tracks. I always feel guilty about defying archival tradition by deploying ink near possibly valuable documents, but I hate using pencils because they lose their points so quickly. The obvious alternative—stopping to take notes with my laptop—always breaks my concentration. Always careful in my professional, if not my personal, practices, I trust my ability to handle indelible fluids. In this, at least, I have never disappointed myself.

With my table set, I should have been ready to begin the feast. I sat down. I stood up. Faint chimes rang deep in the basement. The floor beneath my feet began to quiver in sympathy with the huff of the press two levels below. Were the headlines emerging crisp and clear? Was the shot of Conrad collapsed on the museum lawn going a mushy, unreadable grey? How was Tom Engles's daughter doing flying the press?

Changing into clean jeans that hadn't quite dried from the sloshing I had given them in the sink the night before, I imagined a girl named Sydney or Britney or, better still, an inky Cyan, perched atop the cylinders, holding one arm aloft like a rodeo rider as the old Harris press swooped around the basement.

It turned out to be a Genifer, but she did sport an electric blue crew cut and three earrings in each lobe as she held out her arms to catch the papers cascading from the press. Although the papers were flying high, she was not. However, Genifer did look more cheerful than I would have under the same circumstances, bending over again and again, to grab a bundle and then racing to the freight elevator to drop the stack before rushing back for the next one.

"I just came to see how you're doing!" I shouted above the thudding.

"Do you need any help?" Genifer nodded vigorously, but Rheta was the one who answered.

"No—we're fine." Rheta made her voice carry without actually yelling. "Looks good, don't you think?"

And it did look good: the blocks of copy I had pasted up myself marched in six straight columns across the page, the Bodoni headlines lying plumb above them. I hunted for my by-lines the way people always look for their faces first in a group photo. What I wanted to do was to carry off the paper and chew over my stories in private, but my conscience would not let me leave the scene of unfinished work. (Never mind the task I had left waiting upstairs.)

Tom Engles was stalking back and forth along the side of the press like a pit-bull patrolling a chain link fence. Rheta was holding a paper open to the light as if it contained the first edition of the Ten Commandments. Genifer was bending and running, slightly out of breath. I grabbed a line of papers that was about to tumble onto the floor. "Thanks!" called Genifer, handing me a stick of gum. "Chewing helps you catch the rhythm!" Although she probably was only about fifteen, (the age my mother was when I was conceived, I couldn't help remembering), Genifer obviously had a manager's instincts.

It was a good thing that Bet wouldn't be making her incursion into my life until tomorrow: she believed that women made themselves look like cows when they stuffed wads of spearmint into their mouths. But Genifer was right. You did need something to synchronize your movements with the press.

I was still chewing as I washed my hands and arms at my bathroom sink two hours later. My back ached and the skin of my forearms was flaming, either in reaction to the ink embedded in my pores or to the gritty grey soap that I was using to scour it off.

I picked up the newly-minted newspaper again. I had already read and reread it while Tom was loading a new roll of paper into the press. Despite a few typos, I saw that my work was good—or at least pretty good. I felt like the deity on the evening of the sixth day, already regretting the mosquito and Adam, but admiring the elephant. Unlike the deity, though, I wasn't ready to rest, even though the outside light was dimming. Stripping the brass lamp of its elegant shade, I rescued it from the shame of standing in the corner and settled it into position beside the gate-legged table. Fortunately, the extension cord Stela and Luke had provided stretched to the room's only electrical outlet beside the locked closet on the apartment's west wall. Maybe tomorrow I would remember to ask Rheta for the key to that door. Thanks to the burden of my new possessions, I now actually needed a closet. Of course, if I wanted to use it for everyday storage, I would have to displace the futon to make room for the swing of the closet door. Too many things meant too many complications.

Deciding I'd worry about the closet later or never, I circled the table twice, repositioning the lamp slightly on the first pass and reuniting the table with one of the ladder-back chairs on the second. Evaluating the ledger would be a fussy job—one that would require both concentration and dexterity. My supply of both had to need recharging after four intense days of playing reporter. Evening had taken its seat at the bar and was settling in to finish drinking the day dry. I took few deep breaths to give myself the chance to talk myself out of doing something (else) foolish. By my fifth exhalation, though, I found myself still bound and determined to see what, if anything, I could make of the document.

The outer case of the slipcover parted company with its inner sheath as reluctantly as it had in Bannack, even though I hadn't attempted to force the two completely back together before improvising a wrapping from the paper in Delores's printer. Now I could understand more clearly why Delores had been forced to leave the ledger stuck a third of the way out of the sheath. True, the newspaper clippings stuck in the back of the ledger were part of the problem. So was the water damage, which was worse than I had realized in Bannack. In Delores's office, I had noticed only that the high-tide mark along the sheath's bottom was fainter than the one that marred the outer slipcover. Now, however, I could see swelling that could indicate moisture had penetrated through the boards into the interior. Of course, I wouldn't know for sure how badly the bottom of the ledger was damaged until I could convince the sheath to release its grip—and that wasn't going to be easy. Gently rocking the ledger to test the strength of the bond, I wondered who had forced the marriage between the plain Jane Eyre of a ledger and the aristocratic Rochester of a slipcase, a coupling that nevertheless seemed to have lasted a long, if reluctant, time.

When the ledger surprised me with its sudden decision to divorce, I dropped it onto the tabletop. My hands steadied slowly. Their shakiness surprised me. I harbored no fantasy of communing with the dead by touching the objects they had touched. Nor did I have any interest in collecting the husks of souls the way I had collected beetles and butterflies when I was a kid, impaling them with Bet's dressmaker pins, cringing when my inexperience with formaldehyde was demonstrated in the twitch of a thread-like leg.

Still, I couldn't help feeling a certain reverence for the ledger. Although nothing special, it had survived, bound inexpensively in cloth, the marbleized paper of its cardboard cover still swooping in an intricate pattern of green and red. It had survived even though its back was broken and its tail edge swollen. A member of that humble category that document collectors call "ephemera," it had survived by accident while unimaginable hosts of things more valuable and durable—obsidian arrowheads, gold wedding rings, beaded moccasins, silver-backed hair brushes, ivory buttons, Wedgewood teapots, and bear-claw necklaces—had disappeared.

Yes, it had survived. What good it would do me or anyone else, I didn't know. The solution to that mystery would depend not only on the ledger's contents, but on my skill at sifting the valuable bits from the rest and refiguring them in to a plausible whole.

I thought about prospectors. They had sleep-walked West, dreaming of nuggets lolling under the tumbling, colorless waters of Montana's streams. They had learned to recognize the flecks they'd called "float" and to trace them upstream to the mother lode. Hoping for easy pickings, most had been undeterred when the gold was held tight in gangue—rock valueless because no one wanted to pay good money for the recalcitrant backbone of the landscape. As they probed with their pickaxes, sieved with their rockers, blasted with their high-pressure hoses, tore with their dredges, jabbed with their tunnels, and pounded with their stamp mills, most miners had not possessed the time or the inclination to appreciate the solidarity of the resisting whole. I had resolved long ago I would not be like them.

Pulling on my first pair of cotton gloves, I supported the ledger's spine on a rolled-up hand towel and then nudged its back cover open, using first my largest stainless steel spatula to coax the ledger's last page from its back board. The clippings slipped free with ease: they had been folded in a way that happened to keep them out of the water damage lower down. The outside clipping, a large one that had been creased to create a makeshift folder for the others, seemed to be an account of visitors arriving by train in Misfire—a report that could not have been written until after 1880 when the town was founded as the terminus of the railroad. Obviously, the story was too new to interest me. In fact, the clipping probably would be made redundant by the resources in the *Sun-Tribune*'s morgue, which was, after all, just a few steps away from where I sat.

Tentatively, I tried to lift the edge of creased clipping to see what might be underneath, stopping immediately when the paper began to tear. It was easy to resist the temptation to force a further view: the scrap of type that appeared in the clearing left by the rip revealed "Misfire." Irrationally, I was upset. What had I expected? Cuttings from the defunct and disappeared *East Bannack News Letter*? There might be older documents inside the mass, but chances were that whoever preserved the Misfire story wouldn't have been around in Bannack twenty years earlier to wield his or her scissors. Dismissing the clippings as almost certainly worthless for my purposes, I resolved to set them aside.

Instead, I would follow my usual practice by photographing and then assessing each page of the ledger before I formed an opinion about the usefulness of the whole document. Otherwise, I might race past the significance of a penciled marginal note, misread a blurred word, discount the importance of a sum worked in a ragged corner. Seek and ye shall find; the trouble is that the possibility of finding is limited by what you've set your mind to seek. In 1859, prospectors in Nevada complained about the annoying blue-black mineral that clogged the riffle bars. Because those prospectors were looking so hard for gold, they were slow to notice the silver of the Comstock Lode.

Changing my gloves again, I tried to force myself to assume a properly objective frame of mind. But it was too late for that. I was already fixated on what I wanted to find in the octavo—no less than a revelation. That possibility was what bubbled my blood in Delores's office when I first pried the ledger open to encounter the two lines that I chose to take as a promise:

A True Account
of Bannack Births and Deaths

Even more tantalizing was the fragmentary hint of a third line with tip-of-the-iceberg peaks that might indicate the presence of a set of dates. It was time to test the promise and force the revelation.

Remembering that my new set of Revere Ware included a tea kettle, I felt tempted to boil up a head of steam. I went so far as to fill the kettle and to set it on the stove's one working burner before my responsible self talked my impulsive self into exercising a little common sense. It had been a long time since I'd taken my sole document conservation and restoration course, but I seemed to remember iron gall ink and moisture don't mix. After the kettle whistled, I made tea from a bag I found downstairs in the caddy of coffee-bar sugar and creamer packets. Although the tea was a little stale, the cuppa wasn't half bad.

As it turned out, the steam wasn't necessary. Time, patience, and my document spatulas were sufficient to lift the cover from the front endpaper and then the endpaper from the handwritten title page to reveal . . . nothing much. Looking like the jagged post 9-11 skyline of Manhattan, the line following "of Bannack Births and Deaths" offered an ambiguous and broken tracery of graphite squiggles. Person or persons unknown had glued something over what may or may have not have been a set of dates. Later on, persons or persons unknown had pulled that something off, leaving behind nasty brown blotches alternating with scabby patches where the surface of the paper had been peeled into illegibility.

Things were not going well. Normally, I would have called it a day; the courthouse clock had just intoned nine. Besides, Dame Fortuna might be in a better mood tomorrow. However, I was too tired to feel tired. And my lust to solve this little puzzle trumped common sense, as it usually does, especially after I realized that the ledger's pages beyond the title page were melded into a mess, yes, but not an irredeemable mess.

First, I used first my smallest micro-spatula and then a sheet of acid-free paper to separate the glue-damaged title page and the next leaf. Expect the worst and you won't be disappointed: the recto side was blank and the verso side might as well have been. There were dates inked in the left margin, all from the 1880s and probably referring to articles that I might find mashed in the bundle of clippings—if I bothered to look. Moreover, my magnifier offered a close-up that convinced me that 1880s dates, inscribed quite legibly in a relatively plain Spencerian cursive, had been written by a different hand than the "True Record" lines with their copperplate flourishes. A historian who actually cared about turn-of-the-century Misfire might be fascinated to try to match the pattern of glue blotches on the page to the clippings, but that person wouldn't be me.

"Wait a minute!" I exclaimed. Under the magnifier, a scattering of penciled notes suddenly presented themselves as words that dimmed, but did not always disappear under the glue rash. Although hardly a letter offered itself as immediately legible, I tried to tell myself that things could be worse, that I was lucky that at least the original notations hadn't been obliterated by a crosshatching of new lines, the original plowed over by a thrifty writer trying to make a precious store of paper go further. Still, I hadn't been entirely lucky, because where the clippings had been removed, they had carried away letters, words, and, worse still, stretches of sentences.

Maybe it would be worth examining the mat of clippings after all. I picked up the article I had peeled away from the bundle; it did indeed show a pattern of glue blight that might be distinctive enough to match to the splotches left in the ledger. "Ha!" I exclaimed, unable to help the fact that I sounded like Bet. My magnifier showed at least one scrap of the page had stuck when the clipping had been stripped. If I could match pages and clippings I might be able to fill in at least some of the gaps in the penciled notes.

"Good idea—save it for later," my responsible self commanded. Before messing with the clippings, a professional (and I was one, wasn't I?) would return to the ledger itself. There would be time enough another day to piece together the penciled notes after I sorted out the identity of the ledger writer or writers and worked up a detailed analysis of the document's content.

In penance for my earlier sin of considering using steam, I committed myself anew to the kind of systematic examination that would help me observe details that I might otherwise overlook. If nothing else, the force of professional habit would immerse me in a difficult script that I knew from experience would become easier to read with practice. Deciphering handwriting is a bit like taking a walk in the dark. It's not that the sky grows lighter, but your eyes become acquainted with the denser blacks of buildings or the shadows of the trees.

The task I had set myself, limited though it was, gave me no end of trouble. The list of inked dates was clear enough, but uninformative without the matching clippings. In contrast, the penciled notes were so hard to make out that I couldn't prove that they had or had not been written by the same person as the "True Record" lines. I could, however, decipher enough words to come to the conclusion that the penciled entries had nothing to do with Bannack births and deaths. Discouraged, I slogged on, struggling to compare shapes of letters in words I could definitely not decode to those in words that I felt reasonably confident about. I had struggled with enough 19th century texts to expect that I would have trouble telling the difference between ornate flourishes from any of the lowercase letters. But this document was the most frustrating I had ever attempted. It didn't help that the writer couldn't quite make her pencil produce the alternation of thick and thin lines that made the inked version of copperplate scripts not only beautiful, but reasonably legible.

A further distraction was my tendency to give into the amateurish temptation to guess how the all-too-frequent gaps might be filled. My responsible self realized that playing a guessing game with the document was a waste of time until I developed a reasonable theory of why the ledger had been written and by whom. What I really needed to do was to retreat, to chase down the facts and figures that might offer context for the ledger. Then, after developing a theory about what I was dealing with, I could contact an expert conservator—assuming such an animal ranged within hailing distance of Southwest Montana. Hopefully, a specialist in 19th century documents could advise me on how to deal with the glue splotch puzzle. Or maybe that kind of conservator could tell me if the ledger page was sturdy enough to be scanned by equipment that might reveal more than my magnifier or digital camera. If the ledger turned out to be interesting (so far it was just confusing), I also might try to cajole Luke into arranging an infrared analysis paid for by college funds.

The courthouse clock warned me that it was already ten o'clock. Sensibly deciding to call it a night, I rousted the Glenlivet bottle from its bar shelf. There was too much left in the bottle for one drink, but not enough for two. To resolve the quandry, I tipped the bottle toward my lips in the best Wild West fashion. I deserved a reward, did I not, for behaving so responsibly.

When the bottle was empty, I picked up the journal again, with the intention of stashing it safely away. Three agonizing hours later, I had tentatively determined that the penciled entries on the page were lackluster summaries of letters written in Bannack to "EBP" in Cedar Rapids (Iowa?

Nebraska?) about the tedious challenges of managing her gold camp household. As sketchy as my transcription was, I had learned far more than I wanted about the writer's three children and her husband (referred to as JV), who was preparing to leave for some sort of government position. Three other men also seemed to be taking meals at the writer's table, but they were identified only as HP, T, and S. The entries weren't dated. However, because one letter summary did include references to the arrival of the first territorial governor—Sidney Edgerton, and his family, now I knew the notes had been made in late 1863—twenty years before the inked dates in the margins. Thanks to my preliminary research back in Seattle, desultory as it had been, I also knew that the ledger's notes were considerably more abbreviated than other accounts that had survived from the brief Bannack gold rush. Because I had never expected that my so-called research project would ever develop beyond what I needed to do to hide my real reasons for being in Misfire, I had left my own copies of relevant materials in storage back in Seattle. Not for the first time, I wished that the *Sun-Tribune* hadn't rejected such modern conveniences as the internet. Even a quick search might give me a few clues about exactly who HP, T, and S might be.

Making a deliberate attempt to exercise patience, I started making a list about what I had found out and what I needed to know. I began with what I thought were my most solid suppositions and then leaped into the quicksand of unsupported conjecture. The ledger writer's husband's initials were JV and her sister's were EBP. Because almost every summary mentioned HP and an on-going series of illnesses he was suffering, the relationship between the summary writer and him must have been a close one. He might have been the brother of the writer and her sister, if the sister had been unmarried. Or perhaps the HP was EBP's husband, trying his luck on the frontier while the sister remained in a more settled community for some good reason. T and S were mentioned extensively only in connection with a Thanksgiving dinner that HP (apparently not sick all the time) reportedly was helping to host by importing a costly turkey from Salt Lake City.

I was more than reluctant to entertain the possibility that the initials HP might represent the notorious Sheriff Henry Plummer who had been hanged by the Vigilantes at the start of 1864. How likely was it that such a document connected with that infamous name would have tumbled into my hands? I didn't want to get professionally entangled with a notorious

figure like Plummer, anyway, did I? My (purported) interest was the algo-
rithms of everyday life and death in the gold frontier, wasn't it?

Those questions couldn't cool the series of far-fetched possibilities danc-
ing in my febrile imagination. If HP was Henry Plummer, than T could
be Francis Thompson, who had been the sheriff's friend before he became
the new best friend of the Vigilantes. The reason Thompson's name had
stuck with me was simple: he had been the publisher of the short-lived and
now disappeared *News Letter*. Although (I told myself) I didn't really care
about the notorious sheriff, my heart was going pitter-patter as I scented a
connection between the ledger and the mythical cache of what was arguably
the West's first newspaper. Rheta had waved that possibility under my nose
my very first hour in town in order to bait me into renting the apartment.
That, I realized with a sense of disbelief, had been just one crazy week ago.

To cool the pounding knock of hope, I forced myself to stretch my
mouth into the pretense of a bored yawn. So far, the ledger had offered up
not a whiff of the *News Letter* or, for that matter, the sort of "True Record"
that might move my fictional research into the real world, where I was per-
ishing for lack of publishing. I took a deep breath to slow my pulse. Even
if I were so lucky as to discover a serendipitous connection between the
summary writer and Thompson, Dame Fortuna would have to be smiling
indeed if that link helped me locate even a scrap of a single surviving *News
Letter*.

I stretched my shoulders, wondering if my skin would begin flaking
like good pastry if I took yet another shower. Was I developing some sort
of compulsion about washing? I started undressing anyway. Maybe a hot
shower would help me decide how much I wanted to tell Luke about the
ledger when we met for our appointment. Which, I realized, was just a few
hours away. My impulse was to keep my mouth shut until I had something
to report that wouldn't make me look like an amateur. So far, I felt as inef-
fectual as a bantam hen striving to hatch a goose egg. Maybe I would do
better once I could get to the college's Western history collection.

Any surviving Bannack diary that mentioned a name matching the initials of the summary writer's husband might be enough to make the pieces
of the puzzle fall into place. Surnames beginning with V couldn't have been
that common in the mining camp. There were other threads begging to be
unraveled, especially the summary writer's mention of not only the territo-

rial governor, but of her nearby neighbors Wilbur and Harriet Sanders, important players in Montana's history. The writer's elaborate Thanksgiving dinner hosted by HP also might pop up in period letters. Official sources offered other possibilities. Although the 1860 census did not represent the extensive national efforts of the ones conducted in 1870 and 1880, I might get lucky by hunting up possibilities for EBP in Cedar Rapids in both Iowa and Nebraska.

Despite my exhaustion and my resolution not to get distracted from my real purpose in visiting Misfire, I could feel my enthusiasm effervescing. "Calm down," my responsible self counseled my impulsive self.

But what my impulsive self really, really wanted was immediate gratification, answers to my questions, a game-changing flash of illumination. I closed the ledger and tried to reopen it at random, following Bet's usual system of seeking biblical direction. After I gave divine guidance considerable help with my micro-spatula, the pages grudgingly parted to reveal a verso page that materialized with an astounding line: "Deaths by Violence, 1864." A shocked rictus pulled my mouth into a grin as I recognized the inked copperplate as the obvious twin to the handwriting on the "True Record" title page. Quickly I counted seven—no eight—entries, each indexed in the far left margin with a name, a cause of death, and a date. Only one name meant anything to me. I jerked, my glance caught like a hooked trout on the first cast: "Henry Plummer," it said. "Lynched by a mob, Jan. 10, 1864."

"Don't get excited," I told myself. The fact that the letter writer had recorded that famous death didn't mean much in terms of my research, even though it made it clear my fingers had walked me through a portal into the time period I wanted to enter. But I was excited by the language, an indictment of the men who would soon tout their willingness to act as judges, juries, and executioners as a springboard to prestige and power. "What else! What else!" I burned to reach back through the decades and shake the writer into speaking to me not so much beyond the grave, as before it.

Picked carefully apart, the next two pages yielded nothing much—just more penciled entries that I, blinded by impatience, couldn't decipher at all. Ravenous for more information, I landed vulture-like on the bundle of clippings. After teasing the rough shell of 1880s articles free, inside I found a cache of nuggets. My stomach burned with what felt like a rapidly developing ulcer as I unfolded a brittle, but completely intact sheet of what looked like brown wrapping paper. Only three narrow columns marched across a five by seven sheet under a masthead that proclaimed its identity of the *East Bannack News Letter*, published by F. Thompson Jan. 11, 1864.

Gobsmacked—that's how Bet would have described me. I half-rose, sat down, stood up, and paced back to the kitchen, where habit steadied my hands enough to complete the ritual motions of brewing coffee. I didn't allow myself to even glance toward the gate-legged table while the coffee maker gurgled and hissed. Black and bitter (I must have mismeasured), the coffee burned my tongue. Not bothering to cool it with a swig of water, I returned to the table and bent toward the sheet. My breathing steadied; I had not been the victim of the imaginative equivalent of a hysterical pregnancy. The sheet was what it was.

There were no ads. There was nothing printed on the back. Perhaps Francis Thompson, in hurrying to get out the stunning news in this edition, had skipped the wait for the ink to dry on the first page and hard labor of setting the type for the second page before he could run the sheets through his hand press again. That process would have taken time, and perhaps Thompson didn't feel he had any time to waste. The news of the hangings would have already spread like wildfire through the gold camp. But perhaps this former friend of the dead sheriff had harbored good reasons for wanting to influence where the wind of public opinion would push the flames.

Thompson had followed the common frontier custom of labeling his columns with simple captions in the same size as the body type, noticeable only because they were presented in all capital letters. LAST MOMENTS, the first column was headed. The story was so stunning that I had to rummage in the saddlebag for my inhaler halfway through its lead:

> Will the reader be willing to set aside the rumours and tales that have clouded the truth about the events of the evening of Jan. 10? It is true Henry Plummer was hanged not as the Sheriff he claimed to be, but the desperado he was. It is also true two of his Deputies, Ned Ray and Buck Stinson, died before Henry Plummer did and died badly. It is not true, as this witness can attest, that this nice clean looking man only twenty seven years of age, of pleasing and affable manners and

good ability, showed fear or begged for his life in the moments
before his death. Leader of a group of road agents though
Plummer was, he was a courageous man and should not be
remembered otherwise despite his misdeeds. Neither should
those who conducted an execution necessary to promote and
protect a civil society be reluctant to confess that Plummer
died a death more protracted than justice demanded.

If the ensuing description of Plummer's execution made a remote by-
stander shudder, it would have registered as a 6.0 on the Richter scale of
mining camp public opinion at the time. The Vigilantes, who were already
busy presenting their side of things as the absolute truth must have been
rocked by the potential of the newspaper account to generate sympathy
for Plummer. Perhaps there was a reason that all copies of the *News Letter*,
except this one, had disappeared.

The sheet could be a fake, but I didn't believe that it was. Frontier publish-
ers often had to use any paper they could lay their hands on. If my memory was
reliable—and I thought it was in this regard—surviving references to the *News
Letter* had described it as "small"—so small and intermittent that historians
disagreed whether the publication could be counted as Montana's first newspaper, an argument exacerbated by the fact Thompson himself never staked
such a claim in his late-life memoirs, self-serving as they were.

That academic debate aside, to be taken seriously, the authenticity of this
single issue of the *News Letter* had to be proved, and that meant I'd better
get organized not only to tell Luke what I had found, but to enlist his expertise. It was frustrating that no more intact issues of the *News Letter* had
emerged from the clipping bundle. But I had found a half dozen scissored
articles that might prove to correspond to some of the handwritten "True
Record" notes. For now, I had to be content with one more bit of thrilling evidence: At least three of those articles exhibited a physical kinship to
the complete issue of the *News Letter*. Even though the paper stock itself
did not match in quality and color, the fonts cried out their consanguin-
ity. Both the complete issue and one of the clippings had used two v's to
substitute for the letter w. The letter t was used as a stand-in for f in all four
artifacts. Most definitive of all, one of the lowercase e's was missing its tail
in the complete issue and in all three of the clippings.

It seemed certain that I could make a strong claim to have discovered extant fragments of the *News Letter*. Beyond that interesting fact, so far I hadn't discovered a single clue that could help me interpret the materials the "True Record" writer had preserved. Whoever the ledger keeper was, she hadn't reported any of the other Vigilante-related killings besides Plummer's. In a contradiction of the title page, the writer hadn't listed any births at all, at least not on the pages I had been able to partially decode. Worse still, the death entries seemed to have no common denominator except a time period (the first few months of 1864). Some of the listed deaths were caused by accident and others by sickness, but none but Plummer's by violence. One account reported a street accident that killed a dog.

Like a gambler not wanting to admit luck had run out, I didn't want to stop, even though the courthouse clock was pointing out that it was now four in the morning. Instead of doing the sensible thing—going to bed for a few hours, I found myself trotting down with preternatural energy to the door of the *Sun*'s morgue. Just in case. My responsible self argued it was beyond insanity to start rummaging around in the faint hope of finding something that would have been discovered long ago had it existed. It was an argument my responsible self lost.

[The journalist] realizes vividly the hazard of projecting a complexity in a simple, limited vocabulary, the danger in compressed messages, the difficulty in bringing the remote near, the lack of experience in a single limited life span and the inescapable force of speed, which drives all newspaper workers whether on weeklies or dailies . . . . Because of that conditioning, he should know almost to a scientific certainty—although he calls it a "hunch"—wherein the smooth integument of speed, passion, and false thought hides the truth.

—Robert L Houseman, in "The Journalist as Historian"

Hidden Passages

ENTERING THE MORGUE, I COULDN'T SHAKE THE SENSE I MIGHT BE DREAM-ing. The skeleton key that Rheta had offered me on my first visit to the *Sun* was in my pocket, but the door yielded without it. Fighting a certain sense of furtiveness, I forced myself to leave it ajar.

The light from the stairwell door allowed me to navigate without stumbling on the volumes of bound newspapers strewn across the floor. For safekeeping, I stashed the light bulb I had unscrewed from the silk-shaded lamp in the apartment. If I needed the bulb, I would know where to find it—waiting at the back of one of the empty shelves that should have been filled with neatly cataloged records.

The soft eye of my flashlight opened on the ceiling. But the vista was bland: cracked plaster overlaid by streaky coats of paint. There was no door to an adjoining room. There wasn't even an attic trapdoor, nothing that hinted of anything even as mundane as an overhead crawlspace where a *News Letter* cache might have been secreted. There was, however, a stepladder leaning on the wall directly across the room from me.

After my stretch into self-indulgent fantasy, the climb to the empty overhead socket seemed short. Once all one hundred watts were duly illuminating the disordered room, I lost my impulse to sneak through my work in silence. Instead, I clattered back to the apartment for my boombox and the dust mask Conrad had given me on our trip to Bannack. On the local radio station, insomniacs were shouting about wolves and livestock. The voices crackled with a tension that seemed to go with my mood, so I left the tuner alone and picked up the bound collection that sprawled closest to my feet.

My breath thickened in my throat. The date on the spine—1963—represented a leap of a hundred years beyond the gold camp era. However, it was very much in the chronological neighborhood of my grandparents' death and my own birthday, both in 1966. As I reached with greedy hands to shuffle 1963 aside in favor of what might lie hidden beneath, the reproachful zip of an abused cover separating itself from fragile newsprint stopped me short.

"This is not what you want to do." The radio nearly blotted out my voice, but I couldn't pretend that I hadn't heard it. To give myself the time to assert control, I rustled through the brittle pages of 1963, tucking back into square the issues that had been loosened from their bindings by my careless handling. Still fighting the impulse to give the morgue a burglar's toss, I forced myself to take an interest in the headline "Police Arrest Local Prostitutes" as it emerged with the next turn of a page. Under that banner, a photo showed a cop pushing a knife-thin girl into a car. The cop looked embarrassed; the girl, indifferent in her black sheath. I stared, trying to decide if the girl was Rheta. The deadpan stare, the fringe of hair across the forehead fit into the category of inconclusive evidence. The girl wasn't identified in the caption except as "one of the suspects."

I resettled the cardboard covers of the volume with a soft plop. Resolving anew to sort through the volumes systematically, I set to work. I wouldn't stop to read anything newer than 1900. When and if 1966 emerged, I would set it aside for later when I could examine it dispassionately and carefully in the light of day.

By the time the radio combatants had hurled their last insult at each other, I had finished stacking and sorting the abused volumes into family groups. My hands were filthy. I didn't need a mirror to know that my dust mask was covered (appropriately I suppose) with dust. There were no surprising finds, no slim volume of the *East Bannack News Letter* hiding in the back of another volume or jumbled under a heap.

More than one editor had been careless with the record—a mortal sin to my way of thinking. The *Tribune*, which hadn't begun publication until 1938, was almost as complete as a new pair of false teeth, except as luck would have it, 1966 and 1967. In contrast, the Sun collection was gappy in every decade. I could understand why only one volume from the 1880s had survived and three from the 1890s. But it made me angry to see the long breach that represented the 1940s and the frequent breaks in each previous and subsequent decade. The fact the volumes for 1966 and 1967 were missing from the Sun as well as the *Tribune* felt like some kind of payback for my past misdeeds.

Despite my disappointments, I surveyed my work with the housewifely satisfaction of a good archivist. The representations and misrepresentations of the events of the last century were lined up as neatly as the tombstones in a well regulated cemetery. If carelessness had eaten cavities in the record, it wasn't my fault. Replacing the 1960s volumes shouldn't be a problem. After Conrad recovered (I wouldn't let myself begin that thought with an "if"), he might know where they were. Even if he didn't, the college or the state library might have their own copies.

In the meantime, I might want to rethink the potential value of the 1880s clippings that I had dismissed as redundant as I took them from the ledger. Unless the state historical library had preserved a more complete set, those clippings might be the only fragments remaining of some issues.

A fresh announcer with a perky voice came on the air announcing the six o'clock "March to the Morning." I couldn't tell whether the buzzing I was hearing originated in the broadcast or in my own fatigue, so I pushed the tuner forward until I caught a clearer signal, someone with a Texas drawl reading the livestock report.

Deciding I had to get back to my room before Jana arrived to supervise the mailroom crew in Rheta's place, I took one final look at the now orderly morgue. Returning to the apartment, I tried to convince myself that it wouldn't take very long to transform my new futon into a comfortable bed and to rinse off my newly accumulated layer of dirt. Instead I paced aimlessly, pausing to absent-mindedly rattle the knob of the closet door. It irritated me that the only closet in the place was locked. When Rheta returned from visiting Conrad in Missoula, I would have to ask her for the key. Restless with exhaustion, I checked the Glenlivet bottle. It was still empty. I thought about Conrad's Famous Grouse, but decided another drink would propel me into collapse.

Instead, I retrieved a trash bag from the pile next to the bottle and tramped back to the morgue landing to pick up the empty soda cans and chip bags generated by my cleaning frenzy. Downstairs, a load of the newspapers was waiting on the freight elevator to be labeled, bagged, and trucked to the post office and to the paper dispensers around town. Outside, it was still chilly in the alley, but the rising sun was polishing the newspaper's third-story windows into a temporary glow.

Windows. Third story windows.

Abruptly, I understood what should have been obvious to me my first day in town: The front of the building was divided into just two levels—the newspaper office with those horrible acoustic tiles hiding the original high ceiling and my apartment with its lofty rise. But the back of the building must be stacked like a layer cake—the main floor composing room, the morgue just above it, and a final third floor.

Just as abruptly, I knew how to get up there. I rushed back to the apartment, not stopping until I reached for the dull brass knob that barred me from what I was now convinced was not a closet at all. Might as well try my luck before looking for something to pick the lock. I reached into my pocket for the skeleton key Rheta had given me for the morgue door.

Open sesame: the bolt yielded with a satisfying click that propelled me into a state of shimmering alertness.

Popping through the door like a gopher bursting from its hole, I emerged into a small landing, its blue paint cloudy in the dawn light. To assure myself of an escape route, I scrambled down the dozen steps. Although the glass panel in the door was frosted, I didn't need to throw the grime-encrusted bolt to know where I was. I could see the shadow of a car passing on Main Street. Breathing hard, I ran back up the stairs past my apartment and up another narrow flight to another landing. This time I didn't need the skeleton key: the knob yielded to the twist of my wrist.

Disappointment. The space in front of me was empty except for a carpet so vividly incongruous that it was shocking. Its tree of life design shone through a thick accumulation of dust like moonlight through clouds. I squatted and turned up one heavy corner. Here against the soft gold of the background, the intricacy of the knotted design showed up clearly, the symmetrical knots flattened and polished slightly from long use. When I coaxed open the thick pile by folding the face of the rug in on itself, I saw that the tufts had softened in color as they reached toward the surface. We should all age so gracefully. Tabriz. My adoptive parents would have been proud of me for remembering that Northern Iranian weavers often wove their rugs not only with a silk foundation but with a pile of wool shot through with that gleaming material. Although I hadn't discovered a lost cache of Bannack newspapers, at least Rheta would be glad to know that the Sun might have at least one unrecognized resource. I had seen rugs not half so fine as this one gaveled down for thousands of dollars at estate sales.

Knowing that I shouldn't risk grinding grit into the nap of the rug, I hesitated. In the center of the rug, the branches lifted, festoons of birds flying into vivid relief where someone had recently broken a trail to the door at the far side of the room.

Holding my breath, I listened for the creak of a floor board, the rustle of movement behind that door. The muscles in my calves tightened, arguing for a rapid retreat. I could always come back later. Rheta would probably be back from Missoula by midmorning. If the footprints weren't hers, she should know about them. If they were hers, I could offer to vacuum in trade for a tour. If there was an intruder, he would probably be gone by then. If not, at least I wouldn't face him alone.

But I could no more ignore the invitation of that path than a hummingbird can resist the open mouth of a trumpet vine. Bad guys, like vampires, flee with the dawning light, right? One quick trip back and forth across the carpet wasn't going to do more than add a small insult to a probably insignificant injury.

The floorboards complained despite the protection of the carpet, the squeaks sounding a lot like the noises I had been ignoring every night, hearing them as nothing more dangerous than the sighs of an old building settling to sleep. I decided to worry later about who might have been creeping around on the margins of my dreams. As for now, I told myself, anyone more substantial than a ghost would set off the equivalent of a self-activating burglar alarm with his shoes.

Still, the muscles in my legs tensed again as I dared the door. Someone had left the overhead light burning, a metal chandelier, ugly and dangerous looking, its surface painted in swirls of pink and green. Meant for a higher ceiling, it draped the back of my neck with warmth as I scanned the hall-way, its unpainted pine floor dished in front of each of the four doors facing each other in pairs. The chandelier, bright with four of the oversized bulbs that I'd seen in the darkroom, made me upgrade my personal terror alert level. Rheta would never forget to turn off a light. Careless as he was, even Conrad would think about the *Sun*'s power bill before leaving the chande-lier burning away the hours.

I half-turned to leave when I noticed the unframed photo tacked to the painted wood of the door closest to me. Just one minute. This was some-thing I had to see close up.

A woman who looked more like a French poodle than any human I had ever encountered was attempting a seductive smile above her strapless gown. The photo's colors had faded the material of the dress to dull pastel that I couldn't decide was more pink or orange. Across one corner, large, unformed letters announced: "Love from Peaches!" "Love" was underlined once and "Peaches," three times.

In the windowless room there was no other trace of Peaches. No pictures on the wall. No iron bedstead, no nightstand, no cheap china pitcher and bowl set. If the rough planking had been carpeted once, that carpet had been stripped away. The walls were shelled with the kind of hard enamel I associated with 1950s hospitals run by thin white nurses in white caps starched into wings and white shoes polished into purity.

The other three rooms were just as naked as the first. There wasn't even a photo on the second door, just a tack that held a scab of paper. The picture fastened to the third entrance was of a dark-eyed woman, her face defiant under bangs cut long and perfectly straight. She didn't smile, and her auto-graph was incised precisely with no exclamation point or profession of love. It simply read: "Senorita." The girl had high cheekbones like Rheta's, but her eyebrows had been plucked to dashes abrupt and narrow. She wore an off-the-shoulder black blouse that should have looked cheap, but evoked the glamour it strove for.

Was this the same girl as the one on the front page of the 1963 newspaper? Bending to get a better look at Senorita, I heard someone fiddling with the newspaper's front door below. It must be Jana arriving to organize the mailroom crew.

Without thinking, I reached out and pulled the photo from its holder. I tucked the picture under my arm and padded quietly through the rug room and down the secret stairs to my apartment. I recognized the emotion that was still making my heart pound: a euphoric mix of guilt and excitement. Wasn't that sweet addictive rush why I had made my first excursions into my now ex-husband's bed, undeterred by my betrayal of both another woman and myself? To escape the memory of my lackluster shame, I paused in the apartment only long enough to lock the door to the secret stairway behind me and to stow the photo of Senorita with the ledger.

Jana's head snapped up in surprise when I materialized in the newsroom.

"I thought you were a ghost!"

"I probably look like one." I swiped at the cobwebs clinging to my sweater. "I woke up early, so I decided to play in the morgue awhile."

Jana clattered up the steps and poked her head into a space now orderly enough to warrant the creation of an indexing system. "Looks like you worked a lot more than you played. I don't know what possessed you to tackle that job after the week we've put in. Rheta's going to be surprised when she gets back from Missoula. Want some coffee?"

"No thanks. I want a shower more than anything." I had dared to try Jana's coffee as we pushed to get the paper out and decided never to repeat the experiment. "Oh—and I need directions to the closest laundry. Actually, I'd like the directions first—I need to do a wash before I can get cleaned up. That is, unless you need an extra pair of hands this morning."

Jana gave me an appraising look that clearly was sorting me into the unflattering side of the help/hindrance binary. "Well, thanks for the offer, but our regular crew will be showing up soon to stick the address labels on."

"You do that manually?" I tried to remember where I had been last Wednesday morning when the paper was mailed out. Oh, right. I had been on the road, headed for Misfire. For a micro-second I felt the Chevy's thick steering wheel in my hand, the freedom of the highway stretching seductively away as I shifted the engine's three-on-a-tree transmission into takeoff.

"We have an old machine that speeds up the process. We've had the same bunch of women working together so long that they all know exactly what to do. In fact, they usually won't even let me help. I'll probably take the newsstand copies around while they finish up the bundles for the post office."

I found the laundry with no trouble, despite the distraction of the horrific story Jana had thrown in with the directions: a chilling narrative about the business's previous owner getting kidnapped some years before as she was making her nightly collection of quarters from the dryers. The building didn't look like a Laundromat since it was housed in a neo-classical building faced with rock, twin columns supporting its arched entrance. Everything devolves in the West, everything we Westerners get our hands on.

"I'm really not tired at all," I said to myself, attracting a suspicious look from a mother with two wailing preschool cowboys. The mother moved her sock-sorting operation to the other end of the room, taking the cowboys with her. I didn't mind; their wailing reminded me that I needed to get started on a story about the new Presbyterian minister's drive to halt the daily morning siren. The new minister had been complaining bitterly and publicly that the siren disturbed the peace and upset his digestion.

The members of the volunteer fire department weren't pleased. The fire chief had instituted the morning blast in 1963 to make sure the siren hadn't frozen into silence overnight. Thus traditions begin, a cautionary example for us all.

The firefighters (reportedly) had suggested that the minister move back to California if he liked it so much better there. They argued that silencing the siren would be just as bad in its way as silencing the courthouse clock. The minister (reportedly) retorted that shutting off that bonging reminder of the march of time would be a good idea, too. I was looking forward to the entertainment of interviewing the combatants. Maybe I could put off my appointment with Luke this morning and make an appointment with the minister instead. Otherwise, I would have to decide right away how much I wanted to reveal to Luke about the ledger. One thing leads to another, and I could feel myself in danger of taking a distracting detour that would make me forget why I was in Misfire. Already, after meeting Nancia, my half-hatched plan for using my half-brother to get at Everonica seemed unworthy not of me exactly, but of the person I would like to become eventually—once I was finished with the sneaky stuff I had on my Montana agenda.

Unable to decide between keeping my appointment with Luke or cancelling it, I concentrated on picking out the washers I wanted, each of them blazoned into individuality with its own pretty name painted in cursive across its front. Finally, I selected Angel and Kristy. But later, as I trundled a wobbly-wheeled cart down a line of dryers, I found myself unable to choose among Bert, Don, and Dick. There was a rusty blotch right in front of Ben. I stood helplessly still, staring at it. Rheta said the kidnapper had been a local man who'd done his wash every Saturday night. He had pulled his pickup off a mountain road and committed suicide. He hadn't left a note. The sheriff found the woman's body in the back of the pickup shrouded in a tarp.

I kept staring. My adoptive father once told me you could hypnotize a chicken by drawing a line and forcing the chicken to stare at it. If one of the kiddie cowboys hadn't rammed my cart from behind, I might have been stuck there indefinitely, a tourist attraction for Misfire.

"Why don't you look where you're going!" the mother of the wailers wailed. Since I had not been going anywhere, I had to practice considerable self-restraint not to reply in a way unsuitable for the ears of children. I loaded Ben, not caring that I was mixing the brights with the lights. All I wanted was to be a long way from Misfire, Montana.

By the time my underwear was ready to fold, I felt a slight unsteadiness in my knees and a thrumming that whispered the way a seashell does when you hold it to your ear to pretend the tide you're hearing is the sea, not your own blood. To combat fatigue, I began grading my underwear, sorting panties into categories that I mentally labeled as "embarrassing," "acceptable" or "sexy." When I finished, the "sexy" and "acceptable" slots were empty. Sighing, I decided that it was a good thing my most recent sexual partners hadn't been very particular. I unfolded one "embarrassing" pair and held it up to the light, trying to talk myself into some tolerance for the way its elastic trailed from the waistband.

"I want to talk to you right now!" There he was, John Storey, aggressive as usual, but certainly not courteous in this sudden manifestation. For a second, I thought I might have somehow fallen asleep in the act of evaluating underwear and conjured him up as a nightmare. Startled, I clutched the panties to my breasts like the victim of an X-rated version of a Victorian melodrama.

"What's the meaning of this!" he yelled, waving a newspaper in my face, matching my melodrama with his own. Even though I had long ago learned to hold my own in an argument by coping with angry students, disagreeable colleagues, and an irritable husband, I couldn't think how to respond. But standing there in my dust-streaked T-shirt and cobwebbed hair with a pile of unacceptable underwear clearly visible on the folding table, I took the only refuge that was handy—silence.

"This photo. I'll sue, I'm telling you. I'll sue. Like I told that dumb bitch who's running your mail crew while you and that whore Rheta are slacking off, I have grounds."

I slapped him. He grabbed me and smacked me with a kiss, hard and contemptuous. The cowboys' mother screamed.

I didn't want to feel aroused, but I did.

I didn't want to feel afraid, but I did.

I tried to imagine the scene as a kind of joke, something that would make a good story to tell to friends over coffee or drinks (I would have friends someday, wouldn't I?) after I left Misfire (soon, I hoped) and found myself at last settled and happy elsewhere. I gathered my tattered underwear and my dryer-warmed jeans, daring to turn my back on him.

"Photos don't lie," I said firmly, still refusing to face him as I strode toward the Laundromat's back door with a posture that I held him in complete disdain and myself in complete confidence.

"Well, we'll let the courts decide that—unless the *Sun* prints a front page apology in a special edition tomorrow and again in the regular paper next week. In the meantime, just to show you that I never make empty threats, I'm organizing a boycott of the *Sun*."

With that, he pushed past me on the way to the door, the heels of his tooled cowboy boots drumming out a stride that promised that he wouldn't be the loser in any fight, especially this one.

In its simplest form, placer mining involved little more than scratching the surface. Using simple picks and shovels and usually working in small groups, miners dug up the gold-bearing dirt and then used water to flush the waste material.

—Michael P. Malone and Richard B. Roader, in *Montana: A History of Two Centuries*

Chicken Scratch

SHARP-ELBOWED ANXIETIES JOSTLED FOR THE PRIVILEGE OF BECOMING MY Number One worry as I drove back to the *Sun*. Conrad still adrift in the grey zone. Bet and Chas hurtling my way. My half-brother waltzing out of the grasp of what he was misreading as my romantic intentions. And now John Storey whipping up a boycott that felt distinctly personal.

As I nosed the Bel Air past the *Sun*'s front door around to my alley parking spot, I caught a glimpse of Rheta, already back from Missoula and on duty at the front counter. Her face looked crumpled, even though she waved jauntily when she recognized my car. Had Conrad taken a turn for the worse?

"He was off the respirator last night and already complaining," Rheta called without waiting for my question, as I pushed through vinyl at the back of the newsroom. "They had him scheduled for some more tests this morning, though, so I decided to hit the highway early."

"Well, that's good news." I paused, wondering whether I should tell her now about what I had discovered upstairs. But no—I needed time to figure out how I was going to explain my illicit early morning ramblings.

"I have some bad news," I said, packing my lead with the important stuff up front.

"I know all about it," she said. "You don't have to scratch John Storey very hard to find the asshole underneath."

146

"Do we need to worry?" I didn't hesitate over the word "we."

"Over the lawsuit—no. Over the boycott—probably. The old ranching families like John's carry a lot of weight around here. In fact . . ."

The phone rang, its burr sounding newly ominous.

Whoever the caller was, he or she wasn't wasting any time on pleasantries. Rheta's voice remained calm, but her grip on the receiver tightened as she tried to reason with someone who was shouting. I could hear the sharp bark of the voice, although I couldn't make out the words. Still, their import was clear.

"Well, that's the third ad cancellation already," Rheta said. "John left here not two minutes ago, so he must have started to make his rounds at the break of dawn before giving me a chance to discuss the situation with him."

I couldn't help asking which businesses were lining up against us.

"Well, the bank, of course, and the West Wind Restaurant—John's morning coffee haunt. But the worst so far is the drugstore—they had been scheduled for a nice half-page each week starting next month. But I'll be damned if I'll run an apology."

"Are you going to tell Conrad?"

"Not on your life. His condition is still too shaky. It's just lucky that I talked him into giving me the legal authority to make decisions a couple of years ago. I thought we'd go under for sure when he went on a binge and disappeared for a month. Anyway, I know what he'd want us to do. Conrad has his faults, but he has guts. The best thing for me to do this morning is to go around and try to mend a few fences. Jana can watch the desk for a couple of hours after she gets back from her paper run."

"What can I do?"

"Right now? Whatever you want—we won't start gearing up for next week until tomorrow afternoon. By the way, I've been meaning to tell you what a good job you did on your rewrite of the rally piece. It makes the *Butte Standard*'s article look pretty lame."

The compliment did me more good than another cup of coffee, but it couldn't cure the faint ringing in my ears. I checked the clock on the wall above my desk, suddenly realizing that I had less than a half an hour before my appointment with Luke. Procrastination often makes decision-making irrelevant. That's one of its appeals.

It must have been sleep deprivation that made me fail to notice the Bel Air's gas gauge had sunk to just below the quarter tank mark. It is one of my car's less endearing habits to soften the bad news that the tank is empty and has been for at least twenty miles with this visual white lie. Fortunately, I managed to pull over to the curb just as the engine glided into silence. A full gas can was waiting on standby in the trunk, but the campus was only a half block away. I thought it would be quicker to jog. And it would have been, if not for the stray.

Before I was out of the car, he reached me, panting hopefully and drooling a little on my bare leg. Although I had conceded to a skirt for my appointment, pantyhose had seemed an excessive embellishment—a good thing, as it was turning out. "Go away, dog," I said, but not as forcefully as I should have. His droopy ears and incongruous German shepherd face made me recognize him as the long, low hound I'd dodged when I first drove into town. Either the stray was especially good at eluding capture or the local dog catcher was inefficient. His piano key ribs sang a sad ditty of starvation that had lasted longer than the week I had been in Misfire. I knew better than to encourage a stray, but I reached into my saddlebag for the cracker and cheese snack leftover from my trip from Seattle. Considering his condition, he ate delicately, but with a concentration that let me hustle across the street to escape him. When the fire siren shrieked, he bolted in the opposite direction.

The alarm was the real thing; it was an hour past the daily test time. A good reporter would have figured out a way to follow the sound waves to the story, but a good reporter also would have had her cell handy—or at least a drivable vehicle within range. Out of breath, I stopped at the base of the retaining wall that prevented the campus from crumbling onto the street. As I climbed the steps to the sidewalk leading to Old Main, I noticed a young woman standing in the shade of a blue spruce half way between me and the building's vaulted entrance.

"Can you help me?" she called, looking in my direction, but not making eye contact, one hand held out to block the sun in what seemed an unnecessarily dramatic gesture. She was dressed in jeans and a hoodie that seemed too warm for the morning.

"Sure," I said, although I wasn't all that pleased to have to stop to do the Good Samaritan thing.

"I just need to know what direction I'm facing. The siren startled me, and I stumbled. Got myself confused."

"East," I said. "Actually southeast. All you have to do is look for the mountains and remember the closest range lies more or less to the north." Reaching the end of my sentence, I noticed her telescoping cane, bobbing the way a wand for witching water does in the hands of an adept. I stopped, not knowing what to say.

"That's OK—lots of people don't notice at first," she said, accurately reading my silence. "I'm here volunteering as a mentor at the life skills workshop for the visually impaired."

"Oh, I see." I said and then stopped again. "Do you need me to walk with you somewhere?"

"Thanks, but no," she said firmly. "I'm fine now. Normally, I don't get confused. It's just that I don't know the campus that well, and I forgot my sunglasses this morning. Without them, I can see enough on a bright day like this one to distract myself. How far in front of me are the steps that lead down to the sidewalk?"

"I'm standing right above the first one."

"Oh, I see," she said, and smiled. "Would you mind staying where you are for just a second?"

"Sure," I said, but by that time she had already advanced enough that her cane found my ankle with a gentle bump. She slowed for the first step and then descended steadily, waving her hand in a cheery thank you. Because she seemed to have figured out both where she was going and how she was going to get there, it seemed impolite to watch after her any longer. Wishing I could move as confidently, trusting that confusion would always give way to clarity, I headed toward Old Main. Still bereft of my cell phone, I wasn't sure what time it was. No doubt Luke would wait for me, but I hated to make him think that I was the sort of person who couldn't keep her appointments. As I rounded Old Main, I dodged two middle-aged women, both wearing snappy pants suits and swinging their white-tipped canes with easy rhythm.

"I told Ray that we've just got to get some better recipes for cooking class," one of them was complaining. "He seems to think just because our students have lost their sight, they don't have any taste buds left either."

Old Main's first floor hallway, the one that had been dark and silent during my previous visit, percolated with people bearing canes. A man who looked far too dressed up for the occasion in his white shirt and dark tie grimaced in concentration as he negotiated an obstacle course of desks and chairs. More than a dozen others, all of them carrying canes and what seemed to be electronic sensors, waited in a jostling mass for their try. The cheerful mutter of voices flowed into a shared conversations that eddied around me, a separate island, or maybe just a rock in the stream, a minor barrier to navigation.

Upstairs, I could feel the sigh of a palatable emptiness breathe from the dark space under Luke's office door. The student secretary, who looked about thirteen, but a very competent thirteen, didn't really need to tell me that Luke had already left, but I asked anyway.

"He's a fireman?" she responded, her thumbs flying over her cell phone.

"I believe so," I said, misunderstanding the rising tone at the end of the sentence as a question. After my years of teaching, I should have known better.

"He's a fireman, a volunteer," she said, her overly declarative tone stressing the fact that she found me slow on the uptake. "When the siren goes off, he has to go, even if he's in the middle of a class."

"His students must hate that."

"We don't mind," she said, missing my intended irony. She added, a little sadly, "There aren't that many fires here."

Still not looking at me, the secretary said she would give Luke my message: that I would wait for him in the college library for about an hour. I didn't doubt that she would remember to convey that information even though she disdained to reach for the pencil and message pad perched on the edge of her desk. Instead, she continued to keep an eye on her cell phone, apparently waiting for a reply to her text message while she punched a Facebook comment on the office's desktop computer. The glint of her eyes under her glossy curve of hennaed hair told me that she multi-tasked as easily as she breathed. In the country of the digital, the scattered consciousness is queen. Maybe we could hire her to help the *Sun* join the postmodern age.

Libraries always make me feel better, and this one did, too, even though the front window across from the circulation desk featured a strange tableau: a couple of mannequins, bewigged in Halloween orange, their painted features blurred under a perplexing stretch of knee-high nylon stockings. Their stiff figures supported the flow of graduation robes, wrinkled, blue, and as dusty as the orange beaks of the bird of paradise plant that had been placed between them. What the tableau was supposed to convey, I couldn't tell. I did know it gave me the creeps.

Any library, though, is better than no library. Instead of beginning in my usual way, with a plan and a priority list, I relaxed into the comfortable hush woven from the white noise hum of a bank of deserted computers. Too boggled for serious work, I would doodle through the internet to try to match the initials that the ledger writer had noted in her letter summaries to known residents of Bannack in 1863 and 1864. I would start with the obvious possibility: that the HP mentioned by the ledger writer in her letter summaries and Henry Plummer, sheriff and alleged bad guy, were one and the same.

Of course, I knew that unless today was my lucky day, a desultory search would almost certainly be useless. If the muse Clio did happen to stoop to patronize me by revealing genuine gold winking in some dark corner of the digital bazaar, I would take her gift as a sign. Of what, I would figure out when and if the time came.

The library's research computers allowed a guest log-in; in five minutes I was googling Plummer, an approach that I quickly abandoned since I ended up with an overwhelming number of hits. It was clear from the results list that a great many history buffs were still engaged in the continuing knock-down drag-out fight over the question of whether Plummer deserved hanging. Instead of attempting to pan the gold from the gravel, I went to one of the genealogy research sites I had found reliable as I unraveled my own family history. I hesitated, feeling the impulse to type in Everonica's maiden name, even though I had made that search obsessively and repeatedly and, now, redundantly, since I knew exactly where my birth mother lived.

Wrenching my attention back to the task at hand, it didn't take me long to confirm what I remembered—that the first comprehensive census information available for what is now Montana hadn't been gathered until 1870. The genealogy site did offer a link to what purported to be an alphabetical listing of "Residents of Bannack, City Montana, 1862"—early for my purposes, but at least within spitting distance. It might be worth a gander since the document extended its reach into the winter of 1862-63.

My first quick scan of the listing revealed names that seemed exclusively male. I wouldn't find my female ledger writer here. In fact, only about 300 residents were listed—a mere 10 percent of Bannack's boomtown peak the spring of 1863. The only possible matches to HP on the list were H. Porter, Harry Phleger, and (inevitably) Henry Plummer. My heart went pitter-patter when the sheriff's name popped up, even though its absence would have been a lot more surprising than its presence. What had happened to my disdain for the old-fashioned kind of historian who didn't mind playing a role equivalent to the LA medical examiner's job of coroner to Hollywood stars?

Eschewing both Google and guilt, I decided to switch to the 1890 *Bancroft's History of Washington, Idaho, and Montana*. To stop myself from jumping to facile conclusions, I thought I should find out more about Porter and Phleger and extend my hunt for other HP possibilities. Written not by the notoriously uncritical Hubert Howe Bancroft, but by one of his more reliable assistants, the *History* nevertheless parroted the Vigilante party line. But it dropped a lot of names in the process, ones that might be useful to me. Best of all, it was instantly available from a public access archive. Despite my best intentions to broaden my scope, I typed Plummer's name into the searchable index. Leaning into the screen, I stared intently, the way I used to gaze into my ex-husband's eyes when he was still my esteemed professor, and I, his tremulous teaching assistant. I didn't know what I expected from Litton back then. Nothing much had changed: I didn't know what I expected from *Bancroft* now. What I got was nothing new on Plummer and nothing at all on Porter or Phleger or, for that matter, on any other possible HP.

I tipped my chair back, rubbing the stiffness out of my neck and considering my alternatives. The chances of identifying EBP—the recipient of the ledger writer's letters—seemed exceedingly slim since women tended to appear in public records less frequently than men and in less identifiable ways. Without even a partial name to aid me, I would have to comb through Iowa census records from both 1860 and 1870, both far outside my target year. Although I had only single initials for the two men the ledger writer had mentioned—S and T—at least I knew they had actually been in Bannack in 1864.

Resuming my search, I found that a daunting number of S surnames on the 1862-63 list of Bannack residents. In contrast, only fourteen Bannack residents claimed last names that began with T. One of those names belonged to the sheriff's once-upon-a-time best friend, F.M. Thompson, the publisher of the *East Bannack News Letter*. It seemed I wasn't going to be able to shake Plummer, even if I wanted to.

The online version of Mather and Boswell's revisionist biography of the sheriff reported that Thompson hadn't participated in the hanging. Instead, they said, his job had been to prevent the sheriff's sister-in-law from rushing to the scene to plea for mercy. Should I be chagrined or elated by this information? If true, it meant Thompson couldn't have written the *News Letter* account of the hanging that I'd found in the ledger—or at least, he couldn't have based his article on his own eye-witness experience. On the other hand, Mather and Boswell might have been misled by Thompson's possibly less-than-accurate, late-life memoir, giving me an opening to revise the revisionists.

Confused, I didn't realize for a few breaths that Mather and Boswell had just offered me a helping hand. Sister-in-law. Sister-in-law Martha Vail! Following the link to the book's index, I discovered that Vail was the sister of Electa Bryan Plummer, the sheriff's young wife, who had married him in June and mysteriously left him in September, heading back to the States. If EBP was Electa, then the ledger writer very probably was Martha.

Feeling a sudden need to have a hard copy of Mather and Boswell's *Hanging the Sheriff* in my hands, I located its catalog entry and found it in the library's open stacks, along with Allen's *A Decent, Orderly Lynching,* a newer and, some reviewers thought, a more objective argument. I also picked up Thompson's reminiscences as well as an armload of other possibly helpful books. I quickly paged through the relevant sections. Fate had brought Electa Bryan and Henry Plummer together when Martha's husband had ridden to Fort Benton seeking help to defend the farm he was managing for an Indian agent with missionary aspirations. Plummer offered his assistance. At the farm, he met and fell in love with pretty Electa, educated, but shy and unsophisticated. The two married a few months later and moved to Bannack, where the Vails also ended up living. After Electa left him, Plummer began taking his meals at his sister-in-law's table, an arrangement that continued right up to the day he was hanged. Thompson was there for breakfast that morning, Jan. 10, 1864.

"Remind me to talk to you about getting you a cell phone on the *Sun's* dime," Rheta said after I answered a page to the library's phone. "I'm just glad the history department secretary knew where you were. Your parents walked in the door a half hour ago, and they're getting antsy."

"But they weren't supposed to show up until later!"

"Well, they're thumping around in your apartment right now," she said. "They were up the stairs and in there before I got the chance to head them off at the pass."

"Never mind. That's how they are. Just don't let them take anything, OK?" Rheta laughed, but I could tell that she knew I wasn't exactly joking.

The mirror in the library restroom told me that I was in no shape for a parental inspection. At least I was wearing clean clothes. My eyes looked as though I had used ruby red eyeliner. In the unforgiving fluorescent light, flyaway hair haloed my face, blotchy from too much recent contact with newsprint. I looked like hell, and Bet wouldn't be at all reluctant to tell me so.

Befuddled, I was halfway to the campus parking lot when I remembered where I had left the Bel Air. The afternoon had turned blustery, the sun had disappeared, and the wind felt as though it was flowing off a glacier. The stray was nudged up shaking next to the Bel Air's driver's door. He let me pass, but by the time I hefted the trunk open to retrieve my gas can, the dog had relocated his haunches on the asphalt next to me. "Go home," I said. Instead, he scrabbled into the trunk.

"You can't stay there." He stayed planted.

The gas gurgled into its tank. Instead of resisting as I hauled him out, he thrust his nose under my arm and clung to me. I plopped him down. He jumped back in. When I grabbed him, he relaxed into my arms and closed his eyes. I deposited him into the front seat. Even though I left the door open, he stayed put when I went back to close the trunk.

The mutt's head was heavy on my thigh as I drove back to the *Sun*. He stank. No doubt I would stink too when Bet gathered me into her reproachful embrace.

Although she was socially unacceptable, the western prostitute blended into the fabric of the frontier with easy familiarity.

—Anne Seagraves, in *Soiled Doves: Prostitution in the Old West*

1967: The Long Road Home

"Eat healthy, girls!"

China Rose's voice tumbles down the dark stairwell and pursues Senorita into the bacon-and-sausage-scented dawn. Breakfast is ready for them at the Golden Hour— hot cakes and bacon for Peaches the addled one; scrambled eggs and sausage for Shirley the smelly one; waffles and ham for Lena the educated one; biscuits and gravy for Senorita the practical one.

They eat with their plain wool coats (unimpeachably conservative so as not to offend some respectable early riser) buttoned up tight against the November cold. No use dressing to eat when they'll be back up in their rooms in twenty minutes, at last free to stable between the sheets of the beds where they have labored all night, their faces twisted into imitation pleasure, the mattress under their bare buttocks stabilized by plywood. The girls will sleep right through lunch, so they do eat, but hearty, not healthy. None of them ever orders oatmeal, even though Rose invariably urges them to avoid fried foods that could spot their skins and balloon their thighs. She always gives this advice shaking her finger in mock maternal concern, making them listen before she tallies up the night's take, pressing each girl's percentage into her hand.

"Don't spend it all in one place." As she smiles, her chapped lips crack. Except for her furs, cut to assert a conservative sensibility, she dresses like a secretary in suited jackets. The girls smile back resentfully. They go nowhere in town but the Golden Hour and the bus depot. They save their shopping for their forced monthly "vacations," which they spend in Butte drinking or drugging or visiting children secreted away at a safe distance with relatives who may or may not know what they do for a living.

Senorita wishes as always that China Rose would hand over the take without the lecture and the maternal expressions of concern. She doesn't like to be forced to think about Elsie by her employer's mother-hen pretensions.

It has been almost eight years since Elsie dropped Rheta off by the side of the highway. Senorita still can picture perfectly the way the spinning snow looked as if it were pushing itself up the foothills of the Spanish Peaks, not plummeting down from a leaden sky.

"I'll send for you soon as me and your Uncle Jack get married and find a decent spot for you." Elsie shuddered in her thin coat, her freckled face shadowed by a summer straw cloche that seemed to clutch at her head. When she kissed Rheta, her breath smelled of Lucky Strikes and of the rum and cokes she and Jack had been drinking at the bar in Twin Bridges. Meanwhile, Rheta was sitting up straight in a booth in the adjoining cafe, drinking black coffee and practicing looking sixteen. She had been fourteen for three weeks. The orphans' home was supposed to take you only until you were twelve, but they had never turned her down yet. Rheta had no hope that they would refuse her this time. After all, she knew the ropes as well as the matrons, who didn't think twice about handing her any of the jobs they couldn't get to.

At sixteen, you could get a real job and you could rent your own room, one with a lock. Rheta figured she'd already eaten at least sixteen years of orphans' oatmeal already.

The cold was the type that could marbleize unprotected nostrils, cheeks, fingers, but Rheta's mother hesitated over her goodbyes. "Couldn't we drive her to the door?" she pleaded.

"And get stuck? Hurry it up, Elsie!" Jack repositioned his bulk in the passenger seat, leaned back with his large head, closed eyelids so smooth they almost seemed transparent. He made his living—a good one, he had told Elsie—selling vanilla extract, food coloring, and cleaning products door to door. He had a big territory, he had assured Elsie every day for the last two months. But he was taking a little holiday until the weather got warmer.

Still Elsie hesitated, her ungloved hand trembling in the palm of her daughter's hand-knitted mitten. "Don't forget to go to mass every week, Rheta. With any luck at all, I'll be back to pick you up before Christmas."

Rheta knew her mother's luck was always bad. She didn't think Jack would change it. His eyes opened and began to flicker.

"Elsie," he said softly, his last warning.

And then Rheta was alone, her toes numbing despite the galoshes her mother had stripped off her own feet and made her put on. She waved jauntily into the wind at the farewell tap of horn and pretended to turn toward the buildings stuck like upended bricks among the rising drifts. Snow sucked at her feet. The driveway was as white as a piece of untouched paper. A new sign announced a new name—Montana Children's Center. Apparently things had changed since Rheta had been here last—at least on the outside. When the murmur of treadless tires subsided, Rheta pivoted. She hesitated, picturing what she was giving up: the hissing warmth of steam heat, the strained smile of the hair-netted receptionist. "Here again, Rheta?" the matron would have asked. "Well, your mother should have come in to sign your papers. But we'll manage, won't we? And then we'll see if there's any stew left from lunch."

Rheta had heard the stories of center inmates being hung up by their overall straps on coat hooks, of being thrust into the dark of a cloakroom, of being whipped for bed-wetting. She herself had never suffered anything other than institutional kindness dished out with the same precise measure as the stew, exactly the same amount for each child whose parents had succumbed to death or divorce or illness or unforgiving poverty. She didn't mind the stew, despite its thin gravy and canned peas. Nor the rows of beds, despite the sharp buttons that thrust up from the mattresses to remind each skinny sleeper she was no princess. Nor the disciplined round of school and endless chores that ate up any chance for dreaming. Nor the worn textbooks, the second-hand clothes, the visits from the Butte Junior Leaguers intent on doing good. She didn't even mind the fact that the matrons pressed her into service cleaning, washing dishes, and taking care of the younger children. She did hate the oatmeal, but she had to take it, wasn't allowed to leave it. Wasn't allowed to leave any of it.

Just ahead of her, the highway vaulted over the clear, grey water of the river. When she saw the streak of white coupe speeding over the bridge toward her, the arch of its white tailfins cutting through a white sea, she stuck out her thumb.

"Where you going, girlie?" The woman's vivid yellow-brown face burned a hole in the swirling snow. Beside her, a rat-faced dog wearing a tiny mink vest yapped wildly, stabbing its muzzle through the car window as it powered down.

"Where are *you* going?" Rheta stood up straight and tried to look even older than sixteen. She noticed the dog's vest was of the same glossy fur that muffled the woman to her chin.

The woman made no attempt to quiet the dog. "Just to Misfire—that is, if there's enough of the road left open to take me there."

"That's where I'm going too."

"Runaway?"

"No one will notice I'm gone." Rheta began to shiver.

"What about them?" The woman inclined her chin toward the sprawl of the orphans' home.

"Nobody knows I'm here." Rheta stared into the woman's shrewd brown eyes telegraphing the message: "I'm not lying about anything important, anything that will get either of us in trouble."

China Rose pulled the dog into her lap with imperious decision and gestured with her pointed chin to the passenger's side of the car whose cursive chrome declared it a Coupe De Ville, a fancy new Cadillac.

"OK. But I'll check with the cops to make sure no one's reported you missing when we get to Misfire," she warned.

"No one will notice I'm gone," Rheta repeated, slipping into the car's leather embrace and slipping off her mother's galoshes.

Rheta wasn't so naive that she thought for a minute China Rose had taken her out of the snow because of kindness. And she was right. As China Rose negotiated the ruts that wound with the river, one ringless hand on the steering wheel and the other stroking her dog's hairless forehead, she explained her problem. The proprietor of the Red Rooms, she needed a maid to pick up after the girls who worked for her, to dust the parlor where the customers waited, to empty the slop jars, to run the carpet sweeper over the gorgeous Persian carpet in the central parlor. Easy work. Pleasant work, even.

Rose explained the girls always got their meals at the Golden Hour—breakfast there, covered dishes sent over for lunch and supper—so there would be no grease to scrub off the stove, no dishes to wash. The girls always washed their own pitcher and bowl sets, dusted the commodes that held them, and changed their own sheets. Misfire Laundry always picked up and delivered the washing.

"I don't understand why I never can hire someone for the light cleaning," Rose complained, not so much to Rheta as to the universe. "I pay well, I run respectable rooms. The doc even gives the girls a check every month." Her long unpolished nails shredded the air to illustrate her frustration as she fixed Rheta with her shadowed eyes. Rheta wished she would keep those eyes on the road, which was disappearing and appearing in the white-powdered windshield like an Arctic mirage.

"I don't understand it," she repeated. "My girls don't drink or curse or act up in public or on the job cause I fine them if they do. And I'm community-minded, believe me. Anyone asks—the Business Association, the Kiwanis, the BPOE, you name any one you want—I write out a check. And not a small check either."

Rheta accepted Rose's proposition, and she made more money than a fourteen-year-old had a right to expect, mopping and waxing stairway and the halls every morning, entering the girls' rooms only while they were at breakfast, cracking the window to let the wind rinse away the mingled smells of incense, perfume, and semen; emptying and polishing the always over-flowing ashtrays; carrying to the Red Room's single toilet the chamber pots (at arm's length, even though they hardly ever contained urine, just cold, scummy water from the basins she had learned to call "peter pans").

No cops came calling to ask if she shouldn't be in school. No cops came calling to inquire about a missing juvenile, dropped off in front of the orphans' home in late November. Cops only came calling to smoke a cigarette slumped in the overstuffed chairs, waiting for their favorite girl.

Rheta was neither happy nor unhappy. She turned fifteen and sixteen and seventeen. She went to mass every week. She and Precious Pup slept on the daybed in Rose's apartment while Rose and the girls worked. Her own job (which was easy, but not particularly pleasant) began at five o'clock when the girls went to breakfast. She collected her pay, always presented in cash, and deposited most of it in her savings account. Her stash was growing, but not fast enough for Rheta. At the rate she was saving, she would not be able to leave Montana for somewhere warm and friendly until she was too old to want to.

When one of the girls quit, Rheta applied for the job, explaining to Rose that she hadn't been a virgin since she was thirteen (which was true because of "Uncle" Jack) and that she liked sex (which was a lie, but one that all the girls told).

"I had a funny dream last night," Senorita says, pushing aside memories in favor of ham and eggs. Telling their dreams is the girls' favorite breakfast activity. "I dreamed I saw Miss China Rose flying, her and Precious Pup swooping down the stairs."

"I had a canary once," says Peaches, who could not be counted on to make sense. This morning Peaches can't seem to focus on her heavy plate: pebble grey eyes buzz around the room, lighting on the clumps of other prostitutes who've finished their night's work. Shirley doesn't say anything. She is sensitive about her smell, which disappears only briefly after her thrice-daily baths. By local custom the cafe belongs until five thirty to those who inhabit the Red Rooms, the Crystal Rooms, and (in imitation of the famous Butte establishment), the Blue Range.

"Flying often signifies sex in dreams," says Lena, who finished two years of college in Missoula before she got pregnant by a law student who decided he wanted to marry a girl with an intact hymen. Lena cuts up her ham steak in tiny pieces, her hair bundled neatly in a bun at the nape of her neck.

Senorita never really remembers her dreams, but what else is there to talk about. She opens her mouth to add a few details to her fictional vision of the flying China Rose. Instead, bile more bitter than the underside of a lemon peel floods her mouth: she barely makes it to the feces-flecked ladies' toilet, which won't be cleaned until after the prostitutes leave.

It is the oddest thing. As she heaves into the spattered bowl, her eyes darken into the vision she has just claimed as a dream: China Rose plummeting through a shadowy stairwell, her furs splashing up like a spilled whisky sour.

Senorita decides at that moment she'll refuse the doc's abortion this time, quit the Red Rooms, get work that won't require her to squirt an eyedropper full of antiseptic into naked penises night after night. Whatever she has in her savings account will keep her until she gets a respectable job.

A year or two later, when China Rose trips on her new rat-faced puppy on the very top step of the Red Room stairs, the last madam in a town grown too full of Jaycees to countenance public prostitution, Rheta grieves.

Animals were very frequent visitants of Plains Indians; buffalo, bears, eagles . . . , and sparrow hawks constantly figure in the narratives but also quite lowly beasts as dogs or rabbits.

—Robert H. Lowie, in *Indians of the Plains*

Familiar Spirits

IN THE *Sun*'S ALLEY, NICK WAS WAIST-DEEP IN THE DUMPSTER TOSSING SODA cans into a cardboard box. Grateful that I had deposited nothing more embarrassing in the trash than the cellophane for three packages of Oreo cookies, I nudged the stray's heavy head from my thigh. The dog released the wag in his tail and flowed to the Chevy's roomy floor with a grace that took no account of his long body, bum leg, splayed paws, and oversized head. He sat panting a pleased "ha-ha-ha-ha," nose pointing steadily at the passenger door's handle.

"This way!" The driver's side door creaked slightly under the authoritative thump of my hand. The dog aimed his muzzle in the opposite direction. Taking the hint, I dodged around the Chevy like a high school boy going to a 1950s senior prom with a date who believed in her right to helplessness.

"OK dog, jump down."

The dog didn't budge. "Come on, fellow," I wheedled in a sweeter-than-sweet voice. He stopped panting, looked at me expectantly. "Come on, fellow!"

The mutt disembarked with dignity and trotted away down the alley without looking back, his nose parsing the ground, his head sweeping the terrain like a telescoping cane.

"Here dog! Here fellow!" Against my better judgment, I stepped after him. The dog picked up his pace, allowing his bad leg to jounce in time with his gait. Nick vaulted out of the dumpster, landing with an agility I wouldn't have guessed he possessed.

"Nice-looking dog."

"He's not my dog." The saddlebag, heavy with library books, heavier still with unsolved mysteries, resisted my grasp as I pulled it from the car. Fatigue was making my mind bob like a red balloon on a string. Hurt by the stray's desertion, I decided to let him go, to let someone else save or condemn him. If he chose to turn his back on me, so be it. I needed to get upstairs and see what secrets my putative parents had disinterred from my personal effects. Instead, I stood by the alley door telling myself I really should take a few minutes to fish for information about where Nick had found the ledger.

"Looks as though you've had a productive day." I directed an exaggerated smile toward the cardboard box in his arms. The heartiness in my voice embarrassed me.

Instead of responding, Nick settled his catch of the day in the bed of a Chevy Luv pickup too cheap and scabrous yellow to be considered a classic and too old to be considered a viable form of transportation. Actually, I was surprised Nick owned any sort of vehicle at all, even one furnished with bulging garbage sacks.

"You too. Shall I carry that for you?"

A bit offended that Nick had equated his trash to the treasures that bulged my saddlebag, I forgot to be as charming as an angler after information should be. "No need."

Ignoring my rudeness, Nick opened the *Sun*'s alley door for me. He smelled of orange peels and Old Spice. The mailroom was dim. A buckled board caught my shoe, and I paused to regain my balance and to let my eyes adjust. Ahead, the strips of plastic barring the way to the composing room fluttered as if to wave me off. How should I greet the parents? With hugs and kisses? With careful politeness? With uncurtained anger? Nick seemed in no hurry to move on, but neither was I.

"Somebody told me that sometimes you find interesting old documents, letters and things like that."

Nick didn't reply, just stood in what might or might not be affronted silence. How had I lived with an expert salesman for a father and an accomplished seducer for a husband without learning more about how to

deploy charm? Given the chance to examine my skull, a latter-day phre-
nologist would encounter not a Bump of Diplomacy, but a Slough of
Social Stupidity.

Wondering where the stray would find his next meal, I made a clumsy
cast: "I'm especially interested in old personal records—you know, diaries
or ledgers that you may have found." Silence was a glass that remained half-
empty, until he broke it.

"My retriever just went around the corner. Your dog's probably following his scent."

While I wondered if I should try splashing another conversational gambit in Nick's direction or to give up and to go look for the dog, the strips
of plastic writhed and parted. The stray erupted into the mailroom and
reached for my legs with both paws.

"Fellow! Get down!" The dog subsided, his mouth open in a slight grin.
The black mask of fur surrounding his eyes made him look like a raccoon
drawn by someone who had never seen a raccoon. Trotting to Nick, he sat
and offered his paw, the perfect little gentlehound.

"He needs feeding up." As Nick let his hand bump over the stray's spine,
the bagman gave me a calculating look at odds with his naive redneck act.
The dog muzzled his way lightly down the slope of Nick's paint-speckled
boots, apparently having forgotten me altogether.

"He's not my dog," I repeated. "He was running loose and getting into
trouble. But I guess I can call the local humane shelter just as well as anybody else."

"Ain't no humanity shelter here. Strays get passed out to the local vets.
They get killed after three days if they don't have tags." Nick had waded
back into his folksy shallows.

"Well, I guess I could put an ad in the paper and feed him until someone
claims him."

"You might could. But you'd be wasting ink. He's a stray." Nick offered me an ambiguous glance before he continued. "Anyways, once you've
named a dog, he's yours."

Not sure what to say to this bit of nauseating homespun wisdom, I decided to keep the conversation simple: "I haven't named him."

Nick straightened up. "It might could be that once in awhile I come
across papers that shouldn't be thrown away."

"When was the last time?" I nonchalantly bent to comb the fur on Long-fellow's domed skull with my fingers, afraid to look up.

"Can't say. Maybe around Easter. Maybe at Schooners. Course, might could have been some other place."

"Who are the Schooners? Where do they live?" I asked. Instead of an-swering, Nick simply turned around and left, shutting the alley door firm-ly to keep Fellow—and perhaps me—inside. He needn't have worried. I couldn't postpone facing the parents any longer. Fellow signaled his incli-nation to follow me by standing up when I did. Rather than bolting for the office's propped-open front door as I headed into the newsroom, he took a right turn at the stairs and began snuffling an ascent to the morgue landing.

"Looks like you've got yourself a new friend," called Rheta. "He came galloping in through the front a minute ago like he owned the place."

"He's just a stray—I'll tell you all about it later. How's Conrad? Are my parents still here?"

"Better than he has a right to be. Your father left awhile ago. Your moth-er's upstairs waiting." Rheta offered me a look that I read as sympathetic.

I could already smell Bet's tangy perfume floating in the stairwell—Jean Naté, probably purchased on sale from Walmart.

"Down." Bet's voice refused to sound startled. "Get down." Bet hadn't shut the apartment door, perhaps because of her long-standing conviction that you should always leave someone else's property in the state in which you've found it—after, of course, you've rifled through it sufficiently to ar-rive at an accurate estimation of its value. Or maybe she had needed some air to thin the disinfectant-generated fog that was creeping down the stairs mingled with her perfume.

"AJ, is this your dog? I hope you're keeping him away from that table and off this beautiful rug." I caught my breath at this possible clue that Bet and Chas really had been rummaging around upstairs. Glancing at the door to the mysterious third floor, I refused to feel relief when I saw that it was closed. Bet must be referring to the Ingrahams' gift, glowing under her sandaled feet. "You know what rugs like this are worth, don't you?" She stooped to run her fingers over its soft braided rounds.

Fellow wallowed within an inch of her yellow-lacquered toes, rubbing his filthy underside against the rug. Although I was certain I had left the door secured, I couldn't believe that she and Chas had resisted the temptation to break out their set of picklocks. Perhaps I had dreamed the whole thing up—the secret passageway, the bare floorboards, the Tabriz carpet, the photo of Senorita.

Despite her stated misgivings, Bet reached down to give Fellow a pat. Her hands were encased in rubber gloves; had she been carrying a spare pair in her purse, just in case? They went well with the pattern of the big sunflowers of her blouse and the little sunflowers of her shorts, too brief for the season. She still had the smooth, chunky body of a World War II pin-up girl. Her hair glistened like ripe wheat, a little tawnier than it had been when I was a girl, but just as shiny in the slide of its chin-length curve. I looked nothing like her.

"Sorry you had to wait for me." Bet's perfume, commingled with Pine-Sol, absorbed me. Engulfed by the force of her embrace, I felt the thrust of bones. They felt more breakable than I remembered. Fellow leapt, trying to join the dance. "Down!" I said. Fellow kept knocking at my knees with his ovoid paws, nails, thick, pale, overgrown.

"Down," Bet said. Fellow bounced to the floor and began nosing the perimeter of the room like a demented vacuum cleaner. What kind of history he was absorbing, I couldn't begin to imagine.

"Well, at least he seems to be a quick learner. When did you get him?" She gathered up the shade I had left on the corner of the bar and settled it back on the brass lamp. She pulled a dust cloth out of her pocket and began polishing the lamp's fluted brass column in a way that suggested that she had already appraised it as suitable for resale.

"He's lost, so I'm just keeping him for a few days." I wondered if Bet was as grateful as I was that Fellow had eased us past our moment of meeting. Fellow headed for the futon after he'd lapped up a bowl of water. He propelled himself onto the clean sheets, snorting in what I hoped was ecstasy, not some kind of fit. Recovering, he tramped a circle on its blanket-draped surface and settled down to sleep. I wished I could join him.

"Do you think it's wise to let him sleep on your bed? He doesn't smell very good."

I had long ago decided it was better to ignore discussing matters of even slight controversy with Bet, especially when she might be right. "Where's dad? What time did you get into town?"

"Oh, about two. That nice secretary downstairs told us to make ourselves at home. You know your father. He couldn't wait to set up shop. I'll bet by this time he's cleared a hundred dollars."

Why, I don't know, but it cheered me up to envision Chas, huckster extraordinaire, taking on the treasure-hunters of Misfire. In him, they would meet their match, I was certain.

"I hope you haven't been bored waiting."

"Don't you remember that I never get bored?" She drummed the skin of the word "remember" in a way meant to telegraph the point that she was blameless for the long silence that had divided us.

She paused for two beats for emphasis and then continued in a chipper tone: "I could see right away how you've been struggling to get this place clean, so I thought I'd help you a little." When I didn't react to her underlying message—that I was clearly incompetent when it came to practical matters, she poked at another sore spot.

"How's your research coming along? Your department chair told me that you were on leave to work on something, but I couldn't understand what it was all about except that it had something to do with prospecting. Is there really a need for more of that sort of thing, do you think?"

Again I kept quiet. Instead of snapping back, I moved to the vinyl bar. My cache of personal documents, although still on their shelf, was fanned out in a pattern I hadn't created. Pointedly, I picked them up and tucked them in the manila envelope that still veiled my original birth certificate and the only letter I had ever received from Everonica—a demand that I never try to contact her again. The envelope might or might not have been opened.

Without waiting for any more response from me, Bet began dusting the stove top with cleansing powder; it fell like snow, turning blue as it came in contact with the dampness her sponge had left behind. "I'm just sorry you didn't go into writing—I mean real writing. By this time, I'll bet you would have written a best-seller. Have you heard from Litton?"

Though I was used to her abrupt change of subjects, this one startled me—especially since I was planning what I would say just in case she asked me about the contents of the envelope.

"We agreed not to communicate."

"Such a shame, such a special man. But maybe things will work out. The course of true love never does run smooth."

Bet had adored Litton since the evening of our post-wedding dinner for four at a Seattle Elks Club. Litton danced the fox-trot with her, plying her with Diet Pepsis between sets. Chas, happy to be left in peace with his rib steak and rum-and-Cokes, had liked him, too. The fact that Litton was, like them, an active Elk, and actually seemed to be enjoying their visit, should have given me pause. But I was in love and ignoring far more worrisome signs—including, but not limited to the incessant calls he was getting from his newest star graduate student, female, very bright with a Wonder Woman physique.

I wondered if Bet, who prided herself on being honest to a fault, was still avoiding telling people that I was divorced—not that she had all that many friends to tell. A peripatetic life tends to rasp away the ties that bind.

Fellow's eyes were squeezed shut and his breathing was deep, but his tail whirred into action.

"He's sort of cute in an ugly way. He might make a nice companion for you once you clean him up." For a second, I thought Bet meant Litton until I noticed the direction of her glance. Despite myself, my heart contracted at this sign that Bet continued to cling to her indefatigably positive attitude. The poppy-bright smile kept her face from sliding downward with her glance. But worry lines ran like rivulets to the blurring line of her chin. For the first time ever, I noticed that she resembled the one photo of her own mother that I had ever seen. "Who's that?" I had asked, as she was emptying her bra and panty drawer in preparation for another move. A first-grader, I was fascinated by the red of the woman's hair, the green of her eyes.

"Your grandmother—she died a few months before you were born. Both my parents died then. In a car accident. I've told you that."

Yes, she had told me that once or twice when the topic of grandmothers had come up in some storybook I was attempting to sound out.

"But who's that? Is that you?" I had persevered, pointing at the child sitting in the grandmother's lap, a red-haired child with the same wide mouth and hooded eyelids as Bet.

"Just a relative," Bet said. I waited to hear more. "A cousin," she finally said.

"Do I have cousins, too? What's that on her face?"

"It's just something called a birthmark. I'll tell you all about her when you're older." But she never had. So naturally I never forgot her comment and monitored the photo's continued existence, always in the top drawer of her bureau, even though the bureau itself, the house, and the town changed and changed. Once, after getting tutored in the ways of normal families by one of my rare friends, I had even slipped it from its cardboard holder to check for any writing that might be on its back. Nothing.

Noticing Fellow had emptied his bowl, Bet refilled it. "Well, anyway," she said, reassembling her face into a semblance of vibrant youth. "Let's go see if we can find what our Mr. Charles Armstrong is up to." As always, Bet glowed at the prospect of seeing her husband. Would her passion have withered, I wondered, if hers had been a marriage rooted in the constancy of a clapboard house circled with a white picket fence, if she and Chas hadn't been always already moving or on the verge of moving. In fact, they had met at a gas station, Bet at the pump and Chas waiting. "And we've been on the road since!" Chas always said. There was more to the story than that, I could tell, some secret that Bet and Chas used to hold themselves together and me at arm's length.

"Don't park there, AJ!" Chas boomed as I positioned the Chevy under the awning of an abandoned A&W, a hand-made "For Rent" sign askew in one of its dirty windows. At first, I thought that he looked about the same as the last time I had seen him: like a corruptible white-haired senator from a Rocky Mountain state. It wasn't until he had given me the briefest of hugs that I noticed his shoulders were hunched slightly under the well-cut shirt with the pearl snaps. "Where'd this damn dog come from?"

"I'm taking care of him for a couple of days. I guess his ambition is to be taller, because he seems to want to jump up on everyone."

Chas didn't smile at my joke. "If he was my dog, I'd cure him of that pretty damn quick." Still wagging, Fellow had retreated behind me. Chas and Bet had never owned a pet—too much trouble when you're moving.

"What a perfect sales lot!" Bet said, not gushing, but sincerely impressed. "Although it does make me sad to see the old A&W run down and abandoned. I used to love coming here, sitting in our pink Rambler and sipping away at those frosted . . ." She paused and shot me a look I couldn't interpret.

"When was that exactly?"

It was Chas who answered. "Can't really remember—we weren't here for long. Maybe it was after Billings, but before Denver." He was a plausible liar, but he couldn't fool me. I had watched him lie all my growing-up years.

"No, I don't think so," Bet said, catching hold of her husband's elbow. "We had AJ with us here, but that was before Billings. After we get unpacked, I'll have to look it up in our trip notebook from those years." That last word made me lose interest in the nature of the lie and the motivation for it. I didn't like the sound of the word "unpacked."

Chas had lost interest in the subject. He shook off Bet's hand and gripped her around the waist so that he could propel her through the aisle that separated the four folding tables set up in two neat rows.

Covered with oilcloth, their surfaces were loaded with things that the thrifty generations of the past had stuffed in garages and attics, as if they understood the years would transform junk to junque. As I trailed after Bet and Chas, I spotted a shoe tree, a set of spurs, a buck-saw, a cluster of mason jars blued by longevity and light. A half-dozen hand-made doilies had been given the honor of getting a Coca-Cola tray to themselves. Bet no longer was leaving her handiwork behind on rented kitchen counters, I was happy to see. When I paused to pick up one of the lacey cobwebs, Bet slipped out of Chas's grasp.

"Still crocheting?"

She nodded a confirmation. "I never get tired of all you can do with a little cotton thread and a lot of empty space. That's what I like best—not the stitches, but the holes."

Chas backtracked to reclaim Bet's attention along with her elbow. "It was so late that I didn't want to set out much of the good stuff. But even with only this little bit, I've been hauling it in. Those tourists who roll in off the interstate headed for McDonald's? The first thing they see is my sign. He gestured toward a plywood placard that proclaimed "Antiques" and "Free Coffee" in crude hand-lettering.

"I could probably do a better sign for you with the newspaper's equipment," I offered just to find something to say.

"Thanks, but no thanks. The signs can't look too good or the tourists will figure out we know what we're doing. That's why I parked the RV behind the building. I don't want them spotting our Arizona license plates."

Bet was rearranging a group of old irons with heavy fabric cords. "Don't fuss with that, Bet." Chas firmly subscribed to the idea the man of the family ought to give a lot of orders. If he ever had asked himself how Bet functioned during his frequent absences, he'd given no indication. "We'll only stay open for a couple more hours anyway. Well, here's the cops."

A white man with grey stubble emerged from his patrol car glowering, his hand hooked into the belt above his holster. I recognized him as the only police officer who had seemed more interested in his Big Slurp than Conrad in the aftermath of the rally accident. I went looking for Fellow just in case the cop decided to demonstrate that Misfire really did have a leash law.

I needn't have worried. By the time, I had hoisted him to cling catlike to my shoulder, the cop was sipping coffee from a paper cup and snickering. I guessed that Chas, who was hefting a set of rusty andirons, had told some sort of joke—sexist, racist or homophobic. With the andirons tucked into the back seat of his patrol car and six crisp hundred dollar bills in his pocket, the cop drove away smiling.

"Did you notice that he didn't even tell us to get a business license?" Chas always reiterated his triumphs for Bet, even when she had witnessed them for herself. "Lucky for us that his brother-in-law left him in charge of the place after it folded. Let's have a cuppacoffee and then move the tables inside."

Chas handed first Bet and then me watery coffee poured from a Coleman thermos I recognized from my childhood. My paper cup might as well have carried the legend "Drink me." Like Alice-in-Wonderland, I could feel myself shrinking, my shoulders collapsing in defense, a childlike eagerness to please taking me prisoner. Within seconds, Chas had shaken me down for the scoop on the antiques in my apartment and wrung me dry of information about Luke and his mother's house and his amateur attempt to run weekly rummage sales. At least he made no mention of the *Sun*'s mysterious upper story. The predatory gleam in Chas's eyes warned me to keep my mouth shut, but I was panning for his approval just the way I always had with him, my mostly absent and inattentive surrogate father. Within minutes of working together to haul the loaded tables into the A&W's dining room, we were on our way. Chas had taken over the Bel Air's driver's seat without asking. Bet sat up front. Fellow and I looked out the windows in the back as they plotted their strategy.

Luke glanced at my bulging saddlebag as I introduced him to the parents. With Bet and Chas on the scene, I was keeping both the ledger and my personal documents where I could see them. Luke raised his eyebrows in a wordless question, but I looked away. Although I certainly needed his help with the ledger, my stint in the library had made me broody about it.

Fortunately, he and Stela had more than enough to absorb their attention as they jousted with the parents. As Luke served them up hamburgers with homemade potato salad on the screened front porch of his mother's house, Stela negotiated with deadly courtesy. Apparently she was the haggler in the couple.

"Now Mr. Armstrong, you know that a collection of train lanterns like this one is worth at least a thousand dollars. On eBay, I've seen something that looks a lot like this nice little Colorado piece going for two hundred. I don't know how we're going to do business unless you offer us at least half what you expect to sell something for."

Completely unabashed, Chas held out four bills. "Yes, but most of them of them are just junk," he countered. I wondered how many of those C-notes Chas was carrying.

"Well, I appreciate your generosity," Stela configured her face into a convincing show of sincerity. "But, you know, I might just keep these lanterns. Sometimes I get the notion that I might sell my franchise someday and open up a nice little sit-down restaurant and furnish it with antiques."

Chas held out another ten. Stela didn't take it. He waved a hundred-dollar bill. Stela held out her hand.

"I can tell we're going to enjoy doing business together," Stela smiled, and the talk switched to the question of where on the Ingrahams' property my parents would park their rig and hook into electricity in partial exchange for their sales acumen. They would run their own A&W sales lot Sundays through Thursdays, getting rid of what Chas called "the penny ante junk" there, while reserving the Fridays and Saturdays for "the high-end stuff."

"The good stuff will be safer out here—and that workshop of yours is kind of classy," Chas said. "But I want to make it clear that if we take on this job, we're in charge and you don't even poke your nose in the door while the sales are going on."

Luke opened his mouth in what looked like a rising protest, but Stela stuck out her hand to seal the deal.

Just like that, I was released from my obligation to help Stela and Luke, a development that should have made me happy, but instead made me feel like a high school freshman who had just been unfriended. Even worse, the arrangement meant the parents would be sticking around for several weeks.

At least the sale would keep them too occupied to pay much attention to me. In fact, when I got up to leave, neither the Ingrahams nor the parents took much notice. Luke had already agreed to drive them back to the A&W so they could leave their RV in the shady spot next to his mother's house.

The next couple of weeks pooled into a discouraged tedium. Conrad's doctors recommended surgery. Rheta made two more quick trips to Missoula to see him before the quadruple bypass, but I stayed in Misfire. Conrad made it through the operation, but his doctors weren't making any predictions about when he would be released.

Luke sent word with the parents inviting me to drop out to his house to talk to him. He called the *Sun* and left messages for me. I didn't respond. My half-brother didn't call to report how my bookshelves were coming along. Despite the fact that the arrival of the parents had left me unable to figure out what I should do next about the ledger, about Everonica, about my whole disordered life, I did manage the run to Bannack three times, purportedly to talk to Delores about the ledger, but actually to stalk Adon. Twice I caught a distant glimpse of him rapidly moving in the opposite direction from me, once toward Boot Hill and another time, across Grasshopper Creek in the direction of the defunct cyanide mill.

As for Fellow, frequent bathing had left him smelling more like old leather than roadkill, but no one answered the ad that offered him free to a good home. His limping gait was probably the result of a minor congenital defect, not an injury, the vet said. Fellow would stop throwing up at inconvenient times once his stomach settled into a regular diet of dry dog food, the vet predicted. I didn't tell her that Fellow refused a regular diet. He would take one sniff of his bowl of respectable and expensive kibble and back away. He would deign to return only when I squelched my vegetarian impulses and crumbled in a hamburger patty. I was doing more cooking for Fellow than for myself. No wonder he had been skinny when I had picked him up: he probably hadn't found much garbage that met his high standards.

There wasn't much news, and it was a good thing since Rheta couldn't scare up enough ads to justify even an eight-page publication. The bright spots were few and far between.

"I need an ad in this week's paper," Lena announced one morning at the Golden Hour when she came over to take my breakfast order. I looked at her in disbelief. Rheta had told me the Golden Hour never advertised because Lena believed that any business that had to toot its own horn was revealing itself as a lemon.

Lena scowled. "John Storey isn't the emperor of Misfire, even though he seems to think he is," she said. I got out my notebook and wrote down the particulars.

With all that was going on, I didn't have a chance to think seriously about the ledger until one more publication cycle later as I helped Rheta paste up the week's pitiful collection of ads. She kept lighting one cigarette after another, something I had never before seen her do out of range of the *Sun*'s open front door. My airways begged me to escape. Instead, I offered up the ledger as a distraction less lethal than tobacco. It worked. Tossing her current cigarette in an empty soft drink can, Rheta began speculating about what Nick might have meant when he said the ledger had come from the Schooners.

Nick probably wasn't referring to the local family whose members now mostly resided in the cemetery, she explained. "It's a lot more likely he picked the ledger up at the resort the family used to run." She paused and squinted at the words "All Snow Boots Half Price!" and then repositioned the line to match the faint blue grid revealed by the glow of the light table.

"In the days I worked for the Red Rooms, I wasn't welcome out there— it was a hoity-toity spot in those days. People of means would always take their out-of-town guests to have dinner at the Prairie Schooner because the food was good and the hot springs was a novelty." She set the ad aside and then checked it off her list, a short one, and went on without reaching for a fresh cigarette. "Later on, after it turned into a dive, I avoided it because I was working hard to convince people that I had turned respectable. But Luke's known the family all his life, and I've heard Stela's thinking about buying the place. You know it's just down the road from them, don't you?"

I had not known. Intrigued by the information, I told Rheta I would talk to Stela as soon as the paper was out. "That won't take long—we're done here already." She reached for another cigarette.

With the help of Tom Engles, the press spit out the papers, thin as a whisper, in half the time it had the week before. We didn't even need Genifer. I hurried out the alley door as soon as I could, eager to get out to Luke and Stela's doublewide before the parents came to roost for the evening. If Luke was still at home, I would take it as a sign that I should show him the ledger. If Stela hadn't left for her late afternoon check on the DQ, I would ask her to give me a tour of the Schooners.

As it turned out, Luke was at the college, but Stela seemed happy to see me and Fellow. She recovered the keys for Schooners from a coffee can in the garage. "Well, this is Misfire, Montana," she said, properly interpreting my silent criticism of her security arrangements. The garage was dust-free and nearly empty except for the Model T, undraped, polished, and ready to roll into the arms of a buyer. Bet and Chas were nothing if not competent.

The apex of the Prairie Schooner swelled like an oversized loaf of bread above a clump of scruffy Russian olives even before Stela turned onto the lane that led to its main building. The wind shaking the thorny branches of the trees wasn't stirring a ripple in the schooner's roofline. It must be made of material more rigid than canvas.

"It's just so awful that I can't help loving it," Stela said. As she inserted the key, Fellow leveraged his leash in an attempt to drag me off a long wooden front porch shaped approximately like a wagon tongue. I remembered how impressed I'd been when the parents had moved us to Bemidji one spring: I'd been charmed by the Minnesota town's replica of Paul Bunyan's Blue Ox, Babe. Too bad the Schooners hadn't thought of hitching their restaurant to a bovine star of their own—that would have been really something. Of course, then they would have faced the challenge of providing multiple sets of smaller oxen for each of the schoonerized guest cabins, each with an imitation canvas cover of its own.

"Are you really thinking of buying it?"

"I'd like to, but Luke says he'd be the laughing stock of the Western History Association if I put on a gingham dress and reopened this as a steak house and spa."

Her voice was amused, not angry. Apparently the Ingrahams were simply arguing, not fighting, about the Prairie Schooner. I wondered if the deeper discords that hummed between them had quieted or deepened.

Still determined to go his own way, Fellow sat down and braced his front paws when I attempted to drag him into the restaurant.

"Must be ghosts in there." I couldn't tell if she was joking. "You've heard the story about the hotel in Bannack, how dogs refuse to put one paw past its threshold because of all the haunts that hang out there."

"Bad!" I tried. Fellow put his ears back, licked his lips contritely, and braced himself even more firmly. When I yanked harder, he rolled over, ever the charmer, trying to get his way with guile. I thought of my ex-husband and decided that I would call in another "free to a good home" Tradio ad for Fellow.

"Why don't you just let him chase the gophers for a while—he won't go far."

"I don't trust him," I said, hoisting Fellow to my shoulder. He was even harder to heft than he had been; all those hamburger patties were taking effect. "Once he's on the trail of something, he chases first and thinks later."

In the shadowy interior of the ersatz wagon, Fellow's research focus changed. When I thumped him down, he began casting back and forth across the polished floor, dodging around tables with their freight of up-ended chairs. Above, the ceiling was a perfectly conventional one that made no attempt to imitate stretched canvas.

In fact, everything about the dining room was unsurprising and tidy—in other words, completely disappointing. As I paced down its windowed length, I saw no piles of refuse that could hide an important document like the ledger, just rows of tables that seemed to be eagerly awaiting a call to service. The only unusual feature of the room was the bar that ran perpendicular to the entrance. Inlaid silver dollars glinted like miniature full moons under a sheet of heavy glass.

My hand curled as I remembered the way a silver dollar could warm your hand. I must have been about five when a woman with an auburn ponytail, a stranger, had pressed one into my palm. It could have been any JCPenney in any town. But now, standing with my hand on the glass of the Schooners counter, cold as a slab of raw steak, my memory matched up that long-ago storefront with the empty Penney's showcase around the corner from the *Sun* office. Well, I supposed the match was plausible. Bet had mentioned Misfire had been a stop on the parents' restless leapfrogging across the West. But it was more likely I was falling into the all-too-human habit of refitting the past to suit the present. Although I wouldn't want to bet the proverbial farm on the accuracy of either possibility, I was clearer about what happened that day than about where it took place.

"You wait here while I run in for stockings. If the meter maid comes, hurry up and put a nickel in the slot," Bet had told me. "You remember how?"

"Sure!"

Bet seemed nervous, but not about leaving me. She had been nervous since we'd arrived in this funny little town.

When a tall shadow embraced mine, I thought it might belong to a particularly sneaky meter maid. Looking up, I had at first been frightened. I can't remember why. In those days, stranger-danger warnings had been limited to men offering candy. This was a woman. She had no candy.

"I've been watching you," the woman said, crouching. Her hair glinted in the sun. Happy to meet someone else with hair like mine, I was pleased to see the copper of it and forgot to be afraid. She was wearing glamorous make-up, foundation thick and smooth, eyelids lined in black. Above them, wings of green rose to her brows.

"I've seen that you're a smart little girl and a nice one, too," she said. "Would you like a present, AJ? Your name is AJ, isn't it?"

I nodded and held out my hand, making sure I didn't drop the nickel I was dutifully gripping. The woman cradled my cupped hand with one of her own and slipped a silver dollar into my palm. When I closed my fingers, I expected she would step back. She didn't.

"Mommy, look what I have!" I raised my fist as the stranger's hand fell away.

The red-haired woman shot Bet a look that I could not comprehend. Angry, yes. But not only angry, my memory insisted in a vertiginous revision. Sad. Hungry. Wounded beyond the hope of healing.

"Goodbye, AJ," she said. And turned her back on me.

As the woman disappeared around the corner, Bet reached for my fist. Her hand was so icy that I was surprised into letting both coins drop, my new silver dollar as well as the nickel. Wordlessly, Bet secreted them in her patent leather purse. She never mentioned the gift or the giver, and neither did I. We left town later that day.

I wondered whether Bet still remembered that dollar and whether I could work up the courage to ask her about it.

Absent-mindedly, I polished away the smudge my hand had left on the slab of glass. "I'm surprised no one has broken in and smashed this for the coins," I told Stela.

"Me, too. I guess none of the local felons have wanted to go through all the work of trying to pry the dollars loose. I told Mort—he's the one who inherited the place—he should at least keep it covered up."

"Maybe he thinks it makes a better first impression on a potential buyer this way."

"He's just lazy. He doesn't have the place listed with anyone because he's convinced I'm going to buy it."

"It's really in pretty good shape, don't you think?"

"Mort spent a few weeks after Christmas cleaning the place and doing a little restoration. He planned to reopen it himself, but his wife hated Misfire and said she was moving back to civilization with or without him."

I wanted to ask Stela if she sometimes felt the same way. Instead I got back to business. She listened quietly and, when I had finished, let her silence ask the obvious question.

"I was hoping I'd catch Luke home today, so I could tell him about it," I answered.

She let that fragile substitute for the truth drop without trying to catch it.

Out of embarrassment, I struggled to find something else to say. "I guess it is possible Nick could have found the ledger while—what's his name? Mort?—was clearing the place out. But all this tidiness doesn't look too encouraging . . ."

"Well you never know what you might find in the back of a closet somewhere."

"Hasn't everything been cleaned out?"

"Fraid so—everything's clean as a hound's tooth."

I thought I had better locate my own hound. He had disappeared some time ago under a set of swinging doors that presumably led to the kitchen. All the fixtures had been removed from the kitchen except for a massive stove that looked far too big to fit through any of the building's doors or windows. Maybe they had built the place around it. Fellow wasn't under the stove, and there was no place else for him to hide. When he didn't respond to my calls, Stela fluted her lips to produce a clear, high whistle.

"I've always wanted to be able to do that," I said.

"It's easy; I'll teach you."

"I think the talent's hereditary."

"I've heard Bet whistle." She moved to a door next to the bar that I thought might lead outside. It yielded to the pressure of her palm. Now Stela was the one who looked worried. "I know I left this door locked when I was here last week." I followed her into the bright day as she whistled again.

I couldn't see as much as the tip of a tail above the weedy grass rising toward the mid-May sun.

"Fellow!"

The weeds swayed as he came tunneling through, emerging with a pleased expression on his face.

"See," Stela said, crouching to pat the dog. "They always come back if you give them a little space to run."

Bet had expressed the same idea when she had counseled me not to leave Litton. I didn't point out to Stela that if dogs returned like boomerangs, there wouldn't be so many full-time dog catchers. People and dogs strayed every day; not all of them found their way back, or wanted to. You leave behind what's not important to you, glad to abandon the person, place, or thing that encumbers your trot toward the seductive unknown.

"Bad!" I scolded, snapping the leash onto Fellow's new collar. I had bought it at the store local people still called the "five and dime" even though there was nothing for sale there in that old-fashioned price range and damn little for under five dollars.

The Schooners key ring glinted in Stela's hand.

"Trouble is, these old locks are easy to jiggle open. I did it myself a couple of weeks ago when I forgot the key."

"Maybe the haunts have just been having a little fun with you." Fellow was struggling to haul me in the direction of the closest tourist cabin. I reached out and touched Stela's shoulder, a gesture completely uncharacteristic of me. "I don't suppose there's anything in those cabins."

Stela's face lit with a teacher's pleasure in the epiphany, even if one of a fairly low-wattage, of a C student. "I wondered," she said, "how long it would take you to ask."

Cut—To intersect by driving, sinking, or rising.

—Otis E. Young, Jr., in *Western Mining*

When any leads, lodes, or ledges, shall cross each other, the quartz ore or mineral, in the crevice or vein at the place of crossing, shall belong to, and be the property of the claimant upon the lead, lode or ledge first discovered.

—Section 4, in *The New Mining Law of Montana Territory*, Dec. 26, 1864

Breaking and Entering

FELLOW WAS DRAGGING ME THROUGH THE RIPPLING CLUMPS OF WILD grasses, a tugboat determined to tow a heavy-bottomed barge.

"If you ever have any children, be sure to ask me for a little advice about the value of loving discipline." As Stela caught up with Fellow and me, I shrugged. Did the strap that hung always handy on the back of the parents' bedroom door count as loving discipline?

"I think he recognizes this place." Fellow was sitting expectantly on the cabin's wooden porch his nose pointed toward the doorknob.

"Wouldn't be surprised. Nick sleeps here sometimes, and he feeds any stray that needs a meal. Stela's knuckles offered the door a gentle knock.

"What does Mort think about Nick?" As I intended, my question made Stela pause before she opened the cabin door. Despite my lust for another lucky strike, I was glad for the reprieve. At least in this moment, the cache of *East Bannack News Letters* did exist. At least in my imagination. At least until we opened the door. By turning the knob, I was inviting the dead hand of the past to yank them from the class of the missing, to re-categorize them as irrevocably lost.

Stela explained that yes, the nephew did know about Nick, who had a house of his own, after all, and who, in any case, wasn't hurting anything. On the contrary, Nick was serving as a kind of informal caretaker of Schooners, which otherwise would degenerate into who-knows-what: a handy place for a meth lab, maybe; a secluded spot for unsanctified sex, certainly.

Fellow's leash jumped in my hand. The dim room materialized around the gleam of the bowl from which Fellow was noisily lapping. His thirst satisfied, he began probing a sack of kibble stored neatly in a well-swept corner.

There was no furniture but a folding chair with "Elephant Rock County Museum" stenciled on its back and the battered card table that was keeping it company. There were no stacks of yellowing papers and no closets that could hide them.

Against one wall, a set of bunk beds floated under the fake billow of a canvas top unhidden by an intervening ceiling. The top bunk was empty, anchored by a tautly stretched blanket; the bottom mattress held stacks of canned vegetables and sardines—labels all carefully turned to face the room. A can of store-brand coffee, precisely folded overalls, a pyramid of balled socks struggled for space with the groceries on the narrow mattress. On the wood-burning stove in the corner, a scoured frying pan and an enamel coffeepot waited.

"Nick has another place, his own house, you said." I couldn't deny I was vexed at the blandness of the scene, at its quotidian and completely open aspect. On the other hand, a cache of the Bannack news sheets could well be stashed in one of the other cabins. Never mind that I couldn't quite remember why I had thought finding the cache was so important.

"Sure does, but it's filled to the rafters with things he's collected. That's what people say, anyway—that there's about enough room for a skinny man to slide sideways from room to room, and that's it. Of course, you can hear anything in this town. And since Nick isn't exactly the type to throw dinner parties for his friends, I doubt anyone has ever set foot in his house to see."

I imagined hoisting myself through Nick's window at three in the morning, running a flashlight up and down stacks of yellowing newspaper, making my discovery, and then my ecstatic escape. Perhaps I was my adoptive parents' daughter after all. As a child, I had perched in the back seat just as tense and eager as they were, Chas driving the back roads fast enough to whip a plume of dust into the half-deserted backcountry of Montana or North Dakota or Colorado; Bet keeping an eye out for collapsing homesteads, cabins without locks, any place where a nice bit of china or glass had been left behind, abandoned, belonging to no one, anyway no one who was present.

"Shall we look in some of the others?"

As Stela opened each cabin, I waited on the wooden steps with a catch in my throat. No use getting excited until there was something to get excited about, I counseled myself with the voice of my inner scholar—cold, dispassionate, destined to be ignored. Logic can exercise no real control over the thrust of desire, even (or maybe especially) academic desire.

None of the cabins was locked. None hid precious documents in any of their crannies. But nearly all of them showed signs of occupation. A heap of stained T-shirts and undershorts collected dust under one bottom bunk while the blue stripes of the top mattress sagged under a load of dirty dishes, down-at-the-heels boots, and tattered porn magazines. I worried when I saw ashes mounded in the grate of the squat stove that had been meant to comfort the spa's visitors when Montana's summer nights turned chilly.

"This isn't good," Stela said, following my gaze. "I told Nick to pass the word I don't want fires in these old stoves. The whole place could burn down, especially after the grass dries out this summer."

I was fretting about what the stoves might already have consumed, as eager to burn rare newspapers as they were to consume pinecones or branches broken into firewood. I was not reassured when, in the next cabin, I pinched ashy flakes of paper as fragile as butterfly wings. Ducking my head to avoid the damp diapers that hung from a stretch of twine, I stood up to inspect the rest of the room. Someone with a hunger to decorate or a need to shut out the outside chill had papered the log walls with pages cut from magazines that catered to 1970s working supermoms. Still-glossy photos of eggplant parmesan, mocha cheesecake, chicken noodle soup, broiled Cornish game hens glowed on the log walls.

"Look at this," Stela said. In the corner where a crib stood, its broken slats neatly mended with duct tape, the motif of the decor changed. Well-fed babies smiled in pictures clipped from what looked like relatively recent ads—that is to say, within the last twenty years—for disposable diapers and formula, the photos pieced over thick layers of newspapers, apparently added for extra insulation. I carefully peeled back the layers.

"Oh no," I said.

"It is terrible—someone having to take care of a baby in these conditions," Stela said, mistaking the cause of my distress. "There isn't even any plumbing or electricity out here, just in the restaurant and the spa. No wonder someone picked the lock to the restaurant's back door. Makes me glad I told Mort I'd pay the utility bills while I was making up my mind."

I was too upset to even pretend empathy for the mother who had set up illegal housekeeping.

"This is awful," I said, prying tacks and waving a fistful of crumbling broadsheets that carried World War II headlines. "She's found a stack of these old papers somewhere and stuffed them in here to keep out the drafts."

"Well," Stela said, carefully re-tacking the newspapers I had pulled away. "You don't really care about anything so new, do you?"

"If she found papers from the Forties, she might have come across stacks of older publication too, valuable ones." I tried not to sound as upset as I felt. "Is there any place we haven't checked?"

"Just the spa, and I've been all through that myself. But let's go over there anyway. I think we could use a nice, relaxing swim about now."

From the outside, the spa looked like someone had plopped an oversized shoebox in a grove of cottonwoods not far from the back of the restaurant. A massive willow, its golden branches washed with spring green, swept the building's mottled composition shingle roof with its emerging leaves. Inside, someone—presumably one of the Schooners—had not only painted the pool itself with a blaring blue, but had troweled the color half-way up the wall into a rough approximation of a rising surf. Time and persistent moist heat had skinned away the best of the fanciful veneer, penetrating back to bone grey.

Steaming slightly, the rectangle of water gleamed with a milky pearlescence. Fellow's toenails clicked as he paced the plunge's perimeter, whiffling its medicinal tang, and scowling with the same distaste I felt.

"The dressing room is over there," Stela said.

"I'd really better get back." I had never been skinny dipping, and I didn't want to start today.

"You don't have your period, do you?" Stela's smile was self-contained, amused. I thought of a smooth puzzle box the parents had found once in somebody's attic. Unable to open it and unwilling to smash it, they had sold it at a high price to someone intrigued by its seamless promise.

I shook my head no, but didn't venture another excuse. Still, instead of following Stela, I stopped to study a notice that overlaid the scabby blue of the painted surf in scabby white block printing: "Prairie Schooner Hot Springs is richer than many German spas and holds rare and healthful minerals: 1. Silica. 2. Iron. 3. Aluminum. 4. Calcium. 5. Magnesium. 6. Sodium. 7. Carbonate Radicle 8. Others too numerous to mention." Touching in its decayed self-importance, the listing hovered in the lifting steam.

I could hear the elixir gurgling from the pipes enclosed in the wrought iron cage that ran around the room. Concentrating on the urgent whispering, I forgot not to look when I heard the slap of Stela's bare feet. Unembarrassed, Stela grinned: "Last one in is a rotten egg." Her dive was clean and controlled.

It took me awhile to take Stela up on her invitation, mainly because, back in the ladies' dressing room, I had trouble convincing myself to piss in a steaming toilet. At least the old-fashioned flush cord dangling from above worked. I could only hope the effluvium didn't join the flow into the plunge.

Draped in fog, I told myself there probably was nothing unhygienic in the crusty deposit that ringed the plunge and nothing dangerous in the current of water that streamed from the pipe into the bottom of the pool.

Having taken the plunge, I started to enjoy myself. "I have to admit this is wonderful," I called to Stela. "Once you get used to the smell, anyway."

"What smell?" Stela said floating unembarrassed on her back, her body lifting in and out of the water, a blur. I hoped I would look so good at sixty. Fellow was still slinking around the edge of the plunge looking confused. Finally, he flattened himself into a dog rug, chin and tail and spread-eagled ears tacked down tight on the spa's tile floor, out of reach of the thickest steam.

Swaddled in the pool's white water, I felt well-clothed in an enormously fluid garment. The illusion was aided by the fact that I had left my glasses in the dressing room: The mists of nearsightedness added a reassuring density to the water's warm fog.

"The Prairie Schooner has quite a history." Now Stela's voice sounded very far away. It flowed thicker than the water, warm as honey.

Drifting away on the current it created, I remembered one of the few stories Chas had ever told me about his childhood on a farm in North Dakota, a farm he left after a fist fight with his father, a farm to which, as far as I knew, he'd never returned. The calcimined walls of the house—Chas had called it a shack—had oozed honey every spring.

He said his parents had tried everything—smoke, poison, even cutting a hole where they thought the queen might be. But no matter what they did, the bees stayed. Sometimes, Chas said, he still woke in the morning hearing their humming.

Lulled by the waters, I tried harder to listen to the hum of Stela's explanation. All the rich and famous who happened by Misfire found their way out to the spa for a drink or a swim, even though most of them stayed in the Anderson Hotel downtown, not in the tourist cabins.

"Private bathrooms, there, you know, with claw-foot tubs." Stela's voice was as serene as a lullaby. "Mort said his uncle always liked to tell the story about how President Truman's train made an unscheduled stop on the tracks over yonder before it got to Misfire on the president's explicit request. Apparently even in Washington, D.C., they'd heard about the spa."

Stela interrupted herself to swim a lazy lap around the plunge, her arms reaching out and into the water with a rhythm as steady as the ticking of a clock.

She drifted to a stop, as she approached me and flexed into a float. The milky water framed her face, an island in a warm sea, her body, an island barely submerged at high tide. "Gov. Nutter—he was the one who was killed in a plane crash later. Chief Justice Earl Warren. Even Gary Cooper—he was from Helena, you know. They all ate steak in the dining room. Hemingway is supposed to have said that the restaurant's backbar was the prettiest in Montana."

I hadn't noticed a backbar, only the silver dollars embedded in the bar's counter.

"Did Mort find the guest registers?" My need to solve the little mysteries of the past had resurfaced like a breaching whale. Hard to tell, but easy to fantasize about what else might have been cached with those records: A historian's porn.

"Not that I know of." Stela's weary tone made it clear that she was used to these kinds of inquiries from Luke.

"Do you think Nick might know?"

"Luke's asked him, and so have I. But he's funny about some things. You know how ranchers get offended when you ask them how many cattle they run?"

I'd never had much to do with ranchers, but I didn't want to say so.

"Nick seems to feel the same way when you try to pin him down on what he's found where. Anyway, do you really care? It's the newspapers you're interested in, right?"

I didn't answer Stela, but I did make an effort to quell my free-floating lust for a clue, any clue, even a clue to a minor mystery that I didn't have the time or the energy to chase down. It was clear my desire was an itch that needed to be scratched, a fact that an old-fashioned Freudian analyst would probably find more significant than I wanted to.

To avoid thinking too much about what I wanted to know and why, I used the edge of the plunge to pull myself free of the clasp of the hot water. Fellow reconstituted himself from rug to dog in one movement and galloped toward me, leaping for my bare knees.

"No! Get down!" I pushed Fellow away as Stela's laughter rose with the steam. For a change, Fellow obeyed, whirling to freeze with his nose pointed away from me to the hallway that to my eyes, still innocent of glasses, was a shadowy blotch. Fellow's ruff inflated itself into a reasonable facsimile of a spiked collar; he began vibrating with a growl bigger than he was.

"Who's there!" Stela demanded. The reply stripped me in an instant of the illusion that I wasn't really naked.

"Hello AJ," Litton said in the snarky tone I so well remembered. "I see you still have plenty of bounce even though you've joined the ranks of the unemployed."

My shock at hearing his voice slicing through the fog flared into anger.

Even when I had otherwise adored him, I had hated the sneer Litton had affected. To my disgust, Fellow's tail whirred into a voice-activated blur. My attempt at a dignified exit was undercut by the rage that made my hands shake even after I was safe in the dressing room.

"What does he want, do you suppose?" Stela seemed unruffled as she pulled up the zipper of her khaki pants.

"He's after something, that's for sure. He's coming up for post-tenure review next year without a new major publication. Maybe he thinks I'm onto something. He's certainly narcissistic enough to think that he could charm me into spilling my secrets. Has he contacted Luke at all?"

Stela answered in a way that made me think her honesty was battling with her marital loyalty. I ended up leaving convinced that Luke hadn't exactly been indiscreet, but that he had at least hinted I was pursuing an interesting lead.

Despite the fact that I was now completely clothed and my glasses clung tightly to the bridge of my nose, I felt as tense as I do when I'm faced with presenting a conference paper to a group of academic nitpick-ers from Defoe's flying island of Laputa. Back in the spa's bar, Litton had unstacked the chairs from a table and was scanning the room as though he expected a slow waitress to appear with an apology. Dressed for hunting big game in a made-in-Bangladesh camp shirt that intensified the blue of his colored contact lenses, he leaned like Rodin's thinker on a clenched fist. The biceps emerging from his short sleeves were new, probably ac-quired under the tutelage of the Wonder Woman graduate student.

Having lost the advantage of being the only one clothed, Litton listened with an interest too intense to be sincere as Stela reiterated her stories about Prairie Schooner for his benefit.

"It's just like Christmas!" Litton sang out with a disingenuous enthusiasm; red and green globules of light percolated through the glass blocks of the back bar. When I was his infatuated student, I had loved his childlike outbursts, the oral equivalent of e-mail emoticons. I wondered why Stela hadn't illuminated the backbar for me. I hated Litton as he stepped into the center of the dance floor, a safety net that bounced the globules of light ceilingward.

"What time is it?" I said with intentional rudeness.

"Oh, I think about six." Stela said in the smooth tones of a practiced diplomat.

Litton pulled out a cell, even trendier and more expensive than the one he had carried when last I had seen him. His voice was caressing. "You have quite a time sense, Stel—it's five fifty-nine on the dot." Stela looked amused, but contemptuous.

"Whatever time it is, I have to go," I said. "So why don't you just tell me why you're here and what you want."

"Well, AJ, negative as always. I just wanted to see if I could help you sort out your discovery."

"What discovery?"

"That old fogey Luke hasn't spoken to me ever since I reviewed his last book," Litton said answering my unspoken question despite the fact that the "old fogey's" wife was listening. In response, she strode, pointedly I thought, to the door. "But he let the cat out of the bag to Katharine when she called him to find out if you'd made it to town. Anyway, he told her that you had been handed a document that you weren't eager to share. She happened to mention that conversation when I talked to her after the end-of-year departmental meeting."

Thanks Katharine, I thought as Stela jangled her key ring and Litton rattled on undeterred. He was in the neighborhood anyway, he insisted on explaining, to meet an editor at the University of Utah to discuss a possible project. Instead of challenging that obviously false tale, I cut right to the chase.

"I hope that project had nothing to do with me. Frankly, I think it's strange in the extreme Katharine would be so indiscreet as to discuss my life with you."

"Professional life—not personal. She and I are both concerned about your lack of publication. When I approached her about the possibility of mentoring a junior faculty member with a co-authored project, your name came up. Whatever you think, I still care about your future, and Katharine knows that."

I shrugged an exaggerated shrug, understanding that in Katharine's administrative universe, the suggestion probably made sense. My efficient chair would have seen a collaborative project as an opportunity for moving both me and Litton out of the publication danger zone. Maybe she even harbored the mistaken idea that our marriage might be rebooted.

"It's not going to happen," I assured Litton without denying the possibility that I had struck academic gold: I wanted to tantalize—no, torture—him with that idea. Instead of responding, Litton fussed over Fellow and took his oh-so-charming leave from Stela.

Litton kept his distance the next few days, a strategy that made me nervous. Rheta heard he was staying in the town's only bed and breakfast, owned by the Sundress Woman I had met at the Ingrahams' rummage sale my first weekend in town. Since Litton was the only customer she'd had for a while, he was getting bacon and eggs and Crystal Starr in bed every morning. According to the Golden Hour gossips, anyway.

I developed the habit of passing Crystal Starr's house on my early morning walks with Fellow. The widow's walk encircling the top of the house like a wrought iron crown of thorns was fascinating, I told myself. The mansion had been raised by a local rancher to impress the townies. His last descendent, a grey-haired great-grand-daughter, had lived there with her encampment of cats until the monstrous house got too much for her. After she died without heirs, the house was sold at auction attended heavily by local people, none of whom bid. Too many of them had watched the cracks in the brick walls widening since 1959. The quake that had buried Yellowstone Park campers as they slept had rocked Misfire's windows and walls, too. Passing through town on her way to Salt Lake, Crystal Starr saw the auction signs.

Or so Rheta told me, and I had never once found Rheta to be inaccurate.

Crystal Starr had sunk the money she'd earned running a health food restaurant in Costa Mesa into renovating the house and redecorating it in the touristy Western style that mixed suitably distressed furniture purchased at local rummage sales with neo-Navajo blankets imported from China, cow skulls ordered from a catalog, and fabrics printed with cowboy hats, boots, and spurs.

She had cut down the willows that had wept in the front yard so that the mansion would show better from the street, hacked down the Virginia creeper that had veiled the brick walls. Discovered the cracks and tried, unsuccessfully, to renege on the deal. Gave up and waited for customers. Fertilized and watered the amputated stumps of the vines. Eventually opened an antique shoppe on the first floor, to the chagrin of her neighbors, who had decided too late their traditional Western opposition to the imposition of zoning laws might be a mistake. Got herself written up in the Butte paper as an example of one of Montana's resourceful new entrepreneurs.

By taking up with Crystal Starr, Litton was disappointing me yet again. He should at least have remained faithful to history, if not to me; he should have resorted to a sleeping bag at the KOA before settling into a bed that had to bear the burden of a polyester quilt.

By the start of the second week, I realized stalking was becoming a habit with me. Litton must be enjoying the implication of my strolls past the mansion, my surreptitious glances up at the lace curtained windows. His ostentatious refusal to attempt further contact was no doubt part of his plan to make me regret my hasty refusal and to fertilize any seeds of jealousy leftover from our marriage. Well, enough of all that.

Fellow was getting too used to heading for the mansion: he pulled me in that direction Monday morning with our first step out the alley door. It took considerable tugging and a Milkbone to convince him to take a novel route. "This way! This way!" I said in my jolliest voice. I should have remembered that danger attends every route that leads to the unknown.

We had just crossed the railroad tracks in back of the museum when Fellow compacted himself into an abrupt stop, making me stumble to avoid rear-ending him. His nose stabbed the air. A yellow Lab the size of a small bear stood a few yards ahead, head held down, lips stripped back. I like Labs, but this one seemed to be determined to demonstrate that the famously friendly breed has its exceptions.

"Let's go, Fellow." I forced my tone into a calm, firm register, just the way the dog training book I had checked out from the town's turreted Carnegie library advised.

Fellow stared, his hackles rising like a porcupine's quills. When he moved forward, his legs, stiff with aggression, forgot they could bend. The Lab started bellowing, its ears pressed to the knob of its skull, its tail swishing in a lowdown frenzy. Worse still, reinforcements were arriving: a blue heeler with a mean glint in its mismatched eyes.

"Get away!" I yelled. Fellow was bobbing up and down, his bark ripping through the dusk.

There was a squeal of brakes and the clank of a pickup door.

"Get home, damn you! Get out of here!" It was John Storey swinging a rolled-up *Sun*. The attackers turned tail, and Fellow wasn't fool enough to try to follow them. Instead he converted his energies to groveling his grateful appreciation. I knew that I, too, owed Mr. Courteous-Aggressive a certain debt of gratitude.

"Thank you," I said, my knees locking into a human version of stiff-legged aggression as Storey's fingers found the sweet spot behind Fellow's ears.

"Would have done it for anyone," he said, walking toward his truck, the code of the West as it related to rescuing besieged women having been fulfilled. I noticed he was wearing grass-stained sneakers instead of his fancy boots. Before he mounted the running board, he paused. "Any dog walker with the sense that God gives a sheep carries pepper spray."

Duty discharged, he rode into the sunset, leaving me angry and lustful. One thing for sure, I liked him no better than before.

Back at the *Sun* Rheta was ready with more bad news: Mr. Courteous-Aggressive was organizing a special meeting of the Elephant Rock Business Association to consider upgrading Storey's personal peeve into an official project.

"Picked the evening of our publication day just to spite us," Rheta told me. "He thinks that we won't be able to get anything in the paper about what happens if he waits until after our usual press run. That way we'll either look like incompetent fools the next day when the *Butte Standard* has the story and we don't. Or we'll look like we're trying to suppress the boycott by refusing to report it. But if he thinks he can whip us that easily, he has another think coming."

Rheta dropped her voice on the last few words and turned her attention to the newspaper's front entrance.

"What can I do for you today, Adon?" I took Rheta's cordiality as a personal compliment, even though she had no idea she was addressing my brother. He was alone today—no elegant Nancia in sight.

"I've brought you a news release announcing the Bannack Days tryouts in the hope that you'll be kind enough to get it in this week's paper, preferably on the front page." Adon was dressed in his usual crisp Mr. Ranger shirt and ironed jeans. Over his arm he carried a silver-toned garment bag, zipped tight to protect its contents. Redirecting his glance to me, he added, "Also, if you have time, I'd like you to come out to the truck with me to look at some finish options for your bookshelves."

"So you're that far along already?" The pleasure in my voice was real. The shelves that had started out as a means to an end were about to assert their right to a place in my life. In response to my enthusiasm, my brother offered me a genuinely warm smile. The weird sexual tension between us had disappeared. Perhaps I had imagined it.

He draped the garment bag over the counter.

"Here's your new costume. I wonder if you could try it on because it's the prototype for the rest of the dancehall girl set. I don't want to wait for the dress rehearsal in case there are any unpleasant surprises."

I expected Rheta to tell Adon to return later in the week, after the paper was out. It was, after all, Monday, and we had a lot to do. Instead, she reached for the bag.

"Will you watch the front for a few minutes, AJ—I'll be back in two shakes of a lamb's tail."

In fact, Rheta was gone for at least ten minutes, during which Adon tried to convince me that I should accept a part in the Bannack Days street play myself.

"You would be a perfect Martha Vail," he said with the same sort of frank look of assessment he probably used in high-grading the wood he used in his carpentry. "As a historian, you may remember her, the sheriff's sister-in-law, the one who cooked for him and nursed him through his illnesses after his wife left."

"I do know a little about her." I felt a sudden impulse to run upstairs to check on the ledger. My research project had been stuck in limbo, and not only because of the arrival of Bet and Chas. I knew Martha Vail might help save my scholarly ass, if only I would give her the chance. But in taking that chance I would have to expose the ledger not only to Luke, but to the possibility that my speculations about the clipping from the *News Letter* would be unsupportable by any kind of evidence. I could well imagine how pleased Litton would be to publish a thorough critique of my theories, especially if he couldn't figure out how to reap a share of academic glory from the project,

"Lots of people find the play fun," Adon pointed out. "Nancia thought as long as you're going to be here for a while, getting involved might give you a chance to meet a few more people and to take part in the community."

The strips of plastic at the back of the newspaper swayed, and Rheta emerged swinging her hips in lilac satin with a décolletage that dipped dangerously to advertise just how sexy a woman in her sixties could look. The living embodiment of the frontier myth's favorite woman: the successful lady of the evening, as glamorous and as available as a French pastry in a bakery window, complete with a heart of gold. I saw that Rheta believed in the role, in its seductive blend of epic tawdriness and defiance and soiled saintliness.

"You're perfect, Rheta!" Adon's honest admiration made me smile. My brother really was a nice man. Given his sterling character, maybe his mother—our mother—was a kinder person than I'd taken her for. After all, I'd caught her by surprise on the phone. She'd said some harsh things to me, but maybe the shock of hearing my voice had shaken her into uncharacteristic anger. Maybe she was waiting for me to try again.

"Not half bad—especially in comparison to those tacky red and black costumes we've been wearing since Hector was a pup." I was surprised to hear how normal Rheta sounded, speaking out of all that satin and sexuality.

"Your costume won't be nearly as exotic, I'm afraid," Adon told me. "You'll be wearing grey, but it's real silk, and I think you'll like it."

Rheta grinned at me. "So you've joined the Community Players? You'd be perfect as the narrator."

Adon corrected her gently. "No, Luke will be the narrator as usual. I'm hoping AJ will take on Martha Vail. Do you think Conrad might be well enough by July to glue on his mustaches and pour out the whiskey in Skinner's Saloon?"

Rheta said she expected Conrad would probably rely on grow, not glue, even though they'd shaved the mustache off in the hospital. Conrad had been moved out of the cardiac ICU into a regular hospital room and was talking about coming home, I myself didn't expect to see him anytime soon. In fact, I didn't want to see him anytime soon. When Conrad reappeared in the *Sun*, the need for me to play reporter would disappear. Then I would have to get serious in figuring out what the hell I was doing in Misfire.

As she spoke, Rheta blinked rapidly, perhaps realizing for the first time that she was going to need something to keep Conrad occupied and out of her way when he resurfaced, sooner or later, in our lives. Instead of voicing that thought, she agreed that the play would offer me the perfect opportunity to get to know some folks. I refrained from commenting on the obvious—that I wasn't going to be in Misfire long enough to make getting to know folks a worthwhile activity. Still, I couldn't help but feel tempted: the play would give me the excuse to spend time with my brother without having to reveal my connection to him. Maybe Everonica might even run over from Bozeman and drop by rehearsal some evening. Or she might come to the performance. Recognize me. Feel a surge of maternal instinct. Rush to embrace me. Beg my forgiveness.

Recognizing the milky warmth of rising hope, I was indulging myself in another fantasy. "Thanks, but no thanks," I said. "I really need to concentrate on my research right now. Besides I'm no good at acting."

"Acting!" Bet said in a bright tone that presaged trouble as she sashayed in, a crisp white T-shirt and lime-green shorts showing off her well-toned calves to perfection.

I couldn't stop the flush from firing my face.

"Did I hear something about acting?" Bet asked, her voice a heat-seeking missile. She sidled in a little too close to Adon and struck a pose, hand on hip, chin tipped up.

Oh me. Oh my. There was no escaping this one, whatever this one turned out to be.

Here was a town all full of temptation, gambling, dance halls, etc., and us poor miners had to help them keep up and many a one . . . went to excess . . . .

—Henry J. Bose, in *Not in Precious Metals Alone: A Manuscript History of Montana*, edited by the Montana Historical Society

Side Trip

As I lifted the postcard to the spot just in front of my nose, Fellow nudged my bare feet with his cool nose. His moaning could have earned him an Oscar. Doing my best to ignore him, I pulled the image slowly away, trying for perspective, concentrating on the vines that squiggled across the *Magic Eye* image. Circa 1994, the card was a gift from Bet, who was bubbling after her success in convincing Adon to cast her as one of the dance hall girls in the Bannack Days play. When she pushed the *Magic Eye* booklet into my hand, I shuddered to think of my adoptive mother and my natural brother hobnobbing. Or maybe I had trembled with jealousy. After all, Adon never had offered me much more than the professional courtesy he practiced daily as Mr. Ranger. But he had smiled with real amusement at Bet's fast-talking sales pitch. I tried and failed to imagine how they would feel about each other if the truth came out.

I did know how I felt about that possibility. Misfire was starting to reconfigure itself from a town to a trap, from a quest to a terrible mistake. All the portents were flashing green for "go," for "get out of there."

"That Crystal Starr is a haggler when it comes to buying, but when it comes to selling, she won't give up a penny." Bet was waving the booklet like a guerdon in her upraised hand. Besides the booklet, she handed me an envelope that carried my name written in the ornate cursive that Litton deployed for official purposes.

She had arrived at eleven the night before, precisely when we needed help the most in pulling the papers off the press and getting them into the hands of the efficient mailroom crew. The postmaster had agreed to meet us at the post office ten minutes before midnight so that we wouldn't miss our official Wednesday publication date. "He's an old friend," Rheta said, managing to wink playfully despite everything. Although we had the satisfaction of knowing we had outsmarted John Storey's effort to ensure that the Butte paper wouldn't scoop us, no one was crowing. It was impossible to pretend that the Elephant Rock Business Association meeting had been anything other than a lynching party in dishonor of Rheta and me.

I should have appreciated Bet both for showing up and for bringing along a present to cheer me up. But knowing my adoptive mother, I understood that her gift was meant to accomplish more than one objective. On its thin-skinned surface, the booklet invited me to share Bet's pleasure in a little treasure that, although it cost too much, was almost worth the price. Lurking at the level of the dermis was a reminder that Bet (unlike me) always carried a big wad of cash in her pocketbook. Sunk deeper still in its dank subcutaneous reaches, the statement was veined with a rewrite of the Biblical parable of the foolish (non)virgin (me) who, failing to keep the light of passion burning, had tossed her husband away into the arms of a woman with plenty of heat to spare. The fact the gift arrived in the company of a note from my former husband made Bet's message Crystal clear.

"Well, good luck to Crystal Starr," I wanted to tell Bet and would have, too. But Chas arrived loaded with cartons fragrant with the Golden Hour's bar-hoppers' chow mein special.

"Come on, open it!" Bet exclaimed. I pretended to think that she meant the booklet—a hard fiction for me to maintain: I was already flipping through it. Fortunately, Chas thrust a white carton into her grasp, just as she was about to snatch the letter back to tear into it herself.

Now it was hours later, and I still hadn't broached the envelope. Instead, dawn's early light had caught me pacing, completely unwilling to be subjected to anything Litton wanted, but completely unable to imagine myself going to bed alone.

The *Magic Eye* directions said—in English, in Spanish, in French—that you could see a picture within a picture if you held your eyes right. "The time," the directions said, "it takes to see the image can vary, so don't get

discouraged! El tiempo que tarda en ver la imagen varía, así ¡que no se desa-
nime! Le temps qu'il faut pour voir l'image peut varier: ne vous décourager
pas!"

"Just wait." Fellow's moaning was escalating into a pretty fair imitation
of the courthouse siren. I was unmoved. The alley's gravel was probably still
damp in the spot where he had lifted his leg after we had run the papers to
the post office.

"Does it really matter if we get there at any particular time?" Rheta's
sense of urgency seemed vastly misplaced: we were, after all, hustling to
trumpet our own obituary. Without a word, Rheta kept loading the mail-
bags into Conrad's Scout, but I knew she was as discouraged as I was. John
Storey had all too easily persuaded most of the attending members of the
Association to vote in favor of the boycott. In response to my question,
Rheta should have given me a lecture on the legal and ethical obligations
a newspaper has to meet its own deadlines. Instead, she climbed into the
Scout to ferry the papers the two blocks to the post office. Bet and Chas
departed to fill the newspaper dispensers on the A&W side of town while I
took care of the rest—or at least the ones that were accessible so early. And
then I returned to the apartment, but not to sleep.

"Stop that," I hissed. Fellow was hurling himself in circles, dodging
rocker, table, and brass lamp by fractions. By that time, the oily reveille of
Rheta's coffee had begun seeping into the apartment. Rheta, despite her
midnight veneer of determined calm, must, like me, be tensing herself to
face the ominous new day. The lead headline in our late-night publication
proclaimed the Elephant Rock Business Association's assault with the determined bravery of a late-stage cancer patient announcing her own illness,
along with assurances that chances for survival were very, very good.

As the courthouse clock struck seven, I tried looking not at the card,
but through it, as the directions advised. Its squiggling vines squiggled still.
The elephant refused to appear. I slipped on my shoes, secured the leash to
Fellow's collar. Downstairs, trouble waited in the form of another agitated
early bird: Delores was leaning on the counter, the blades of her cheekbones
sheathed in her hands, her elbows tacking down a fresh newspaper. Rheta
was nowhere in sight. Perhaps she had gone to check on her mother in the
nursing home.

"Did I quote you correctly?" I asked Delores. Fellow's toenails scrabbled for a purchase as he endeavored to haul me to the purple stroller parked just inside the office's front window. Baby Jack was sprawled with his head back, his eyes closed, his mouth slightly open. I couldn't help remembering one of the irrelevant details I'd learned as the parents' unwilling sidekick: collectors loved rare closed-mouthed dolls because the open-mouthed ones, presumably modeled after real babies, were the common ones.

Delores straightened. "If you don't pull this story, I'll hire a lawyer. You have no right to mix me up in this fight."

I didn't feel strong enough to argue with one of the few people in town I counted as an ally. But, I had no choice. For now, at least, I still represented the *Sun*.

"It was a public meeting; you're a public employee. We had the perfect right to quote you. You were the only one who had the knowledge to explain how difficult it is to keep the ghost town from sinking into ruin, even without a mine in its backyard."

"I was there only as an observer. If Rheta hadn't asked me all those questions, I wouldn't have said a word. Your story didn't make that clear at all. Where is she, anyway?"

I explained I didn't know. That in any case the papers had already been delivered to the newsstands and the post office. That the *Butte Montana Standard* would probably quote her as well. Emotion—anger? fear?—sharpened her face.

"I don't think you need to worry," I added. "You didn't do anything wrong."

Delores turned to her son and scooped him up as if he needed waking from a bad dream. With the baby out of reach, Fellow settled for snuffling around Delores's legs.

"You don't understand. At my pay grade, I'm not supposed to try to influence public policy—just carry it out. When my superior reads this, she's going to have every right to call me on the carpet, and maybe worse." She jounced the silent baby on her shoulder as if he were crying.

"I'm sorry," I said. "You're welcome to write a letter to the editor clarifying your position."

For a few heartbeats, I imagined myself back safe in my academic cubbyhole. Historians expose secrets, destroy reputations, impugn the honor of whole generations. But their subjects are usually safely dead. The men and women once extolled as intrepid pioneers, now impugned by many as destroying invaders, continue to disintegrate in their graves, as indifferent (although far less durable) as granite. Sheriff Henry Plummer does not care that revisionists are trying to salvage his reputation a century after he asked for a good drop on that bitter January night in Bannack. Nor does he know his sister-in-law fainted at the news of his death and later carefully preserved the record of his death in a homely ledger that had swum upstream into hands that were grasping for a life preserver, namely mine.

Wondering whether I was sinking or swimming, I winced when Delores abandoned her attempt to save herself through intimidation and offered me an apparently genuine smile.

"Oh well. As you already know, I've been thinking about resigning anyway. And that is not for publication."

"No," I agreed, relieved (and hating myself for that relief) that Delores hadn't mentioned the ledger—demanded it back or tried to use it as leverage.

"If there's anything I can do," I said, meaning it—at least meaning it within certain limits, but wishing Delores would leave. Besides, Rheta would be back any minute, and she didn't need any more problems this morning.

"You *could* try to retrieve the papers left on the newsstands and print a different version, leaving my name out of it."

Delores did not bother to pause to wait for my response, obviously not expecting me to take the suggestion seriously. "Just take care of that ledger," she finally said, returning Jack to the stroller and agitating Fellow into keening a protest and lurching into an attempt to follow.

"I'll talk to you about it one of these days when things calm down."

"That may be never, the way things look now."

By the time Fellow had finished galloping through our morning walk, Rheta was ripping tear sheets for the advertisers at the front counter, a task that would require a pitifully small expenditure of time and effort. Her normally creamy complexion had soured to a yellowish tinge; her lips were colorless and chapped without their usual sunset glow.

I should tell her now, but I didn't want to deepen the shadows under her eyes. I should tell her that Delores wasn't the only one planning to quit. After all, the lie I had concocted about my sudden need to depart would be better delivered now while Rheta was too beset to question it closely. I had received an urgent call from my department chair, I would tell her. I had to pack up and leave town by the end of next week in order to prevent my leave from becoming a termination.

I should tell her. Instead, I asked, "Any reaction around town to our new competitor?" The association, besides officially endorsing a boycott of the *Sun* and re-affirming its support of GoldPro, had announced the Butte paper would immediately begin a daily "Misfire Edition."

During the meeting, John Storey had tried to stare me down as he urged local readers to drop their subscriptions to the *Sun*. The Butte reporter had drummed a frantic rhythm on his laptop as if the announcement were news to him. He was introduced later as the new Misfire bureau chief.

"Do I have to report that," I had asked sitting down to the Underwood after the meeting ended.

"Report everything important," Rheta had replied. I had typed:

> The acting editor of the *Sun-Tribune* last night vowed to continue reporting all sides of local news while reserving the right to take editorial stands on controversial issues. Rheta Fox's statement came in the wake of the Elephant Rock Business Association's decision Wednesday night to boycott the local newspaper and to support the out-of-town *Butte Montana Standard*'s new "Misfire Edition." Association members approved the resolution, unprecedented in the organization's history, 24-18, after a heated debate in which some members blasted the *Sun*'s stand against a proposed mining development near the historic Grasshopper Creek that runs through the historic ghost town of Bannack. (See related story on this page.) Citing the newspaper's First Amendment right to freedom of expression, Fox asked local merchants how they could in good conscience ask county residents to support their businesses while urging local readers to subscribe to the *Standard*'s new publication.

"I'd like to point out that the *Sun-Tribune* is a taxpaying member of this business community—not to mention, a member of this group," she said in casting the *Sun*'s negative vote against the proposals "If you boycott us because you disagree with our editorial stand, maybe we should urge local residents to go out of town to buy their cars and clothes and even groceries because we disagree with you. But we won't, because that's not the American way—or at least it shouldn't be. The American way should be to talk things over not try to kick in the face of the guy you disagree with.'"

Looking over my shoulder, Rheta had directed me to write a sidebar explaining that the newspaper had been published late to allow for coverage of the meeting. Despite her exhaustion, she also took the trouble to pat my back and praise the improvements in my news writing style—comments I once would have resented.

Now, whatever personal reserves Rheta had exhausted to get the paper out the night before seemed to be regenerating themselves. As I helped her load the last batch of newspapers, the ones meant for local businesses that wouldn't open until nine o'clock, I thought of the way the hot springs at Schooners drew replenishing water from stone as fast as its flow was being sucked away to feed the plunge. With determination rehydrating her face, she announced, "When I dropped the Snappy Service's papers off a little while ago, Matt Loomis said he wasn't going to support any damned boycott."

"Can I quote him?"

"Better ask. In fact, it probably would be good to get started right away on a follow-up. I suppose I'd better drive up to Missoula after we get finished here and break the news to Conrad in person. It's just a good thing my mother is making a good adjustment to the rest home. Anyway, this is getting to be a big enough mess the *Missoulian* might run a few inches on it. I don't want Conrad to find out about that way—it's liable to give him another heart attack, just when they're talking about releasing him."

In fact, I did not spend the afternoon polling local merchants on whether they planned to join the boycott. Instead, a few hours later, I was 130 miles away twisting enthusiastically under the weight of my former husband, having rashly remembered on the way back from a trek to see dinosaur eggs what I had once liked about Litton. In truth, it had to be either Litton or Mr. Courteous-Aggressive. Better the devil I knew.

Showing up at midmorning, Litton had repeated the contents of the note Bet had delivered for him: an invitation for a quick trip to Bozeman, a roadside picnic and a drop-in visit to the Museum of the Rockies, where a mutual friend of ours worked as education director and documents curator. He gilded his invitation with what he no doubt imagined was an irresistible tease: "I made the appointment before I left Seattle because I have something interesting to show him, a letter from—well, probably I shouldn't say."

He paused expectantly, his offer clear: "I'll show mine if you show yours." When I didn't respond, he upped the ante. "If I ask him, Harold might have time to look at your document, too." He paused a little too long to achieve the off-hand effect he was aiming for. "What is it, exactly?"

"No thanks." Harold had been my friend longer than Litton's, but never mind. Despite my negative response, I did feel a little tempted to disentangle myself from Misfire for a few hours so I could decide exactly how I was going to deliver my bad news to Rheta. Actually, I wouldn't mind getting another opinion on the ledger if I could carve out a few minutes with Harold without Litton. Perhaps I could even think of an excuse to get Litton to drive me past Everonica's house.

"Come on," he wheedled. "It'll be fun. And I promise not to ask one more question about your secret project if that's what you're worried about."

"Ha." But my resolve was weakening even as my suspicions worked up a sweat.

Then Litton offered his final bribe: a stop at a real coffee shop for a cup to stay and a supply of fresh roasted beans to go. I'd been making do with the grocery store brand since I ran out of my own supply. Besides, I had heard good things about the espresso bars of Bozeman, not only the one owned by a film star, but its half-dozen competitors. Apparently there was no shortage of customers willing to stand in line for latte and biscotti in the former cowtown, which, despite the recession, was hanging onto its status as a get-away destination for three subspecies of the well-to-do: the rich and famous, the merely rich, and the fortunate offspring of one or the other—the trust-fund babies who, despite the reversals of the recession, were optimistic enough to keep pursuing big skies and snowlight. If the economy didn't improve, they would have to go to work. In the meantime, they adopted a Montana address as their privilege. Nor was there a shortage of the kind of well-educated underachievers willing to grind beans and foam milk in genteel poverty in exchange for winter skiing at Bridger Bowl and summer backpacking into the Crazy Mountains.

I got through the first half of the trip well enough by plopping a Johnny Cash CD into the car sound system, my best candidate for a singer certain to make Litton subside into irritated silence. Maybe I did need one of the fancy new whatever devices with earphones. For now, I would have to rely on my growing skills of deception and misdirection.

"What?" I would ask every time Litton opened his mouth to compete with Johnny. Eventually he gave up.

Even after he stabled the car in a spot where the shoulder of the road widened, I kept the conversation pointed away from myself and to marshlands. Thank goodness for the borrow pits and the life they supported. Litton, who obviously still considered himself a better-than-average amateur naturalist, couldn't resist showing off. I let him run with his lecture, refusing his wine, munching his Safeway French bread, and concentrating more on the flash of red-winged blackbirds than on what he was saying.

The sun reached down through the bursting leaves of the willows to lightly touch the back of my neck. Litton was swatting at something considerably more substantial than filtered light. I considered offering him a spritz of the insect repellant in my saddlebag, but decided a little suffering would be good for his soul. Sheep blatted from the field across the road as vehicles passed at long intervals, most of them pickups, all of them branded with local plates. As each driver took the curve past us, a sun-baked arm saluted us, fulfilling the Montana dictum that hospitality must be offered to strangers, if only with the flash of an open hand.

We took the long way around. After Twin Bridges and Silver Star, the road undulated up and down hills that overlooked hay fields, spring bright under sprinkler-induced rainbows. The green softened outside the territory patrolled by the massive wheel lines. Beyond the irrigated fields, wild grasses drifted to foothills still cloaked in winter browns and then climbed to the shifting border where the soft grays and purples of the higher slopes gave way to the gleam of peaks where the snow never completely melted. I wondered how soon global warming would change that.

When we returned to the car, Litton held silent, limiting himself to asking me if I wanted to explore the gravel road that slid off the main road behind a fishing access sign that announced "Parrot Castle." Later, I looked up Parrot Castle, finding the name represented just another dreary instance of emigrants trying to mark the landscape by calling it after themselves. R.P.

Parrot had built a mill to process ore and left his name on the place, proof of his existence.

"Better not," I said, my voice blending with the air rushing through the window. I didn't want to leave Fellow alone too long. Litton accepted my refusal with no comment; the summer-like warmth of the day had seemed to leach his usual bright volubility away leaving only a quiet glimmer. I thought of the difference between mica and real gold. Mica glitters wildly and shatters under pressure. Gold glows softly and can endure the blow of a hammer. Maybe I needed to re-assay the character of my former husband.

Maybe not. Approaching Whitehall, where we would have to leave the two-lane to join the interstate race toward Bozeman, Litton squinted at a mountain scoured into a massive cliff stained with vertical streaks of rust and dirty yellow.

"That's an interesting formation. It reminds me of the ones I've seen in Southern Utah." His voice had taken on the unctuous slickness of someone who believed he ought to express an opinion, even without the grounding of relevant facts.

"It must be the local gold mining operation." I struggled out of the clasp of the seat to sit up for a better view. I shuddered at the idea of this stripped and sterile mountainside transposed on the slopes that climbed the sky in back of Bannack.

"Well, for my money, it doesn't look half-bad. Just another variation in the landscape. And think of all the local jobs."

I refrained from commenting about the ditches that still etched Bannack one hundred and thirty years after the mining boom, the heaps of tailings where mosquitoes had bred every summer since.

My ersatz contentment chilled further when Litton pushed the buttons that sealed the windows and activated the air conditioning. Soon the atmosphere chilled to temperatures that reminded me of my last snowy trip to Bozeman, ill-conceived, cold, and futile. At least it wasn't snowing this time. As the Taurus sped past rumbling recreational vehicles and trucks and Trailways busses, I glimpsed a meadowlark on a fence post, beak raised skyward. I tried to run down the window to catch its song, but my ex-husband had activated the vehicle's child lock system.

"Look at that oriole!" Litton said. No longer content with wordlessness, he launched into an extended description of the construction of interstate highways contrasted to the building of the railways in the Intermountain West, a topic that I did not find riveting. Really, I decided, Litton wasn't worth either liking or disliking; he was just another pedantic professor, as common as the dandelion and just as persistent.

When it turned out Harold was in the hospital with a broken leg sustained in a hang-gliding accident the weekend before, I felt so pleasantly detached from Litton that I easily restrained myself from mentioning he should have called to confirm his appointment.

Instead, I circled the exhibits as placidly as if Litton had been a stranger who just happened to be passing through the dinosaur hall at the same time as I was.

"Don't you just hate all this plastic and papier-mâché, or whatever it is?" Litton said, not bothering to whisper. His voice reverberated against models of three quetzalcoatlus models, immobile in imitation flight over our heads.

"Not really," I said, stopping to examine a collection clustered under glass: unremarkable ovoids to an untutored gaze like mine, just another clutch of stones laid down by an earth fecund with stones. It was impossible for me to imagine they held unhatched dinosaurs—tightly curled embryos trapped unborn in the uplands between the rising infant mountains and the spreading ancient seas. No wonder the museum devoted so much of its floor space to reconstructions that revived the ghosts of a presumed deep history. "Now why don't they have more of this sort of thing," Litton said, rapping his knuckles on the glass, but his eyes fished other corners for color, life, entertainment.

Freed by the divorce from any obligation to curb Litton's behavior, I loved not having to cringe at his pretensions. Still, a little distance might be in order. Anchoring myself on the outer rim of the tour group, I noticed how its members stood politely attentive, bearing up well despite the weight of their fanny packs and cameras. Frozen in stereotype, they might have been part of the exhibit, a diorama of the behavior of domesticated tourists. At what age do people fossilize themselves into their roles? When did John Storey become Mr. Courteous-Aggressive? Conrad, the hard-drinking editor? Rheta, the prostitute with the heart of gold? Bet and Chas, peripatetic prospectors after good fortune?

"Now, I want you all to take note of the many features of this exhibit, which features maiasaura, the dinosaur whose name means Good Mother

Lizard," the volunteer docent said in a voice that had probably carried to the very back of the classroom for at least forty years. I cringed a bit at the volume and retreated a couple of paces, stumbling over Litton's feet, size sixteen pickaxes, thinly gilded with polished leather, probably Italian. He steadied me in a grip that I waltzed out of, but not before startling at the zing of static electricity. Hoping he hadn't felt the charge, I concentrated on the exhibit, a mild-eyed maternal monster perched at the edge of her nest, her head bent protectively toward her hatchlings.

"Let's get out of here," I said, wanting the slapping rush of a very hot cup of very good coffee.

And the jolt of two double espressos sipped in quick succession under track lighting did push me into a facsimile of jittery happiness.

"Want to go see Harold in the hospital?" Litton's voice vibrated in counterpoint to the hiss of steam. He looked good under the glare of the lights, his shirt collar open a calculated two buttons, his eyes, vivid.

"No."

"I like you like this, AJ."

The third double espresso was curling my tongue.

"You should have liked me sooner."

Litton and I always had been good at repartee, dueling wittily even when enraged. Perhaps we thought someone was listening and making notes for a new screenplay. Litton's hand reached for me, caressed the tips of my fingers to communicate a facsimile of regret. I expected that. Didn't expect the shudder.

"Do you mind, then, if we make another quick stop? There's a restored Milwaukee Road hotel I'd like to see just out of town."

Everything was settled. I didn't protest when he signed us in Mr. and Mrs., just waited in the gleam of the black and white tiles of the lobby floor, stared out to the lawn through the length of the veranda. The sun was catching the whipping twist of translucent fishing line as a blonde man in khaki shorts and a T-shirt that said "Princeton" practiced his casting again and again, undiscouraged that he'd never catch a rainbow trout in the short-clipped Kentucky blue.

Litton made a tentative pass toward the cavernous lobby with its fireplace as big as an elevator. But I reached for his elbow and ushered him to the staircase, to our room, which had traded nineteenth-century authenticity for twenty-first-century comforts. Opened my mouth in hunger as he opened his, my vagina flooding. Shed my clothes in a cascade, as he, just as needy, shed his. It wasn't love, but it was good. Afterwards, when I urinated, I smelled coffee.

... the Wah-clel-lars stole my dog this evening [April 11, 1806], and took him toward their village; I was shortly afterwards informed of this transaction . . . . and sent three men in pursuit of the theives with orders if they made the least resistence or difficulty in surrendering the dog to fire on them . . . .

—Meriwether Lewis, in *Original Journals of the Lewis and Clark Expedition*, 1804-1806

Lost

I, THE-ALMOST-ALWAYS-PREPARED, SPENT THE QUICK INTERstate FLIGHT home silently castigating myself for allowing—no, encouraging—a reunion as sweaty as any of those in Binah's "Lasso and Leather" romances. Litton, with just one hand on the steering wheel, the other cutting the space between us, was running his mouth even faster than he was pushing the car. He was much too proud of himself to realize all was not well with me.

"Admit it, AJ." His voice was fletched for target practice. "You made a mistake divorcing me. I'm willing to forgive and forget, even though everyone on campus knows your reputation as a good-time gal."

One thing about Litton, he was always a wonder of consistency. I should have been able to armor myself against him. But, sharpened by the day's events, his slings and arrows quivered, then penetrated. Struck by the crossover of the metaphorical with the biological, I thought about how humiliating it would be to turn up accidentally pregnant at my age. For the first time in my adult life, I had let myself run out of birth control pills, not wanting to transfer my prescription to the local drugstore, one of the first businesses to join the boycott against the *Sun*.

Shivering in the gelid micro-climate of the car, I ran down the window and let the flap of the warm wind deflect the lift of Litton's voice. It seemed a long time before the old highway slipped into Montana Street. The Taurus seemed to be creeping more slowly with every passing block. I had enough time to catalog the distinctive bouquet from each of the bars on drinkers' row, from the Club, the Shoestring, and the State; from the Stockman's, the Mint, the Moose; from the Crystal, the Prospector's, and finally the Antler, its neon sign in this context looking like the lights of home.

"You must have a protest on your hands." Without the competition of the wind, I could hear Litton perfectly well, but I didn't answer. On the sidewalk in front of the *Sun*, Binah was marching a groove into the sidewalk with her crimson cowgirl boots. In contrast, Brownie Brown, her reluctant suitor from the rummage sale, was leaning the back of his bibbies against the newspaper's stretch of plate glass. Placards bobbed.

"Don't park—just let me out." The handle resisted my fumbling grip. The lock yielded suddenly, thrusting the door into the street. The driver behind us braked without apparent resentment and waited, swiveling his neck from our car to the picket line, his car engine snoring gently.

"What about having dinner with me a bit later?" I ignored the wobble of hope in Litton's voice, concentrating only on the way it slipped into the path of practiced seductiveness.

"No," I said, too angry to try to clothe what had happened in a cliché, to chirp my usual exit line on such occasions: "Thanks, that was fun." My stomach lurched. He looked hurt.

"You know I have to get back. I probably will leave in a couple of days." His voice begged me to talk him out of it. "Unless you want me to help you with your research. Remember, my name could open a lot of doors for you."

"Have a nice trip back." Was Litton really signaling willingness to give up on his attempt to elbow into my research, not to mention my life, without a fight? Maybe I could stick it out in Misfire awhile longer.

"I can make things difficult for you, you know," he said.

"You've already done that."

Distracted by that tidbit, Litton drove away, chewing it over and probably liking the taste. Binah had tipped back the brim of her straw skimmer to better evaluate what kind of drama Litton and I were staging. Now that she had let the placard come to an uneasy rest on a lace-shrouded shoulder, her hand-lettered exhortation to "Save Our Newspaper" made the situation clearer. Evidently the Sons (and Daughters) of Bannack were casting themselves not as protesters, but as rescuers.

"I see romance is in the air." Binah hiked the hem of her drooping skirt to show off her petticoat and curtsied. I wondered if the costume had come with today's wig: Goldilocks curls that sagged against the thicket of her overgrown collar. Silence was ever my first defense, and I took it.

One thing was certain: Binah was badly in need of a cold front, even though the unseasonable warmth of the day probably hadn't reached the weather report's predicted high of 78. Nevertheless, the skin of her face sagged like the leaves of a tomato plant transplanted in the heat of the day and left to wilt. Under his Prospector's Bar cap, Brownie looked cool in comparison. Still, because he was inching himself toward the Antler, I guessed he would melt into the tinctured shadows inside first chance he got.

"So are you two getting back together?" Binah demanded, not noticing that her own intended beau was slipping between the swinging saloon doors.

A good rejoinder would have combined wit and evasion, but I managed only an ambiguous mumble. The vision of Conrad snugged in behind the Underwood Champion, his face greenish under his eyeshade banished cleverness. Unexorcised by my blink, Conrad wadded his face into a greeting.

"Reinforcements have arrived." He stood up no more unsteadily than I remembered his doing my first morning in the *Sun*.

The strips of plastic in the composing room doorway parted like the Red Sea. "His doctors were ready to release him anyway," Rheta explained, "although I don't think they wanted him to head for the office his first hour home."

I leashed my impulse to leap forward and enwrap Conrad's stooped shoulders, and not just because his resurrection meant I could extricate myself more easily from the *Sun*'s problems. "It's good to see you back," I said, meaning it.

"It's good to be back." His eyes glinted. Jumping from a hospital bed into an old-fashioned slugfest clearly had given his heart a reason to chug on. "Rheta has apprised me of our situation in full. On our journey from Missoula, we devised a stratagem that may not only help us weather this storm, but rain down a little revenue as well."

I squelched my inclination to ask how. I wanted to go feed Fellow and then run to the drugstore before it closed at six to demand a morning-after pill.

"Maybe you'd better not tell me too many secrets because, now that you're back, I won't be a member of the staff much longer." When Rheta frowned, I wished I had formulated a more gracious exit line.

I waited for her to respond. And she did, but not in the way I expected: "AJ, there's something you should know." Rheta face showed more concern than her voice was admitting. "Fellow got out after lunch. Your mother went up to the apartment to leave you something, and when she opened the door, he took off like a shot. Ran down the stairs and out the front door before anyone could stop him." She paused. "Now don't look so worried—he's a smart dog. He'll show up as soon as he gets hungry."

I could tell that Rheta believed what she was saying, but I couldn't take any comfort from her words. Fascinated by the fizz of the world's fragrances, Fellow had never shown any inclination to backtrack during the two weeks I had been taking him for walks. He seemed to have only two gears: fast forward and full stop. And he only used the second one when I tried to herd him home.

"You're probably right, but I'll feel better if I look around for myself."

By this time, Binah had given up her parade and had settled herself into the scanty shade of the bench. "You had quite a surprise waiting inside, didn't you? You can't keep a good man down, can you?"

Ignoring her, I glanced up and down the street. I half-expected to see flattened fur crushed into the asphalt. Joining me on the sidewalk, Rheta put a hand on my arm. "Your mother's out looking for him; she suggested you stay here and wait. I'll go out, too, now that you're back."

"No. I'd really like it better if you'd stay here and let me go. I know the places Fellow likes."

"Is something wrong?" Binah chirped.

"AJ's dog has run away."

Binah's face crumpled with what looked like real concern. "The only thing to do when a situation like this arises is to take measures. A stitch in time saves nine. I'll roust Brownie out of the Antler and we'll take from here south and east to the college. You'll go north and west?"

I nodded, grudgingly grateful for Binah's help. I didn't have to ask which way was north; I knew. Apparently the direction-finder in my mind was now sweeping without hesitation to the correct bearing no matter my state of mind. Jogging across to the museum lawn, I glanced under the canopy of the blue spruce. It seemed to me a bad sign the cave of living branches was empty. Nick almost always settled himself in the deep shade around supper time to share out whatever he had gleaned from the dumpsters in back of the grocery stores and restaurants.

"Fellow! Fellow!" I shouted. A tourist family steamed down the board-walk, their conversation hissing with irritation. A woman with a soft midriff and crackling hair was dragging a pubescent girl by the leash of her arm.

"I want to go to McDonald's. I don't want to go here. Why can't we go to McDonald's!"

"I don't want to hear another word out of you," the father said. He had a bandage on his cheek that might have covered a skin cancer excision.

"Look at that weird lady," a skinny boy who was wearing his brush of hair saturated with what looked like carmine paint. "This town is random."

"Shut up," the father said.

I screeched for Fellow again. Impressing adolescent tourists was not high on the list of my priorities. No Fellow leaped out of the long grass. The railroad tracks behind the museum lay as an empty contradiction to the warning I could hear jangling the nearby crossing. Scrambling up the gravel bed of tracks, I paused at dead center. No Fellow anywhere.

"Stupid dog." I slid down the other side of the tracks. The wooden bridge across the creek swayed under the tramp of my feet. No Fellow in the cool crevice under the cottonwoods where Nick and his cronies sometimes slept away the afternoons now that it was turning mild. When I'd walked him here just a few days ago, their branches had been budding but bare. Now the trees had draped themselves with sexy summer green. The stream, run-ning strong and muddy from the spring run-off, burbled over the wink of water-logged pop cans. I slapped at the gnats rising from the tangled grasp. I gasped when a section of log about Fellow's size bounced past.

The afternoon cooled into a long twilight as I systematically drove up and down Misfire's streets, stopping to ask people if they had seen Fellow. It was full night when I found Bet waiting white-faced under the buzz of the newspaper office lights. One of her sunflower earrings was missing.

"I'm sorry." Bet waited for me to say something. I refused her even one word of comfort. She sighed the sigh I remembered too well from my child-hood. "Well, at least I tried to find him. And so have your friends. Even that sick editor of yours was out driving around before Rheta made him go home. She said not to waste time with the subdivisions west of town—she's checking them now. What do you want me to do next?"

"Go on back to the RV." I succeeded in keeping the anger from my voice. "I'll take over from here. There's another place I can look."

"I'll go with you."

I grimaced and gave in. There was never any use arguing with Bet.

Nick seemed unsurprised when we drove up. In the glow of the gibbous moon, the canvas roof of his schoonerized cabin had been whipped into an immaculate meringue. He nodded a greeting as I climbed out of the Bel Air, but didn't stop to answer my question about Fellow until he finished draping a wet pair of overalls over the rail of the cabin's porch. The eerie white light frothed in the residual suds slipping down the denim.

"Nope, ain't seen him, but I'll keep my eye peeled." He gave Bet a glance. In response, she cranked up the car window and snapped down the door lock with unnecessary force.

"My mother. She's a little upset about my dog." My face was blooming so rapidly into embarrassment it must be mimicking a time-lapse video of a pink peony unfurling.

Nick didn't seem to notice. His glance had set into a stare.

"That's my mother," I repeated. "She's helping me look for my dog." I didn't know what to say, so I said that.

Polished by moonshine, Bet's eyes gleamed like aquarium glass. The tears must be an illusion: I was certain Bet would never cry for something as inconsequential as a lost dog. Maybe to escape my scrutiny, or Nick's, she slammed her eyes forward like a closing door.

The force of that swing bounced Nick's attention back to me. "I'll keep my eye peeled," he repeated in a mumble.

"I hate thinking of him roaming around in the night—it's chilly," I told Nick. Still distracted, it took him three beats too long to reply. He didn't say Fellow would be all right.

"He don't look out for cars too good, that's for sure. And there's people that'd just as soon shoot a stray as look at him. You've got to really watch a dog in this town." Nick paused to upgrade his articulation. "Someday, when you have time, I'd like to show you a few things that you might find interesting."

The Chevy's horn bleated. Bet had angled her chin straight ahead to insist that we needed to leave immediately. I waved in acquiescence, but she wasn't looking at me and Nick.

"OK, thanks," I said absently, my hand already on the car door.

"Creepy," Bet said vehemently as I eased back into the car. "How in the world did you ever come to know someone like that? Who is he anyway?"

"Did you really have to lock the door like that?"

"Really, AJ, what do you know about him? He looks dangerous to me."

"Don't worry about him. Nick is just Nick."

"Nick?" she asked. "What's his story?"

I shrugged. Neither of us said another word.

Chas was standing outside the RV smoking, his cigarette a tiny spark floating in the moonlight. My mother disembarked from the Bel Air's passenger side. She didn't bother to offer me a goodnight.

"You know what they say," he said, punching me lightly on the shoulder through the open car window. "Leave them alone and they'll come home, wagging their tails behind them."

When I didn't respond he tightened his fist and pounded into his open palm three times and then waited. I had never liked the game. Paper. Rock. Scissors. Paper wraps rock. Rock breaks scissors. Scissors cut paper. I sighed, reaching my hand through the window. The best thing to do would be to get it over with.

My fist lifted and pounded in time with his. On the third stroke my fist unfurled while he clipped at the air with his first two fingers.

"Scissor cuts paper!" he said, punching my shoulder, this time hard—his reward as the winner. As he smiled his best salesman's smile, his cheerful indifference made me want to weep. From the beginning, I had been Bet's project; Chas had always found other fish to fry. My throat and my shoulder aching, I went back to patrolling the dark streets for another couple of hours before giving up.

Without Fellow anchoring me to the futon mattress, I could toss and turn without impediment. I was free to hear noises, cook anxiety up into an asthma attack. As the courthouse clock struck three, I realized I should have checked with the cops hours ago. If I asked for information in person, I still might get lucky. Throwing on jeans and my heavy Seattle sweater, I decided to walk the few blocks to the courthouse in case I might spot Fellow curled up next to a building or under a bush.

The Antler slumbered in its post-closing hush. Downtown was deserted, the moonlight transforming it into a stage set by washing its daytime colors into the sepia of iron gall ink. I walked quickly, more out of hope than fear. The dispatcher in the law enforcement annex's glass cage was filing her short, unpolished finger nails, ignoring the line of TV screens in front of her. Cameras scanned cells where prisoners slept in double-decked bunks, faces wall-ward. Their shoulders heaved in black and white.

"I've already checked for that dog once tonight—for Luke Ingraham," the dispatcher said. Her voice was sieved by the microphone just under her slightly doubled chin.

"What time was that?" I wondered how Luke had heard about Fellow. I had purposely not called him. "I feel lower than a snake's belly," he had drawled two days before when I had stopped in his office. And he had looked terrible. Spring fever was his unconvincing excuse.

As the dispatcher bent forward, I noticed how whitely her thin black hair divided. I thought she needed to learn the Shoshoni trick of enhancing a wide part with a line of red.

"I thought it was just after I came on shift—at nine. As usual, we've had a bunch of dog-at-large complaints, but none matching the description you've given me."

"Could you call me if something comes in?"

"If your dog is tagged, we'll phone."

"He is."

"What's your cell number?" Of course, I had to tell her that I didn't have one and gave her Rheta's contact information instead.

"Well, okie dokie, then. You might contact the local vets, too, after they open. The dispatcher's eyes were losing their glaze of boredom. "Sometimes people drop off strays at their offices, especially if they're hurt."

I couldn't bring myself to ask what people usually did when they came across dead dogs, but the dispatcher told me anyway. "The dead ones usually just get left where they're at until somebody calls us to complain about the stink or tosses them in a garbage barrel. Mostly, though, strays show up back at home after a few nights on the town. Your dog been fixed?"

Lack of time and money had kept me from attending to that detail, I had to admit.

"Well, that explains it," the dispatcher said, waving me away and turning back to her TV screens and nails. I imagined the file dust sifting down night after night onto the prisoners below, flouring them with a fine grit that they rubbed from their eyes, blew from their noses, washed from their skin until it disappeared, until it was converted, like everything else, into garden dirt or desert sand or the nuclei of raindrops.

Too tense to return to the apartment, I let the street lights lead me back downtown. A bus was belching diesel in front of the Golden Hour. The driver was grunting as he threw taped-up boxes into his coach's underbelly. Not a single passenger had abandoned his or her seat to inhale carcinogens under the café's pulsing neon sign.

A waitress I didn't recognize was bending over someone's bald spot. Hollow if not quite hungry, I went in, ignoring the tables and sliding into a booth. The swipe marks were drying on the top of the chrome-banded surface as slowly as the approach of dawn. I tugged a couple of napkins from a dispenser that had been jammed too full and folded them into coasters for my elbows. The damp seeped through. Somehow I found it comforting that at the Golden Hour it was business as usual.

"What can I get you, honey?" The woman was massive, at least six feet tall with upper arms that bulged hard muscle under her uniform sleeves. Her wide-set eyes were the verdurous green of an irrigated field. A real orchid perched in auburn hair that had been frosted by nature, but curled tight by artifice. The blossom matched the yellow stains on her broad apron. It was clear she felt herself competent to handle the night shift.

"A coffee, please, with cream and sugar."

The waitress paused, her pencil poised, willing me into a larger order.

"And a piece of pie—chocolate."

The pie case was smeared with fingerprints and caked blobs of whipped cream: testimony that Lena was not yet on fastidious duty. But the slices themselves stacked up high, wide and handsome—the crimson cherry as seductive as a lipstick ad, the golden custard as smooth as the underside of a thigh, the burnt umber chocolate as erotic as accidental sex.

"That's all, honey?" The "honey" was a disguise. I could see through it to the rock-solid will beneath as easily as I could see the pink slip announcing itself through the waitress's uniform. Out of habit, I peered into the woman's face, searching for some resemblance to my own, the way I always did with women of a certain age, especially red-haired women. If I ever met Everonica face to face, what would I see in her eyes?

As though I had conjured him up, my brother slid in beside me. Adon was out of uniform tonight. He wore jeans and a sweater that looked a lot like mine, except that on him the tan of the yarn was lighter than the permanent tan of his skin.

He explained that he had spent the day in Bozeman to help his mother with a few house repairs and to lend a hand in planting her garden. "She never wants to come here, so Nancia and I try to take the kids there every other weekend. But she didn't want to lose the good weather by waiting. Then she forced me to play three games of Scrabble after dinner." I carefully stored away the facts that my mother was a gardener and a Scrabble player—and that she avoided Misfire.

"Are you two twins?" the waitress said, smiling at our matching sweaters. She splashed more coffee in our cups without asking if we wanted more and then hustled away without waiting for an answer to settle a noisy herd of twenty-somethings in scuffed cowboy boots.

"Do you have any siblings?" I heard myself asking after we agreed on our mutual good taste in apparel, and I asked how Nancia and his daughters were doing. It was risky to nudge him into the topic of family so early in our relationship, but I couldn't seem to help myself.

"I'm an only child," he said, sloshing cream into his cup from the stainless steel pitcher that stood at his left hand where the waitress had left it. Evidently, my brother was a late-night regular at the Golden Hour, or she wouldn't have known he was a leftie. "I always wanted a sister, but my parents wouldn't cooperate. They're divorced now."

I let silence settle between us. The cowboys were making enough noise to fill in the blanks.

I closed my eyes briefly and decided.

"Actually," I said. "I believe we're related."

He held my gaze for a minute and read it accurately.

"Well, I'd better get home," he said, sliding off his stool.

Ignoring his unspoken response, I stood up. "We're not twins," I said. "But we're siblings. You're my half-brother."

"My mother warned me earlier this spring that something like this might happen."

I waited.

"That some cr—confused—woman had called claiming to be her long-lost daughter. But it can't be, you see. My mother married when she was barely 17 and I was born just nine months later."

"Would you like to see my birth certificate?"

Without answering, he turned his back on me and walked into the night. Blindly, I stepped out of the restaurant's island of light to try to follow him. He had already disappeared. The Golden Hour's coffee was wearing off fast. I didn't know what to do next. Only one thing seemed certain to me: I could not allow myself to think about what had just happened. The half block to the *Sun* walked like five miles. I stood outside the alley door, wondering if there was some place else I could look for Fellow. Behind me, a car rumbled and slowed. I glanced back over my shoulder, big city wariness instantly reactivating itself.

"AJ! What are you doing wandering around out here!"

It was Bet, her eyes and lips ghosts of themselves. I took an involuntary step back before I realized my mother wasn't wearing any makeup.

"Guess I'm doing the same thing you are."

"But I went back for my car. What can you be thinking! That dog of yours isn't that important."

"If you were really my mother, maybe you would understand."

There. The words I had ached to say since I was thirteen pinged against the dark like hail against a tin roof.

Bet looked not so much hurt as outraged. "Get in this car right this . . ."

"I'm not a child."

"You could've fooled me. Do you think you're the only one in the world who has troubles?"

This time, I was the one who turned my back and headed into the charcoal shadows.

Rocks so filled the road, that anyone who had not begun to
see the elephant would have been afraid . . . . We, however,
were well-seasoned by this time and simply kept pushing.

—Abigail Scott, quoted in *Seeing the Elephant: The Many
Voices of the Oregon Trail* by Joyce Badgley Husaker

Seeing the Elephant

THE MOON BRIMS SO COOL, NICK FEELS TEMPTED TO REACH OUT WITH THE
plastic mug he carries tied to the hammer loop of his overalls. After a luminous draft, he might be able to float through the next hours transformed:
his skin, snow-white vellum; his veins and arteries, vines writhing up and
down the text of his life; his heart, the quivering initial of the last word he
would ever speak.

"Alph!" he whispers, his voice fragile. "Alph!"

The ryegrass shudders and parts, each of its arrows sharp as a black and
white photograph of itself. The retriever trots straight to Nick and seats
himself, dark eyes lifted.

"Stay near me?" Nick speaks in the same tone of voice he would use to
ask a favor of a friend, if he had one.

The retriever's rusty nostrils quiver. The acrid scent of skunk carries a
long way on air chilled by spring moonshine.

"Alph?" The retriever licks his lips in assent.

Stepping carefully to avoid gopher holes, Nick forces himself through
rabbitbrush and thistles, tender with rising growth. It has been years since
he last visited the marker. He can't think why he feels the compulsion to
seek it out now, when he has so much to do before dawn. But he ever has
been a man to fall back on instinct; he doesn't intend to change his habits
now. His bath wasn't really an aberration: although mortification of the
flesh is a useful tool, he didn't want to go about this night's duties stinking
of stale sweat.

He moves his lips in a 13th century supplication, the Latin tasting good on his lips and refreshing his resolve. There are times in his career as a scavenger that he appreciates his Jesuit university training. Of course, he failed as a scholar, just as he failed as a husband and a father. He has failed at everything. All that's left is to try to repair some of the damage.

"Just fifteen more minutes." Alph's tail is waving like a flag. The retriever stops and squares the apex of his ears. When Nick doesn't say anything more, the dog sniffs a hillock and then squats.

Nick almost smiles: how impressed he had been as a nine-year-old with the wondrous tumble of manure from the circus elephant's vent. His mother—a shy woman who was ashamed of her German accent—had placed her gloved hand firmly over his mouth when he tried to shout out the elephant's prodigious accomplishment.

"Come, we must go now," she said. Nick could tell that she was worrying that he would catch a cold if the wind-driven storm drenched them. Never did she seem to realize that he was growing up.

Alph barks a sharp warning and then thrusts his nose toward the moon. Blinking, Nick sees the elephant, too. There she is, silver-plated by the moonlight, but otherwise as substantial as Alph, her Asiatic ears draping neatly from her domed skull, her trunk hovering curiously above a clump of rabbitbrush.

Alph yelps again and moves to Nick's side; the elephant turns her head slightly and gazes at them calmly with one lustrous eye. The moonlight washes down her high, straight forehead, revealing the streak left by the lightning, dark and unbroken.

Nick advances. Entranced, he forgets to pay attention to where he is going. He recovers immediately from the stumble, but by the time he looks up again, Alph is nosing the ground where the elephant's splayed toes had covered the flat tablet that marks the grave. Vanished is the fence that cages the grave in the bland light of day. Missing is the tree planted to mark the site where the massive body had been buried after the storm. But Nick knows he isn't dreaming.

He kneels to sweep back the grass with his hands. Alph presses in, sharing the warmth of his tattered fur. In the moonlight, the engraving on the brass plaque is perfectly legible:

Pitt
Killed on this spot
by lightning Aug. 6, 1943

"POOR BOY," HIS MOTHER HAD SAID, PATTING HIM DRY IN HER KITCHEN with a towel that had dried rough in the Montana wind. "To see the elephant struck down and then to suffer the rain too." She always spoke in full formal sentences to him, as if to teach him the language she had worked so hard to learn. In wartime, speaking German was dangerous.

The boy's father was slumped over the yellow Formica table, forking in his noon dinner of chicken and homemade noodles before going back to his job as a house painter.

"You worry too much," he said. "He won't melt. And now he has a story that he can tell the rest of his life."

Nick raises himself to his feet. A long low shadow trots toward them, separating itself from the night. Alph whimpers a greeting.

"Well, I suppose you'll have to come with us," Nick says. He strides away, in a hurry now, fearful of lingering, whistling sharply for the dogs to follow. He doesn't want to tempt the elephant into rematerializing. Into sounding his last trump too soon.

Must these like empty shadows pass/Or forms reflected from a glass?/Or mere chimæras in the mind,/ That fly, and leave no marks behind?

—Jonathan Swift, in "Stella's Birthday"

Stela by Moonlight

STELA BLAMES THE GLANCE OF THE MOONLIGHT ON THE GREEN ASH and cottonwoods for making her miss the I-15 exit ramp. At five minutes after four in the morning, Montana Street is broad and empty enough to accommodate a leisurely U-turn by a semi, but she keeps on driving. As for the parking lots that stitch a straggle of businesses to the street, she lets them slide by too. The A&W that Chas and Bet have revived and renamed The Last Chance. The Dave-Elaine Bowling Palace. Misfire Implement. The State Liquor Store. The Pizza Towne. The Sunrise Inn. The Elephant Rock Country Club with its wide circular driveway.

Streetlights are redundant tonight. Swollen on the edge of fullness, the moon blots up their lesser lamps. She veers right as the town yields to farmland. The ripple of the road is dull aluminum in the silvery light. Halfway up the hill, she realizes she is climbing to the cemetery. Nevertheless, she lets the road take the car, telling herself it will be easier to turn around at the graveyard's gates than to chance one of the farm lanes meandering off the main road into the night.

Stela doesn't know that what she really wants is to sing in the graveyard. Nevertheless, she pulls up by the fancy wrought iron gate inserted into an equally fancy rock wall: a padlock gleams in the moonlight. Acting on impulse, she parks and steps out, the gravel shifting uneasily under her soles. She has dressed too nicely for the trip to the Bozeman airport, in an ivory suit and matching high heeled shoes. The still soft tips of the foxtails reach for her stockings and the hem of her skirt. She follows wrought iron to where it angles into a simple page wire fence, crowned by the unequivocal hostility of two barbed strands.

The headstones on the other side of the fence quietly absorb the moonlight in the same way they sponge up sun and rain and snow. Stela slips out of her skirt and jacket, hangs them neatly on the nearest fencepost, strips off her pantyhose as well and pushes the bundle into the jacket pocket. Straightening her slip and putting her high heels back on, she precisely positions one palm down on the bottom strand, and then presses up on the safe, smooth length of wire beneath the set of twisted barbs. Through the void, she shimmies unscathed except for the warning bite of a single barb through the collar of her silk blouse into the vulnerable skin at the back of her neck. She has forced plenty of barbed wire out fishing, Of course, it's easier if there are two people, one to hold the barbed strands while the other thrusts first one leg and then another into forbidden territory.

Standing erect in the graveyard, she immediately wants out. But she wants even more to answer the invitation that has called her again into the company of the family dead, Luke's family. She believes it will be the last time. The grass is soft and black under her feet, dense enough to support her heels without a twist.

She hasn't lived in Misfire long enough to know many of the people here, but she recognizes names from her encounters with their surviving kin.

"Your grandson is on my bad check list." The granite monument, which is etched with a complicated mountain scene that suggests no place in particular, doesn't reply. But a far older monument, an urn draped with a stone pall, glows momentarily whiter, a trick that startles Stela, until she realizes the worn marble has caught the lights of a vehicle passing through a distant lane.

The urn orients her to her place in the graveyard—not far from where Luke's parents are buried. Before she moves toward the twin markers that she can now distinguish just beyond the most heavily populated part of the cemetery, she turns her head to assure herself she can still see the ivory marker of her jacket. She walks on. Only occasionally does she slow to sidestep the depressions of some of the cemetery's oldest graves.

The geraniums in front of the two-sided rose granite marker exude an astringent greenhouse smell, so she knows Luke must have watered them recently. Stela avoids setting foot on the hump above Luke's mother or into the grassy basin above his father. But she plants her heels firmly as she traverses the plots Luke has bought for himself and for her. The cemetery is perfectly silent. No owl calls, no dog barks in the distance, no breeze rasps the needles of the giant blue spruce that protects her grave from the moonlight.

Stela opens her mouth, not knowing what will emerge. As her lips part, she feels Mahler's "Magna Peccatrix" rising from her throat, even though she is not a first soprano and even though she is not a sinful woman. She presses her fingers against her mouth. For the first time she is a little afraid, remembering the European fairytale of the virtuous maiden who speaks pearls and diamonds while her evil stepsisters drool toads and snakes. She drops her hand. Not just her lips and her mouth, but her throat and her diaphragm open. A song she doesn't remember having heard floats into the air—a soft song, a lullaby, she feels sure. The words are not French, German, or Italian—her tongue knows the curves of those languages. She thinks the rhythms are African but she cannot be sure. Long ago, she accepted adoption into the white sweep of European operatic tradition. It happened the moment her seventh grade music teacher asked her to stay after class. "You are a voice," he told her.

How long she sings she doesn't know; she hears the chiming of the courthouse clock without counting the strokes. When the fire siren wails hours too early, she subsumes its sobs into the song.

The song slows, softens, and stops. The chill demands access to her skin. The dew soaks her shoes. Stela bows her head and feels the silk of her collar tug itself away from the dried drop of blood on her skin. The moon has set. Her jacket beacon no longer glows white, but her feet, now bare and cold, find their way. She doesn't remember taking off her high heels. The barbed wire allows her to escape without another scratch. Out of the car's back seat, she retrieves her suitcase. In the privacy of the near dawn, she pulls on jeans and warms her feet in heavy socks and sensible shoes. She exchanges the suit jacket for a sweater, climbs into the rental car, and drives toward the sunrise.

I had the misfortune to lose my memorandum book which contained all the family likenesses—I miss them very much—and if you can afford the expense—I would feel very glad if you will have the picture taken which I mentioned to you last summer and send it as soon as is practicable—I feel lost without even the shadow of my family to look at occasionally . . . .

—F.L Kirkaldie, in an 1866 letter to his wife, quoted in *Not in Precious Metals Alone: A Manuscript History of Montana*

A Fine and Private Place

IN WALMART, BET IS ALWAYS HAPPY.

"Chas, I need to go to Walmart," she demands before dawn the next morning, still boiling mad, glassy-eyed from rage and lack of sleep. Chas is playing solitaire and drinking instant Folgers at the RV's tiny kitchenette table. He has slept, showered, and shaved. There is a smudge of egg yolk left on his plate. He smells like cedar. And bacon. The lock of gray hair that swoops across his brow has been smoothed into its Gary Cooperish wave. He's not the sharpest pencil in the box, but he sure is handsome. Life long ago taught her to be wary of smart men.

Chas doesn't ask why. Instead, he simply hauls himself to his feet, recombs his hair using the screen of the tiny TV for a mirror, and reaches for his leather jacket.

He has just one question: "Butte or Bozeman?"

She chooses Bozeman. It's farther, and today, that's what she wants. Always Chas is ready for a trip. Never does he want to discuss the meaning of life. In under ten minutes, he is herding the RV down Montana Street.

"I just don't understand our daughter." She raises her voice to make herself heard above the courthouse siren. The fire truck speeds in the opposite direction as Chas takes the state highway out of town. Neither wonders aloud where the fire is.

"How sharper than a serpent's tooth it is to have a thankless child," Chas quotes King Lear. He can do that, recite poetry at the drop of his baseball cap, even though he never finished high school. He can't say where the lines come from, though, except his favorites from "The Cremation of Sam McGee." Bet never lets on to him or anyone else she knows Shakespeare when she hears it.

"Amen," she says, and then expounds on the theme as he pushes the RV to a steady seventy, taking advantage of the fact that the two-lane highway is empty. Bet repeats what AJ dared to say to her outside the Golden Hour and what she said back and what she should have said instead. Chas, on the lookout for potholes and any deer intent on predawn suicide, makes no further comment.

The Walmart parking lot is surprisingly full, considering how early it still is. They return the greeter's chipper "Good morning" with even more chipper replies. Bet thinks (and not for the first time) she'll apply for a greeter's job herself if she and Chas ever dare to settle somewhere. Chas has known the score since the beginning, not that he has minded the footloose life that he suggested was best for both of them. A traveling salesman he was when she met him, and a traveling salesman he has remained, by his choice, not just hers.

Once she nabs a shopping cart, Chas abandons her to seek more coffee and an Egg McMuffin. She doesn't mind. In fact, she prefers to shop alone, propelling her cart with a sense of purpose that materializes like a will-o-the-wisp shining all the more brightly as it beckons her down one aisle and turns into the next, out of reach. Too bad AJ is such a pill. She could have come, too, and they could all have had a nice time together.

Suddenly Bet realizes she needs at least three new outfits, each suitable for wearing to the Bannack Days pageant rehearsals: cool, cute, and youthful, but comfortable, too. And matching earrings. And sandals. And lipstick. And nail polish. She is sure that anyone who knew her when she was young and completely lacking in fashion sense could not recognize her now. That certainty is the one good thing that came of her night-time hunt for AJ's damn dog. It was a shock seeing Nick staring and staring at her from the porch of his cabin. What had possessed him to return to Misfire? Despite the overalls and the slouch, she had recognized him immediately. For a few liver-chilling moments, she had been convinced he had known her too. But no. Despite the way the moonlight must have washed the years from her face, he blinked and looked away. She must be safe. Otherwise he would have given some sign.

In the happy glow of the cosmetics aisle, she decides to buy the lipsticks first and then find the outfits to match. That will be different. That will be fun. "Pick Me Up Pink" seems a perfect place to start. She blushes her hand with a streak from the tester. She turns to the woman picking through the rack of concealers crammed next to the lipsticks. The woman is too old for the designer eyeglasses she's wearing—dark red with a flash of forest green outlining the lenses. The green of the frame matches the green of the woman's eyes and the dark red, the auburn of her hair, which either has resisted graying or has been skillfully tinted.

Those eyes. That hair. The shadow of a birthmark on her cheek.

Bet steps back into a downdraft from an unseen air conditioner, a cold spot that freezes her into a pillar of salt.

"Don't say a word," the woman hisses. She slams Bet with a look of glacial hate. She pivots. She leaves without looking back, a point of light receding forever. Still gelid, Bet wonders if she will ever thaw again.

One winter evening, Coyote went outside to defecate. He looked down as he was squatting there, and noticed a fire below. He thought he saw it right in his anus and jumped up. Then he saw that it was way down the mountain. He asked his anus, "What's that fire for?"

—Robert H. Lowie, in "The Northern Shoshoni," *Anthropological Papers of the American Museum of Natural History*

Burnout

"Fire! Get up, AJ! Fire!"

The pounding of the words against the apartment's door—or maybe the wail of the siren—penetrated my dream, evaporating the deep pool through which I was swimming, swimming, swimming after someone who was drowning. That's what you get for going to bed with your clothes on. At least I'd taken off my shoes.

"Where?" I stuttered, even before I noticed the aching absence of Fellow, who was not nudged tightly against my thigh and might never be again.

"Where!" I called again, pulling on my shoes. The atmosphere smelled of nothing more dangerous than the cranky plumbing.

"Bannack." Luke sagged into the room, looking grayer than he should have, even considering his news and the predawn hour.

Still groggy, I noticed that Luke's hands, instead of gripping a hose or an ax, were flapping empty at his side. But he was buckled into the rest of his gear, an old-fashioned red fireman's hat and a black bunker coat.

"What?"

"Bannack! If you want to ride with me, we have to leave now." He paused, his eyes telegraphing another message, one even more painful.

"What else? Is it Fellow?"

"Stela's left me." He pivoted, rescinding with his back the offer of a ride.

It took me no more than ten breathless minutes to turn up the volume on the police scanner, pull on my clothes, load ten rolls of film to supplement the one already in the Nikon, and to phone Rheta on the receptionist desk's phone. I decided that no matter what happened today, tomorrow I was going to replace my cell, either on the *Sun*'s dime or my own.

"Whatever you do, don't call Conrad." Rheta's voice sounded as collected as if she'd been up for hours, as though she had accustomed herself to sleep deprivation, even grown to like it. In contrast, my voice quavered.

"Don't you think he's heard the siren?"

"Since the whole town including the dead in the cemetery is probably awake, I imagine Conrad is too. Well, leave him to me. You get going fast as you can. We've got to beat the *Standard* on this one. I need to call the nursing home to let them know that I'll be out of town for a few hours, but I'll be right behind you."

My key was in the Bel Air's lock when I realized my saddlebag was still upstairs. In a flash, I decided to leave it behind. The highway patrol would have more pressing things to do than to pull me over to demand my driver's license. My documents were safer upstairs than at the scene of a fire. And I had a spare inhaler and the credit card I used for gas in my glove compartment.

The Chevy proved it could hold onto a shuddering eighty, a speed the cop who flew past me must have considered reasonable and prudent, given the circumstances. As I swung off Highway 278 onto the Bannack road, I could see three separate geysers of smoke piercing the still morning air. Under the bluing sky, the bunchgrass held itself as motionless as a jackrabbit being stalked by a coyote.

Asthma might have had something to do with the constriction in my chest, but after fishing my inhaler out of the glove compartment with one hand and taking a quick hit, I ignored the spasms. There were more pressing things to worry about than breathing.

"You can't go any further!" In uniform—a nicely pressed uniform at that, Adon stopped me at the entrance of the ghost town, clearly too preoccupied to give a thought to our last angry conversation.

I grabbed my camera bag from the passenger's seat and held it up. "I've got to get in there!"

"Back up and leave your car in the lot!" Adon's eyes were wide with fear disciplined into resolve. Instantly dropping my law-abiding habits the way some lizards shed their tails between a predator's teeth, I forced the Chevy full speed ahead. Dust exploded from under the car's wheels. But I surged only to stop. Bannack's main street already was saturated with vehicles abandoned higgledy-piggledy, lights flashing and doors ajar, open to the smoke reaching for them. There was no place for me to park in the ghost town without making the blockage dangerously worse. Adon shot me an angry look as I reversed past him. To avoid confronting him again, I took a few seconds to position the Chevy at the far end of the ghost town's parking lot with its nose aligned for a quick exit. If a rapid departure became necessary, I wanted to give myself room to maneuver. Grass fires could explode with the slightest breeze.

By the time I ran back to the entrance, I could see my brother ahead of me jogging in the same direction I was—toward the fire chief's white helmet visible even in the dawn's half-light at the far end of town.

My feet knocked against the deserted boardwalk with the hard beat of panic. Smoke runneled the face of the cloudless sky. I sprinted on, noticing a mechanical thrum. Pushing past the Brother Van's church, I could now see the congregation of cabins at the far end of town. Three wore a crown of flames. Each floated in a pool of flickering grass and blackening sage.

"Can I help!"

"Stay out of the way!" said Delores, not taking her eyes from the stream of water she was wielding like a sword. She was wearing a bunker jacket, but no helmet. I wondered where Baby Jack was. The nozzle in her grip trailed a taut length of hose across the road to a fire truck, its paint an incongruous smiling yellow. Like the other two tankers nudged up tight to the creek, it vibrated with the throb of a mobile pump. At least water supply wouldn't be a problem.

Rock, paper, scissors.

Water douses fire.

But the flames dripping down the sides of the trio of cabins weren't playing the game.

Fire eats wood.

Wind scatters water. Drives it into waves. Splatters or absorbs it.

And the sun was whistling up the wind with a warmth that seeped into the rugged topography in fits and starts, creating a roller coaster from thin air. Delores was hacking away, cutting against the rising wind with the arc of her liquid blade. Flames hissed and then flared up again and again. A woman's voice parted the crackle: "Keemo and Brownie, help Delores!" The white-helmeted chief materialized shouting directions. Before the men could leave their attempt to wet down the roof of a nearby hut, the cabin imploded with a bang reminding me what I was supposed to be doing.

Just as the camera lens began tracking the steady trickle of fire from the cabin into the surrounding grass, a gush of wind swelled it into a breaker. "Look!" I was the one who had screamed. In response to the warning or to the toss of the wind, the chief—Binah I now saw— snapped her head toward the flare-up.

Pointing one hand at Delores to hold me in position while using the other to redirect the men, Binah re-orchestrated the crisis. The wind worked itself into a thin wailing as the prickly pear cactus on the nearest cabin's sod roof charred and smoldered. But the tide of flames in the grass was falling back.

I took a half step toward the two men, but stopped in midstride: I didn't have the equipment or the know-how to help. Instead, I swung the Nikon to my eyes and faced the stony ridge where a line of volunteers were chopping out a fire break with picks and shovels. An abrupt gust churned up a dust devil that leaped the earthen barrier as easily as the fire would if it advanced another hundred feet.

I kept swinging the camera back and forth, finger pressed down on the trigger of the motor drive when one of the faces in my viewfinder came into sudden focus.

"Conrad!" I hollered. "Put that shovel down!"

Startled Conrad paused, the tails of his shirt flapping in the wind.

"God Almighty!" I heard the grief in his voice as I dodged a clump of sage. "God Almighty!" he repeated returning to his digging before I could reach him. "If that wind makes up its mind to start really blowing, the whole place could be gone in an hour."

I reached for Conrad's shovel, but he yanked it from my grasp.

"Conrad, give it to her!" It was Luke, red-eyed from smoke. He was holding what looked like an Aladdin's lamp veiled in soot.

"Are you saying that you don't need my help?" I waited for Luke to order Conrad out of the way. As Conrad's spade rang again against the rocky ground, Binah's voice sliced through the falling ashes. "Shovel crew—move down the road to this side of the church on the double. Luke, get over there—Tanker Two's about to lose it!"

Tucking the Aladdin's lamp into my gaping camera bag, Luke shouldered his way back, into the smoke.

"What do you want me to do?" I wasn't going to fiddle around with my camera while Bannack burned.

"Keep shooting," Binah shouted as she jogged after Luke. "We'll need a complete record." She stopped and gave me a hard stare. "For God's sake AJ, stay the hell out of the way!"

Later, I remembered the fire as a patchwork of scenes sliced into squares by the black edge of my viewfinder. The camera watched as the miners' cabins demonstrated that nothing, especially nothing built of wood, resists its return to dust and ashes.

Fire eats wood.

By the time reinforcements arrived from Butte, the volunteer department had dammed the fire halfway up Boot Hill—far enough from the center of ghost town to dry the sheen of fear on the volunteers' faces. Some of the firefighters had breath enough to sing as they circled the blaze, raking back wisps of grass, saturating the ground one more time, or beating out a stray spark with a blanket. Luke had a voice of iron. It sank beneath the song: "Row, row, row your boat." Not the best song to fight a fire by, but I couldn't think of a better one.

I trudged back toward the Visitor Center on a boardwalk now slippery with a slurry of mud and ash. With relief, I saw Conrad just ahead shaking his fist in the face of a firefighter encased in high-tech armor. Obviously, the stranger was an outsider, a member of the professional emergency crew from Butte. A few feet away, Rheta was holding a sleeping Baby Jack on her shoulder as she poured coffee from an over-size Thermos on a card table already burdened with paper plates of pastries deflating in the sun. Brushing a fly away, I began wolfing down a maple bar without bothering to ask how she had come to cater this event.

I paused before reaching for another. "I see you managed to stop Conrad from killing himself."

"All I had to do was point out that those galoots from Butte were likely to start shooting off their high pressure hoses like this was the Fourth of July and these old buildings were their firecrackers. He made like Crazy Horse at the Little Bighorn. At least this particular cavalry knew when it was surrounded." Rheta was right: although the saloon's false front was dripping, and two or three of its front panes had been knocked out by a hasty jab of water, the Butte crew had retreated.

Thinking about what could have happened to the saloon, the hotel, the Masonic Lodge, all the fragile relics of the otherwise disappeared past, I felt the blessing of relief.

"I brought you some more film," Rheta unsnapped the clasp on her purse. I started to reach out with sticky hands, but Rheta shook her head and instead pulled open the unzipped top of my camera bag.

"What's this?" she asked when the snout of the lamp thrust itself into the light. "Where's the genie?"

"It's something Luke pulled out of one of the cabins before it burned." Tears washed the smoke from my eyes.

Rheta touched me lightly on the shoulder. "I know you're exhausted, but can you stick it out to shoot another few rolls of film? I'll take what you've already shot back to town and soup it: we won't be able to scoop the *Standard*'s web edition, but they just got here, we were here first, and we can stay here until the last dog is dead." I tried not to wince. "Sorry," she said.

A sudden cramping interrupted my acknowledgment of her apology.

"Are you OK, kid?"

"Yes," I stopped. "I think I'm getting my period."

Rheta offered me a knowing wink and smiled.

After a quick trip to the Visitor Center restroom—surprisingly clean, empty, and functional—I felt an easing of tension. I wasn't pregnant. I had a quarter in my pocket for the Kotex machine. Bannack was apparently out of danger. The *Sun* had one hell of a photo story. Maybe Luke and Stela could patch things up, and maybe I could, too, with both Bet and my brother and maybe, eventually, my elusive mother. Maybe Fellow would be waiting for me when I got back to the newspaper office.

As I emerged into a morning—or was it afternoon by this time?—that seemed to have settled back down to a stillness thick enough to smother any sparks the firefighters may have missed, I felt weirdly happy. I even waved politely to the *Standard* reporter bobbing down the road, his camera poised, but nothing much ahead of him to shoot but smoldering sagebrush and firefighters sweeping their hoses back and forth with the bored rhythm of homeowners hand-watering the perennial beds after a long day's work.

Because I was basking in the pleasant glow of false hope, I didn't pay attention at first when the police scanner in my hip pocket—which had dropped into low-key spurts of chatter as the fire had subsided—began buzzing with an uptick in conversational traffic. But when at least a dozen firefighters abruptly detached themselves from the mop-up crew and began running, I knew enough to run too.

The Chevy cut a clean, quick path out of the parking lot, but as fast I had forced it, the city's fancy yellow fire truck jostled past me less than half way to the intersection with the state highway. Both my hands were occupied in keeping the Chevy speeding over the Bannack Road, so I waited to snaffle the scanner out of my jeans until after I turned onto the state highway. Even then, I couldn't make the words I was hearing string together in a way I wanted to make sense.

The newspaper.

Upper story.

Need an ambulance. Stat!

Rheta! How long ago had she left?

The Chevy skimmed Badger Pass at ninety. I reined in as I exited into town and passed the college. Skirting a couple of cop cars blocking Montana Street, I rolled to a stop on the far edge of the museum lawn. Bursting from the car, I didn't recognize the *Sun*'s silhouette at first. The newspaper office had hidden itself for more than a hundred and thirty years behind a sheet iron facade meant to imitate distant Eastern grandeur and to intimate a prosperous Western future. Now the facade teetered forward, leaning heavily on a power pole, a section of the street-side roof smoldering behind it. Tripping, I fell to my hands and knees on the museum boardwalk and looked up, scanning the street for Rheta's white hair.

Buried somewhere under the collapsing upper story was the rocker that had belonged to Luke's mother. The brass lamp. The gate-legged table.

My birth certificate. The ledger.

The morgue. The third floor's secrets.

At least, Fellow couldn't be curled into charred lump under the gate-legged table, his fur singed away, his pink tongue bulging from his open mouth. Instead he was lost. A word that carried more hope than I had before realized. A word that invoked the possibility of its opposite.

I tried to calm myself.

Things could be worse.

As long as Rheta wasn't in the darkroom.

But it was hard to hang onto hope at the sight of the *Sun*. Collapsed above, axed open below, all its dignity had been stripped away with the shattering of its plate glass. It might have been better if the contents of the office had burned completely. The main floor office lay exposed, drenched and blackened—the wobbly desks, the sodden stacks of newspapers, the rickety steps now weaving up to nowhere I could go anymore, the slumped ceilings, all open to public view.

I tried hard to look away. I didn't want to see anything more. I didn't want to find someone to ask about Rheta. Instead, I concentrated on the tiny clank the camera made as it made contact with my glasses. Forcing myself to view each scene in black and white, I mentally captioned every picture I encountered in the small safe frame.

I caught the arc of water dousing the roofs of the Antler on one side and the abandoned JCPenney building on the other. I caught the knot of early afternoon drinkers who had been forced out into the asphalt, but who had hung onto their shot glasses and beer mugs. I caught the skinny cop clamping Conrad's arms behind his back, restraining his rush toward the still-smoking building. I caught the *Standard* photographer and the crew from the Butte television station aiming their lenses, their faces bright with a lambent pleasure.

I caught the expressions of the EMTs who were loading a gurney into an ambulance with a care no longer needed by the body hidden beneath the blanket.

I caught frame after frame until I ran out of film. I caught myself thinking, "That's OK, I'll just run downstairs to the darkroom and . . ."

Lacking the camera to hide behind, I let the Nikon dangle around my neck and then forced myself to look for Conrad. He was sitting in the passenger side of one of the police cars, Rheta bending toward him over the open door.

I ran, catching her up in my arms so abruptly that she startled in my grasp. Then she reached for me and whispered, "It's all right. I stopped to check on my mother first. I didn't even know the *Sun* . . ."

She turned back to Conrad, who was leaning like an old tombstone. I could not ask who it was who had been found in the *Sun*. It was within the realm of possibility that Bet or Chas could have been poking around upstairs. But surely the coroner, who was also the undertaker, would have arrived by now to grasp me by the shoulder with professional gentleness had that been the case. Jana wasn't scheduled to work. So who?

Conrad kept his gaze fastened on the street where an old-fashioned red fire truck sat, polished and parade-ready, probably the only vehicle that had been left in the stable when the race to Bannack began. It had clearly been nudged into the background again when the city's yellow behemoth arrived on the scene from Bannack.

It was Rheta who stood to face the ruin of the *Sun* and then me, her creek-colored eyes luminous. But she didn't speak. The ambulance pulled away.

Who?

"Nick." Rheta seemed not to believe her own words. "The police think he's the one who started it, either accidentally or on purpose. They found him on the landing outside the morgue. They think he passed out from the smoke."

I blinked. My eyes had squandered their tears and left me none. I wondered briefly if any of this could really be happening. Maybe I had been the one asleep upstairs when the smoke started creeping under the door. Maybe I was in a coma now, dreaming all of this.

It would be possible, I decided, to dream in such detail, to generate these images: the smudges on Rheta's pearl-buttoned shirt, the stink of smoke in my own hair, the gleam of the *Sun*'s toilet through a burned wall.

There was nothing here my mind couldn't supply, no particular that my memory couldn't have manufactured. Except Nick. No matter how deep my coma, I wouldn't cast him in the role of arsonist. Besides, my imagination was not so extravagant that I would have dreamt up not one fire but two.

Sighing, I felt grief tremble for a man who had been nothing to me but a secretive stranger. All I wanted now was to go up to the apartment, take a shower, and settle into Luke's mother's rocker with Fellow resting his chin on my bare feet.

Conrad, finally propelling himself free of his lassitude, propelled himself out of the patrol car.

"Well, that's a damn lie." He slapped the car's roof. "I'm sure it's John Storey they took out of there. I've got to get to a phone, to call the state attorney general. If those GoldPro miscreants think they're going to force the *Sun* out of business and burn down Bannack for good measure, they most certainly have another think coming!" Despite the fervor of his words, his gaze was fixed thirstily on the Antler, which was reabsorbing its drinkers, even though its facade was weeping sooty water.

"All right, Conrad, you do that." Rheta stepped back to give the editor passing room. In the meantime, you won't mind if AJ and I try to work out a deal with Elephant Rock Printers to get a special edition out, will you?"

Conrad wasn't so enraged that he couldn't hear a call to duty when he heard one. He paused, letting his priorities battle themselves out.

"Yes," he said quietly, some of the color coming back into his face. "I do mind. I'll take care of that job myself."

The last thing I should have wanted to do was to somehow help manufacture a special edition under makeshift conditions with begged and borrowed materials. But suddenly I was possessed with a manic enthusiasm for the project.

"Too bad we don't have time to sell advertising," I said, my voice edgy with goofy glee. "We'd probably force our boycotters into supporting us or looking like assholes."

"Who says we don't have time?" Rheta bounced on her Keds. "It's only two: I'll head for the bank first, and you trot right over to the Elephant Rock Printers and bat your big green eyes at Tom Engles and ask him to set you up in his darkroom. He doesn't use it anymore, but I'd bet a million dollars he still has all the makings."

"Why don't I find Luke instead? He could probably pull the strings at the university to get us permission to use the art department's darkroom—the one they're using for their Maymester history of photography class? If so, we could save some set-up time."

Rheta stood bouncing back from one foot to another, her car keys jingling in her fingers. "Well, OK, but we'll still have to get Tom to do the press run for us. I really don't want to have to drive clear to Hamilton and back tonight. Tom can only do tabloid-size, but we won't worry about that. Getting the papers labeled for the post office could be a major problem, though—but maybe the damage didn't reach into the mailroom."

Ignoring the fact that I stank of sweat, smoke and menstrual blood, I made a mental checklist of what I had to do next. Get to a store—I felt uncomfortably damp and my teeth needed brushing. Scan the streets for Fellow, just in case. Somehow locate Luke without the aid of Stela or a cell phone. Drive out to Bannack again to find him if necessary and to get updates from Binah and Delores. Drive back to Misfire to squeeze all the official information I could from law enforcement. Try to dig up enough information to write Nick's obituary. Check with the dispatcher about any dog-at-large reports. Make a brief appearance at the door of the parents' RV to let them know I was alive and reasonably well. Call Litton in case he had heard about the fires on the news and was worried.

No—that's one task I could skip. But I would need to figure out a place to crash and clean up, a cheap place. Fatigue was making my ears ring, my eyes lose their focus.

Reviewing my mental list, I was sorry I had started it. Sometimes it's better not to know what you have ahead of you until you see the headlights coming.

I found Luke hunkered vacant-eyed on the front porch of his mother's house, still buckled into his bunker coat, apparently unwilling either to insert himself into the cobwebbed clutter of his childhood home or to reopen the door of the empty doublewide where he had been playing house with Stela.

"You'll stay in my mother's house, of course," Luke said with no preliminary discussion. "Here, I've written up Nick's obituary—I doubt there's anyone else to do it, and I don't want him portrayed only as the man who burned down the *Sun*."

I scanned the hand-written article and then raised my eyes. "Why?" I asked. "Why did he end up the way he did?"

Luke shrugged. Instead of answering my question, he asked me what else he could do to help. Within minutes he had arranged for me to get access to the college's darkroom. "You'd better take this," he said, handing me his phone after I asked him if he knew how to contact Binah and Delores. There was something disturbing about his willingness to part with his cell so easily. What if Stela tried to call? Instead of asking that question, I accepted the mobile with no comment but my thanks.

His contact list was surprisingly complete for a man who spent his professional life in the 19th century. Still standing outside Luke's mother's house, I reached Binah and Delores right away, jotting down their comments on the back of Nick's obituary. The parents' RV was dark and the workshop lights were on. I convinced myself later would be a better time to deal with Bet. For now, a note stuck under the RV's windshield would suffice.

At the courthouse, the dispatcher still didn't have any information on a dog matching Fellow's description. I had to appreciate the fact the police chief ushered me into the county sheriff's office while the Butte TV crew and *Standard* reporters waited in the foyer for the official press conference. "I'm not going to announce this yet for public consumption, but we're fairly certain it was arson and that Nick started the fire at Bannack, too." the police chief said.

I couldn't begin to believe such an absurd accusation. "Arson? Why?"

"Who could tell with Nick? We'll start sorting out possible motives tomorrow after the Fire Marshal arrives to help us sort out the crime scene. In the meantime, don't even think about trying to get in there. I've had to threaten to arrest Conrad twice already for trying to slip in the alley door."

After the press conference, I scanned the bottom of my to-do list where the parents waited. Bet stood on the top step of the RV, her arms folded across her chest. She looked frozen. I felt chilled myself in the grip of the nightly spring cool down.

"I'm glad you finally are getting around to us, AJ." Bet's voice cloaked an emotion that, for once, she wanted to keep to herself. Let her.

"We got back from a quick trip to Bozeman to find Montana Street all blocked off and the *Sun* smoking."

Since my note was sticking out of the pocket of her sweater, I decided not to present it as evidence for my defense.

"Well, what's done is done. You'd better come in to get cleaned up— you'll have plenty of privacy because we still have a few things to do out in the workshop for the sale tomorrow. I've already made up a bed for you on the little pull-out couch."

"That's OK," I said brusquely. "I don't want to crowd you; Luke has invited me to stay in his mother's house. Besides, I've still got film to process and stories to write." Before Bet had the chance to chastise me further, I scuttled away.

"Are you sure you don't want to bed down on my roll-away?" Adrenaline depleted, Rheta had to boost her words by making a megaphone of her hands. I wouldn't have been surprised to see her slide gently to the floor next to the copying machine that was spitting single sheets into the hands of the *Sun*'s mailing crew. They had reorganized themselves to do a mass hand-delivery of the flyers that carried only seven words and an URL in Bodoni bold 72 point type: "Complete Coverage of *Sun* and Bannack Fires: www.elephantrockprinters.com"

"I can print the damn special edition for you, sure, even though I don't relish the thought of another midnight press run," Tom Engles had told an enraged Conrad when we had first converged at the print shop. "But what are you going to do then? There's no electricity in the *Sun*, and you know that law enforcement isn't going to let you drag your mailing equipment out of there while the building's still smoldering. Besides, you'd need four weightlifters to budge that dinosaur you call a labeler—and you won't even know if it still works until you try it."

"We'll manage!" Conrad shouted, but it was clear he knew Tom was right.

Tom pushed even harder: "If you go digital, I can get the web edition up just as soon as Rheta gives me her ad copy and AJ types the stories to go with the photos she's printed up, as many as she wants. The sky's the limit. How long will that take you?" He directed the question at me. "An hour?"

"Maybe two."

"While you're doing that, I can scan in the photos you've printed and put together the basic design. It won't be fancy, but it will be fast and accessible to everyone with an internet connection."

"But what good will a web edition do if no one knows it's there?" Conrad said, brightening at what must have seemed to him an irrefutable clincher. Genifer, waiting to be given something to do, snorted with the contempt of the young for the aging. "Believe me, they'll know," she said. "Probably everyone in Misfire is googling the fires right now to see what's been posted. The *Standard* has already posted the photos they've bought off some of the firefighters."

"No," Conrad said. "We need at least some kind of paper publication. We'll run flyers on your copying machine and rustle up the mailing crew to blanket the residential areas with them."

Genifer didn't try to mask her astonishment. "Are you kidding me? Just call the radio station—they'll probably announce the internet coverage as a public service just to help you out."

However, Conrad wasn't one to take the advice of an adolescent girl with cyan hair, so flyers it was. He left as soon as he scanned my story on Tom's computer screen. "This is the beginning of the end," he said. He didn't specify the end of what.

"Really, AJ, you are more than welcome to stay with me," Rheta said, repeating her earlier offer after Tom had finished uploading my stories and photos to the *Sun*'s smoking-new digital edition.

"I'm tempted." In fact, I was dreading the prospect of trying to set up camp in Luke's house, so dusty and sad. But I didn't think Rheta needed company for what was left of the night. "Thanks a lot, but Luke's expecting me, and I can't even call him since I have his cell."

"He's kept the landline in the house, but I doubt he would hear the ring from the doublewide. How was he when you went over to pick up Nick's obituary?"

"Shell-shocked about Stela—but I'm certainly not the one he'll want to confide in. And Bet's in some kind of snit, so I think she'll leave me alone. With luck, I'll be able to slip in and go straight to bed without seeing anyone."

The moon was rising full and bright, but my vision was so blurred by exhaustion, I might not notice Fellow even if I passed him. Still, I spent another hour randomly driving through Misfire's quiet streets. All I accomplished was to prove to myself that you can't force your luck. The Ingrahams' yard light shone like a solitary star as I drove over the cattle guard and past the unlighted humps of my parents' RV and of Luke's doublewide. The glassed-in porch of the house was illuminated with the same sort of teardrop bulbs that dangled in the *Sun*'s darkroom. Had dangled. The porch's screen door squealed as I opened it. Inside, the air was poulticed with the sour smell of recently washed fir flooring. I pulled down the blinds and locked the door. Luke had already made up a bed for me on the wide window seat that spanned one end of the enclosure. Had the sheets not been ironed, I would have crawled in smoky clothes and all.

Although the porch was fresh and clean, the interior of the house was a different matter. Feeling my throat close, I dodged towers of half-sorted boxes. The only washing machine I could discover was an old wringer model in the basement. Too exhausted to trust myself to keep my hands out of its rollers, I swished the only clothes I now owned in the adjacent laundry sink and tossed the sodden mess into a dryer of relatively recent vintage.

Upstairs, the bathroom was immaculate. The claw-footed tub was too tempting to pass up, even though I wasn't sure that I should trust myself to six inches of soporific hot water. As it turned out, the rising tide woke me up every time my chin started slipping beneath the waves.

Luke hadn't set out towels for me, so I dried myself with a brown wool robe that probably had waited on its hook ever since Luke's father had last worn it. My body felt strange under the rough cloth, as though it belonged not to me, but to an accident victim I'd happened upon. Despite the cramping in my uterus and the inhaler-induced burning in my throat, sleep was reaching out for me before I even pulled the lavender-scented sheets around my shoulders.

That's when I remembered Nick's retriever.

I groaned, trying not to picture him wandering terrified and hurt through Misfire's streets. Surely Nick, if he had been planning burglary and arson, wouldn't have taken the retriever with him. Surely he would have left the dog somewhere safe provisioned with food and water. Surely the dog would have sense to pee on the floor if no one appeared to let him out. Surely the dog could wait for a rescue until I got some rest.

Surely.

I dragged myself out of my fragrant nest, shimmied into my damp clothes on and set myself to facing up to the new thing on my list.

Even the seeker after gold is not always rewarded but often, after enduring hardships that he would be unwilling to endure in an old settled country, goes home poor in purse and broken in health or toils on in search of the phantom of fortune, which may never be his lot to find.

—James Fergus, in a Jan. 1, 1863, letter from "Bannock City," quoted in *Not in Precious Metals Alone: A Manuscript History of Montana*

High Beam

STILL SHIVERING, I CLICKED THE CHEVY'S HEATER ON. AT LEAST I HAD THE benefit of shelter against the nightly spring cool down. If Fellow was outside tonight, he would be chilled no matter how tightly he curled. Or not. Maybe the chill I was feeling wasn't a result only of the external weather. Maybe I was generating my own cold front, one as personal and portable as loneliness.

Because the full moon was on high beam, I didn't think about headlights until an on-coming police car went into beacon mode. Annoyed, I pulled over to my side of the two-lane road and flicked my lights on to show I understood. Instead of letting me go on, the cop got out.

"You OK, AJ?" the cop asked as I cranked down the window. Although at first I couldn't put a name to his earnest doughy face, I recognized him from somewhere.

"Just looking for my dog—he's sort of a basset hound. Seen him?" The cop scrutinized my face with an attention that made it obvious the moonlight wasn't working magic on my bleary eyes and half-washed and far-from-dry shirt.

"May, may, maybe you ought to get some rest? You must be exhausted after the fire and all." It was Bruce Storey, the museum docent. He must be supplementing his salary by literally moonlighting for the city. Thinking how pleased John Storey would be to hear that I had been taken into custody by his son, I considered fleeing the scene of whatever this was.

"Got a place to stay?" Since Bruce didn't seem to be arresting me, I pointed back toward Luke's, close enough that the yard light was still visible. Oddly, I recognized something like gratitude swelling under my breastbone in response to the question. Or maybe it was just the tidal sweep of acid in a stomach that had been offered nothing but the maple bars and bad coffee Rheta had been handing out to the firefighters at Bannack.

Rest, Bruce suggested. I considered taking his advice for a whole half second after he waved me off. Wandering around the Prairie Schooner might not be the safest thing to do alone in the middle of the night. Still, a quick check wouldn't take more than a few minutes. I had everything I needed for this little job: the spare leash I'd been carrying around in the Bel Air since Fellow had gone missing, the emergency lantern from my trunk kit, and even Stela's set of Schooners keys, which I had found right in the coffee can "safe" where she had left them.

Stela by moonlight: where had the highway taken her?

I pushed that question away as something to worry about later. I had more than enough to worry about now. As I turned into the resort, the canvas top of the Prairie Schooner glowed, a phosphorescent mushroom. Inside the main building, the glare of electric lights slapped me out of the silver of the night. The dining room was dead quiet. The dollars embedded in the bar glinted lifelessly. Stupid with fatigue, I opened my mouth to call the retriever and then closed it. I didn't even know the dog's name.

A sharp creak in the dark passageway that led from the restaurant to the spa building triggered something like the panic attack equivalent of a gag reflex. Sprinting out of the empty restaurant, I raced for the Bel Air.

Back in the Chevy's steel shell, I struggled to quiet the drum of my own panting, to decide what to do next. Really, there was only one logical way to proceed. I sat there breathing deliberately, trying to discipline myself to take it. If courage came in finite portions, apparently I had used up my day's supply. Despite my growing sense that something else very bad was about to happen, I would have to go back to the restaurant to make certain the retriever hadn't made the noise that had spooked me.

Shaking and ashamed of shaking, I forced myself to backtrack. This time, I checked not only the restaurant's dining room and bar, but the kitchen, the restrooms, and the half-dozen luxury guest suites upstairs. Nothing bad happened. I did allow myself to give a bye to the spa; clearly Nick wouldn't abandon his dog to dankness. However, I couldn't talk myself out of the necessity of checking the cabin Nick had claimed by virtue of squatter's rights.

The deep shadows under the cottonwoods made me glad of my lantern. At first, it seemed nothing had changed since my brief stop with Bet the evening before. Even the overalls Nick had draped over the railing to dry were still there, flapping disconsolately. Inside, my probing light showed that Nick had left the place in perfect and unrevealing order, the bed stripped, cans of pinto beans and soup stacked neatly in a cardboard box by the door. Then I noticed it: a half sheet of paper on the card table with a key taped to its center. Two words were printed neatly at the top in an editor's blue pencil: "For AJ." There was no other message.

Later, I didn't remember pocketing the key or walking back to the Chevy. But I must have, because I found myself behind the steering wheel with the car on its way downtown. Just in time, I stopped myself turning automatically onto Montana Street. Instead, I let the Bel Air take me away from the ruin of the *Sun* to the bright windows of the Golden Hour.

The vinyl of the booth I had occupied the night before was streaked and damp. I settled in anyway, needing someplace familiar to plant my backside. The café was absolutely empty except for the same formidable waitress who had waited on me almost exactly twenty-four hours before.

"What'll you have tonight, AJ? Another slice of that chocolate pie?" I felt disproportionately pleased that the woman remembered my name. Tonight, she wore a tag that made a further introduction unnecessary.

I stared unable to answer, even though Sue B. and I now knew each other on a first name basis.

"Hard day, huh. Well, I bet you'd like steak and eggs with biscuits on the side? Right?"

I didn't protest. Lacking the energy to specify that the steak be cooked until the description "well done" would constitute an understatement, I sat inert.

After two cups of coffee, the saucer-sized biscuit, half the T-bone (medium rare) and both eggs (sunny side up), I asked Sue B. for a telephone book.

Nick wasn't listed, but then, I really hadn't expected him to be. I placed the phone book neatly beside my plate and let my chin sink into cupped hands, shaking despite the unsteady support of my elbows.

"Do you have a city directory?" Although vastly out of date, the old-fashioned reference was still useful because people in Misfire tended to stay put. I imagined walking to the *Sun* and pulling Conrad's copy out of his desk drawer.

"Who you looking for?" Sue B. plopped a waxed sack with a cartoon of a panting dog on it next to my plate. I didn't answer: I needed what remained of my energy to coax the big chunk of uneaten steak into the small bag. I didn't want to offend Sue B. by leaving it behind.

Sue B. tried again. "I don't mean to be a busybody or anything, but I know phone numbers. I mean, I see them once, and they stick in my head."

I imagined Nick's ghost hesitating over a ringing phone. What would I ask if he answered?

"Go ahead—try me," Sue B. urged. Her hair glinted insistently. I didn't want to hurt her feelings.

"Do you know Rheta Fox's?"

Sue B. rattled off a familiar number, put her hands on her substantial hips and waited for my confirmation.

"The *Sun*'s?"

Before I could utter the last sibilant, Sue B. had propelled the number into the café's bacon-infused air.

I was impressed. "Can you remember addresses in the same way?"

Sue B. shook her head no, sorry to break the bad news. "It's funny that I don't—it's just phone numbers I have the knack for. But, whose house do you want to find? I know where a lot of people live."

"Do you know Nick Stanislavsky's place?"

Sue B. stared intently at me and then decided: "If anybody asks—the cops, for instance—I'll have to tell them I gave you directions."

"That's OK. I'm worried about Nick's dog. I think he might be shut up in the house."

"That nice old retriever? He wasn't burned up in the fire with Nick? Are you sure you want to be the one to take him on? Maybe you should call the cops."

"They would just stick him in the pound. Besides, Nick gave me his key, so it won't be breaking and entering." I fished it out of my jeans pockets and held it up like an icon. Sue B. paused long enough to let me know she saw holes in my story big enough to toss an Angus through, but was going to help me anyway. I didn't know why. After all, this was the second night in a row she had been called upon to administer first aid to me in the form of strong coffee and high-fat food. In ten minutes, I was on my way with a map sketched on the back of a paper napkin.

Although the diagram was clearly drawn, finding Nick's house was difficult. After I spent what felt like an hour wandering up and down the series of unmarked lanes winding off the road to the cemetery, the moon finally revealed the cluster of mailboxes I had been hunting.

The courthouse clock struck five. I pulled up in front of a flat-roofed house circa 1955. A chain link fence, tight and straight, surrounded a lawn that smelled as though it had been recently cut. Weeping willows swept the front door behind a twiggy curtain. White petunias frothed and spilled from a planter made of stacked tires. When I turned off the engine, I heard a crescendo of howling inside that would have done justice to a pack of wolves.

As the gate yielded with a screech, the barking stopped and reconfigured itself into the lash of a growl. I hesitated. The retriever had never shown himself to be the least bit aggressive, but the decibel level promised violence. Approaching the door, I tried peering into the window, as much to let the retriever see me as to get a look at him, but the plastic trash bags serving as curtains blocked my view. Frantic nails scratched at the door as I unlocked it and pushed it in a cautious half inch. A black snout wedged itself into the breach. Gasping, I hopped out of range.

Fellow tackled me hard before he whirled a circumscribed circle around the chain-linked yard, pausing only to lift his leg twice. I blinked in disbelief. When I opened my mouth to shout him back to me, my throat creaked into a sob. The retriever followed, dodged past me and trotted to the gate with an expectant air. When Nick didn't appear, the retriever marked the fence and then planted himself by the closed gate, his face pointed down the lane.

Swaying with confusion, I reached for the support of the door, a grin stretching my face. Rushing to me, Fellow made a leap that allowed him to snag the doggie bag that I had absent-mindedly stuck halfway into my pocket. He tossed it in the air, carried it once around the yard like a banner, and then settled down to gnaw bag, meat, and bone together.

"Why?" I demanded an answer from Nick, but a conversation with the dead can never be more than a conversation with yourself. It's not enough, but it must suffice.

The retriever showed no interest in Fellow's prize, instead holding his pose by the gate. When I crouched to pat his head, he looked away—pointedly, I thought. I stumbled back to the house, trying to decide whether I still needed to assail Nick's privacy. Neither dog tried to follow me as I entered.

I'd expected a labyrinth of tightly packed trash. Instead, a spotless strip of hallway linoleum, its pattern of yellow and grey squares worn almost white, gleamed. My nose told me the wax was fresh, and I inhaled the homely fragrance to calm myself. Except for three pools of piss and two piles of dog shit deposited neatly near the door, the living room was as orderly as the cabin had been, but infinitely more illuminating. Neatly constructed shelves of unfinished pine insulated all the walls but one with books, all perfectly aligned. The remaining side of the room was dominated by a desk fashioned from a smoothly varnished oak door balanced on two painted saw horses. Here the linoleum gave way to a worn square of carpet cleaned so recently I could see the trail the vacuum had blazed. In one corner, a spot was reserved for the dogs with a folded wool blanket. Centered precisely under the desk was an incongruously elegant Queen Anne chair, its back vase-shaped, its cabriole legs curved. Stationed in a corner on a rubber mat was a tub of kibble and a tub of water, both at least two thirds full.

Folding my arms, I gripped skin so cold that my fingertips didn't recognize it. Without considering what I was doing, I walked to the chair and unfolded the cardigan that was draped over its back. I had never seen Nick in anything like it. The sleeves dangled and my elbows fell short of the hollows his had left. The cashmere enfolded me with the warm fragrance of incense. Closing it with buttons of bone, I let my eyes skid across the cleared desktop to a lamp that looked like a real Tiffany. When I switched it on, the twisting stems of daffodils flowed to the wide open faces of trumpeting blossoms.

More surprising than the lamp was the altar next to the desk. Crafted from the shell of the kind of massive stereo cabinet popular in the fifties, it had been repurposed into a mahogany cave. Inside, a plaster statuette stood lifting her arms, a cloak of blue silk unfurling from them like gold-embroidered wings. Despite her finery, Mary accused fallible humanity with an agonized stare, painted tears flowing from her painted eyes, a lace handkerchief ready in her grasp. I wondered how Nick worked at his desk within the splash of so much grief.

At Mary's feet was an offering of stacked parchment sheets that I at first took to be especially fine reproductions of an illuminated manuscript. The enameled glory of the document transfixed me for a heartbeat. It was no reproduction, I realized: Leaning close, I saw the initial letter of the phrase "In the beginning" had been crafted out of the image of a cottonwood tree bearing dozens of minuscule birds that flew and nested. I recognized a magpie, a robin, and a mixed cloud of mountain bluebirds and goldfinches. Leading a parade of dogs sniffing around the base of the tree and along the margins was Nick's retriever. I laughed out loud when I saw that the hound at the end of the line was Fellow.

Fellow? I rushed back out to the yard. My dog was where I'd left him, the bag and the steak consumed, but the bone grating between his jaws. Kneeling, I embraced him, taking in his leather smell, feeling the vibration of his jaw against my cheek. He leaned into me, but kept on gnawing. The retriever had planted himself like a boulder next to the gate. When I stroked his back, his muscles tensed, ready to resist. The goldfinches were greeting the first intimations of the dawn. I would need to leave soon, to wake Luke to tell him what I had discovered. He could take steps to protect the manuscripts. It was certain law enforcement would be investigating the house sooner than later.

Inside, the altar drew me back, but I refused to sully the ivory vellum with ungloved hands. Where had Nick acquired such exquisite materials? Had he scraped and cured skins himself? The man was a cipher, and one I wouldn't be able to solve in the few minutes more I could allow myself to spend alone in the house. And yet, I was unwilling to leave.

Just as spartan as the living area, the kitchen had been equipped even more eccentrically than the living room. A table, another Queen Anne piece, was squeezed against a dented stainless steel sink and counter that looked as though they had been salvaged from a school kitchen. The counter's well-wiped surface held five—no six, boxes. Several lengths of strapping tape sealed each and at least three labels were visible, but I had to bend over to read Nick's handwriting, precise, but tiny. Rheta's name was the first I saw and then Conrad's, the tags affixed to flat cases that I immediately recognized as archival storage cartons. A container that looked like an old-fashioned hatbox was designated for Delores.

The sight of those labels transformed me to cold stone: Nick had been preparing for his death. The question was which death? The death that engulfed him in the *Sun* or the eventuality that waits for everyone?

Without considering the consequences, I scooped up the three boxes. I emerged into a dawn that was getting serious about getting the new day on the road.

Fellow immediately tried to induce me to play a game of keep-away with the remainder of the bone. Stooping to him, I let my fingers trace his flying ears as he whipped under my hands to the corner of the fence; he went to work to scrape up a bare patch of ground.

Icy dew was drowning the grass, soaking into my shoes. The Chevy's back seat would easily accommodate the three other boxes still in the kitchen, even though one of them was sizable, a Butte Brewing Company box whose fancy red script had outlasted one of Montana's most famous beers. I felt an icy compulsion to leave them undisturbed on the kitchen counter. The moon had forgiven my intrusion in a way the rising sun would not.

Still, it didn't seem right to let the cops dig through Nick's legacy, rifling through whatever he had gathered for others. I didn't allow myself to think about the legality of what I was doing. Fellow barked sharply once and pointed his nose at the Chevy to indicate that we should get going.

"I'll just be a minute." My own name buzzed at me from the top of the beer box, jerking me into a shock that felt not at all metaphorical, but the kind of zapping that strikes when you unwisely plug in a rummage sale coffeemaker. With the muscles in my arm still jumping, I picked up the carton. It not only dwarfed the others, it was much heavier. Too cowardly to look at the labels on the remaining packages—both more archival cases, I stacked them on mine. Feeling more like an invader with every degree the sky brightened, I scanned the remaining two rooms—a spartan bedroom and a prosaic pantry—and was happy to find nothing I needed to take an interest in. Until I had slept, acquired somewhere a set of clean clothes, and reacquired somehow my clarity of mind, I wanted no more surprises.

The retriever refused to follow Fellow into the Chevy's backseat. When I attached the spare leash to his collar and pulled, he simply settled more deeply into the wet grass. Stymied, I couldn't figure out how to coax him, and he was too big to lift. I unlocked the house again. When the retriever saw what I was doing, he bolted for the opening door. He settled under Nick's desk, chin steadied by his front paws.

"What's your name?"

He closed his eyes to make me disappear.

Nick's Kelvinator not only was completely empty of snacks that might be used to bribe a dog, it was clean and defrosted, a rolled towel propped in the door to keep it from closing. Lacking the heart to rummage through Nick's cupboards, I refilled the water tub. I cleaned up the mess by the front door with paper towels I found in a cupboard and deposited them in a garbage can behind the house. Too late, I realized that in doing so, I had confused the time line law enforcement would try to infer from the condition of the house. The retriever didn't raise its head as I left.

Luke was standing at the cattle guard watching the traffic on the interstate. His own truck was parked just off the driveway, poised for what looked like the same kind of quick getaway I had arranged for myself in Bannack. He forced a grimacing smile and a victory sign when he caught sight of Fellow balanced with his front feet on the dashboard. The lenses of his smudged glasses magnified the shadows under his eyes.

"She's not coming back," he said, as I got out of the car, letting the door close as quietly as possible. Fellow subsided into the passenger's seat and buried his head as far into the back of the seat as he could.

Confused, I didn't reply.

"I found her good high heels by my mother's headstone."

No less confused, I waited.

"She used to go out there every Sunday. She called it 'singing them to sleep.' She would dress up, make an occasion of it. When the grass was wet, she would wear her walking shoes and carry her heels to change into them there."

"I'm sorry." I wanted to ask, "Why?" but now was not the time. Instead, I started unloading the boxes from the back seat. I handed him the one with my name on it and told him where I had found it. He tested its weight and then gave it back.

"Anything for me?" He looked hurt when I shook my head in the negative. "I mean, no, I don't know, I haven't looked at all of them yet."

He didn't ask why not, and I didn't tell him, mostly because I scarcely knew.

"Well, you'd better keep all of them unopened and together for now—at least until you know what your legal position is." I expected Luke to help me carry the cartons into the house. Instead, he walked down the drive empty-handed. His gait was stiff.

"Wait," I called. "Come back." His eyes were empty, devoid of interest. But this was no time to offer tea and sympathy. A shot of scotch was what he could have used, but my replacement bottle of Glenlivet had added fuel to the fire. Balancing the cartons against the Bel Air, I told him about the manuscript and the retriever. "What's his name?" I asked.

"Alph." His voice was hollow. "Like Alpha and Omega. He knows me. I'll get him into the truck somehow and keep him here in the trailer until we can decide what do with him."

Before I could reconcile my memory of dumpster-diving Nick as the sort of man who named his dog after a letter of the Greek alphabet, Luke returned to the trailer without a word. To prepare a place for Alph? To shed more tears out of my sight?

Waiting for him to re-emerge, I gave Chas and Bet's RV a nervous glance. It remained dark and quiet. But I couldn't believe Bet, who was ever a light sleeper, wasn't awake with her ears pointed to full attention. She must be seriously angry with me; otherwise she would have been at the door of the Bel Air before I even stopped the engine.

Fellow lifted his head and then let it drop. Luke reappeared with a pair of white cotton archivist's gloves and a handful of white plastic trash bags. "They'll do to protect the manuscript for now." He had to try twice to master the tall step into the cab of his pickup.

I knew I should go directly to the porch, settle Fellow, and go to sleep. But what if the cops came looking for me? Worse still, what if Bet and Chas stirred themselves to find out what was going on?

I remembered the way Fellow had safeguarded his bone by scratching a quarter of an inch of dirt over it in the bare corner of Nick's lawn. I resettled the cartons in the back seat and moved the car as close to the house as I could. This time Fellow stood up on the front seat, his eyes wide. Leaping out the car door, he was waiting for me on the front porch when I arrived with my first armload. He was still waiting when I carried in the second set.

He watched with interest as I lifted the top of the window seat where I had almost slept. I deposited the cartons in the roomy storage compartment below, closed the lid, and re-straightened the sheets of my makeshift bed to discourage the parents from poking around. Dissatisfied, I yanked off the sheets and retrieved the three cartons on top—my beer box and the two whose owners I carefully had postponed identifying.

Fellow trotted alongside as I slipped into the back of the house, leaving the lights turned off, making do with the seep of the early morning light. In what must have been Luke's mother's room, I pushed the boxes under the high-framed bedstead. There was plenty of room, even for the beer box. As I shoved, the label on one of the cartons insisted on turning its face to me, revealing its intended recipient. I sank to the floor, stunned. Could I be mistaken? With my heart thumping, I pulled the box back into the light: Mrs. Bet Armstrong. I paused trying to call my breath back. Wanting no more surprises, I rustled the other carton out of the dark and was relieved to find Luke's name. Fellow inspected it with his nose and then sat to see what I would do next.

Bet. She couldn't find out about this, at least not yet. I gathered up the boxes remaining in the window seat and added them to the collection under the bed. Retreating to the bedroom door, I saw my work wasn't yet finished: the first row of boxes was clearly visible. Rummaging through the linen closet in the hallway, I found a chenille spread I had noticed earlier. I draped it unevenly over the bed, letting its long side sweep the floor on the side facing the door. Fellow used the cedar chest at the foot of the bed as a springboard to the mattress. He circled himself a new place in the world just as I noticed his paws and my feet had blazed a path in the dust that dimmed the planks of the floor. I needed a broom.

The kitchen was dark, its drawn curtains dingy for lack of washing. Something fluttered in my peripheral vision. A short, stocky woman scowled until she disappeared into an old-fashioned dressmaker's form standing in one corner. Except for the accumulation of dirt, the kitchen waited for Luke's mother to return—the family of bluebirds flying over the arch above the sink, the sturdy white china in the glass-fronted cupboards ready for a family meal, the iron skillet on one of the stove burners, at hand to fry up bacon or pork chops or hamburgers. I sighed when I thought of the shiny copper bottoms of the lost Revereware. Those pans must have lived in the lower cupboards. I opened all the cupboards; yes, they were empty. Luke had progressed thus far and no further.

I found the broom along with a mop and a pail in a narrow closet next to the stove. Motivated by some reason I didn't care to think about, I not only swept away the tell-tale path, I mopped the floor. Twice.

Feeling better, I sat on the chenille cover and then stretched out beside Fellow, my face pressed against the tracery of a floral pattern too fanciful to identify with any real blossom. I sneezed. Although closeted, the bedspread hadn't escaped the house's accumulated dust. I knew I should return to the clean porch. Instead I remained planted. "Let's just stay here for a minute," I told Fellow, but he was already asleep.

When he finally nosed me awake, the Big Ben clock on the bedside table told me it was noon. Feeling better despite the secrets under the bed, I tripped over a sack propped against the outside of the bedroom door. Inside were nested serviceable cotton panties in a close-enough size and a tank top with a self bra that didn't require a precise fit. Good. I was less pleased when I unfolded a T-shirt that depicted a grizzled prospector crouched over a gold pan and a rumpled pair of jeans two sizes larger than I usually wore. Luke? No—probably Bet, even though she usually had a better eye. Maybe this was her revenge, just an innocent mistake on the surface, but spring-loaded with a little slap underneath. That would be Bet. Yes, it would.

The bed of the creek is rich in the shining treasure but has not been worked on account of its expensiveness. The creek has to be flumed, and the rock bed is from 15 to 30 feet deep, upon which the gold is deposited. This has to be reached and then mined which is attended with danger and expense.

—Kate Dunlap, in *The Montana Gold Rush Diary of Kate Dunlap*, edited by S. Lyman Tyler

Boxed In

AT FIRST, I IGNORED THE KNOCKING. BUT WHEN I HEARD BET CALL my name, I stumbled to the porch holding up the oversized jeans with one hand. Fellow bounded ahead, yelping with what I felt was excessive joy.

"I'm so sorry!" I couldn't tell whether Bet was apologizing for her part in our argument the evening before or for my ensemble. Without another word, she swept me, baggy-assed jeans and all, into an embrace that reminded me of how good a mother's arms can feel. Then she spoiled it. "We've decided to cancel the rummage sale today because of everything, so I can take you right downtown and get you presentable in no time."

Irritated, I tried to pull away. It was Bet, after all, who was responsible for my currently unpresentable condition. Never mind the excuse she whispered in the ear smashed against her face: that by the time she had thought to go shopping for me, the only places she could find open were the Dollar Store and Crystal Starr's antique/souvenir/used clothing enterprise.

At least the underwear was new. But the idea that my jeans might once have strained over Crystal Starr's voluptuous haunches made me try again to shudder out of Bet's embrace. She pinioned me for a one beat longer before giving me up. The sudden release sent me collapsing into an unintended crouch, which I converted into a hard sit onto the top step of the outside entrance. Bet thudded down next to me in a movement that fell significantly short of her usual grace.

"Now, don't jump." Bet's voice wobbled. Fellow didn't seem to notice. He threatened her crisp trousers with an uplifted paw. Bet grasped it firmly while she babbled about how she and Chas were "thrilled" that things had worked out. Fellow backed away when I tried to use his collar as a handle to force him to my side of the step. Jealous, I wanted to feel the sandpaper of his pads against my palm and the tattoo of his claws in my grip. "Shake?" I asked to entice him to me. He shook me off and wallowed at Bet's right ballet flat. I noticed its pearl gray toe was smudged.

Bet was making me worry. She never apologized. She wasn't the type to ignore the threat posed to the seat of her trousers by unswept concrete. She wasn't a dog lover. She wasn't a babbler. Things had not worked out. Chas never was thrilled about anything connected with me. Bet polished her shoes every morning.

And then there was the box Nick had inexplicitly addressed to her. But my adoptive mother had never laid eyes on Nick until the night before he died in the fire, had she? I pictured Nick's face in the moonlight outside his Schooners cabin. Had there been recognition in the stare he had shot at Bet as she shielded herself with the Bel Air's window?

I didn't want to think about what any of this might mean. In fact, my mind wasn't working well at all. I could remember everything that had happened yesterday and early this morning. But I couldn't figure out what to feel, let alone do, about any of it.

It was relief when Bet leaped to her feet and demanded that I help her scout the house for something I could use to secure my jeans. Inside of five minutes, she had pulled open all the closets and drawers in that bedroom and the other two, stopping only when she found a narrow leather belt that looked as if it had once done duty for a man's suit trousers. Incapable of speech, I waited for her to lift the bedspread and discover the boxes. She didn't.

"OK, then. Now we can go." She sounded almost normal.

"Go?"

"Yes. We need to go shopping!"

I insisted on doing the driving, hoping to reassert some control over the situation, whatever the situation was, but my hope was futile. Bet demanded I pilot the Bel Air as close as possible to the newspaper building.

"Maybe things aren't as bad as they looked yesterday," she said. "Besides, it's always better to get things over with."

"Ha," I said. However, I turned on to Montana Street because I was certain that, Bet or no, we wouldn't be able to get nearer than a block to the *Sun*. To my chagrin, traffic was moving normally through downtown Misfire, except directly in front of the newspaper building, where a barrier forced drivers to give the *Sun* a wide berth. As Bet predicted, the *Sun* did indeed look better than it had the night before—less like a victim sprawled at the scene of an accident and more like a corpse that had already kept its appointment with the undertaker. The newspaper's false front had been pulled more or less erect and secured to the Antler on one side and the empty JCPenney store on the other. The *Sun*'s front door was propped open as usual with the newspaper dispenser. It was streaked with soot, but furnished with what looked like the flyers we had run off the night before. Clearly visible, the reception counter seemed neither more or less disordered than usual.

Conrad was pacing back and forth out front. Noticing the Bel Air, he waved to signal me to park in front of the museum. I looked for signs of exhaustion in his face, but the swing of his shoulders communicated the fact that he was fired up, not burned out.

"This might take a few minutes," I told Bet. I needed to keep her at a distance while I let Conrad know about my finds in Nick's house. "Why don't you go over to the Golden Hour and order us lunch? I'll be over as soon as I can."

Bet brightened. "If we're lucky, your father will still be over there. Don't be too long now." She hopped out of the Chevy and hurried away without looking back.

"A deputy from the state fire marshal's office is in there, but he wouldn't let me go along for the inspection, the simpleton." Unable to wait, Conrad was already shouting to me as I dodged across the street. "He said it was too dangerous—he even intimated that he hasn't entirely ruled me out as an arson suspect, the pluperfect fool. But I did get down to the press this morning before he arrived—the cop on duty owed me a major favor. Anyway, the basement stairs are intact. And I'm sure there's no major damage to the press. The floor drain took the worst of the water that came down the stairwell from the fire hoses."

"Oh good," I said, wondering if Conrad's doctors had cleared him to climb stairs. "All you have to do now is figure out how to get it out of there and where to put it and we'll be ready for the next edition."

Conrad agreed vigorously, missing my satiric intent. "Yes, we'll be ready with our own story about the fire. I already have made it clear to the marshal that he must at least consider the possibility that John Storey and Gold-Pro have conspired to destroy Bannack and the *Sun*, too."

I hated to disabuse Conrad of that convenient notion, but as I summed up what I had found at Nick's house, he listened intently, interrupting only to ask questions and to take notes. Whatever else Conrad was or wasn't, he was a careful reporter.

"Did the contents of the boxes reveal his motives?" He reached for my shoulder. My shrug out of his grasp was meant to communicate my irritation at being asked this question for at least the third time. He engaged me in a staring contest, daring me to lie. After I repeated what I had already told him—that I hadn't opened any of the boxes, not even the one labeled for me, he seemed satisfied.

"Who else knows about them?" This was another question he had already asked.

"No one but Luke," I said, carefully omitting, as I had before, any indication of where exactly the cartons were stashed.

"Well, good, then," Conrad said. Oddly, he didn't urge our immediate departure on a mission to disambiguate the boxes. A long silence, at least long for him, let me know he was searching for a safe spot in the intersection between his personal curiosity, his journalist's sense of ethics, and his legal obligations.

"We'll have to turn them over to law enforcement," he finally said, and not happily.

"No," I replied. "I can't imagine why Nick left me anything at all—I've spoken to him only a half dozen times at the most. But I don't want the police or the fire marshal grabbing whatever's in my box before I get the chance to see it. All the cartons must hold materials that are private. Otherwise, they wouldn't be so elaborately sealed. And otherwise Nick would have just handed them over to us without all this drama."

"I agree with you about that much, AJ, but, ethics aside, we don't want to subject ourselves to criminal charges, do we?" I was tempted to mention that entering a crime scene when you hadn't been ruled out as an arson suspect was worse than failing to mention a few sealed boxes to law enforcement. However, I stopped myself from interrupting Conrad to say so.

"You can't prove what Nick's intentions were in leaving you his key, even if you might be able to argue that you had the right to enter his place. The cartons weren't in the same part of the house as the dogs, were they?" I had to shake my head no. "So you had no real reason to even go into the kitchen or to assume that you had any right to take possession of the cartons. Even had Nick died of natural causes, your actions would have been problematic. But since his death is part of a criminal investigation, I think you might be facing real legal trouble."

"No one knows about the boxes but us and Luke," I pointed out again. "So who's going to tell the police?"

Conrad might have answered, but Binah, who was wearing her fire chief's helmet with authority, materialized from behind the newspaper's reception counter accompanied by a balding man in an official-looking dark blue jacket. Conrad waved his notebook in the marshal's direction. I decided to get away while the getting was good.

Bet was sitting alone in a booth at the back of the Golden Hour, her pork chop cooling on her plate under its thick blanket of gravy. The slump in her shoulders worried me. "Bet," I said softly. She startled and blinked, as if she had been asleep. I waited until she had rearranged her features into their usual perky contours.

"Ready to go?" I asked as though longing for a rare treat.

"You bet," she said, but a beat too late to reassure me that my worries about her were misplaced.

"Is this your sister, AJ?" The owner of Misfire's only women's wear shop made her inquiry a little too sweetly. I didn't really know her, but I tend to dislike women of my age who wear their hair dyed black and sprayed into the Big Hair of a collectable Barbie. Besides, she had been one of the first to raise her hand to vote aye for the Elephant Rock Business Association's boycott against the *Sun*. On the other hand, that meeting had receded so far from relevance, I could hardly recall its details. And there was something else: yesterday she had bought an ad from Rheta for the web fire edition and had promised an insert for our next regular publication. People in small towns are like one big unhappy family, I decided. The fights stop, at least temporarily, for intensive care and funerals as everyone tries to out-nice each other.

"Yes, AJ is my sweet little baby sister," Bet proclaimed, cinching me around my waist. Don't you think we look alike?"

In fact, the two of us had never looked anything alike. I remembered squeezing into a photo booth at Woolworth's once when I was about ten, pressing my head against Bet's softly powdered cheek (she was inflicting one of her occasional freckle-hiding campaigns on herself) and smiling shyly into the camera. "Come on! Be a clown!" Bet slipped her lipsticked mouth into a rubber grin. No one could see us. Nevertheless, I was embarrassed.

"Come on! Don't be such a pill!" Bet crossed her eyes so vigorously I was afraid I would vomit. The camera caught me looking away as Bet stuck out her tongue.

That memory did nothing to boost my mood today, especially when the shop owner smirked "The family resemblance is absolutely clear, especially around the eyes!"

"Come on, sis," Bet said, winking at me. "Let's shop."

I determined that I would maintain a diplomatic silence no matter what manner of polyester horror Bet pulled from the store's racks, but as it turned out, I didn't have to. Within twenty minutes, she had helped me find two pairs of reasonably flattering khaki pants, three well-cut T-shirts free of synthetics and slogans, a flowing sweater in white cotton, and an assortment of underwear more luxurious than anything I had troubled to buy for a while. Bet only made one suggestion: that I try on a jade green sundress. It turned out to be both comfortable and flattering. Adding it to the pile at the counter, I turned to Bet and offered her a genuine smile.

"Thank you."

Bet handed the store owner a shortstack of hundred dollar bills. "Ha! I think the last time I heard those words from you was when you were about fourteen."

My smile vanished and a headache went from bud to blossom in about three seconds.

The owner called after us, "You two girls have a real nice day, now."

Bet's face configured itself into the mischievous mask I had disliked as long as I could remember. "You know," she said as we back-tracked to the Bel Air. "I think she really does think we're sisters. Now, don't you go telling her any different next time you see her. What she doesn't know won't . . ."

"That's what you always used to say to me." My tone struck even my own ears as petulant.

Bet's eyes glinted. "It's been a long time since you've asked any questions, AJ."

"What?"

She didn't answer, pretending to be oh-so-busy with the task of settling our parcels into the Bel Air's back seat.

"What!" I demanded.

"You heard me."

My ears were buzzing and the headache was spreading into my field of vision like thistles invading an untended garden. The acid bubbling up in the back of my throat was about to erupt into bitter words when Conrad loomed large in the driver's door window. I cranked it down, grateful that he was saving me from discovering what stupid thing I was about to say.

From the flare of Bet's freckles, it should have been clear to Conrad that he had blundered into an argument, but he was too intent on his own news to notice the fire and ice inside the Bel Air. "I've talked to Luke, and he's proposed what I think is the only practical solution. Bet, this concerns you, too. Can you come along right now?"

"To a party?" she asked, shifting into such a false cheeriness that my earlier worries about her multiplied themselves by a factor of a hundred.

"More like a wake."

Why wasn't Bet insisting on being told what was going on?

"Will there be whisky?" she asked disingenuously. I stared at her in disbelief.

"There'd better be," Conrad said grimly. "Rheta will meet us there, and so will Delores. I caught her on her cell, so she shouldn't be long."

Again, Bet failed to demand more information. Which meant she already had somehow figured out all that she needed to know. But how?

As everyone assembled at Luke's mother's house, we hauled the chairs from the dining room into the bedroom and pulled them up to the chenille bedspread as if it were a tablecloth and we were guests at a formal dinner we didn't want to attend. From the porch, Fellow was whimpering rhythmically to let me know he needed to participate in whatever we were doing.

"How's Alph?" I asked Luke while I finished arranging a buffet of sorts with the collection of sealed boxes. The four flat cartons suggested that pizza was on the menu. My Butte Brewing Company box promised the beer, and Delores's hinted at party hats.

"Not so well. After I brought him home, he curled up tight next to the trailer's toilet and stayed put, his face against the wall. I moved him outside to my mother's old fenced herb garden about an hour ago in the hope that some fresh air would cheer him up."

"Well it hasn't," Bet said. She had been absent much longer than the "minute to freshen up" she had requested before hunching away to the RV like someone trying to evade a stalker. "That poor dog didn't even look up when I walked by his pen just now. Isolation is about the last thing he needs." She straightened out of her uncharacteristic slouch to stiffen her argument.

Luke didn't defend himself. "I wish I knew what would help—and that I could offer it to him," he said. "If you have any ideas, you're welcome to try."

"Maybe some company would help," Bet suggested. "OK if we take him into the RV tonight?"

Luke nodded, looking grateful. "In the meantime, we'd better get started here."

"What's going on?" I whispered to Bet as Luke called the meeting to order.

"Nothing. I'm just worried about that dog."

And I'm starting to worry about you, I thought as Luke turned the floor over to me.

It took me only a few minutes to explain the provenance of the boxes. Everyone boiled over with comments, but Bet. She didn't say another word and held her face as still as her tongue. As the master of ceremonies at this strange banquet, Luke outlined the procedure he thought would allow us to keep the contents of our boxes private for now, but would document what we found in case of legal exigency later on. "I do want to make it clear that it would be better if we collectively turned over all of this material to law enforcement." His voice was as flat and official as the papers he had distributed to us.

"All right," he said in response to the murmur of protest. "We may live to regret it, but since we're all in agreement, let's get started. You each have an individual receipt. Sign it to confirm that you are receiving the carton with your name on it. Then pass your receipt to the rest of the group so they can sign as witnesses. Don't forget to note the date and specific time where indicated."

Everyone was paying close attention to Luke, but Delores. Still in uniform but with her holster empty, she was frantically texting.

"Is everything OK?" whispered Rheta, ever interested in babies in general and Jack in particular.

"Jack's teething, and the babysitter says she can't get him to stop crying." Delores's eyes flashed with worry. "I'll have to stop at the drugstore to pick up some teething gel on the way home. Will this take very long?"

"Probably," said Rheta, always the realist, and then began advising Delores on the efficacy of frozen washcloths. Not for the first time, I wondered if Rheta had ever been married, had babies of her own. Delores returned to her texting, jabbing rapidly at her device. "Thanks," she told Rheta. "Maybe that will hold him until I get back to Bannack."

Bet, usually more than willing to put in her two cents worth on any topic whatsoever, was hunched into herself like a woman waiting for a bus in a snow storm. I offered to pull a blanket from the linen closet, but she shook her head in refusal. Documents started piling up in her lap. She had not glanced at one of them. She had not signed her own.

"Do you have a concern?" Luke asked her, sounding more lawyer-like than I imagined he could. Bet shook herself into a tinfoil smile. "Oh, no. Well, yes, actually. I'm worried about that retriever in the backyard." She scratched her name on the first document without reading it first and passed it on to me. Her signature had fallen into a splat that little resembled its usual peachy cursive.

Luke repeated his directions for the next step of the process. Each of us would leave the bedroom with Rheta (we had unanimously elected her as our official witness) to open his or her carton in the kitchen. Rheta would note and describe the contents; she would seal the lists into individual envelopes, which she would mail to herself after we were finished. Luke would hold the postmarked lists in a safety deposit box in the local bank.

Subsiding into silence, Luke bowed in Rheta's direction. Rising, Rheta held up her hand in one of the few gestures that have survived the American obsession with informality. "I swear not to divulge the contents of what I'm about to witness unless called upon to testify in a civil or criminal case."

Rheta had to choose someone from the group to witness the opening of her own box. She chose me.

"I'll show you mine if you show me yours," she joked as we settled down at the solid oak table in the kitchen placing our boxes before us. Vulgarity is ever an effective antidote to fear, and I was grateful for hers. Under my hands, the table's raised grain testified to decades supporting elbows and coffee cups over an unbroken procession of breakfasts, lunches, and suppers. The day outside was bright, but we left the curtains closed. Rheta switched on the overhead light. It illuminated the cobwebs clinging to the flock of plaster bluebirds on the arch above the sink. Rheta found a paring knife in the first drawer she opened and used it to slit the strapping tape on our cartons with a few precise cuts.

She folded two napkins from the holder in the center of the table into thick squares and then set a jelly glass of The Famous Grouse on each of them. I wondered if Conrad had retrieved the bottle from the *Sun*. Rheta held up her glass. "Here's how." She raised her drink in the best John Wayne style.

"Here's how!" I echoed her words and tried to grin what we were doing into a joke. I took three big gulps—swallowing more fire than smoke—to Rheta's single sip. I wanted more, but I set the glass down. Rheta's jelly glass was still nearly full.

"I don't like scotch," she explained. "Besides, I have four more packages to face after we open ours."

She lit a cigarette. "OK?" she asked waving it in my direction. I nodded. If the dust in the kitchen wasn't choking me, I didn't think Rheta's coffin nail would batten down my airways. In fact, since the fire, my asthma had gone back into hibernation. Maybe my airways had acclimated.

Rheta lifted the lid of her carton, her hands steady. She sat staring for a full minute and then angled up the carton in my direction before setting it down again and using her cell to take a photograph of the contents. The baby album had once been a satiny pink, but its rosy-fingered hue had been dimmed by the creep of a stain. When Rheta lifted the album's cover, a half sheet of official-looking paper fluttered out. Without a word, Rheta picked up the document, scanned it rapidly, and then set it on the kitchen table facedown. She lifted her glass and drained it. Then she handed the paper to me: a death certificate for one Janice Ann Payne, age 14 months, deceased July 18, 1969, pertussis.

"Funny, I've been thinking about her all day," she said quietly. "It's her birthday. But, then again, I've thought about her every day of my life since she was born."

I had sense enough to keep my mouth shut.

"My baby. Didn't they care enough to get her vaccinated?"

"I'm sorry."

Rheta shook her head helplessly. In a few minutes she began paging through the rest of the album—photos of a happy infant. One studio photo that displayed her naked on a blanket like an oyster on a half shell. The rest were the usual snapshots—baby held loosely in the arms of a woman in pedal pushers and a polka dot blouse; baby sitting in Santa's lap with a bow in her scanty hair; baby laughing in her bath; baby waving a piece of birthday cake at a table, frosting smeared on her face; baby napping with a large dog of an indeterminate breed. There were thirty- four shots of baby—I counted and described each and every one. Thirty-four shots and then nothing.

"I imagined a lot of things, but I never imagined this," Rheta said. Her voice was clear and her eyes were dry, but her hands were trembling. "It looks as if Nick found it in the dump." Her voice thickened on the last word.

"Why would he want you to know?" My voice was tight with anger.

She shook her head.

"Who were the adoptive parents?"

"It was a private adoption, so I knew them. You wouldn't recognize their names. They moved out to Oregon a few weeks after the adoption was final—I think they didn't like running into me around town. They had cousins here—that's how the album must have ended up back here—so I might have been able to keep track. But I had promised never to try."

We sat in the dim light and listened to the ticking of the wall clock. It looked old enough to require regular winding. Luke must make his way into this dim kitchen every few days to keep it running. Outside in the hallway, I could hear the comforting clack of Fellow's toes; someone must have released him from his imprisonment on the porch.

"Well, we shouldn't keep the rest of them on pins and needles." Rheta was making an obvious effort to move on. "Are you ready to open yours?"

She poured herself another drink—but a short one. I drained mine, wishing I could put off the viewing for another day, another month—hell, maybe another life. But I could almost feel the anxiety seeping down the hallway, so I got on with it. There was no use taking the time to wrap myself in my new sweater: the chill I was suffering couldn't be thawed from the outside in.

I carefully peeled the tape from the beer box, mindful of its status as a collectable. Fortunately, Nick had sealed it with the kind of tape that lets go without a trace. "Oh!" I said with more pleasure than I wanted to express in front of Rheta. Her face had lost its usual alabaster luster, maybe forever.

"He must have made an extra trip to cart everything home before," I said, carefully not specifying the "before what." I forced myself not to grin, but my voice leapt high. "Not only the Bannack ledger! Everything! My personal papers, my maps, my research notes!" I couldn't help raising my voice in delight, as I retrieved my homely treasures, formerly lost. "My laptop and my saddlebag! Even my document kit!"

I stopped, realizing with a thud that Nick had just offered an unequivocal answer to the question of whether he had started the *Sun* fire on purpose.

"Why?" Rheta's voice was so soft I could hardly understand it. "What could he have been thinking?"

"I wonder if this means we should turn all this over to the police."

"Wouldn't undo the past," she said, her voice weighted like a rock.

"There's more," I said showing her a sealed envelope and a parcel wrapped tightly in what looked like a couple of old IGA grocery bags—paper, not plastic. An index card carrying a hand-printed message was taped to the front of each: "To be opened by Luke Ingraham in the presence of AJ Armstrong."

Coffin: Old workings open to the day.

—Otis E. Young, Jr., in "Glossary of Mining Terms,"
Western Mining

Where There's a Will

"WHAT'S THIS ABOUT?" LUKE USED THE TOE OF HIS BOOT TO NUDGE FELLOW
back into the hallway as he joined Rheta and me.

Wordlessly, I pointed toward the contents of the carton that Rheta had
spread out on the table. She moved the glasses of scotch to the stovetop, well
out of tipping range.

"Do you have your cell?" Luke asked Rheta after reading Nick's notes.
Rheta pulled it from her purse. He asked her to take photos of everything
on the table and to get closeups of the envelope and the parcel.

"Shall I stay?" she asked after she had finished.

"It seems to me that Nick didn't intend another witness to what comes
next, so I think not."

After Rheta closed the kitchen door behind herself, Luke opened the
envelope and quickly scanned the contents—two yellow sheets torn from a
legal-sized tablet and covered with precise and wholly legible handwriting.
"It's a holographic will," he said, handing me the first page. "It designates
me as Nick's personal representative responsible for overseeing the dispensa-
tion of his estate. It also directs me to see to Alph's welfare."

Confused, I glanced at the first paragraph. Shock made me stumble,
stop, and start over. But I had read it right the first time. There it was, my
name specified as Nick's sole beneficiary, excepting only the contents of the
five cartons designated for recipients other than me. A list identifying his
assets followed: two Butte bank accounts; an investment portfolio; and several real estate holdings, including Nick's house and four rental properties
in Misfire, an apartment complex in Billings, and a commercial building in

Bozeman. I was also to inherit everything else Nick owned, including all of his personal possessions and household goods—if I complied with "the conditions listed on page two of this document."

"I don't understand," I said, knotting the fingers that held the first page of the document into fists. But I was lying. I had to lie. I wanted—I needed—another ending to this story.

"Really? This first page makes Nick's intentions completely clear, I think."

"It can't be legal." I kept my voice calm, my sentence short. Words were dangerous. Words would open the channel that would release the flood. Everything I supposed about myself would get swept away.

"Handwritten wills are perfectly valid in Montana, even if they aren't witnessed."

"But it was signed and dated the day before he died!"

The cold water slap of fear kept me from taking in Luke's response, I asked him to repeat himself.

Luke deliberately slowed his speech. "As I said, the date isn't a source of concern. In fact, because the document opens by stating this will supersedes any and all previous ones, the date tends to support its authenticity. However, the listed conditions do complicate things considerably."

Luke waited until my eyes focused on the second page. "Notice that here Nick reaffirms your status of sole heir, but does so with one condition— that you stop trying to locate or contact your natural parents or any other blood relatives. Have you been making such attempts?"

"I have." The words erected a temporary levee against my rising outrage.

"I think we should halt this conversation now until you have the chance to at least consider hiring your own attorney. I can't represent the estate and you at the same time, and you should have your own legal advice about this situation."

"I don't want anyone else involved in this mess. Just ask me what you need to know."

"OK—but let's just consider this an informational conversation, one that won't bind you to any course of action. Have you already found any of them?"

"My mother—she refuses contact. And my half brother—he doesn't believe me."

"What about your father?"

"There was no father's name on my original birth certificate. But that hardly matters now, does it?"

We let the clock on the wall talk to itself.

"Well," Luke finally said, "I guess if you agree to Nick's terms, you'll never know who he was. With absolute certainty."

I spit out the words I could not swallow: "It's absolutely clear to me who Nick was. But I'm not going to let that unfortunate fact force me into doing anything that I don't want to do."

Luke rubbed his bloodshot eyes. He scraped his chair out and lumbered to his feet. Circling to the kitchen window, he converted his back into a wall, allowing me privacy to pull myself together as far as I was able. I stifled my impulse to sob with disappointment, anger, and purely selfish grief. The evening sun slanted past Luke. It had dimmed halfway to dusk by the time he faced me again.

"You notice he does offer an alternative heir—the Montana Ghost Town Preservation Society—an irony I'm sure he intended you to notice. Even though I can't serve as your attorney, as a friend, I strongly recommend that you resist the temptation to make a quick decision. There's more at stake here than the property and the money. You need to consider why Nick might have gone to such extremes to throw up a formidable barrier between you and the past before you insist on breaking that barrier down."

"If I agree to the terms of Nick's will, I'll never know the answer to that particular question."

He looked away.

"But Luke, you know, don't you."

"You're mistaken."

"Let me rephrase the question." Fellow growled from the other side of the door, anxious to protect me from whatever enemy I was facing without him. "Do you have any idea what the hell is going on here?"

"Yes." The clock on the wall ticked out another minute

"Then tell me!"

"I can't."

"You won't!"

"Speculation based on hearsay and rumor won't do you any good and might do the others involved real and permanent harm."

"So you knew my mother."

"I don't remember meeting your mother. If she was who I think she might have been, she was several grades behind me in school. It is true that I knew Nick back in the day, but under another name and only as a high school student knows a principal and a mentor who moved in different social circles from his parents' friends. By the time you were born, I had already moved away for what I thought would be forever. I'd like to think Nick and I became friends after I returned. But he never acknowledged his past, and I never asked him to."

Stubbornly, I demanded more with a silence thickened by bitterness.

"Shall we open the other package?" Luke finally asked. I shook my head in an emphatic negative.

"You shouldn't relinquish your rights to the estate unless you know everything it contains—and that package is part of Nick's estate."

Reluctantly, I had to admit Luke had a point. I signaled acquiescence by pouring myself another generous slosh of scotch and finding a clean jelly glass for him. Neither of us offered a toast. But we both drank.

A shriek permeated the house. Startled, I jumped to my feet before I recognized the forced hilarity in Bet's voice, the unsettling antonym of her earlier mute nervousness. Everyone else in the bedroom seemed to be moaning dramatically in response to some joke. Chas's deep bass enriched the mix—when had he showed up? If Rheta was in the bedroom, I couldn't hear her. Fellow muttered his anxiety in the hallway and then receded, his nails clicking faintly away. I wondered how Alph was doing in the abandoned garden. Whatever Bet's motivation for taking him in, I was glad he would be getting the benefit of her attention.

As I sat down again, Luke pushed the package in my direction. I carefully stripped the tape from the wrappings, not daring to risk a knife against whatever was hidden underneath. What felt like a book came away; it was neatly wrapped with more yellow legal paper. The sheets were incised with the branching charts of a long genealogy, but I set them aside with hardly a glance when I caught sight of what they had concealed: a ledger nearly identical to the one Delores had given to me in Bannack. Luke lifted it from my hands, tugging it away when I tightened my grip.

Even though this ledger lacked a slipcover, I could see it was in better shape than its battered and water-damaged twin. A thin bundle of what might be folded clippings from the *East Bannack News Letter* protruded, revealing type-set lines bumping against a narrow margin. I gripped the edge of the table in frustration. As a bribe, the ledger offered me a temptation that was going to be hellishly hard to reject. Had Nick meant this offering to be consoling or cruel? I would never know if I accepted the terms of the will. If his intention was to punish me for my inconvenient existence, he was succeeding.

"I would like to look at the cover sheets first, if that's all right with you?" Luke's glance was kind, but sympathy is cheap when it is bereft of the support of action. The situation, like the documents that Nick had left me, was literally out of my hands. Luke picked up the legal sheets, shuffled them into order, and began reading the first paragraph of the first page to me. "This family tree and the enclosed ledger include informa-tion that may allow Dr. Armstrong to revise long-held suppositions about Henry Plummer and his wife, Electa Bryan Plummer. However, should Dr. Armstrong refuse the conditions of my last will and testament (first page of this document), this material must be burned by my personal representative."

My face stiffened with outrage both at Nick's attempt to blackmail me from the grave and at his tone—impassive and cold, with no mitigating hint of paternal affection. Luke's face was folding itself into an expression of agonized amusement. "I can't help it," he said stifling a painful laugh. "He didn't know you for very long, and yet he understood his money and his property wouldn't be enough to persuade you. So he upped the ante with an offer he thought you couldn't refuse."

"Well, he was wrong. I don't want anything at all from him—and I want to end this conversation now." And I meant what I said. I wished I could escape into the Bel Air and to drive far and farther until I found refuge. Maybe I would head for Alaska. If I could just get away, I would never again look back.

"But it's my clear obligation to assess and summarize these materials for you."

Realizing I wasn't going to shake his sense of duty, I shoved the docu-ment kit that Nick had restored to me across the table. "Let's get it over with, then."

Instead of starting with the ledger, he turned back to the genealogy. The clock ticked for a long time before he summed up what he had found:

the chart did seem to support the long-standing rumors that Sheriff Henry Plummer had not died childless.

"It also ends with a clear indication that there are living descendents. Indeed, it lists them by name," Luke told me.

"Let me see!" So much for my resolution to cut my losses and leave this mess for someone else to clean up.

"I can't, not yet."

"What about the ledger?"

"You know very well that I'll need at least a couple of hours for even the most superficial initial examination. A complete evaluation by someone with more expertise in authenticating documents than I have could take months, even years." An abrupt knock jerked us to attention. Fellow scrambled inside and pressed himself whimpering against my right leg.

"They're getting hungry out there," Rheta reported flatly from the threshold. "They're playing poker," she added in a detached monotone after Luke invited her in. "AJ, your mother is hooked on some kind of crazy winning streak. Your father's in there with them. If I can get them to interrupt their game, he can make a food run, you can take a break, and maybe I can pry someone away from the table to get another box opening done."

"I'm sorry to say this, but I think you should stick it out here as witness while I look over this material," Luke told Rheta. "AJ can't stay because she can't be privy to the specific contents of these documents unless she accepts the conditions of Nick's will."

Expressing no surprise, Rheta refilled her jelly glass and handed the bottle to me. Not at all woozy, I poured a full measure and drank it right down. Still shocky, I thought about taking another. Fellow leaned into me determined to stick to me like Velcro wherever we were going next.

We didn't make it very far—just to the bedroom. After Chas left for the Golden Hour, I joined Delores and Conrad at a 1950s style card table, covered in a pink leatherette material striped with silver. Because of Bet and Chas's larcenous tendencies, I didn't dare ask where it had come from. Having abandoned the comfort of a chair, Bet stood arms folded in the threshold, her carton within stooping distance at her feet. For the first time during the plodding course of this strange day, I allowed myself to admit that my adoptive mother might have a set of secrets at least as complicated as mine. I remembered the window she had cranked up defensively between herself and Nick the night we were looking for Fellow, the questions she had asked afterwards in the silvered night.

Without a warning, Conrad produced a pocket knife and began slashing at the tape that battened down the lid of his box. "This is nonsense. All this secrecy runs against my grain. Besides, everybody in town already knows the worst about me."

"Wait!" I said. With Rheta stuck in the other room, someone had to at least take notes. But Conrad had already snaffled a mounted eight by ten photo from his carton. The picture showed Conrad with a woman I recognized as the Theme Parks International honcho who had led the museum lawn rally. Although Conrad was wearing the same wide tie I remembered from that disastrous evening, the photo probably had been taken a year or two earlier; the businesswoman didn't look as sumo as I remembered and her hair was both shorter and darker. For the camera's edification, Conrad and the executive were stretching between them a highly colored rendition of a gondola system ferrying smiling tourists up Boot Hill toward an outsized Ferris wheel. The name of the studio, Wakasa's Fine Photography, was imprinted in silver foil into the lower edge of the cardboard frame.

"Well, this is nothing new," Conrad said, his voice sounding more tired than disappointed. For the first time in hours, I remembered he wasn't taking care of himself the way someone recently released from a cardiac care unit should.

"This wasn't taken at the rally, was it?" I asked, more to get a sense of whether he was running on empty than to confirm what I had already figured out about the photo.

"No—Theme Parks International wanted a formal photo made to document their new alliance with Save Our Bannack. It must have been one of the last photos Mrs. Wakasa took before she died." When Conrad removed the picture from its holder, an invoice slid out.

He unfolded the statement. "Well," he said. "Well." His voice thudded with exhaustion.

Everyone waited politely for him to explain, everyone but Bet. "Well what!" she demanded.

He handed me the slip that had been attached to the proof sheets. "Would you read this to the group?"

There didn't seem much worth declaiming, but I enunciated the words in my best professorial style: "One set of studio portraits, to be billed to Theme Parks International."

Conrad gestured toward the invoice. "Would you read the text on the attached business card as well, AJ?"

I announced the name of the executive and the address of the corporation.

"Delores, would you mind using your phone to see if you can find the address for TPI online?"

"I've got it," she said a couple of minutes later. "In a New York office building."

"That's where we've always contacted them," Conrad said slowly. "Now would you see if you can find the contact information for GoldPro?"

Delores looked annoyed, but she turned back to her phone and in a few minutes recited an address that featured the same street and building as TPI's office.

"Could be a coincidence," I said, feeling vastly indifferent to the proceedings. A sorbent numbness seemed to be gobbling up my anger and disappointment.

"I doubt it." Cynicism is the first resort of a journalist, and with its help, Conrad seemed to be already recovering from his love affair with TPI.

Sounding like someone I had never met, Bet chuckled like a strung-out hyena. "Pretty sharp of them! TPI must be a subsidiary of GoldPro, so you'll be dealing with them no matter which way you jump, right?"

"Unfortunately, you are absolutely correct," Conrad said as Chas reappeared to thump a bulging plastic bag onto the card table. The reek of hot oil and soy sauce fogged the air. Without stopping to distribute the food, Chas hurried to Bet's side. I couldn't hear what he asked her, but it didn't seem to have anything to do with chow mein. "No," she said, her eyes wide. Numb as I was, I recognized fear when I saw it. No one else seemed to notice.

I knew I should do something for Bet, but I couldn't force my mind to think what that might be or to move my muscles in her direction.

Still surfing the net, Delores ignored the food: "A computer would make searching easier, but from what I'm gleaning, I think TPI might be the parent company. Don't quote me, though. I really don't know much about corporate structure. OK—that's it. I really have to go now."

"No," Conrad told her, working his chopsticks, the only one in the room who had reached for sustenance. I wondered what his hospital dietician would think of Golden Hour chow mein. "There's still your box and Bet's. I suppose Luke will open his in the kitchen, since he's in there with Rheta anyway. Shall we do yours next?" Conrad was brightening rapidly. Maybe he was already planning to scoop the *Standard* with the TPI story.

"OK—but then I'm absolutely going," Delores agreed. "You'll have to finish up without me." Delores set aside her cell and retrieved her box from the bed, giving the carton a slight shake. "It's light for its size. Maybe it really does contain a hat." Deft with Conrad's pocket knife, she cut the lid free in seconds. When she raised her face, her cheeks were shining with a trail of tears.

"Take a picture before you touch anything," I said, still too boggled by Nick's will to figure out what I should be doing to make up for skipping both the notes and the photo for Conrad's package. Instead, Delores tipped the carton toward us. The hat was more grey than white. It was impossible to guess its original color.

"My three times great-grandfather's," she said. "Chief Tendoy's—I'm sure of it. I've looked at this hat almost every day for the last five years. It's the one he's holding in the treaty photo hanging on my office wall. See the stain on the brim—it shows up in the picture."

She gently disinterred the hat and cradled it in her lap, just as her grandfather had held it for the photo. "I've got to figure out how to get this home," she said, standing up.

"If it actually is the chief's, it ought to be in the museum, not out in Bannack where the mice might ruin it." I hadn't intended my suggestion to clank like a bunch of aluminum cans bagged for recycling. But it did.

"Not Bannack. Home. The Lemhi Valley," she said. "I'm sorry, but I need to leave now."

Without her, the bedroom felt bleak. "Well, I guess it's your turn," Conrad said to Bet, who was standing with one foot inside the threshold and the other, outside. "Do you want to wait for Rheta? Or do you want us to serve as your witnesses?"

"Neither." Bet swept up her carton and fled, Chas a whisper behind. Fellow tried to catch up, but the front door slammed against his muzzle. There was a yelp of pain: it was mine.

Geologists often call the granites, gneisses, and schists of the continental crust "basement rock," because they seem to continue down to indefinite depth without any surface indication that anything may lie beneath them. If you drill deep enough almost anywhere on the continent, the hole will eventually penetrate basement rock. Echoes of reflected earthquake waves show that the basement rocks probably continue to the base of the continental crust, where they lie on the heavier black peridotite of the mantle. No one has ever drilled that deep.

—David Alt and Donald W. Hyndman, in *Roadside Geology of Montana*

Drilling Down

BET'S NOTE WAS NEARLY IMPOSSIBLE TO DECODE. HER HANDWRITING WAS AS uncharacteristically illegible as it had been the day before, and her message was deeply creased besides. I had jammed the paper into a hard wad after finding it stuck under the Bel Air's windshield wiper. Now I was holding it stretched under my chin like the prisoner identification number in a mug shot.

Opening her screen door, Rheta ignored the note. Her eyes were cloudy, as though she had developed cataracts overnight. In truth, I wasn't feeling so hot myself. I stepped over a wide swath of black construction paper taped to the floor as a buzzer sounded somewhere in the house. "It keeps mother in—she thinks it's a hole," Rheta called over her shoulder as she turned abruptly. "But latch the door anyway. I've got to check my pies."

The dim hallway was infused with apples and cinnamon. I saw myself materialize in a mirror above a narrow console table. My hair, in urgent need of skilled scissors, recalled the fork-in-a-toaster look of a young Bob

Dylan. I was still wearing my baggy-assed jeans and prospector's T-shirt, having collapsed into bed in a cloud of scotch and confusion.

From the oven, Rheta was pulling a pie bubbling golden through its lattice top. The linoleum rug glowed with so much wax that the faded pink roses under her feet looked wet. At least a dozen aluminum pans, each wearing a tiara of a scalloped crust, were cooling on the tiled counter of the kitchen. Rheta's mother was sitting at the kitchen table, her hands clasped in front of her on a pink tablecloth. Her walker waited in the corner, just as it had my second day in town when I had showered here.

"This is AJ, mother—I work with her. Do you remember that I've told you about AJ?" Rheta raised her voice slightly and the older woman's eyes flickered. Her shoulders, under a braided crown of white hair, were as straight as Rheta's.

"I must be crazy to be doing this today," Rheta said, refocusing on me. "But I'm good at pies, so the American Legion Auxiliary manages to overlook my past every year, at least long enough to solicit a donation for their Memorial Day fundraiser." Rheta tried for a smile. Her lips were pale and dry. I'd never seen her without lipstick.

"Now taste a piece from Number Thirteen, my tester. I figure if any of the pies are going to be off, Number Thirteen will be the one."

"I don't have much of an appetite." In fact, my longstanding ability to drink deep into the night without paying the usual morning-after consequences had lit out for the Territory.

"Truth be told, neither do I. Let's try a little anyway." She handed me two plates, vintage Franciscan Desert Rose, I couldn't help noticing. "Cut us a couple of big slices while I make coffee. We'll need something to keep us going for the rehearsal this afternoon."

I'd forgotten all about the Bannack Days play. I hadn't seen Adon since our confrontation in the Bannack parking lot the morning of the fire. Which followed our confrontation in the Golden Hour. What would I hate to do more? Embarrass myself by reneging on my commitment to play Martha Vail? Or embarrass myself by participating in a travesty of truth directed by my now-hostile brother. Deciding not to decide, I took a big bite of the pie.

Pastry shattered between my lips, and tart juice cleansed my mouth. I was careful to keep crumbs off the crisp cotton of the tablecloth. Contrary to my protestation, the pie helped.

"Yellow Transparents—from the two old trees in back. These are from last year's harvest. Transparents bear early, but not this early. I freeze a bunch every year. Not as good as fresh, but quicker. I suppose the trees will give up the ghost one of these days, but until then the Auxiliary will get my pies—even though they always seem to forget my name in their list of contributors."

While I sipped a cup of Rheta's oily coffee, I told her about finding the note from Bet. "No one would answer my knocking last night, so I got up early to try again. But they were gone, and they must have sneaked off pretty damn quietly. Otherwise I would have woken up—their RV sounds like a semi when it starts up. I guess I shouldn't be upset. But my head is already spinning from this weird thing with Nick's will."

And from residual scotch fumes, I could have added.

Rheta, who seemed dead sober and self-possessed despite her own impressive intake of jelly-glass scotch the evening before, didn't comment. Instead she read Bet's note out loud: "Have important business to take care of. Don't look for us until you see us coming." Instead of a signature, Bet had signed with a cupid's heart pierced with an arrow. Rheta skipped it with no comment, finishing with the postscript: "Alf is going with us—a little car trip might make him feel better."

"My mother the dognapper," I said. "I hope Alph doesn't mind that she misspelled his name."

Ignoring my attempted joke, Rheta put the message face down on the tablecloth. She covered it with a napkin, either to protect it from pie juice or me from the backsplash of Bet's words.

"Well, I suppose what was in her box figures into all this somehow, but you won't know how unless she decides to tell you. And given the way she bolted last night, she may never do that."

"May not what? Come back? Or reveal her secrets, so lovely, dark, and deep?"

Rheta again ignored my strained jest.

"Let's have another piece of pie and pretend everything is hunky dory. All I can say is that it's a good thing that it's Sunday, and we won't have to face the world until tomorrow." Her own tone was determinedly light, but the slice of pie tumbled heavily onto my plate from the silver server in her hand.

"Are you ready for another piece of pie, mother?"

"Who are you?" The mother's voice was clear, well-modulated and puzzled.

"I'm your daughter, Rheta. You've been living with me for the past six years."

"Where was I before?" The older woman looked seriously interested. Rheta turned to me. "God only knows. A Miles City social worker tracked me down after mother started wandering the streets half dressed. The call took me completely by surprise. The last time I'd seen her before that was a few weeks after my fourteenth birthday. She and her boyfriend of the moment dropped me off in front of the Twin Bridges orphans' home, but I hitchhiked into Misfire instead. The Red Rooms madam was the one who stopped to pick me."

To fend off my look of pity, Rheta waved her empty fork in the air and explained she hadn't gone to work for the Red Rooms in an official capacity until a few years later. "I don't know what would have happened to me without China Rose—she let me work as a maid until I insisted otherwise. Tutored me so I wouldn't end up ignorant. She was an elegant writer herself and good at numbers. Still, somehow mother did keep track of me. They found my name and the *Sun-Tribune*'s address in her purse. Made me wonder . . ."

I waited for more explanation, but Rheta ended the sentence with a sigh.

"Do you want more coffee, mother?"

"You make terrible coffee." Rheta's mother pushed away her cup.

Rheta managed a laugh. She touched her mother lightly on her elbow. "Would you like some ice cream on your pie?"

"Who are you?"

"Your daughter, Rheta."

The older woman stared intently, deciding. "No," she said, picking up her fork.

"That's all right, mother," Rheta said. "Just eat your pie. AJ, why don't you just let things settle for a while? Since Luke is executor of the estate, I'm certain he'll drag out the probate process as long as possible to give you the chance to think over Nick's conditions. At the very least, he'll figure out some ethical and legal way to preserve the information on the historical documents, even if the originals end up getting burned."

I appreciated the passive construction at the end of Rheta's sentence. She could have said "even if you force the originals to be burned."

I nodded. After all, Luke had said as much to me this morning while he was packing his truck. He was headed off on a mysterious trip of his own, but at least he had—unlike Bet and Chas—warned me he was leaving. He also had given me the keys to the house, his trailer, and all the outbuildings. Before climbing into his truck, he pressed a fistful of hundred dollar bills into my hands. Probably Chas's originally. When I tried to refuse the money, he waved me off. "I need a caretaker until I get back, and you're it. This should cover your groceries and any incidental bills for the next couple of weeks. If your parents get back before I do, don't let them sell anything else. Don't let them take Alph again—I owe it to Nick to see how he's doing. Call my cell if there are problems and, for God's sake, get one of your own."

I repeated the conversation to Rheta, inflecting my report with a hefty dose of self-pity. "Everybody but you seems to be abandoning ship just when I need them most."

"I think there's something else you aren't telling me. What happened last night when I wasn't in the kitchen?"

It was a relief to tell her. I assumed my conclusions about Nick would be a shocking revelation, but she didn't even pretend surprise.

"It would seem you've hit on the only logical explanation," she said, her tone matter of fact. "But I can't help wondering how in the world he came to recognize you as his daughter. If we could sort out the answer to that question, it might help you decide what to do next. It's just too bad that Luke can't find it in his heart to come clean about what he knows. To hell with his hearsay and rumors excuse."

She took a pack of cigarettes out of her shirt pocket. Unlike me, she had forced herself to climb into clean clothes this morning. Instead of opening the pack, she slapped it down next to her coffee cup. "I've decided to quit," she said.

"Well, I can't help thinking and thinking about the night Bet and I drove out to Schooners looking for Fellow. Nick did seem to react when he saw Bet, but I can't imagine . . ." My sentence shattered against evidence that my mind was still determined to rule as inadmissible. Uneasily, I described the encounter that wasn't an encounter—Nick's lapse into speechless surprise, Bet's stubbornly averted eyes. "There must have been some shared history between them, and it's not only the whole strange business of her box that makes me think so. She hasn't been herself since the fire. But I don't have a glimmer . . ."

Rheta let me hide in silence for a few minutes. "Let's think about the situation from another angle. The will prohibits you from attempting to find out more about your natural family. But it doesn't prohibit them from getting in touch with you, does it?"

"No. But that isn't likely to help." Summarizing my unsuccessful attempts to contact Everonica and to create a relationship with Adon, I began to feel worse than worse.

"Adon? That's a bright spot in all this! He's a brother worth getting to know." She studied my face intently. "Now that I'm looking for the resemblance, I can see it: you have the same kind of eyes. But he doesn't have red hair."

"Unless he dyes his brown." Rheta didn't smile at my second failed attempt at a joke. "Have you ever met Adon's mother? My mother."

"Don't think so. Have heard of her somehow, though. Everonica. It's a strange name, one you don't hear very often."

Rheta sloshed her coffee down hard.

"Oh shit!"

"Be careful, Rheta!" her mother scolded, sounding completely in her right maternal mind.

Rheta leaned toward me. "Now that I think about it, I know where I've heard the name, and in connection with Nick, too—although it was when he was T.N. Smith—Thomas Nicholas Smith. Nick to his friends, even back then. You remember from the obituary Luke wrote that Nick was the high school principal here in the 1960s?"

"Right," I said, waiting for the point, acting as though this was no more than a moderately interesting conversation about someone who had nothing much to do with me.

"Luke didn't tell the whole story in the obituary. Nick was forced to resign. He was married to a Bannack girl, and her little sister Evie—Everonica—boarded with them when she started high school. Then she got pregnant."

Rheta let me absorb that information. Finally, I dipped my chin to indicate I was ready to hear more.

"The girl went up to the home for unwed mothers in Helena for the duration. In the meantime, Nick and his wife—I'm pretty sure her name was Elizabeth—whispered it around that the father was a high school student Evie wouldn't identify. With the help of the home, Nick and Elizabeth made arrangements to adopt the baby. They even ran an announcement in the newspaper about the new addition to their family. Just when it seemed the town was buying their version of the story, Everonica showed up in Misfire again and went straight to the county attorney. She accused Nick of statutory rape—how she discovered that concept I never heard. When Nick was charged, both the *Sun* and the *Tribune* ran the news on their front pages—the papers were still separate in those days. The stories didn't name Everonica, but everybody knew she was the one involved. Lots of folks went directly into blame-the-victim mode. You can imagine what fun the gossips had."

I swallowed hard against the bile rising in my throat. For years, I had been dying of thirst for my backstory. Now the deluge of information was threatening to swamp me.

"What happened next blew the situation up into the scandal of the decade: Elizabeth left town and took the baby with her, even though the adoption hadn't been finalized."

I shuddered with disbelief.

"What's wrong? What's wrong?" Rheta's mother wailed. Her coffee cup split into two neat pieces as it hit the floor.

"It's all right, mother. Just close your eyes. Everything is OK."

"Lucky the cup was empty," Rheta said holding the halves together. "It's a clean break. I might even be able to mend it."

Rheta's mother not only closed her eyes, she dropped into the sudden sleep that attends infancy and mitigates infirm old age. Too bad that escape wasn't available to me.

Rheta was waiting for me to ask her to go on. I didn't. I couldn't make my hands stop shaking. I watched the easy rise and fall of Rheta's mother's breathing and tried to match my own to it. "How did you forgive her?"

Rheta didn't hide her confusion.

"How did you forgive your mother?"

"I don't know exactly. I didn't want to have anything to do with her when the social worker called, but once she was situated here, things changed. She had lost the ability to tell me her side of the story, and I realized I was partly to blame for that. All those years, I never even tried to find her. For a while, I ended up hating myself almost as much as I hated her. But one morning, I woke up, and I made breakfast, and we ate it. And I didn't hate her, and I didn't hate myself."

She paused. "I'm afraid, AJ, you may find that you can't will anger away, and you can't force forgiveness, no matter what the self-help books say. But you can do something. When you're ready, you can unlock the door. If someone finally knocks, you sure as hell can get up and answer that door. And, here's the only piece of advice I feel qualified to offer on this subject: Try not to drag your feet."

But I was dragging my feet even now. I knew I had used my question to delay Rheta from telling me what had happened next.

"Are you ready to hear the rest now? I should warn you it's not a happy story."

"It's better to know than not to know." There it was: as close as I could get to truth in this imperfect life.

"OK, then. Because the adoption hadn't been finalized, a warrant was issued for Elizabeth's arrest."

"For kidnapping? I was kidnapped?" I choked on the words.

"That's what they called it. Nick disappeared the same day. I guess the bail bondsman must have ended up with the house. It was at least ten years before Nick resurfaced here alone. Not many of the people who knew the principal Thomas Nicholas Smith recognized him as the bagman Nick Stanislavsky. I did."

I raised my eyebrows. Rheta confirmed my guess with a quick nod. Yes, Nick hadn't limited his attentions to fifteen-year-old girls.

"It's too bad he didn't stick to the Red Rooms," I said.

"A lot of people who know you would disagree. Anyway, Luke's mother did recognize him—she'd been a school board member, and she told Luke after he moved back here. Luke told Conrad, who passed the information on to me. I pretended to be surprised."

It was a futile gesture, but I covered my ears. I had wanted the truth, but not all at once in such a big and bitter dose—and one that left the poisonous aftertaste of unanswered questions. What story had Nick told himself to justify sex with a tenth grader? Had his wife abetted him by feigned ignorance? Or had she been a victim as well?

No wonder Everonica had refused me. Sometimes a life raft has room for just one.

"What happened to them—Everonica and Elizabeth?" I had to force the words out in a stutter.

"I don't know what became of either one—or about the baby. You."

"But none of this explains Bet and Nick." My voice sank like a rock.

Rheta waited for me to see it.

"Bet couldn't have been Nick's wife!" I objected with real horror to what Rheta had not said. "Bet's name is Lisette, not Elizabeth. Her family name was Parsley. My mother's family name was Ohm, so Elizabeth must have been an Ohm too."

"Maybe, but maybe not. It would have depended on the family situation." Rheta was soft-talking me, the way you do an accident victim or a panicked animal. "Right now, you probably have a lot more solid information about Bet's family than about Everonica's. Did you know your adoptive grandparents?"

This was a simple question, one that I could answer, and I seized it with gratitude: "Bet's parents died before I was born, and Chas didn't get along with his family, so he kept away from them."

I halted, struck for the first time by an unlikely coincidence.

"God save me, Rheta. Bet always told me her parents died before I was born. In an accident. I've seen an obituary for Everonica's parents, my natural grandparents. They died in a car accident. Just before I was born."

She calmly stirred a little more cream into her cold coffee, miming the message that the two of us could cope no matter where our conversation led. I struggled to believe her, to force my breathing to relax.

Enunciating her words with great care, Rheta agreed the coincidence was a little too coincidental. "Have you ever seen the obituary for Bet's parents?"

"No. I was never interested enough to look it up. But I've seen Bet's birth certificate, and it definitely lists Parsley as her maiden name." My voice creaked with a conviction that was receding with the speed of light.

"Did she have any brothers or sisters?"

"Rheta, you're acting like you're the prosecuting attorney and I'm the hostile witness!"

"I'm sorry, AJ." We sat without speaking, the only sounds in the kitchen, her mother's sleeping sighs and my rasping breath. "Do you want to drop it?"

"Too late for that." I pictured I-15 rolling north and south, intersecting with a network of other highways. The woman who used to believe in no regrets squeezed her brimming eyes shut. Dizzy, I let my chin sink into the support of my cupped hands for a moment. When I sat up again, I told Rheta what I knew.

"Bet always said she didn't have any brothers or sisters—although, oddly, when I was a kid she mentioned a cousin." I disciplined my breathing to a normal rhythm as I described the photo of Bet's mother that had fascinated me as a child and of the little girl who also had appeared in that picture. But by the time I finished, I was starting to wheeze.

"Well," Rheta said, but it was clear she was merely playing devil's advocate. "Maybe Bet wasn't Elizabeth. After all, the real Elizabeth could have dropped you off at a hospital emergency room or left you on a doorstep when she realized she was wanted for kidnapping. Once you were in state care again, Bet and Chas could have adopted you."

"Is that what you think happened?"

Instead of responding, Rheta waited for me to fill in the blanks.

"Of course," I said. "It could have happened just like that. Except . . ."

Except: how could Nick have suddenly realized I was his daughter unless . . . ?

I was running out of oxygen too fast to ask the question aloud.

Those who say drowning victims don't suffer haven't drowned. Bet was Elizabeth? She had snatched me away from her own sister? Instead of a chosen child, I had been a stolen child? She had hated Everonica and Nick so much that she had been willing to spend her life looking over her shoulder? In Chas, she had found not so much a father for me, as a partner in crime for herself?

"I need my inhaler. From the car." I was gasping. I had waited too long.

Rheta fumbled the Bel Air's keys out of my jacket pocket. The Albuterol didn't start working until the third dose. My breathing eased the way a glacier moves, but the bitterness at the back of my throat stuck. I doubted it would ever go away.

"You're right. We are jumping to conclusions." Now there were tears in Rheta's eyes. "It's too bad the fire destroyed all the papers in the morgue—otherwise we could get to the bottom of all this right now. I'm sure photos of both Nick and Elizabeth got published after the kidnapping. If only we could see Elizabeth's photo, we might be able to tell if Bet really was Elizabeth."

The punch of those words knocked the breath out of me again. Saliva flooded my mouth. "Sorry!" I staggered to the bathroom, choking, my vomit erupting in a greenish stream before I could brace myself against the sink.

Rheta gripped me under the arms and lowered me to the toilet seat with a practiced grip. She held the inhaler to my lips.

"It's not your fault," she said wiping my face with a wash cloth, wet and cold.

"It was. Why else would Nick have set fire to the morgue? Here I was in Misfire, the place where I was conceived, poking around more or less promiscuously, grabbing at whatever caught my interest. He must have realized I wouldn't limit myself to Bannack if it was an easy reach to the materials that really concerned me. And he was right."

"He didn't have to burn down the newspaper and kill himself to get rid of a few articles."

"But the volumes from those years were missing. I noticed the gap when I put the morgue in order. Nick may not have been planning to burn the *Sun* at first. But when he discovered that the volumes from 1966 and 67 were gone—and not only for the *Sun*, but for the *Tribune*—he must have thought I'd already stashed them in my apartment or somewhere else in the building. He knew I was perfectly capable of asking the questions that could expose Bet before I understood the danger to her. He also realized he didn't have that much time to search for them. Even if he did decide to set the Bannack fire as a diversion, he knew that it wouldn't keep us occupied forever. In fact, if it hadn't been for the wind, the fire fighters would have had it under control hours sooner."

"But AJ! Wouldn't any reasonable person have talked to you before going to such extremes?"

"Maybe Nick wasn't a reasonable person. Maybe he was feeling, not thinking." I remembered the silence of Nick's immaculate house, gleaming with the residual relief of a man who had decided to put his burdens down. He may not have closed his door intending to burn the *Sun*. But he had determined he wouldn't be coming home again. And now I understood why. I understood his guilt, and Bet's and— however undeserved—Everonica's.

And now mine.

Even in brushy terrain, surface anomalies were the first to be investigated, since they hinted that the rock of which they were composed was either softer or harder than the country rock and hence probably of differing composition.

—Otis E. Young, Jr., in *Western Mining*

July 20, 2010: Brushgold

THIS WASN'T IN THE SCRIPT. DURING SIX WEEKS OF SUNDAY AFTERNOON rehearsals, nothing like this had happened: Martha Vail's gray silk sleeve gave way with an audible rip as she jammed her elbow backwards into Francis Thompson's ribs. His grunt of pain made her feel better than she had for weeks. But then his hand tightened around her upper arm hard enough to hurt as he struggled to force her to stand still. She tried again, this time missing his booted toes with Martha's buttoned shoe. The crowd twittered uncertainly. Was this supposed to be funny? Martha didn't hear them. She couldn't feel the July sun. For her, it was January, dark and relentlessly cold.

Her high cold scream exploded into shrapnel as it pierced the frozen ground. Rage wasn't fire, it was ice. From the porch of the hotel, a dog began braying with throaty fury. The horse that had been bobbing nervously under the facsimile hanging tree bolted. Facsimile vigilantes scattered. The facsimile noose didn't tighten. But the facsimile Henry Plummer screeched as his shoulder harness snapped him into a swing. Confused, the Bannack Days audience gawked from the boardwalk.

Ever a quick thinker, Luke, all decked out in the narrator's stovepipe hat and black frock coat, hardly paused: "And that, ladies and gentleman," he boomed from the steps of the Meade, "was that. For the sheriff, anyway, if not for the men who hanged him. They went on to become celebrated for what they claimed was a necessary and civilizing act. As far as the right or wrong of what happened that winter night in 1864, the jury is still out."

The crowd waited momentarily for a more conclusive finale and then began clapping with a distinct lack of enthusiasm. Becoming aware that the day's heat was converting Martha Vail's silk dress into a sweaty cocoon, I was tempted to stretch out on the dusty road and sink into reptilian lethargy. Guilt was exhausting, and I had been caged by guilt for weeks. Rage was just as exhausting, and I had been ensnared by rage for weeks. I needed to get free. But the rescue I had planned for myself could fail. I had come to count on Rheta, Conrad, Luke and Stela as friends—truth be told, my only friends in the world. But was I presuming too much too soon? Would they find my request not only strange, but silly?

I caught a glimpse of Adon's shoulders squaring with displeasure as he stalked away from the scatter of spectators. During the weeks of rehearsal, he had been far too courteous. Except for avoiding eye contact with me and sidestepping any conversation unrelated to the play, he had treated me with the same impersonal professionalism he routinely applied to the more obnoxious Bannack tourists. Clearly, he was clinging to the pretense I had never made the crazy claim that he and I were brother and sister.

Right now, he must be deciding (and who could blame him?) that the Armstrongs were an unstable lot. First, Bet goes AWOL after cajoling him into letting her play a dancehall girl, and now, I transform the street play from a history lesson into a personal melodrama. To distract myself from a stabbing conviction that Adon might very well be right about Bet and me both, I offered John Storey another sharply aimed elbow: I was as mad as hell, and I wanted to make certain he understood I wasn't accepting his abuse as a compliment. I could already feel a five-fingered bruise forming on my upper arm. It was some comfort to realize his bruises probably would hurt longer than mine. Still, he wasn't letting go, even though the play had ended. This time Martha Vail's shoe made contact with more than boot leather. "You cunt!" John Storey swore. Francis Thompson would have been shocked. Released, I sprang out of Mr. Courteous-Aggressive's grip, glad that I didn't feel the merest twinge of lust.

"Do call me!" he managed to hiss. To save face, he was reconfiguring the ugly little event into a joke. I didn't look back as the Meade's steps carried me away from him into the deep shade of the hotel's front porch.

"I don't think that went over so well," I told Luke, who was wasting no time stripping off his authentically scratchy wool coat. "I can't imagine what made me scream like that."

Luke shrugged. "The audience expected a grand and glorious tale of the Golden West, and we served up something a little less shiny. It's the 'print the legend' syndrome. Don't worry about it."

Taking his own advice, he turned to Stela, who looked as cool as the limeade she was sipping out of a real glass. "Hungry?" Fellow was the one who answered first, swishing his tail, but remaining in an ostentatiously obedient sit-stay. Apparently Stela's hand on his leash was enough to quell him into a semblance of a well-behaved dog.

"I sure am, and I think we have just about enough time for a buffalo burger before we have to go home and start loading up the U-Haul." Before she had left Luke, Stela almost certainly would have said, "I sure am, sugar."

As she relinquished custody of Fellow, he literally jumped for joy at our reunion. Panting that something really, really delicious was cooking nearby, he tried to drag me in the direction of the hotel's dining room. Apparently, he hadn't heard the story that nothing canine would enter the Meade for fear of haunts.

"Sit." Stela said quietly. Fellow subsided. She reclaimed his leash from me, heeling him toward the dining room. Fellow looked desperately back over his shoulder, but gave in to the higher force of Stela.

Luke was not invited to follow, and neither was I. Abandoned, we were left to keep each other company. Although Luke had returned with Stela from his road trip, evidently she had not made up her mind to forgive whatever there was to forgive. Although not the forgiving sort myself, I hoped she would rule in his favor.

For now, Luke was stuck in marital purgatory, even though he had agreed to transform his sabbatical into retirement and to leave Misfire with Stela. The U-Haul he had rented was the smallest the company makes. I wondered, and not for the first time, what Luke's box had held. He hadn't volunteered the information, and I hadn't asked. But I couldn't help but think that its contents must be connected to their decision to leave town.

Luke had promised Stela whatever remained in his mother's place would go to whoever bought the house. That "whoever," he hoped, would be me. I would have the means for the purchase if I agreed to the terms of Nick's will. Luke would provide a way otherwise. He was also pushing me to apply for his position in the history department, but the application deadline was coming up, and I still hadn't decided. Quitting the *Sun* would feel too much like setting aside a mystery half-solved and shelving a project just started. With the help of the *Sun*'s insurance, the newspaper office was undergoing not so much an evolution as a revolution, one that Rheta insisted would ensure its survival in the digital age.

"Want to join us?" Luke asked three trotting steps into his race to catch up with Stela.

"I do—if you don't think a lynch mob will take the opportunity to organize while we're eating."

"They just might," said Delores as Luke departed, her tread solid on the hotel's porch, her uniform in an unusually crisp condition. For once, she was almost as well turned out as my ever-starchy brother. The overall effect was challenged, however, by her grandfather's hat, stained and smudged, and drooping over her brow. "I've already had to listen to one complaint about the play, all wrapped up in a very loud promise that 'your superiors will hear about this.'"

"That was fast." I had enough to feel guilty about, but I added the play's failure to my list. After all, I had been the one who had talked Adon and Luke into letting me write Francis Thompson into the scene of the hanging and to present the sheriff's sister-in-law as Plummer's enraged champion. My iconoclastic revision of the standard story was based in what I considered solid, if as yet unpublished, evidence. Determined not to be bribed or coerced into letting Nick dictate my options, I had been working steadily transcribing the first journal and reading every extant Bannack diary or letter.

I needed the distraction—and not only because Nick's will had left me in limbo. Even after all these weeks, Bet was keeping herself out of my reach as I struggled not to drown in the mire where she had abandoned me.

There were other major frustrations as well. Without the aid of Nick's research, I had been unable to find a trace of Electa and Henry Plummer's supposed descendents. Nor had Luke deigned to offer me the slightest hint about what that genealogy revealed. Lacking a photographic memory, I had only myself to blame for having handled the chart so casually during those few seconds I'd had it in my hands. As for the second ledger, its existence reminded me that although I had resolved to give up gratuitous sex, I was still prey to lust of a scholarly kind.

"Never mind," Delores said. "Pretty soon, rants connected with Bannack won't be my problem." She must have seen my confusion, because she repeated the comment. Certain that I was finally paying attention, she explained, "I'm finally turning in my resignation. Next week."

"When next week?"

"Don't worry—I've already asked the powers-that-be to get the press release out Wednesday so you can scoop the Butte paper. Not that I think many will see my leaving as hot news."

"So you have a new job?"

"What I have are my savings. I've decided to take on a project for the Lemhi Shoshoni—fundraising for a new Tendoy museum that will raise awareness about our history and give us a boost as we keep trying to get the feds to recognize us as a separate nation." She gave me a long look, but refrained from making any reference to my new status in life as a potential heiress, information that the megaphone of gossip had vastly amplified from the documents that had so far become part of the public record through the probate process.

Rheta appeared in the hotel's doorway, her dancehall girl costume well-protected by a big white apron. "Better come on and get something to eat while the getting's good," she said. "I thought hot weather was supposed to take away people's appetites, but the way those burgers are selling, they'll run out before noon. Besides, Stela won't be able to hang onto the table she's saving for much longer."

Delores declined lunch. She needed to give the hotel a quick walk-though before she continued circulating to make sure that all was well. Problems in Bannack were a certainty when tourists were as thick as sage-brush. I did follow Rheta, but slowly, pausing in the cool shadows of the foyer to make sure that I'd left Martha Vail outside, wondering whether I would ever be able to discover more about her and her sister Electa without Nick's help. Nothing in the ledger Delores had given me revealed why Electa had left Bannack so early in her marriage or why Martha had changed her mind about a man she originally distrusted. True, Electa would have been terribly lonely in Bannack had not the Vails followed her there for a temporary stay. Their imminent departure prompted her to reconsider her own immediate future, or so she told her good friend Francis Thompson.

The gold camp was no place for a woman alone, and Plummer's job required him to travel the length and width of his large jurisdiction. When the easy gold started giving out—the sort that fortune hunters could find by pulling up a clump of sagebrush—most prospectors moved on, many of them to the new hotspot, Alder Gulch, some distance from Bannack, but still the sheriff's responsibility.

Still thinking hard about Martha and Electa so I wouldn't have to think about what I was planning to ask my friends, I wondered how Plummer, a man with a reputation for violence, had earned the regard of such respectable sisters. Knowing him well, were they the ones who understood his character the best? Or did the reddish glints in his dark hair blind them?

I thought of another man who had been charming enough to make two sisters love him. Had Nick ever tried to reach out to Everonica after her marriage? Had he traced Bet? Those were questions that could only be answered by the people involved. And one of them was dead and the other two, silent.

"AJ!" The call shook me back into the present. Binah, not Conrad, was holding court at the telegraph table, so the editor must still be playing bartender in Skinner's Saloon. "Are you here to get photos of the Hang 'em High Flower Show?" she asked. "Mine is the one with the little scaffold made out of cinnamon sticks."

"That, I've got to see," I said, trying and failing to imagine how anyone might work an instrument of execution into an arrangement of the peace roses that I knew were blooming in Binah's yard.

Mistaking my comment as a compliment, Binah decided to take advantage of the moment. "Do you want to send a telegram? An heiress like you ought to be able to help us out." Rather than going into my standard speech—that I wasn't a heiress yet, and even if I did end up with Nick's estate, it would be all I could do to pay the attendant taxes, I accepted the telegram form. To Conrad, I wrote, "Must see you immediately. Meade Dining Room. Urgent Question."

"That will be five dollars, including delivery any place in Bannack." Realizing I'd left my cash in the Bel Air because Martha Vail's dress had no pockets, I grimaced.

"Well, it is a fundraiser," Binah said.

"I know. But I don't have any money with me."

"That's what they all say, but I'll be happy to allow you credit enough to cover five telegrams."

"I appreciate it, but one will be enough." I tugged at the neck of Martha Vail's dress.

The message I really wanted to send was to Bet, whereabouts still unknown.

She had been texting me on and off since I had tried to baptize my new cell phone with a call to her. To my combined chagrin and relief, she didn't answer, but the next day she sent a message: "Alf fine. Miss you. Love you. Making progress."

I winced at the "Love you." But instead of the cramping anger with which I had become all too familiar, all I felt was a leaden sadness.

"Oh really, Bet?" I wanted to respond. Instead, I texted: "Making progress where with what?"

"Important business."

"When will you be back?"

No reply. No responses to my next three calls. More than a week later, Bet finally texted me again: "How are you? We're fine. Will explain everything soon."

That will be quite a trick, I thought. "Where are you?" I texted.

No reply.

At least she and Chas were alive somewhere doing something, presumably to do with the box Nick had left her.

I considered inquiring what she wanted Luke to do with Nick's ashes, but forbore asking that inflammatory question. I did need to see her again. I didn't want to make her disappear by bringing up what was her recently resolved state of bigamy.

The Meade's floorboards squeaked under my feet as I followed them through the dim passageway to the sudden windowed brightness of the dining room.

"Over here!" Stela called, her singer's voice projecting over the worried buzz of a crowd convinced a "closed for restocking" sign was about to be posted.

Fellow was sitting between Stela and an empty spot at the long table with his nose pointing to a plate heaped with two steaming burgers, a rather limp iceberg salad, and a mountain of potato chips. He dug his nails into my knee in greeting and then subsided back into his food trance.

"Don't worry, I'll save you some," I told him as I maneuvered my folding chair into place. He looked doubtful, so I passed him a bite before I took my own, being careful not to drip ketchup on the silk dress. "More," Fellow indicated, lunging up and reaching for the edge of the table.

"Down," said Stela. "I have to ask, AJ, why in the world did you bring him along today?"

"Ever since he got lost, he chews up anything chewable if I don't make it home in the middle of the day. Anyway, I want to hike up to Boot Hill for some photos, and I thought it would be fun to take him with me." I was lying again—I'd dragged Fellow with me for moral support.

"Who's having fun?" Rheta co-opted an unoccupied chair from the adjacent table. We all shifted in a friendly accommodation and then reconfigured again when Conrad arrived. I huffed in a breath of grease-slicked air. "I want to ask a favor of you all before Stela and Luke leave," I said. Then I made my request while flies buzz-bombed our plates.

No one said anything.

To my alarm, Rheta laughed. "I know what I'd name you." She waved away a particularly juicy fly away. "But I'm not going to tell you."

"Me neither, sugar," Stela chimed in. "It's one thing for babies to get stuck with whatever names their parents get a wild hair about, but at your age you should be happy to get to do your own choosing."

"I've tried. But naming yourself is like buying yourself a birthday present. You can do it, you can even get yourself something really nice or something you really need. But the gift you buy yourself is a lonely one."

My words reverberated in the dining room, almost empty now that the volunteer cooks had gratefully announced the kitchen was closed. What I didn't say is I thought a new name would help rescue me. I wasn't sure how much longer I could carry AJ's burdens.

"Why now?" Conrad said from his station next to me. "If you've lived as AJ for thirty-five years, why do you need more?" Grateful for Conrad's graceful underestimate of my age, I did something uncharacteristic of me. I squeezed his hand. And then I told the truth as I understood it at the time: If I couldn't make peace with the past, I needed a new name to build a future on. If I did accept the terms of Nick's will, I would never be able to fill in the gaps of my own history or weave myself into the fabric of my family. If I didn't accept the terms of Nick's will, in all probability I still would never be able to fill in the gaps of my own history or weave myself into the fabric of my family.

My own sense of culpability, I didn't mention. What was done was done.

"It's hard to argue with that," Stela said. "But it still doesn't seem like a good idea to me."

"I agree," Rheta said. "What if we come up with just a middle name for you instead? Then you can choose your own first name? Or why don't you just ask your mother?"

"Which one?"

That stopped the conversation.

"OK," I said, avoiding surliness by a hound's whisker. Fellow whined and stood when I did. "Well, I guess I'd better go retrieve my camera and change my clothes. I have work to do."

"Why don't you just think about what we've said?" Conrad suggested.

Apparently, I had friends who liked me well enough to make me unhappy for my own good. As a bonus, I even had a dog.

But for all that, I felt no less adrift.

The Bannack Management Plan is quite clear that lost elements are not to be replaced. We respect that decision, but believe that it is appropriate to mark those gravesites where grave fences were originally located but have now disappeared.

—Michael Trinkley and Debi Hacker, in *Assessment and Management Plan for the Bannack State Park Cemeteries, Bannack, Montana*

The Past in the Present

BEFORE SETTING FOOT ON THE STEEP PATH UP TO BOOT HILL, AJ STOWS the digital Rebel in her camera bag, exchanging it for her faithful Nikon. For today's task, the camera wears its telephoto lens, 300-millimeter and hefty. Old-fashioned film is the right medium for the story AJ wants to tell; at least she hopes it is the right medium. Fellow lowers his head and digs in his front paws until she holds out her fist and lets him smell the napkin-wrapped fragment she has saved from lunch for just this purpose.

The ploy works. Fellow bobs a half-step behind her, leaping every few trotting steps to bounce his cool nose against her tightly closed fingers. He is almost all the company she needs. His bounce is easy through the shimmer of the late afternoon heat and rising wind. The two Klean Kanteen water bottles clipped to belt loops on her jeans jounce happily in a matching rhythm. The combined weight of the camera bag on her shoulder and of the camera strap against the back of her neck is not too heavy to bear.

AJ has been thinking for a couple of days about trying to shoot a long view of the ghost town from the Old Cemetery. By slowing the Nikon's speed, she plans to blur the people moving through Bannack's dusty streets into indistinguishable figures, gray ghosts of themselves. She hopes to frame the photo with a recognizable element from the graveyard. She can already picture the print layout in her mind: a stark black and white photo bordered by the easy color of the transitory images she already has stored in the camera's memory. The dance hall girls leaning against the bar in Skinner's Saloon, hips thrust forward in a pose too exaggerated to be provocative. Tourists splashing their T-shirts as they slosh gold pans through the stock tank set up on the edge of town by the Jaycees. Kids being hauled by a horse-drawn wagon up and down Main Street. Members of the Elephant Rock Homemakers Club all dressed up in gingham to sit in the shade with their spinning wheels. For the online edition, she hopes Tom Engles will know how to make the photos materialize against a panoramic stretch of the graveyard.

The grade of the trail not only rises more sharply than AJ expects, its rocky and eroded surface demands that she pay attention to where she is going. Her new hiking boots are already proving themselves a good fit and a smart investment. Fellow is panting by the time they reach the jack fence that defines the graveyard against the elevated sweep of sparse bunchgrass and wheatgrass, so dry and colorless as to deny their recently green past as a mere rumor. AJ pauses at the cemetery entrance, her bra damp with sweat. Dust and sagebrush saturate the rising wind, which also carries the incongruous smell of kettle corn from a Bannack street vendor below.

There isn't much to see in the cemetery burdened by the glare of the afternoon sun. Most of the graves—gravelly mounds or subtle depressions—are unmarked within their straggling five rows. A collapsing heap of wood fragments occasionally sketches the existence of an otherwise invisible plot. Posts, rails, and even a few surviving pickets suggest the borders of a few graves. Defined by what is missing rather than what has survived, the fences seem more metaphorical than real. AJ thinks about what Bet likes about her crocheted doilies: the gaps that make the pattern.

Asserting pride of place, a tall pedestal monument—shocking white and draped with a carved pall—shames the rest of the cemetery by the refusal of its marble tassels to yield to the wind. The sandstone slabs of the low wall meant to protect an important family's eternal rest have been heaved into disarray. AJ can almost feel the vibration from the pendulum that ever swings Montana between molten heat and iron cold, time rocking human artifacts and nature in the same rough cradle.

As Fellow tries to pull AJ through the cemetery's open gate, she realizes how selfish she has been to bring him along. Of course, she can't take him into the historic site of the graveyard. And although the jack fence along the perimeter looks sturdy enough to serve as a hitching post, it would be cruel to leave him tied up with no protection from the wind or sun.

AJ fishes a collapsible water dish from her camera bag and offers Fellow a drink from one of the Klean Kanteens. He wags his tail in appreciation before dipping his nose to its cool surface. It's one of the things she likes about him, his uncomplicated canine courtesy. He drinks the dish dry splattering droplets that evaporate instantly from the ground, packed hard and worn bare by the tramp of tourist feet. Perhaps she should head back to town and return here alone. Rheta would babysit Fellow for a while, she is sure. AJ listens to her own breath for a few minutes and then unfastens Fellow's leash.

"Have fun," she says. "But don't forget where you belong."

Turning himself into a burger-seeking missile, Fellow launches himself against her fist. She raises her hand to communicate to him that she is keeping the morsel safe, but that she doesn't intend to part with it in the immediate future.

"Later," she says, tucking it in her pocket with an exaggerated motion he is sure to understand. Her camera trigger finger isn't greasy, but she swipes it across her jeans to make sure. Commenting on her refusal with an annoyed shake, Fellow noses his way over the barren plateau toward clumps of sage that rise like fountains from the stony ground, raining dry shade. Abruptly he bolts, hurtling along a trail invisible to AJ's eyes.

"Fellow," she calls after him, already regretting her decision to let him go. "Fellow!"

A woman steps out from behind the south side of the marble monument. AJ gasps and then laughs a little in apology: "Sorry—I didn't realize anyone else was up here." The woman doesn't say anything. Her face shines cool and pale despite the burden of her bustled dress, authentic in every uncomfortable detail. "I didn't realize anyone else was here," AJ repeats, scanning the sagebrush for the tip of Fellow's tail.

"Fellow!" she yells again, her attention so distracted that she doesn't notice how the woman disembarks from the elevated and overgrown plot.

"If you call or pursue them, they won't come back." The woman speaks quietly from beside AJ with the conviction of someone who has dealt with a great many dogs, children, and men. However, AJ silently rejects the truism as only sometimes true: Stela would not have returned had Luke not pursued her. A chase is sometimes necessary to demonstrate the depth of your caring.

The woman's skirt does not sway in the wind; it must be anchored very securely with complicated underpinnings. A trowel dangles from her left hand, which is gloved in what looks like kid leather worn to ivory from its original white. With her other hand, she tucks a stray tendril of rusty hair into a feathered fluff of a hat that somehow is staying anchored. Dust has muted her outfit into a close match to the tawny landscape, but she doesn't seem to notice.

As uncommunicative as the woman is, AJ welcomes the break in her solitude. "I thought I'd have the place to myself this morning—except for the ghosts."

The woman doesn't smile at AJ's little joke or offer an explanation about why she is standing here in the heat-baked cemetery with a trowel instead of enjoying the jollifications below.

AJ tries another conversational gambit: "That dress is beautiful, and it looks so authentic."

"It's a family heirloom, my mother's, and I always wear it for this occasion." She lifts the long skirt slightly with what looks like a practiced gesture and picks her way across the cemetery to the jack fence on its east side. She surprises AJ by mounting its bottom pole with one handsome boot with laces up the front. The woman lightly navigates the barrier, her skirts floating back into place as she kneels on the rough slope that falls from that side of the graveyard. By the time AJ catches up, the woman is widening a freshly worked patch of earth under a wild rose bush, its five-petaled blossoms startling in their pink contrast with the high desert tans and grays. A depression, perceptible—but barely so, stretches from under the rose's branches, dark red and prickly. The woman must be tending a grave that lies apart from the rest.

"Are those canteens you have tied to your belt?" the woman asks. "I wonder if you would mind setting one under the fence where I can reach it?"

AJ pushes the fuller of the two bottles toward the woman. Picking it up, she struggles to figure out how to open it and then gazes at AJ directly for the first time: "Do you have enough for your walk back to town?"

"More than I need."

The woman anoints the ground under the rose and then returns the bottle to the cemetery side of the fence. "I'm expecting rain, but on this slope, it will simply run off unless I break up the ground." The woman glances at the sky, which indeed shows a distant cloudbank gathering itself on the horizon. "In the meantime, your water will help keep the earth I've dug damp and open."

"I'm surprised to see a wild rose growing way up here. Did you plant it yourself?"

The woman doesn't answer. Instead she rises bonelessly and bows her head to inspect her work.

AJ finds herself glad for the woman's reticence. She turns back toward the cemetery, scanning the surrounding slopes for any sign of Fellow. Without considering a possible alternative, she follows the paths the tourists have pounded into the earth. She stops frequently to focus the Nikon toward Bannack, watching for the ghost town to resolve itself into an image. She can't see as much as she hoped from here, even though the gold camp is less than a half-mile away. She'll have to move down the trail to get the photo she wants and give up the idea of working a fragment of the graveyard into the image. Of course, if she switches back to the Rebel, she might be able to Photoshop the image into being. But technical manipulations seem dishonest for this particular photo.

The woman taps AJ lightly on the shoulder, making her startle. "I've noticed that there is a clearer view of Bannack from the entrance side. Perhaps if you can balance on the fence to get a little height, you may see what you want to see."

Returning to the other side of the cemetery, AJ courses around until she finds a likely spot and finds her balance on the second pole. Farther than that, she doesn't trust her equilibrium. The woman follows soundlessly and waits behind her.

"So, do you come here often?" AJ adjusts her light meter. Lacking the digital camera's ability to conjure a photo even before it has been taken, AJ uses her imagination to coax the picture into taking shape behind her eyes. She presses the camera's trigger, but she knows that the image has flown free of the film.

"My father is buried back there." The woman points her chin back toward the wild rose. "I'm the only one who remembers."

"I didn't know there were any modern graves up here," AJ releases the camera's shutter and then climbs down to kneel for a lower angle. Fellow re-emerges from the brush, circles the cemetery, and bolts once more without pausing to acknowledge AJ or to demand an introduction to the woman.

"I guess he's too busy for us right now," AJ says, scrambling up to see if she can frame the ghost town with a slice of the monument. From here, the Meade, plain and dowdy when seen from the back, seems about to capsize under waves of sagebrush. On the far end of town, the scorched patches from the May fire already have been partially hidden by their obscuring reach.

Nothing below is clear. Although she knows plenty of tourists are trudging along Bannack's boardwalk, AJ is beginning to doubt they'll be able to insert themselves into her viewfinder from her present perspective. Unidentifiable figures do appear intermittently in the gaps between the ghost town's surviving buildings, only to disappear again. Their entrances and exits strike her as too transitory to register.

The woman raises her pale face, apparently unconcerned by the scour of the sun. She must be wearing a very good sunscreen. The old-fashioned scent of dried lavender rides the wind from her direction. Belatedly, AJ senses a story. "You're not from Misfire, then? I'm AJ Armstrong, a reporter for the local newspaper." AJ extends her hand, trying to force contact.

"Most pleased, Miss Armstrong—you'll forgive me if I don't offer my dusty grasp. No, I'm not from Misfire. I only visit here once a year to tend my father's grave, although I can't think why I feel compelled to do so."

"You still must love him very much to make the trip every year. Where did you say you're from?" Somewhere out of sight Fellow barks with sharp excitement.

"No, I don't love him. I never knew him. And, from what I gather, that's just as well. I understand that, although well-intentioned and possessing intelligence and courage, he was sadly lacking in both luck and foresight. Is that a snake in your dog's mouth?"

After AJ makes Fellow drop a ropy length that hasn't been alive for some weeks, she snaps his leash onto his collar and clips the other end to one of her belt loops.

The woman continues the conversation from the cemetery side of the jack fence without acknowledging the interruption. "Of course, it is impossible to know what might have happened if my mother had stayed here with him instead of leaving." The woman stays on her side of the jack fence but keeps pace with AJ, who is working her way down the sloping trail that parallels the cemetery, pausing frequently to scan the ghost town through the camera's viewfinder.

The woman is beginning to make AJ nervous. Her story about her father seems incongruously personal given the fact that she hasn't even offered her name. Re-enactors sometimes have trouble separating the past from the present, and her companion is showing signs of suffering that malady. The woman stops at the end of the graveyard jack fence, and AJ for some reason feels compelled to halt as well.

"Mother said she fully expected him to follow her back to civilization. She told me that much before she died, but I don't know whether she told the truth. I don't know why she told me anything at all. Until that moment, I thought my stepfather was my father—and there I was, a grown woman with children of my own. Did I not feel foolish? Was I not justified in my anger?"

"Sometimes it's better to let the dead bury the dead," AJ says, surprising herself by repeating Everonica's words from their first and only conversation—words she neither understands nor endorses. The woman offers AJ an ambiguous stare: "But if we don't look back, how can we see a way to go on?" She turns away and begins making her way back to her father's grave, favoring a path that she finds for herself, rather than following the wandering tourist loop.

AJ is happy to let her go. When Fellow balks, she retrieves the burger bribe from her pocket. When he is satisfied that she has nothing more for him, he matches his pace to hers. The ghost town's streets buildings are becoming more distinct as AJ negotiates the downward path, and she is encountering people in the viewfinder who are almost recognizable as individuals. As she uses her telephoto lens to inspect the three cabins at the trailhead, she notices someone in uniform waiting near the door of one of the cabins, someone whom she thinks is her brother.

When Adon comes into soft focus, AJ realizes he is not alone. He is standing like a gatepost between Bet, who is clearly recognizable in her bright sunflower outfit, and another woman. AJ doesn't recognize the stranger's face, but she does see her auburn hair glint. AJ reaches for a breath: "Mother!" she shouts.

Pushed by the wind, her voice flows downward. The camera lens shows both women looking up in her direction. Bet reaches for the red-haired woman's arm with one hand and waves frantically with the other. Adon stays frozen in place. The red-haired woman jerks away. Heedless of the blinding sun and the treacherous trail, AJ runs.

"What shall we tell her?" Bet asks her red-haired sister. She feels warm for the first time in weeks, too warm to tolerate the weight of her sunflower earrings. She takes them off and secrets them in her pocket.

"What we decided in Bozeman. The truth." Everonica's concealer has melted away under the sun. Her birthmark glows like a wild rose.

"The truth might be just too complicated," Bet says.

"Damn Nick for leaving you that box." Everonica's face has slammed the door against her anger, but it's seeping through the crack in her voice. "He must have known you'd feel compelled to move heaven and earth to deliver my share to me."

"I couldn't very well ignore a certified check for a hundred thousand dollars."

"What in the world are you talking about?" Adon asks, looking baffled.

His mother takes his hand. "Go help your sister. She's fallen."

He barely hesitates before he jogs up the incline. Bet watches him lift AJ to her feet while Fellow races a circle around them. "He's not calling for help," she tells Everonica, "so she must not be hurt too badly. Let's get out of here and find somewhere cool to talk things over one more time before we say something to them we may regret."

"We *have* talked it over." Everonica says. Up above, AJ is looping her arm around Adon's shoulder and attempting a tentative limping step. "It's time to bring all our secrets to light. That was Nick's problem. He was too much of a coward to face the truth. Otherwise, he never would have shipped me up to Helena for the duration just weeks after mom and dad died—or asked you to believe that I was pregnant by some nameless high school boy. I really don't think he ever changed. Forgive and forget indeed! How did he convince himself that the right thing to do was to hand us the responsibility of sorting out the whole shameful mess after he was safely dead!"

"You're flattering yourself if you think that I ever believed his story or yours." Bet's freckles seem to darken as her skin pales. "I was crazy with grief over Mom and Dad and crazy with rage about you and Nick, but not crazy enough to show it. Your baby needed a home, and I needed a baby. You certainly weren't equipped to be a mother, fifteen years old with no resources, not even a high school diploma. If you'd had a grain of sense, you would have let the whole thing play out according to Nick's plan. Instead you cut off both AJ and me by going to the county attorney with that ridiculous charge."

"I cut you off? You're the one who kidnapped AJ and tried to disappear for the next forty years, committing bigamy, I surmise, in the process."

"Well, here they come," Bet says, reaching blindly for her sister's arm to steady herself against the beat of the sun. Everonica hesitates only for a heartbeat before she steps near enough to close the gap between them.

For now we see through a glass, darkly; but then face to face: now I know in part; but then shall I know even as also I am known.

—in *The King James Bible*, 1 Corinthians 13.12

Telling Time

WE WERE IN THE KITCHEN, THE ONE PLACE IN LUKE'S MOTHER'S HOUSE I was beginning to think of as mine. The plaster bluebirds still flew above the kitchen window, but they were free now from their burden of dust. I opened up the new curtains, fresh and white. Despite the harshness of the mid-summer heat, I wanted to give the sun the chance to clarify what it could. I offered no scotch, but, despite my still-swollen ankle, I coped with my fancy new coffeemaker—a parting gift from Luke and Stela to replace the one lost in the fire. With so much else.

Bet took her brew black as usual. Like me, Everonica didn't disdain a healthy splash of cream in her cup. Adon was sticking to bottled water. Chas had absented himself—to leave us in peace, he had said. Chas really was an optimist if he thought that's what we would find in the kitchen today. Rheta had offered to come by to hold my hand—literally if necessary—but I thought this encounter was something I needed to face by my lonesome. Now I wished I hadn't felt such a need to play the heroine.

"I have several questions," I said in my most officious academic voice. Fellow was stretched out beside my chair, his claws clicking against the floor as he galloped through his dreams. At least I had him in my corner.

"I don't want to be unkind, AJ, but let's not pretend that we'll ever have any kind of relationship." Everonica, sitting straight and self-contained in the kitchen chair, was elegant in a forest-colored linen sheath the color of her eyes. Her ballerina flats in a rich top-stitched leather echoed those greens. "It's too late for that. Although Bet chose to preempt me as your mother, I'm certain she was a good one. She's the one you share a history with, not me."

Ah, Everonica, I thought, I'm not the only one to cherish my anger.

"Mother," Adon said softly. I used my eyes to broadcast gratitude in his direction. It was clear that my brother had steeled himself to serve as mediator. He might be the only true adult in the room. Then again, his life had not been blighted by betrayal and abandonment. He seemed unembarrassed that he and I both had armed ourselves against this day with nearly identical khakis and shirts. We even had hiking boots in common, although I had left the laces untied to accommodate my injured foot.

Bet was holding her face in a stiff smile. Her crimson lipstick and blanched skin made a patriotic match with the navy tie of her snappy little sailor outfit. Like Everonica's shoes, hers conversed with her outfit: bright blue Croc knock-offs. A stranger would have taken her for the younger sister, vulnerable and unstrung. Alph—now Alfie—was sitting with his head on her knee. I was glad Bet had someone in her corner, too.

"She *is* a good mother—and I'm grateful to her," I said, surprising myself. Rheta had been right: You can't force forgiveness, but it can catch up with you when you're not looking. Who was I, after all, to judge Bet? She reached for her phone and bent over its keypad. My cell pinged with its text alert: "Thank you."

You're not welcome, I thought. So much for my brief hope that I had left my anger at the kitchen door. The decantation of grace may be as welcome as rain in the drought-prone West. But it apparently could also be just as transitory.

"You may be right. But I still have my questions," I told Everonica. Because I had come prepared for rejection, I wasn't expecting to be susceptible to wounding. I was. My skittish fingers drummed the tabletop. I picked up my cup of coffee. My heart skipped a beat.

Yes, indeed I did have questions. More than that, I had lots of answers to the questions I hoped Everonica would ask—about me, my life, my work. I was hungry to see some slight sign that she ever had given me a second thought. But if she harbored a spark of maternal interest, she was hiding it very well, her face as impassive as someone waiting in an airport for a flight to nowhere particularly interesting.

Never mind: It was almost enough for me to hold her in my gaze, to search her face for resemblance to mine, to experience her not merely as an idea or a collection of documents, but as a living presence, no more or less ineffable than the average human being. The clock on the wall was ticking away another and then another and then another moment, each definite, discrete, and disappearing fast. I had better make the most of an opportunity that would probably never come again. Although Bet and Everonica had engineered this meeting, it was clear which of my mothers had decided to secret herself in a cocoon of indifference in order to survive it.

"Write them down, those questions, and I'll see if I can answer them." The line fell so naturally from her lips, I knew it was one she must use routinely with her high school students, but perhaps with more sincerity than she intended with me. Only time would tell.

Her green eyes closed briefly with the ironic flicker I had noticed all my life in Bet's hooded gaze. We wore our DNA on our faces. I looked like Everonica. But I also looked like Bet—why had I never allowed myself to see the resemblance?

"What about you, Bet, then?" I asked.

Despite the tension in the kitchen, Bet couldn't suppress the little smile that she had always deployed to mask immodest pride in a job well done. I was tempting her into full disclosure, but, after glancing at Everonica and Adon, she paused to separate what she remembered happening from a story she could safely tell.

"I didn't start out planning to take AJ." Bet directed her answer to her sister, not to me. "The minute Nick told me you were pregnant by some nameless high school boy, I knew in a flash what had really happened. You were a shy kid, no one ever called you, and you hadn't once gone out during the school year with even a girlfriend." She hesitated. "Besides, I had noticed how eager Nick had been to help you with your homework."

If this assessment hit too close to the mark, Everonica refused to reveal it. Her face remained indifferent.

"But I pretended to believe Nick—I was used to acting like the good little wife. I let him drive you away to Helena without even saying goodbye to you—and that I'll regret to my dying day. Instead, I should have marched right up to your room. I should have told you it wasn't your fault. It was Nick's. And it was mine, too. I should have been paying closer attention." Bet ducked her chin to hide her face.

"Yes, you should have been paying closer attention." Everonica's voice was distant, disconnected. She kept her hands in her lap as though she couldn't bear to share a glimpse even of her polished fingertips. She added just as calmly: "But I was the one who let it happen."

"You were barely fifteen." Bet's voice firmed with the conviction of an older woman speaking to a younger one. "No fifteen-year-old girl deserves the blame for a pregnancy when the man is in his thirties. That's what I should have told you. Instead, I let Nick take you away. I was hurt. I was furious. After you two left, I spent the day packing. I had just sold Mom and Dad's Bannack property to the state—they'd been after it for years. It didn't bring all that much, but I wouldn't need a fortune to get a fresh start somewhere. I still had my English degree, and I thought I would be able to find a job. I cashed out the proceeds because I didn't want Nick to be able to trace me."

English degree? That minor revelation shook me almost as much as my earlier realization that Bet was a fugitive. I had never known her, really. And if I had never known Bet, I had never known anyone.

"I was efficient, and it didn't take me long to get organized for my trip. But Nick got back sooner than I thought he would."

I tried to picture a suited version of Nick, clean-shaven and guilty looming in the door of a handsome house. My imagination failed except in the matter of guilt. The guilt I could understand. "And he talked you into the adoption," I said, certain about what must have happened.

Bet glanced at me, but then turned her attention back to Everonica. "We had a terrible fight. But he could be persuasive when he wanted to be. I knew the pregnancy wasn't your fault, but he convinced me—and maybe even himself—that it was. I found it convenient to accept his story. I'd been wanting a baby forever—and even more so after the board of trustees strongly suggested it wouldn't be appropriate for me to continue teaching in Nick's school district once we were married. When I couldn't get pregnant, I tried to keep busy doing volunteer work. But it wasn't enough, not even close to enough.

"For the next few months I was happy getting ready for the baby. I thought the baby would make everything OK." Bet shifted her focus to me. "AJ, you were born three weeks early. The social worker reported that the birth was hard and that Everonica refused to see you afterwards.

I thought I would go crazy during the six weeks it took for the state to release you to us."

Her voice dropped. "I kept picturing you lying alone in little crib in a big room full of rows of unwanted babies. The first time I held you, I fell absolutely in love with you. I decided that it wouldn't be hard to forgive Nick for your sake."

Here was a woman, I realized, who had her regrets, but who had found a reason to live with them. I was that reason. What was I supposed to do with that responsibility?

Everonica aimed herself at her sister like a spear. "Because I'd agreed to give up the baby before the birth, they didn't *let* me see her. They didn't *let* me hold her."

It was probably the light, not tension, that had winched Everonica's face into a pale oval as tightly stretched as a tea towel in an embroidery hoop. Between blinks, I thought I saw her as she must have been at fifteen, skin smooth but already sharply marked by someone else's careless stitching.

"They did let me stay in the Home for a few weeks until I recovered from the birth and figured out what to do next. The other girls told me about statutory rape laws and pointed out that if the father of my baby was an adult, I probably could use that fact to get some financial compensation from him. I knew they were suggesting something like blackmail, but I didn't even hint to them or anyone else what my situation was. It gave me some comfort to think how grateful Nick must be that I was protecting him."

She found her sister's eyes. "I knew that it would look odd if he came to visit me on his own, but I did expect you to come to see me, Elizabeth—especially after the Home's social worker told me you and Nick had been appointed foster parents as part of the adoption process. I guess she assumed our family connection made the usual confidentiality requirements moot. At first I was happy. I even had the crazy idea you and Nick would stop in with the baby on the day you were scheduled to pick her up. If you believed the story about the high school boy—and I was sure you did, I thought you might even invite me to come home with you."

"Please believe me, Evie. I didn't imagine you would want to see me." The crack in Bet's voice suggested she didn't expect to convince anyone at the table, including herself. "You hadn't made any effort to get in touch

with me. All I knew was that you had petitioned the court for legal emanci-
pation as an adult on your sixteenth birthday."

Bet's voice flew apart into silence. When she began speaking again, her
tone was weighted with what I took to be shame. "Mostly, I guess I wasn't
thinking about you at all. Before I held AJ, I thought I would be a clumsy
mother. But she was mine right from the first. Everything seemed perfect.
You would go on to live your life, AJ would have a good home, and Nick
and I would have a child. I told myself everything had worked out for the
best."

Everonica yelped with a cough or a laugh, I couldn't tell which. But Bet
didn't stop again. Now that she had decided to tell the truth, the words
tumbled link by link, chained tightly, no space left between them.

"But only a week later you filed charges, and Nick was arrested. It took
him by surprise, but not me, not really. You can only hold your tongue
so long before you have to speak out or resign yourself to shutting up forever. I should have gone to you then, Evie, but I was paralyzed with fear. I
knew someone could be coming any minute to take AJ away. I grabbed the
money from the sale of mom and dad's Bannack property—I'd stashed it
in the sewing machine cabinet the day Nick had driven you to Helena. And
then I took AJ. And I ran."

Everonica slid her chair back with a screech. "Please, Mom," Adon said
quietly.

I could smell Bet's anxiety in the rise of Jean Naté evaporating from the
heat of her skin as she forged her story into shining fetters meant to hold us
until she finished.

She had begun her escape by driving to Bannack to exchange her pink
Rambler for her parents' nondescript second car, which she had left stored
in their barn, figuring the state wouldn't be in a hurry to inspect the property. In Bannack, she also found the essential elements that would allow her
to leave her identity as Elizabeth behind.

"You weren't the only one who spent a lot of time in Mrs. Parsley's
house, Evie." Even in these circumstances Bet couldn't conceal a certain lift
of pride from buoying up her voice. "You wouldn't remember much about
her daughter Lisette, but we were best friends growing up as the only kids in
Bannack. One of our favorite things was going through her mother's cedar
chest. Lisette loved making up stories about the people in the old photo al-

bums. I guess she wanted some adventure in her own life, because she took off for Las Vegas the summer after we graduated from high school. Her mother didn't know she was going, but I did. She sent me a lot of postcards the first year, and then nothing. Mrs. Parsley was worried to death about her and even hired a private detective to find her, but no one we knew ever heard from her again."

"So you became Lisette Parsley—Bet, for short," I said, not knowing whether I admired Bet's cleverness or was horrified by it.

"It was an easy switch. We were the same age and even looked a little alike. After I met Chas, it wasn't long before I became Bet Armstrong, so there was even more space between me and Elizabeth Smith. He knew what the situation was from the get-go. He was the one who said we would be safest if we didn't settle down for a while. At first we traveled because we had to, but then we got to like the freedom of picking up and moving whenever we wanted."

Bet stopped abruptly and looked directly at her sister. "Evie, after I married Chas, I felt secure enough to send your share of the money from Mom and Dad's property. I always hoped that you got it and understood I was sorry that things turned out the way they had."

I touched my own face when Everonica's expression ripped and frayed. So this is what my anger looked like. "Yes," she said. "I got the money, and I laughed and laughed at the idea you couldn't live with the idea you had cheated me of a few thousand dollars when you were apparently just fine with having stolen my baby! What really hurt was that you didn't bother to include a note to let me know how she was doing. I would have given anything for even one photo."

Everonica swept herself out of her chair. Fellow jumped to his feet and barked.

"But you did track me down, didn't you?" My voice creaked into a high register. How could I stop her from leaving? "That was you that time in Misfire, wasn't it?"

My words froze her in midstep. "I always wondered if you would put two and two together someday." Still perched on the edge of flight, she paused behind Adon's chair, gripping his shoulder. Emotion colored her face, but I couldn't tell what kind. "But I didn't track you down. It was just by chance I stopped in Misfire that day because I was on my way to pick up some things from Mom and Dad's house the park manager had set aside for the family. Of course, Elizabeth had disappeared. But by that time I had passed my GED and was working on my degree in Bozeman. I hadn't made any secret of my whereabouts; I didn't have anything to hide, so I'd been easy to find. Anyway, I was driving down Montana Street when I caught sight of you standing by a parking meter outside of Penney's, your red hair shining in the sun. You looked like an Ohm. You looked like me."

For the first time, Everonica unshuttered her gaze. "You were sweet and smart and completely trusting. When I put that dollar in your hand—your fingers were so small and warm—I felt . . ." She stopped. Her voice hardened. "I'm sorry, AJ, but this isn't going to work. Give your questions to Adon, and I'll do my best to answer them. But I can't see you again."

"I remember your hair," I said desperately, touching my own. Everonica didn't slow her retreat.

"But won't you at least tell me my name, my *whole* name?" I called after her.

She pivoted. Behind the stylish fence of her glasses, Everonica stared in disbelief.

"She doesn't know her name?" she asked Bet.

"You're the one who left that line blank on her birth certificate." Bet's voice invited Everonica to quarrel.

"But the social worker told me that you and Nick had agreed to name the baby after mom." She redirected her attention to me. "Artemisia Jane was our mother's name. Father always signed her as AJ, so we—all of us—decided to keep that tradition as well. Did you know they were both deaf?"

"No," I said, trying to thread myself into the eye of my personal hurricane. My joy and my rage swirled into a tangle. But grace descended again. I found the quiet at its center. "I didn't know. I've seen the accident report from the Butte paper, but the article reported my grandmother's name as Amanda."

"That's a newspaper for you. Well, now you do know," Everonica said, disciplining her voice back into containment. "So that's that." She shook me off the way Fellow shook off rain. Adon trailed her out of the room. I heard the thud of the front door and the growl of her car engine idling.

"I'm sorry, AJ." Bet said. I had never heard her sound so sad.

I blinked back tears. At least I finally did indeed know my name. Artemisia Jane. I had always feared there was a plain Jane in me somewhere. But Artemisia was lovely, redolent of sagebrush and open spaces full of light. Who could I become as Artemisia?

"We were afraid mother's name would make you easier to find," Bet said. "When Chas adopted you—you were only three—we kept it simple. We had always called you AJ anyway. I was planning to tell you everything once you seriously asked."

"How in the world did you end up working out a legal adoption?" My voice was harsh. Grace had again been swept away. "I suppose Chas crossed someone's palm with a few hundred dollar bills to smooth away the little matter of the kidnapping."

Bet winced at my sarcasm. "I'd been appointed your foster mother while the adoption was pending, so I had your paperwork. I took your original birth certificate with me when I left. I knew I wouldn't need it for a while, but even in those terrible moments when I was rushing around getting ready to leave, I realized that I would eventually have to work out a way to claim you as my legal daughter. As it turned out, Chas figured out all we had to do was to arrange identification for someone willing to temporarily play the role of Everonica—"

"No more," I said. "I don't want to know—not right now anyway."

Bet stuttered to a stop, hating to give up her chance to tell the rest of the story. "What *do* you want then, AJ?"

"I want to be left alone." That claim, of course, is the biggest lie of all, the last stand of those who don't believe they have any choice in the matter.

"Chas and I are going on a little road trip to let things cool down. Come with us?"

"I can't—the *Sun* needs me." My words were glazed in ice. I recognized Everonica's voice in my own. I could hear Everonica's car shifting into drive. It bumped over the cattle guard and was gone.

"AJ, I don't know how to make you understand . . . will you keep in touch?"

I thought about it and then drilled into my reserves. "Do you want me to?"

"You are still my daughter, AJ."

Adon rapped on the casing of the kitchen door. I struggled to get to my feet: I wanted to stand to face him. He hurried to help me up. "I have something I want to say before I leave, AJ. You'll have to give our mother a little room. She gets all wooden and withdrawn when she gets scared."

"I noticed." Like mother, like daughter, I thought.

"Why don't you have dinner with Nancia and me next week, and we'll talk things over."

Something had changed. I wasn't sure what. I had changed. I wasn't sure how. But I did know I was willing, finally, to hope for the best.

"I'll be in touch, Artemisia," my brother told me.

It is not known at what point on Electa's journey Plummer finally left her and turned back, but wherever and whenever, it was the last time they were to see each other.

—R.E. Mather and F.E. Boswell, in *Hanging the Sheriff: A Biography of Henry Plummer*

September 1863: Dust to Dust

"We must look a fright," Electa laughs. She is making a conscious and continuous effort to maintain good cheer despite the alkali dust clinging to everything—the box wagon that styles itself a stage, the mules, their clothes, and food. Even the skin of their faces has been transformed to a ghostly dirty white.

Still, Electa does not complain. She does not ask how long Henry will ride with her as the stage lurches its way toward Salt Lake City, and he does not say. She hopes the disappearing miles will seduce him, lull him into traveling on to her destination, which is not just a place, but a goal: to detach her husband from his low-paying and dangerous job and to resettle him where he will never need to wear a sidearm again.

Electa knows the memory of an unhappy woman won't hasten Henry to her side in Iowa. So she smiles a gritty smile and whispers to him about the baby as he reins in his horse to keep pace with the plodding mules. Normally she wouldn't speak of her pregnancy in any but the most private of circumstances, but the driver is drunk by midmorning and oblivious except to the demands of remaining upright in his seat.

"I'm convinced we shall have a daughter, and if so, I'll name her after you: Henrietta."

"Never will you do that with my consent, dear wife, but I do hanker to have a daughter named Electa."

"Well, if you keep your promise to join me, husband, I'll allow you the full naming of the child, whether boy or girl, as long as you arrive before the baby does."

Plummer has promised to join her, but he will not assure her that they will see each other before the birth. He has a goal of his own: to overcome the persistent rumors that frame him as a desperado by standing those rumors down. To leave another frontier town under yet another cloud would be to relinquish forever his hope of becoming a man worthy of his wife.

Even though he knows Electa is in all ways his moral superior, he has scruples of his own about matching his words to his deeds. So he makes no promises he cannot keep. They ride along in silence, the sky vivid above, the sun warm, but the wild grasses already brittle and the snow on the distant Tetons already giving evidence of its growing seasonal reach. Electa took this stage knowing it would probably be the last one before winter shut down human ambitions. She is betting that Henry will not be able to stand the sight of her receding back. Even if his sense of responsibility wrenches him from her side, she is convinced he will hurry back to Bannack only for the few days it will take him to prepare for a permanent departure. On his fast horse, he can catch up to her before their parting becomes irrevocable.

She has conjectured wrong. Tomorrow they will meet a wagon heading to Bannack with the new territorial chief justice, Sidney Edgerton, and his family; they will all like Plummer—at first. In one hundred and twenty six days, Edgerton will be instrumental in hanging the sheriff and two of his deputies. Others will die—so many that historians can only estimate a number between thirty and fifty-five. None of those "executed" will be given the benefit of due process under the law.

Those events, however, lie in the still malleable future. Today Henry and Electa are riding through a dream, although not the same dream, side by side, the bright light sparking the red in the sheriff's brown hair. "I hope," she says, "that all of our children will look like you."

THE END

Acknowledgments

If not for the venerable Utah Original Writing Competition, sponsored annually by the state Division of Arts and Museums, I never would have revised this novel to completion. Since 1958, this annual event has gifted hundreds of writers with the incentive of a deadline, the hope of state-wide recognition, and the promise of a close reading by at least one knowledge-able reader—the judge of the our genre category. The writer Brian Evenson served as judge of my manuscript, and I am forever grateful that he saw potential in my manuscript.

For me, the announcement that *The Ghost Town Preservation Society* had won the 2013 novel contest was bittersweet—the news came within days after my husband's funeral. Duane had read each succeeding draft of the manuscript with the supportive conviction that it was already good, but that it could be still better. How much better, I didn't realize until Chris Cauble of Riverbend Publishing took the manuscript in hand. Demon-strating the rare ability see both the trees and the forest, he cut through the underbrush to help me find coherence in narrative that had not so much come to a conclusion as it had simply stopped. By the end of the multi-stage revision process, Chris probably had labored over the novel nearly as much as I had.

My challenge in trying to figure out where the novel really wanted to go was complicated by the fact that I had worked on the manuscript in fits and starts for a long, long time. *Ghost Town* really got its start when I ar-rived as the Butte *Montana Standard* newspaper's wet-behind-the-ears Dil-lon Bureau reporter. The *Standard*'s parent company had decided Dillon was about to explode with a shale oil boom, which, as it happened, soon went bust in the usual Western fashion. I was a last-minute substitute hire, taken on despite my short resume because I was between jobs and ready to jump in my car that Thursday to drive straight across North Dakota from Minnesota to occupy my new Montana office/basement apartment by Monday morning. Before I had unpacked all of my boxes, I was assigned to trot downtown to the Dillon Elks Club to cover a meeting of The Montana

Ghost Town Preservation Society. I learned a lot about false front architecture at the convention and even more about ferocity that fires Montanans deeply in love with the heroic version of their history.

A few months later, my future husband drove me out to Bannack, where I saw for the first time the ghost town rising like a mirage in the sharp and slanting winter sun. It was the contrast that hooked me: between the silvering structures and the frozen stretch of sky far above the narrow valley; between the fragmentary history of the place and the shining myths built on its crumbling foundations and splintering timbers.

After the economic opportunity seduced me into leaving Montana again, I had cause to be grateful to those who had halted the ghost town's disintegration—chiefly, the Beaverhead Museum Association, whose members were animated by the spirit of the Sons of Bannack—not the fictional SOBs of my novel, but the descendents of those who kept the town alive for decades after its brief 1862-63 gold rush. I couldn't go home again, or at least not very often. But thanks to them and to the earlier perseverance of the Montana Sons and Daughters of the Pioneers in persistently pestering the state to save the ghost town, I could revisit Dillon and Beaverhead County in my imagination, a process that became accessible to me through the door of fiction.

Of course, I write not about Dillon and Beaverhead County in this novel, but Misfire, a town that represents an alternative reality that sometimes overlaps and sometimes departs from both geography and history. Southwest Montana's literary great Tom Savage anchored his fictional town of Grayling with the real Dillon streets of Rife and Pacific. Following his example, I attempted to be faithful in my fashion to the geography of Southwest Montana (even though I allowed myself such bold liberties such as transforming the famous local landmark Beaverhead Rock into Elephant Rock), and to recorded historical events (except at points where the fiction forces me to refashion them to its own purposes). For example, to see the disappeared landscape of Bannack's Boot Hill in what remains at the site, I needed Michael Trinkley and Debi Hacker's *Assessment and Management Plan for the Bannack State Park Cemeteries, Bannack, Montana*. To understand the Bannack townscape, I drew from Kingston Wm. Heath's "False-Front Architecture on Montana's Urban Frontier" in the journal *Perspectives in Vernacular Architecture*. The Dillon *Tribune-Examiner's*

"Centennial Edition," which I helped compile in 1980 as a young reporter, was a starting source for descriptions of many local places and events.

The novel draws from a wide variety of other sources in order to pick its way between the historic record and the kind of variable truth that depends on lies. Because that useful academic tool, the footnote, isn't much used by fiction writers, I imply my considerable dependence on the work of others with the epigraphs that begin the chapters. However, this askance glance toward documentation isn't sufficient to acknowledge the extent to which R.E. Mather and F.E. Boswell's iconoclastic scholarship in *Hanging the Sheriff: A Biography of Henry Plummer* caused me to doubt the story I had learned growing up in Montana public schools: that the vigilantes were heroes who brought justice to the state's gold frontier. Of course, my purpose in the novel is not to settle or extend the debate over the question of whether Plummer was an outlaw or a victim, a bad guy or a good guy. But I could not write about the past that lives in the present of the novel without feeling history quake under my feet. In this I was aided by many and various sources in addition to Mather and Boswell, most importantly Lee Graves' *Bannack: Cradle of Montana*, a book that encapsulates for a popular audience the heroic view of the vigilantes' role. Graves also recounts two of the ghost stories important to the novel—the haunting tale that asserts the cries of children dying in an epidemic can still be heard in a Bannack cabin and the story that the real Bannack resident Bertie Mathews told about seeing her drowned girlhood friend appear in the Hotel Meade. Scholar Frederick Allen should also be noted for offering a more recent and scholarly exploration of executions carried out without benefit of a trial with his important *A Decent, Orderly Lynching: The Montana Vigilantes*.

I also found significant help in a set of diverse sources in my framing of alternative reality of the novel as it involved Francis M. Thompson, who was first a friend of the sheriff, but later an intimate of his foes. Dorothy M. Johnson, a historian as well as the grande dame of Montana literature, lists *The East Bannack News Letter*—either printed by someone else on Thompson's press or published by the young man himself—as a possible contender for the honor of the first newspaper in Montana. In an essay appearing in Warren J. Brier and Nathan B. Blumberg's *A Century of Montana Journalism*, Johnson ultimately rejects the *News Letter* as fitting the definition of a true newspaper. Supporting the *Montana Post* instead, she cites evidence that the publication wasn't regularly published and did not persist beyond a few numbers. However, drawing on two early sources, she also offers a tidbit of information that interested me extremely—that the *News Letter* was published in the winter of 1863-64, or, more specifically, in February 1864, a month or so after Plummer's hanging. Telling myself that close counts not only in horse shoes, but fiction, I seized upon this tidbit with enthusiasm, by elevating the role of the *News Letter* in the narrative and allowing myself to ignore the actual timeline to make the story work.

Although I also exaggerated the *News Letter*'s importance in the alternative reality of the novel, I tried to be precise about the practical details of frontier publication, drawing most heavily from a variety of essays in the aforementioned *A Century of Montana Journalism* and the carefully researched *The Business of Newspapers on the Western Frontier* by Barbara Cloud. Also of aid was the general audience book *Newspapering in the Old West* by Robert F. Karolevitz. As for the pre-digital routines of small town publishing, I checked my own recollections against descriptions in period manuals and textbooks, some of which I had retained from my undergraduate days. (Sometimes it pays to hang onto things.) I was boosted in my description of the *Sun-Tribune* office by Arthur A. Hart's "Sheet Iron Elegance: Mail Order Architecture." Former *Tribune-Examiner* editor John Barrows and, more recently, J.P. Plutt, took time from fighting the good fight of old-fashioned journalism to allow me to wander through the newspaper offices to refresh my memory of what it was like to work for a small-town weekly. Barrows also served as my telegraph tutor at a public demonstration of the skill, although he probably doesn't remember doing so.

I should mention one more major instance in the way the novel crosshatches accepted historical accounts with its fictional alternative reality by altering some accepted facts of Thompson's life, this time in connection with his role in Plummer's hanging. Thompson's description of the event was not published until 1912. In the world of the novel, however, Thompson authors an account of the hanging and publishes it in the *East Bannack News Letter* within days of the event. As a starting point for the novel's alternative history, I began with Mather and Boswell's carefully documented representation of the day of the hanging. The historians offer considerable detail, starting with Thompson's breakfast with Plummer at his sister-in-law Martha Vail's table that morning and extending through the evening when Thompson expends considerable energy to keep Vail from realizing what was happening until it is too late for her to intervene. In the fiction, Thompson becomes an eyewitness of the execution, something that more than one source contemporary to the event would indicate as highly unlikely. The novel's first-hand account, then, clearly is fiction, but perhaps it should not be considered pure fiction. The *News Letter* news story does draw heavily from Thompson's description of the hanging in his 1912 memoirs, first published in *Massachusetts Magazine*. More specifically, the description of Plummer in the novel's fictional news story includes wording drawn directly from the memoir.

Readers interested in learning more about Thompson and his brief frontier experience may want to seek out the 2004 Montana Historical Society Press edition of his recollections—*A Tenderfoot in Montana: Reminiscences of the Gold Rush, the Vigilantes, and the Birth of Montana Territory*. In an introduction to the memoir, its editor Kenneth W. Owens argues Thompson offers a more objective vision of Plummer and the Vigilantes than other participants' accounts, offering a "complex" view of the sheriff. Of particular interest is the way Owens contrasts Thompson's memoirs with the standard history by Thomas J. Dimsdale (*The Vigilantes of Montana, Being a Correct and Impartial Narrative of the Chase, Trial, Capture, and Execution of Henry Plummer's Notorious Road Agent Band*, first published in 1865) and by Nathaniel P. Langford's (*Vigilante Days and Ways: The Pioneers of the Rockies, the Makers and Making of Montana, Idaho, Oregon, Washington, and Wyoming*, 1890). Even though *Ghost Town* paints a far darker picture than Owens would regard as fair, I was indebted to the editor for his insights and also for the practical information he offered on Thompson's life. Owens notes, for example, that Thompson returned East to do well for himself in New York by marketing Montana mining properties and also by acting officially for Montana Territory by promoting western emigration.

Even though Thompson finished out a respectable life in his Massachusetts hometown as a public official, a lawyer and probate judge, the simple facts of his biography and his memoir recollections don't resolve a mystery: What kind of man sits down to breakfast with someone he once esteemed as a friend with the knowledge the man would die within hours? Mather and Bowell explore Thompson's internal dilemma by suggesting the way his positive personal relationship with Plummer conflicted with his esteem for his powerful Vigilante friends. The alternative reality of *Ghost Town* allows Thompson to resolve that conflict in a somewhat more complicated way than he did in actuality.

Of course, the genre of memoir allows individuals to assert versions of events that sometimes extend and sometimes contradict standard views. Here would be a good place to note that my ideas about the interaction of memory and history were greatly enhanced by the assertion by Clyde A. Milner, II in his *Montana: The Magazine of Western History* essay on the way memoir is shaped by and shapes shared identities. In "The Shared Memory of Montana Pioneers," Milner does a particularly good job of exploring the way Dimsdale's early narrative influenced those that followed, even though the writer himself was not present in Bannack at the time of the hanging and was subject to the influence of those who benefited by being part of the Vigilante movement. Mather and Boswell argue that Dimsdale's picture of the sheriff's supposed "reign of terror" as a highway man rests on "suspect evidence." For example, they challenge Dimsdale's statement that Plummer was implicated in more than a hundred murders. After reviewing Dimsdale's own sparse documentation against other records, the historians conclude the following: "During the nearly fourteen months Plummer lived at Bannack, eleven robberies occurred in the mining districts east of the Rockies and two more were presumed." The historians could document only twenty-one crime-related deaths in the area and they found no convincing evidence that implicated Plummer in any secret society of criminals, if it indeed existed.

It should be apparent by now that, on one level, the novel owes its framework to Mather and Boswell's revisionist history. However, on another level, it does take great liberties, including one that I haven't yet discussed: the novel's answer to the question of whether Plummer left any descendents. Mather and Boswell explore and convincingly reject the long-standing rumor that Electa, Plummer's wife, bore a son after the sheriff's death. Although the historians find no evidence of such a child, they do note the mystery of a girl born a few months after Plummer's death. Vital statistics indicate, the historians say, that the girl, Rena, was born in Iowa, where Electa had moved after leaving Plummer in Bannack the fall of 1863. However, other documents indicate Rena's parents were Electa's sister Martha Vail and her husband, James, who by that time had moved from Bannack to South Dakota. The historians report without endorsing the speculation that Rena's parentage had been mis-ascribed so the child wouldn't be tainted by Plummer's reputation. Since Rena apparently died young, the question of her parentage seems of limited importance to the historical account. However, as a novelist, faced with a mystery, I wasn't limited to the sparse and ambiguous facts in pursuit of a resolution.

The reader may be interested to know Electa avowed Plummer's innocence when she heard of his death, a protestation that may call into question that she left her husband months after her wedding because she had discovered him as a bad man. It took ten years, but she did remarry, according to Mather and Boswell. After moving from Iowa to take a teaching position in South Dakota nearer her sister, Electa met an Irish widower with six children. She and James Maxwell had three sons of their own, two of whom survived into adulthood. Although she suffered from rheumatism, she lived until age seventy. Electa's stepdaughters remembered her fondly and praised her for "loving sympathy." Although Electa lived out her life in South Dakota, Mather and Boswell say that the Vails returned to their native Ohio. After her husband died, Martha became a matron of an orphan's home with the help of her daughter Suzie, who acted as her assistant.

Besides the demands of creating a plausible alternative reality from the materials of the historical record, I needed to come to understand why the fictional characters AJ, Bet, and Everonica feel about each other as they do. Towards this end, I considered dozens of sources ranging from scholarly studies of the effects of adoption to anonymous internet stories about attempted birth parent/adoptee reunions. Early on, the Montana Post Adoption Center helped me understand the practical and emotional challenges of an adoption search within the context of Montana law. Janet Carsten's study "Knowing Where You've Come From: Ruptures and Continuities of Time and Kinship in Narratives of Adoption Reunions" was essential to letting me see adoption as a multi-dimensional process with life-time effects. The study also revealed a theme that emerged in almost every source I encountered: Anguish is the most frequent outcome of a situation when there's no way to answer the questions "Who am I?" and "Where did I come from?"

As for the organized prostitution that persisted in Montana towns through a considerable stretch of the twentieth century, I was lucky enough to be able to interview someone who remembered the details of how the system worked. The source asked not to be named. For wider context, I relied on "The Devil's Perch: Prostitution from Suite to Cellar in Butte, Montana," by Ellen Baumler. This study appeared, like so many that I have already mentioned, in *Montana: The Magazine of Western History*. The full-text resources of this important publication are widely available through the JSTOR index offered by many university libraries, including Southern Utah University, my research home. I also was helped over the course of many summers by librarians at the University of Montana Western and by archivists at Montana State University's Special Collections. The indexes and resources mentioned during AJ's research into the ledger that figures importantly in the plot reflected my own searches using the indexes and resources at UM-Western. Charles S. Petersen, a longtime and well-published Utah State University professor, helped educate me about the ways in which historians approach research. I was lucky enough to take two Western history-focused graduate classes from Dr. Petersen and later to audit the SUU undergraduate senior thesis seminar that he taught in retirement. If AJ's research approach doesn't meet professional standards, however, the fault is entirely mine, not Dr. Petersen's.

I don't doubt that the novel contains unintended factual errors despite my best efforts to be accurate. However, *Ghost Town* hopes for authenticity as it gives its characters the opportunity to work out their lives. Of course, fictional characters are always (or at least often) assemblages of fragmentary experiences transformed by imagination: a favorite catchphrase here, a garbage bag stuffed with cans there, the angle of a Stetson reflected in a shop window. But except for the real people referenced by name and their place in the community or in the larger historical context, the characters presented are indeed fictional even though they may inhabit spaces many in Dillon might recognize. For example, a marked grave does really denote the spot where the circus elephant was buried after she was struck by lightning. But the Nick who hears the elephant's trumpeting exists only within the world of the novel—even though on my office wall I have a portrait of the late Dillon "can man" who looked a little like my fictional character.

There is, of course, the real Montana Ghost Town Preservation Society, but it is an entity with not only conventions but with officers and bylaws, quite in contrast to the novel's Society, an undefined congregation of fellow travelers who reach out to hold each other steady against the buffeting of time.

About the Author

After earning her undergraduate journalism degree from the University of North Dakota, Montana native Julie Clark Simon worked for newspapers in Minnesota, Montana and Utah, winning several awards for her feature stories and news writing. During her years as an editor for the Logan (Utah) *Herald Journal*, Simon completed her master's degree by virtue of taking two Utah State University evening -courses per quarter. Following a subsequent stint teaching composition at Southern Utah University, Simon and her husband, Duane, attempted a return to Montana. However, a winter spent washing dishes in the Bozeman food co-op convinced Simon that grading stacks and stacks of freshman essays every evening wasn't the worst way to earn a living. She returned to SUU as the English Department's director of composition. One long leave and a PhD later, she became director of the Writing Center as she continued to teach writing, grammar, and literary theory courses. After winning the state of Utah's Original Writing Competition for the manuscript of *The Ghost Town Preservation Society*, Simon decided to fulfill a long-held ambition to write full time. In between trips to Montana, she continues to live in Utah.